J.M. Hall is an author, playwright and deputy head of a primary school. His plays have been produced in theatres across the UK as well as for radio, the most recent being *Trust*, starring Julie Hesmondhalgh on BBC Radio 4. His novels, *A Spoonful of Murder* and *A Pen Dipped in Poison*, are about retired primary school teachers who turn to sleuthing.

Also by J.M. Hall:

A Spoonful of Murder

A
PEN
Dipped in
POISON

J.M. HALL

avon.

Published by AVON
A division of HarperCollins*Publishers*
1 London Bridge Street
London SE1 9GF

www.harpercollins.co.uk

HarperCollins*Publishers*
Macken House
39/40 Mayor Street Upper
Dublin 1
D01 C9W8
Ireland

A Paperback Original 2023
2
First published in Great Britain by HarperCollins*Publishers* 2023

A catalogue copy of this book is available from the British Library.

ISBN: 978-0-00-850964-4 (PB)
ISBN: 978-0-00-853891-0 (TPB)

Typeset by Palimpsest Book Production Ltd, Falkirk, Stirlingshire

Printed and bound in the UK using 100% Renewable Electricity by CPI Group (UK) Ltd

This book is produced from independently certified FSC™ paper
to ensure responsible forest management.

For more information visit: www.harpercollins.co.uk/green

To Sally. Thank you.

PROLOGUE

We're gonna be bringing out the bunting this Friday for our St Barnabus PTA Summer Fayre! Stalls, games, delicious hot dogs – not forgetting our Mega Raffle! Plus, your chance to soak Mr Berryman with wet sponges! Come along from 6 p.m. and help us raise money for school resources – all welcome!

July

(i)

There are many signs that a school summer fayre has gone well – a bare tombola littered with discarded tickets, a cake stall with a few scant Krispie buns remaining – a teacher wet and shivering after a stint on the 'Soak Sir' stall. Many signs of things going well – but an empty school office, door wide open, piles of change left unattended is not one of them.

Thelma stood in the doorway; in her hands a Tupperware container neatly labelled 'Change Bookstall'. Looking round the abandoned room, she felt a prickle of unease. Where was everyone? Linda Barley, cheerfully scooping the change into piles of pound coins? That buttoned-up office manager with her pained air of holding things together, just?

She scanned round looking for some clue. Scattered across Linda's workspace was a fan of white envelopes that Thelma knew to be the raffle prizes. Apparently there had been a bumper crop this year: tickets to Newby Hall, a free appointment at Curl Up and Di, afternoon tea at the garden centre. One envelope lay apart from the others, crisp cream paper as opposed to white, a slightly different size from the others. Angling her head, she was able to read snatches of the letter protruding from it.

. . . seven years . . . great regret but no other
choice . . . Impossible to remain as chair . . .

She guessed immediately what this letter referred to, and who it was from – there had been little talk of anything else amongst the volunteers at the fayre, particularly Izzy, the garrulous lady running the bookstall with her. Some spat had blown up between the parent–teacher association (Friends of St Barney's) and the school's executive head Mrs Kayleigh Brittain – something about how the money raised was to be used. The Friends of St Barney's had proposed their usual end-of-term ice pops and bouncy castle; the head teacher, however, had decreed the money be spent on new maths resources.

'Blood on the walls I heard.' Izzy Trewin had spoken with cheerful relish. 'Absolute carnage.' Indeed, so bitter and so acrimonious had this spat been that Donna Chivers – the breezy, force-of-nature chair – had apparently been reduced to Absolute Floods in the middle of the school playground, and the entire PTA had walked out en masse. Hence the eleventh-hour drafting in of volunteers such as Izzy, a parent new to the school, and people like Thelma and her friend Liz, retired staff members.

'At the end of the day, your head teacher isn't here to make friends,' Izzy had pronounced. 'I should know – I used to work in a school for my sins, back in the Dark Ages!' She gave one of her merry trills of laughter as she thumped a pile of Biff and Chip books into some semblance of order. 'I mean I've not met Mrs Brittain yet, but she'll have had her reasons. The wisdom of management and all that.'

Thelma had said nothing. To her it felt like no sort of wisdom whatsoever to alienate the entire PTA the day before the summer fayre. But then Mrs Kayleigh Brittain, executive head teacher of St Barnabus's Lodestone Academy, did have the reputation for being One Tough Cookie.

In the year and a half she had been in place, it was fair to say she had neatly divided opinion in Thirsk. On the one hand her toughness – cracking down on absences (pupils and staff alike) and her relentless focus on the end of Key Stage Two tests (the results were apparently the highest the school had ever seen) – was welcomed by many, particularly those who sought to get their children through the hallowed gates of Ripon Grammar School. But on the other hand, if you were one of those parents who could only afford cheaper term-time holidays, or one of those children who struggled with endless tests, or even a staff member in need of medical or dental appointments – in short anyone not totally comfortable with the Lodestone Academy Trust ethos embodied in Mrs Brittain's designer-clothed form – then she was never going to be your favourite person. 'More like a blumin' CEO than a head teacher,' was the verdict of more than one person.

All this was running through Thelma's mind as she scanned the empty office. Could the absence of office staff be connected in some way with what Izzy kept referring to as PTA-gate?

'I need change!' The voice that echoed Thelma's speculations was hoarse but penetrating; standing behind her was a short dumpy figure with wild magenta hair and even wilder eyes. Bunty Carter, the Nursery Nurse, was one of the increasingly few staff who had worked in the school in Thelma's day.

'Where is everyone? They shouldn't be leaving all the money like this!'

'They must have just nipped out,' said Thelma calmly.

'I tell you, Mrs Cooper . . .' Bunty shook her head darkly, eyes wide with potential catastrophe. 'It's been just terrible here. Terrible!' Her dire tones were ones Thelma had heard many times over the years, describing everything from a playground fight to a jammed photocopier. She took a surreptitious sniff. With Bunty Carter one could never *quite* be sure. That awful incident at the Teddy Bear's Picnic.

Bunty took another step forward, eyes darting round the room. She *seemed* steady enough. 'Do you think maybe something's happened?'

Thelma was thinking exactly that but had no wish to join in with any fevered speculation that was likely to end up on the Sowerby Girls WhatsApp group.

'If you stay here, I'll go and check,' she said.

Bunty opened her mouth, obviously to protest, but there was something about Thelma's voice – the calm authority of someone who had taught for thirty-seven years. 'I can make a start on counting the money,' she said, eyes again roving round the office.

Thelma noted the many bottles lined up as raffle prizes and offered up a quick prayer.

After leaving the office she turned left, away from the swell of noise from the school hall. The first door she came to was one that was also open when it should have been closed. This one bore a name plate, gold letters on a tasteful crimson background: MRS KAYLEIGH BRITTAIN – EXECUTIVE HEAD.

From within the room came raised voices, sharp with panic.

'I say we should call the police, Mrs Brittain!'

'No.' The negative held authority – but also a distinct twinge of stress.

Thelma knocked and without waiting for an answer went in.

That she'd walked into the middle of a crisis she could tell instantly from the body language of the four women she faced – three standing, one sitting behind an imposing wooden desk that wouldn't have looked out of the place in the study at *Downton Abbey*. On this was an unfolded sheet of paper, which they were all looking at with various degrees of wariness and concern.

One of the women she knew well, Linda Barley – number two in the office, wife of Matt the site manager, famed for her love of rich tea biscuits and the Spice Girls. Next to her was the neat figure of Nicole the office manager, looking accusingly at Thelma. Both women were wearing corporate-looking grey blouses that Thelma knew represented some sort of academy uniform. Nicole's neck was swathed in a thick turquoise scarf – surely an odd choice for such a warm night? The other woman standing was that tall red-headed girl, the one who had been darting about all evening with a ferocious energy, organizing volunteers and dispensing change. She was now bent over the desk, fingers splayed against the surface, frowning at the paper that lay white against the rosewood. And seated in an opulent office chair was the fourth person in the room, wearing a designer cream jacket and with abundant chestnut hair. Her very presence meant this could only be Kayleigh Brittain, executive head of St Barnabus's Lodestone Academy. However, it was not her, or any of the other three, who made an immediate impression on Thelma.

It was the room itself.

It was a space she knew well from the days of Feay, the previous head teacher; like the school itself, it had undergone a massive change. Gone was the genteel clutter, the bookshelves rammed with assembly books, the inevitable Mike Hopper calendar and the open cupboard leaking ring binders and magazine boxes. The drab North Yorkshire Local Education Authority olive green had been repainted a refined shade of dove grey, the carpet tiles replaced by something altogether plusher in a shade of crimson. The whole effect was corporate and somewhat spartan; the only breath of something more spontaneous was a large seascape that dominated the wall facing the desk, a vibrant swelling mass of greys, greens and oranges.

'Can I help you?' Kayleigh's chilly tones plus the differing expressions on all four faces made it crystal clear she should not have just walked in. 'This part of the school is closed to the public.'

'It's not the public, it's Thelma,' said Linda Barley in relieved tones that she obviously felt explained everything. 'Thelma Cooper. You can trust her, Mrs Brittain. She used to work here.'

Thelma registered Linda's use of her head teacher's title and surname. It struck something of a jarring note from the usually free and easy Linda, who invariably used first names, or more often the term 'lovey'.

'I came looking for change,' said Thelma.

Nicole, fingering her scarf, turned to Linda. 'I hope you haven't left the office unattended.' There was a far from subtle subtext of 'it's not my fault, miss!' in her voice and Linda's mouth drooped uneasily.

'There's someone in there keeping an eye on things,' said Thelma, firmly pushing away the images of all those bottles of Orchard Hooch with a further prayer.

'As long as they're not making off with the money,' said Nicole.

'People.' It was the red-haired girl talking for the first time. 'If we *are* going ahead with drawing the raffle, we need to move *now*.' Her voice was abrupt, almost gruff.

'Becky – how *can* we?' Kayleigh Brittain's voice was almost incredulous. '*Anything* could happen if I go out there.' The girl flushed, in the way red-haired people can. 'I was just seeing if that's what we had decided,' she said gruffly.

'Someone else could draw the raffle,' suggested Linda.

'I'm not being funny, but should we even be even talking about this?' said Nicole, sliding her eyes towards Thelma. 'In front of strangers.'

'Actually, I really don't think you have anything to worry about.' Thelma spoke directly to Kayleigh Brittain. 'The person who wrote this horrible letter almost certainly isn't here.'

The reaction to this statement was dramatic. All four sets of eyes instantly jerked back towards her, and Nicole swiped the paper on the desk, holding it protectively against her trim figure. They all stared at the slight woman with the grave face and large glasses, wondering how on earth she knew what was going on. Thelma, however, had seen all that she needed to see; years of working in a classroom had made her something of an expert at reading text upside down – besides which the note on the desk had been written in leering block capitals:

I HOPE YOU REALISE JUST HOW MANY
PEOPLE HATE YOU. YOU'VE UPSET SO
MANY PEOPLE! WHY DON'T YOU GO
AWAY – YOU'RE NOT WANTED HERE!

Now she spoke directly to Kayleigh. 'It's a horrid thing to receive. I quite understand why you're upset.'

'I thought it was a raffle prize,' blurted out Linda in distress. 'Thank God I thought to check them all. It could have been opened in front of all the parents.'

'I rather think that was the idea,' said Thelma.

Kayleigh regarded Thelma thoughtfully. Even at such a time of stress she cut an imposing figure, and Thelma found herself contrasting her own M&S skirt and blouse with the cream designer suit. 'You said the person who wrote this *isn't* here tonight?' said Kayleigh Brittain.

'I don't see how you can possibly say that,' said Nicole dismissively. 'I really don't think you should go out there, Mrs Brittain.'

'How can you even know?' The red-haired girl's voice could have been interpreted as abrupt and challenging, but Thelma recognized it as that of someone who genuinely wanted to find out.

'Of course, I can't be certain,' said Thelma. 'But I haven't seen Donna Chivers all evening, and I understand . . .' she paused tactfully '. . . I understand she has said she won't be coming.'

'*Donna Chivers?*' said Kayleigh.

Thelma nodded.

'How can you be so sure it's from her?' said Linda.

'The envelope.' Thelma indicated the white torn-open object discarded on the desk.

'I don't see.' Linda picked it up and scanned it, as if it might say 'Donna Chivers sent this'. 'It's even not like the ones she usually uses.'

'No,' said Thelma. '*But it's exactly the same as the ones the raffle prizes are in.* And Donna organizes the raffle. Or at least she always used to.' Again, the four women looked at her. 'As I say, I imagine the plan was for the letter to be revealed in front of parents at the raffle draw.' She remembered the chair of the PTA – all breezy good humour to your face, and then behind your back . . .

'I believe,' she said, 'her Jake is finishing this time?'

The red-haired girl – Becky – nodded.

'So, in a week's time she won't even have to come near the place.'

Kayleigh nodded. She appeared to have come to a decision. 'Right,' she said standing up.

'I'm not being funny,' said Nicole. 'But this lady could be wrong.'

'Not Thelma,' said Linda with a laugh.

(ii)

It was still uncomfortably warm in the school hall, despite no less than three floor fans racketing away on the stage. The sight of Izzy Trewin energetically fanning herself with one of the Biff and Chip books made Thelma feel even hotter.

'It's still red hot in here,' said Izzy, strands of permed curls plastered to her temples as Thelma set down the tub of change. 'Some sort of issue with the heating, someone was saying. Not that I'm moaning! Hey, I grew up in Cornwall for my sins! Talk about wall-to-wall mizzle!'

At that moment a rather overweight woman – presumably a parent (so many people Thelma didn't recognize) – brandished a copy of *New Life, New You!* which was Izzy's cue to enthusiastically embark on the subject of her recent relocation to Thirsk from Luton (Hey! This is my time now!) leaving Thelma free to reflect on what had just happened. She hoped she'd been right about Donna Chivers; she was as sure as she could be. She remembered that awful incident with the lollipop lady and social services – all Donna's handiwork.

She glanced around the hall. Everything looked very much as the summer fayre had always looked, no sign of Donna, but as for people sympathetic to the PTA, well, there were so many people she didn't know . . . Parents . . . staff . . . That large lass on the cake stall surreptitiously polishing off a stray Krispie bun. A plump girl, pink-faced in the heat, half-heartedly selling raffle tickets. Across from her running the whack-a-rat stall was someone she did know – Sam Bowker, the Year Six teacher.

Once upon a time and many moons ago, she had taught him. His rather cadaverous face (his nickname had been Zombie Boy) had not really changed, rather elongated, along with his body. Watching him, Thelma sighed to herself – yet another example of the passing of the years, like the hall she was in, with its smart blue paint job and enormous interactive whiteboard where once there had been the Superstar of The Week display. And above that, dominating all – the logo. Blue, brash letters LAT (Lodestone Academy Trust) with the caption 'Strive for success and reach for your dreams'. Of course, academies were very much the norm these days. So many schools seemed to be – what was the word? – federated into groups of schools administered by these trusts with their brash-sounding names, dotted randomly across the country. St Barnabus's was, she knew, federated with schools in Bradford, Leeds and – rather bizarrely – Felixstowe.

A grating whine from the PA system drew her attention to the stage where an energetic man in a tomato-red tracksuit was adjusting the microphone. Thelma knew him to be Ian Berryman, who taught Year Five. Not unattractive (a shame about that livid shaving rash) with hair wet and tousled from his stint on the 'Soak Sir' stall. 'Ladies and gentlemen.' His voice was distorted with that weedy resonance peculiar to school public address systems. 'Ladies and gentlemen – I am now going to draw the raffle!' He said it in a way that invited laughter as if it was some colossal joke – but no one did apart from Izzy and the plump girl with the raffle tickets.

Thelma frowned and looked at the door to the hall. Had Kayleigh Brittain had second thoughts about making an appearance? But at that moment the door opened, and the head teacher of St Barnabus's Lodestone Academy made her entrance.

For indeed 'entrance' was the only appropriate term for the way she appeared and then progressed with easy, smiling confidence through the crowd of parents. Thelma found herself watching her with the same fascination with which she'd watched Helen Mirren at Stratford a few months previously. If Mrs Brittain was uneasy, she gave absolutely no sign of it; the smile was calm and gracious, not giving a hint of anything untoward. As she passed the tombola, Liz's friend Jan Starke called out something cheerfully to her. Kayleigh's response – or lack of response – was striking. The smile didn't slip one jot, but at the same time she paid absolutely no attention to Jan, not even turning her head. There was no doubt in Thelma's mind that it was a deliberate snub and from the slapped, hurt look on Jan's face and the grim set of Liz's mouth she could tell that was how they saw it too. Had Jan somehow fallen foul of her boss? Knowing Jan Starke, that wasn't beyond the bounds of possibility.

Kayleigh ascended onto the stage and took her place before the crowd of parents, looking totally composed and confident. 'I just want to say thank you so much for coming along and supporting the St Barnabus summer fayre.' The voice was poised and confident. 'This is my second summer with you. As ever, I am so impressed by the way you all turn out and support your children's school.'

The parents regarded the designer-clad figure in watchful silence. Had Thelma been wrong? *Was* someone going to shout something out?

'And it's a good school. There's so much to be proud of – your children have worked so hard! We're on track for an excellent set of results and indeed our Year Six writing is not only the best across the trust but has scored very highly in the north-west league tables!' This time there was a faint murmur of approval – after all, good results were good results. Kayleigh smiled down beneficently. 'As a result of this, I'm happy to announce that from September we're going to become a Beacon of Writing Excellence!'

Again, only Izzy Trewin and the girl selling raffle tickets reacted with whoops and cheers; but then many people (Thelma included) had no idea what a Beacon of Writing Excellence was, except that it sounded to be a Good Thing. There was the faintest spattering of applause, but it struck Thelma how very subdued the parents were; there was none of the cheery warmth and support that former head Feay had engendered whenever she spoke.

Thelma regarded the staff, now assembling on the stage carrying the various prizes, looking like the cast of a play preparing for a curtain call with Kayleigh as the leading lady. There was Ian Berryman holding a bucket containing the tickets; beside him stood Sam Bowker hefting a pamper hamper. Nicole and Becky stood to their left holding the basket with the prize envelopes. Across the other side was Raffle Ticket Girl, Linda, and Jan holding the bottles; between them glumly clutching a tub of Quality Street was Bunty Carter. All were watching Kayleigh Brittain. For an absurd instant, Thelma was seized by the fancy the woman might be about to break into a rendition of 'Don't Cry for Me Argentina'.

'And now,' said Kayleigh, extending an exquisitely manicured hand into the bucket of tickets, 'let's get this raffle drawn!' The staff all smiled dutifully but it suddenly occurred to Thelma that none of the smiles seemed genuine.

'I never win anything me,' said Izzy Trewin cheerfully.

'Blue 279.' Again Ian's magnified voice sounded weedy.

Thelma's attention was not so much drawn as grabbed in a headlock as Izzy let out a piercing whoop and waved a blue ticket in the air.

'It's me,' she said. 'And I don't win anything ever!'

She continued to both whoop and repeat how she never won anything as she proceeded to the stage and chose a course of sunbed sessions at Bronze and Beyond. All eyes in the hall were on her – all except Thelma's. Her position at the side of the hall meant she was the only person in the hall able to properly see Kayleigh Brittain's face.

The head teacher of St Barnabus's Lodestone Academy was no longer standing on the stage but had removed herself to the bottom of the steps, looking up at those clustered together holding the prizes. *And her face . . .*

Her gaze was completely devoid of any expression – and yet it was by no means expressionless. Indeed, she looked so ghastly that Thelma felt a prickle in the nape of her neck. Was she going to faint? There was something in that gaze, that unwilling stare, as though Kayleigh possessed no power to take her eyes off whatever it was she was looking at. Was it shock? Or fear? None of these, and yet somehow . . . both.

Thelma swiftly scanned the hall but there was no sign of Donna Chivers. She looked on stage to see who on earth it could be that Kayleigh was staring at in such a way. Ian Berryman? Nicole or Becky? Sam Bowker or Raffle Ticket Girl? Then there was Jan Starke . . . Linda . . . Bunty Carter. Had one of them prompted this awful, stricken look? It *couldn't* be the letter; it had been well over half an hour since she must have seen it.

So what was it?

Thelma looked back at Kayleigh and was just in time to see the cream jacket retreating discreetly across the hall and out of the door.

CHAPTER ONE

A second envelope is found and sad change is observed in the emotional heart of the school.

September

Face impassive, Kayleigh Brittain stood in the centre of Elm Base, gazing round the classroom. In her hands was an iPad in an expensive-looking leopard-skin case; on this she was making intermittent light taps. As she did, a faint chinking sound could be heard from her gold charm bracelet, which winked and glittered in the September sun streaming through the windows.

From her vantage point in the reading corner, it seemed to Liz that the class were largely oblivious to the presence of their head teacher. She couldn't help but contrast their reaction to the one Feay, the previous head, invariably provoked from children, fending off barrages of news about trips to Center Parcs and parties and guinea pigs. There was something about Mrs Brittain's presence that seemed to somehow repel the children – or at least not attract their attention.

She was expensively dressed; even Liz could tell that. The apricot suit was crisp, clean and elegantly cut. The abundant chestnut hair shone in the sun without a trace of a grey root showing. With some shame Liz noted her own appearance, faintly reflected back at her in the classroom window – the helmet of greying hair, the white blouse and faded blue skirt, resistant to most things a primary classroom could throw at them. Her cardie had been consigned to the back of the chair within thirty seconds of entering the room – it really was fiercely hot.

If the children were oblivious, her friend Jan, gamely teaching phonics to her Bumblebee table, was anything but. Her voice had gone up at least two notches since her head teacher had materialized for one of her infamous Wednesday drop-ins. 'Split digraph, Randeep!' she was saying in tones that were warbly with stress. No, not stress.

Fear.

Which of course, was the reason that Liz was sitting here helping the children of Elm Base plough their way through various split digraphs and consonant blends. Her thoughts spooled back to the night at book group when this had all started – well, it must have started before that, but it had been that night when she became aware of her friend's problems.

When Kayleigh Brittain had first started at St Barnabus's and the school had become an academy, Jan had been an ardent advocate. It was high time, she'd say, that the place was taken by the scruff of the neck and given a jolly good shaking! The energy and enthusiasm of her words had the effect of making the recently retired Liz feel like some decrepit old has-been.

Then, subtly, things had changed.

Jan had begun dropping out of book group meetings, citing the pressure of work. When she did come, she said little (for her) and the comments she did make lacked their trademark authority.

The big reveal had come the previous June. The group had been meeting at Liz's house; the book, some first-hand account of a drug addict's hell in a Malayan jail (*The Moon Through the*

Bars – not at all Liz's cup of tea) had been Jan's choice. But despite this, Jan had barely spoken . . . almost as if she hadn't actually read it . . .

After seeing the others out at the end of the evening, Liz half expected Jan to be clearing away the coffee cups when she came back to the living room, but Jan was still sitting on the sofa, gazing unseeingly at the remaining crumbs of a piece of Busby Parkin (all of their cakes were named after local places). It was a look Liz recognized instantly and one that made her deeply uneasy.

'I suppose I better be making a move.' Jan's voice had been dull, weary, in the way it had not been for some years. 'I've work I need to do when I get back.'

Liz couldn't remember exactly what she'd said in response, something along the lines of 'surely not at this time,' at which point Jan's face had slipped and screwed up, followed by sudden sobs and hot tears. Jan wasn't an easy crier. Her face looked ugly and helpless, her sobs rasping and nasal. She cried for seven and a half minutes (during which time Liz's husband Derek came in, took one horrified look and hared upstairs with the *Yorkshire Post*) and then, through fistfuls of Liz's balsam tissues, the story staggered out.

It was the national Year One phonics test. That year, a number of Jan's class, for a variety of reasons ranging from a chicken pox outbreak to plain lack of ability, had failed to achieve the golden pass mark of thirty-two. This had not gone down at all well with Lodestone Academy Trust, who had subsequently pronounced an 'All Achieve!' policy for the following year's test. This, it transpired, meant that every child in the Year One class – especially those deemed to be Phonically Vulnerable – MUST have a Quality Bespoke Phonics Experience at LEAST three times a week. Which was all well and good in theory but as Liz knew full well, the simple truth was that some children could spend all the hours God sent having Quality Phonics Experiences and still remain stubbornly and cheerfully Phonically Vulnerable. This view, however, was not shared by Kayleigh Brittain.

'She has this way of just looking at you!' Jan had wailed like a hurt child. 'You just feel completely rubbish!'

Which explained why Liz had found herself on Wednesday mornings since the start of the autumn term steadily dispensing bespoke experiences to the phonically vulnerable of Elm Class. Plus – crucially – to be there on hand to give extra support in the event of any of Mrs Brittain's infamous Wednesday drop-ins.

Derek hadn't been at all keen about this arrangement. 'Don't be getting involved,' he'd cautioned. But then Derek was someone who spent his life living with a horror of Getting Involved. Involved with what exactly was something that was always fairly opaque and differed from situation to situation – but Jan crying on the sofa certainly qualified. And of course, there'd been that time the previous year when Liz had very definitely Got Involved in a situation surrounding the death of a former colleague, one that had resulted in three people going to prison.

All of which meant that on these Wednesdays, Liz never said that much about these trips to her former workplace.

'It's all looking lovely in here, Mrs Starke!' Kayleigh's warm but curiously flat voice broke into Liz's thoughts. She looked round the room, smiling, taking in the walls with their laminated labels, plus the crayoned vegetable hats strung across a wall ready for the forthcoming harvest assembly. 'It's evident a lot of quality learning is going on.'

Jan looked up at her, her eyes wide, her expression vulnerable, hopeful. 'We have a new home learning system,' she said with a wide manic smile. 'The children all take their sounds home to learn in their "Funky Phonics" envelopes.'

'I can see you've got it very organized,' said Kayleigh. 'And I see you've got your friend helping you.' She bestowed a gracious smile on Liz, who felt a sudden impulse to curtsey. 'I'll give you more feedback later – but well done! And just a thought to park with you, as t'were. Consider a phonic-rich environment to support all the lovely learning going on.' She gave a final smile, turned and left the room.

Liz looked over to her friend, giving her a 'well done, now relax!' smile. But Jan was staring after her boss. A stare the Liz had not seen for a few years and one that made her deeply uneasy.

'Right!' As the children streamed noisily out to play, Jan stood frowning in front of a display of autumn words. 'A phonic-rich environment!' Liz noted the edge to her voice and looked at her friend in concern. 'At least have a quick break,' she said to Jan.

It was as if she hadn't spoken.

With a grunt of determination Jan proceeded to fall on the display, ripping off paper and words (words that Liz had spent an hour laminating only the previous week).

'You go get your break!' Jan spoke in that gung-ho way she had when the mood was on her. 'You don't mind fending for yourself?' She vigorously scrunched up words and paper in a way that told Liz it mattered little whether she did or not. 'Help your-self to my red bush!'

Outside in the corridor, Liz paused and frowned back at the door, unsure what to do. She'd seen these bursts of activity in her friend before – they were never a good thing. That time she feng-shuied Liz's conservatory . . . the look on Derek's face.

It was then that she noticed the envelope. It was sticking out at an angle from under one of the benches by the reading books, pristine white against the smart blue carpet tiles. A 'Funky Phonics' envelope, no doubt. Liz picked it up; she'd need to see that it was returned to its rightful owner before Jan started stressing.

Making her way to the staffroom, Liz reflected on the last twenty minutes. Could Jan have been exaggerating these past months? Blowing things up out all proportion was, after all, a characteristic of hers. Fair enough, there had been the way Kayleigh Brittain had snubbed her at the summer fayre back in July – but with everything going on that night surely it was no wonder? She remembered everything Thelma had told her – all that upset with the PTA – and then Kayleigh getting that awful letter. It was enough to make anyone look like they'd seen a ghost. And as for the 'drop-in' this morning, Liz had seen no evidence of Kayleigh being out to get her friend.

. . . angry hammering at the front door . . . 'Is she in there the mad bitch?'

Liz shook her head. *Come on, Liz, get a grip . . . All that was ages ago . . .*

Suddenly ahead of her down the corridor appeared the faintly lurching figure of Bunty Carter. Liz felt a twinge of guilt. After Thelma had shared her worries the night of the fayre, she'd had it in her mind to call or even drop round. But as was the way of these things, somehow it had never happened, and in school so far that term their paths had never seemed to cross. She focused on the figure ahead; was she all right these days? She looked a tad unsteady . . . but then she did have that hip. Liz called out, 'Good morning, Bunty!' and waited for a pause in the unsteady progress.

The reaction was marked.

With a distinct increase in speed the dumpy figure hurried round the corner, flashing a quick wild-eyed glance over one shoulder. *Odd.* Bunty was *always* up for a chat. Maybe she was in need of the ladies'?

The staffroom was filling up with people queuing by the water boiler, making themselves a drink, spooning coffee into the Lodestone Academy blue mugs arranged neatly on trays – so different from the old mishmash of crockery . . . Topsy's Viva Las Vegas mug and the hoo-ha if anyone else dared drink from it! Liz looked with longing at the various jars and tins in the cupboard. She'd kept meaning to bring a jar of coffee in with her, but so far, she'd not got round to it, and she didn't feel right asking anyone for a spoonful. She sat herself in a corner of the once well-known room, feeling that familiar sense of dislocation on seeing again how very different it was. Corporate blue chairs instead of the saggy olive-green ones. Noticeboards with their inevitable Lodestone logos. One thing, however, had not changed.

'It's that time, folks!' Margo Benson – the Year Three teaching assistant – waved the brightly coloured Know-body Indulgence cosmetic catalogue; her glasses on their gold chain winked invitingly. 'Orders in by Friday!' There was a quiet response to the fluting announcement and Liz smiled to herself. One of the many perks of retirement from St Barnabus's was being able to stop forking out £9.99 on Indulgence Gardeners' Hand Gel, which had always left her palms feeling slightly sticky.

'Plus, I'm thinking about the Christmas do! We need to get moving before everywhere gets booked up!' Again, a muted response, just a few half-hearted smiles, which was slightly surprising as talk of the Christmas do usually stirred some response from people, if only a lament about how quickly the year was passing.

On the staffroom whiteboard, Becky Clegg was writing in uncompromising red handwriting: *All baseline data to Becky by Friday AT THE LATEST, thx!* At the end she was drawing a smiley face, as if this could somehow soften the directness of the demand. Liz wondered whether now was the time to approach her. She had seen her a couple of times already that morning,

21

charging up and down the Key Stage One corridor with a focused purpose that had deterred Liz from talking to her.

Jan had none too high an opinion of the girl. Last time Liz had been in Jan's class the two had had a decidedly heated exchange about phase-five phonics (whatever that was) leading Jan to label her (with trademark lack of self-irony) a Bossy Madam. But since the other week, however, Liz had seen her in something of a different light.

It had been in the garden centre. Liz had been on the first of her September bulb-buying expeditions, when she'd noticed the tall figure looking rather flurried, arms full of bamboo poles. It had been one of those instances when she was unsure whether she knew someone sufficiently to speak to them, or whether only a vague smile of recognition was required.

The question had been resolved when Becky, in fumbling for her purse, had dropped the poles and Liz had helped her retrieve them. They weren't, it turned out, intended for any plant-related purpose, rather something to do with a puppet workshop being run in school. Becky, who always seemed so focused, had been surprisingly eager to pass the time of day. She had been most interested in the trolley of bulbs, which surprised Liz who had only ever seen her in the context of brisk and brittle exchanges about phase consonant blends or split digraphs. She looked wide-eyed at the varieties of bulbs in Liz's trolley with their lyrical names: Whispering Dream, Pink Sorbet.

'I thought they were just red or yellow or orange,' she'd said with an air of wonder, and it suddenly struck Liz she was quite a lonely figure. With her tall stature and red hair, she reminded her of a childhood rag doll, Raggedy Ann.

As they loaded up the poles into the boot of her trim red Fiat, Becky had said how due to 'unforeseen circumstances' she was renting a flat by the canal in Ripon. (Liz guessed this referred to a rather messy relationship break-up earlier that year – details of which had been avidly supplied by Jan.) She had been thinking about getting some tubs of flowers out on the balcony but wasn't sure where to begin, and it was with this in mind Liz fingered the bulb catalogue in her handbag. Was this the right moment?

'Data time, people,' said Becky, snapping the lid on the pen with a smart click. She was, Liz noted, one of those people incapable of making a request seem anything other than a barked order. Cravenly she decided the bulb catalogue could wait for another time.

'Here, Mrs Newsome.' It was Sam Bowker, his death's head features composed into an undertaker's smile proffering . . . relief! A cup of coffee. 'Milk, no sugar?'

'How kind! Thank you so much!' She smiled at him, thinking as she always did when she saw him how the years flew. Memories of him in times past flashed through her mind: hearing him read, playing Joseph in the Nativity, picking runner beans on his Grandad Billy's allotment – the one across from theirs. Would she ever get used to seeing him as a twenty-something teaching Year Six? With this in mind she said, 'I can't get used to seeing you here.'

He smiled, yawned slightly. 'I can't get used to being in here. I still keep expecting Mrs Joy to walk in and tell me to get out.'

Liz smiled sadly at the mention of Topsy Joy, her late colleague who had died the previous year in such awful circumstances. Deliberately she turned her mind from those upsetting events. 'So how are you getting on?' she said. 'I've not seen you at the allotment recently.'

'I've had to give that up,' said Sam, looking sad. 'I know it was Grandad's, but with a kiddie – and with work here – I just wasn't getting the time.'

Liz nodded philosophically. As a one-time primary school teacher she knew all about shortage of time. 'Anyway,' she said, 'I've been hearing such good things about how you're doing! This Beacon writing thing Jan was telling me about?'

Sam smiled, but this time not quite so fully – almost awkwardly one might say. Abruptly his face was broken by an enormous yawn.

'Sorry,' he said. 'Disturbed night.' Now he mentioned it, he did look tired. His face, always on the sallow side, was looking decidedly pasty.

'The little one been keeping you awake?'

He nodded, yawning again. He seemed about to say something but at that moment the large Year Three teacher – Tiff was it? – began speaking to him about writing assessments. 'I need to push the fronted adverbials,' she kept saying plaintively.

Although Sam's answers came easily enough, he kept fingering his shirt collar, and Liz noticed a livid red mark on his neck. Just the same as Derek would get after finance meetings in Tadcaster. Stress neck he called it. But what did Sam of all people have to be stressed about? Apart from the understandable issues of a wakeful infant?

All of a sudden, she felt tired. Tired and old and out of place in that bright corporate room with this focused chat about fronted adverbials and baseline assessments. She had a sudden poignant flashback to the old days – herself, Pat and Thelma, tense from assessments, fraught from Nativity practices, floored with laughter about something some child had said or done.

All at once she realized how quiet the room was, despite being more or less full. Such conversations as were taking place seemed to be all about work – otherwise people were sitting in muted silence, staring down into their drinks. And there'd been the lack of response to both Margo and Becky. It had never used to be like this . . . Back in her day the staffroom had been a place that was pretty much the emotional heart of the school – a place where plans, gripes, worries, problems had all been shared. Had something happened?

'Okay, chaps and chapesses!' It was Ian Berryman, standing in the doorway, in a purple tracksuit today, gesturing comically at his watch. ''Tis time!' Immediately the staff began stirring, even though by Liz's watch it was a good three minutes before the end of break. The staff were obviously well trained – one of Feay's more persistent gripes had been the time it took the staff to vacate the staffroom. On one famous occasion she'd even stood outside the door with a football rattle.

Instead of heading back to Elm Base and whatever state Jan was in with the phonics display, she nipped into the ladies', took out her hairbrush and fluffed her greying helmet of hair. Not that it needed it; it was just something she always found comforting to do.

What a strange break time. That queer muted atmosphere . . . like people were walking on eggshells. *Had* there been an argument or something? She took a deep breath and looked in the mirror, seeing a worried face staring back at her.

Something felt very wrong.

All at once she remembered Bunty Carter hurrying away down the corridor. Why hadn't she been in the staffroom? It wasn't her duty day, and for Bunty to miss her coffee was unthinkable.

And that look on her face as she'd glanced back at Liz.

Shifty – almost furtive. Almost . . . afraid . . .

The metallic rattle of the bell signalled the end of break. Liz sighed – time to get back to Elm Base. Harvest practice next. Sighing she placed her brush back in her bag and braced herself for a run-through of 'Once upon a time in the cabbage patch'. As she did, her elbow caught something sticking out of her pocket. The envelope! She gave a guilty start; she'd forgotten all about it.

She needed to identify who was missing their home learning – the very last thing she wanted was to set Jan off worrying again. She opened it, as carefully as she could.

For an uncomprehending moment the words failed to make sense.

CALL YOURSELF A HEAD TEACHER?
YOU DO REALIZE THERE ISN'T A SINGLE
PERSON IN THIS PLACE WHO RATES YOU!
YOU'RE NOT WANTED HERE. *DO US ALL*
*A FAVOUR AND PISS OFF . . . **BITCH**!*

CHAPTER TWO

In the garden centre café evil is recognized, and there is news of a surprise request.

'I thought Donna Chivers had nothing to do with school anymore, not now her Jake has left.'

'She hasn't.' Thelma took a sip of her coffee. 'She's joined the PTA at Ripon Grammar School. Busy organizing a sponsored bed push to Fountains Abbey so I hear.'

'So what's this about?' Liz gestured at the piece of paper on the table.

The spiteful text shouted out, jarring against the reassuring atmosphere of the Thirsk Garden Centre café. She had hoped that seeing the words in this comfortable, familiar context would somehow reduce, even trivialize, their sheer nastiness. But no, even seen upside down, as Thelma scrutinized the document, she felt the frissons of shock that had given her such a sleepless night.

She looked round the familiar surroundings for comfort. The café was, as it always was on Thursday morning, about half full. The retired, those off work, those with time to chat, to do the crossword, to linger over their phones or tablets. One of the staff was balanced uncertainly on a chair, winding orange fabric leaves round a light fitting; another was drifting round the tables calling out 'cheese and ham panini?' in hopeful tones. Ordinary and reassuring.

Again, Liz looked down at the hateful sheet of paper. Thelma finished her scrutiny and was about to push it across the table, when she caught sight of her friend's expression. 'I can hang on to this, if you'd rather?' she said gently.

'If you don't mind.' Liz's words came out in a sort of relieved rush. 'I know I'm being silly, but there's just something about it . . . *something* . . .'

'Something evil.' Thelma supplied the words with calm, unfussy certainty. 'Yes, I agree.' Liz looked gratefully at her friend, so calm, so reassuring, the sensible glasses, the wavy brown bob (now showing more and more strands of grey). As always Thelma *understood* – as she had on so many countless occasions in the past, one of the many reasons why they met here every Thursday for coffee despite having both stopped working together some six years previously.

'And you say you told no one about it?' asked Thelma, putting the letter into her handbag.

'No one.' Liz shook her head vehemently, remembering the fevered, almost guilty way she'd stuffed the thing to the bottom of her handbag, her one instinct to keep such a poisonous document away from where anyone could see it. Definitely from Jan in the full throes of harvest practice. And certainly from Kayleigh Brittain. Of course, strictly speaking as head teacher, and the intended recipient – well, surely, she had a right to know? But even so, Liz's cheeks burned at the thought of those wide grey eyes scanning those venomous words. 'Why? Do you think I should've?' she asked Thelma. 'Told someone there was another letter?'

Thelma shook her head. 'No,' she said. 'A dropped letter isn't

28

exactly the same thing as a *sent* letter. I find it's always better to be careful.' She briefly put her hand on Liz's. 'No, I think you did the right thing.'

Liz smiled wanly, feeling a brief, treacherous surge of tears. She took a sip of coffee and steadied herself. It was *awful* how the whole thing had got under her skin – she'd even blurted out the story to Derek, despite her desire to downplay any mention of her involvement with the school.

Frowning in distress she said, 'I just don't see why Donna Chivers would still be sending letters.'

Thelma looked at her. 'I don't think she is,' she said.

'I thought you said she sent that letter, the one at the summer fayre?'

Thelma nodded. 'That's what I thought,' she said sombrely. 'Obviously I was wrong.'

Liz frowned worriedly. 'Maybe I should have told someone. What if one of the children had picked it up?' There was real outrage in her tone.

'But they didn't,' said Thelma calmly. She knew exactly how Liz felt. All of their working life had been spent in schools – teaching children so many things . . . the importance of reading, the tying of shoelaces, the ins and outs of the Nativity, the thorough washing of hands after using the toilet. Nurturing, if you wanted to give it a title. Like Liz, she felt something evil had entered a place where it had no right to be.

'Tell me again,' she said, 'where you found it exactly.'

'Outside Elm Base, on the Key Stage One corridor,' said Liz. 'Where Marni Barker used to do special needs.'

'And where was it? In the middle?'

Liz shook her head. 'At the side,' she said. 'Half under a bench.'

'And you say you found it at break time?'

'I was on my way to the staffroom.'

'You probably can't answer this,' said Thelma, 'but I don't suppose you know if it had been there before?'

'It hadn't.' Liz sounded definite. 'I'd been out earlier changing the Bumblebees' reading books. I'm sure I'd have seen it, or one of the kiddies would have picked it up.' She shuddered again.

'And have you any idea who might have been going down the corridor?'

Liz frowned, trying to remember. 'There was the woman from the office – that Nicole – bringing the dinner menus. Becky Clegg bobbed in with a note for Jan. But really people are always going up and down that corridor – anyone could have dropped it.'

A thought occurred to Thelma. 'If it *was* dropped,' she said.

'I told you, it was just lying there in the corridor.'

'I mean, it could have been left there deliberately.'

Liz frowned at her friend uncomprehendingly.

'Think about it. You want to send an anonymous letter to someone – to your head teacher – but you don't want to run the risk of being found out. So, what better way than to leave it where it'll be found by someone else.'

'But there was no name on the envelope.'

'Exactly. *So, the person who finds it opens it to see what's in it.* That way other people see what's been written, *as well* as the recipient. Remember, the one at the summer fayre was tucked away with the raffle prizes.'

'*Oh!*' Liz's startled cry made more than one person look round and almost made Thelma slop her coffee. 'I nearly forgot. *Bunty.*' Briefly she told Thelma what had happened. '. . . and when she looked back at me . . . I'm sure she was *scared* about something. Maybe *she'd* dropped it and thought I'd seen her.'

Thelma looked at her, trying to find the right words. 'You don't think . . .' She let her words tail off delicately and she made a small but discreet gesture with her coffee cup.

'I don't know.' Liz shrugged. 'I didn't get close enough to her. But I'd have thought not. I mean Kayleigh Brittain isn't like Feay – any sign of Bunty drinking and she'd be out on her ear.'

Thelma nodded. 'It might be worth giving her a ring,' she suggested.

'Yes, I was thinking I might,' said Liz. There was a pause. The patio doors were wide open, admitting the warm September sunlight. 'Remember you said you saw Kayleigh Brittain looking funny – the night of the school fayre. Could that have something to do with all this?'

'I don't know.' Thelma stirred her coffee in that thoughtful way she had.

'I mean to have two horrid letters written to her . . . I know she isn't everyone's cup of tea, but even so . . .' Liz's words tailed off.

'What *is* she like?' asked Thelma.

Liz considered. 'I don't really know,' she said. 'From everything Jan told me, I'd have said a nasty piece of work. But then she didn't *seem* like that yesterday.'

'How did she seem?'

'Okay.' Liz shrugged helplessly. 'Friendly. A bit stand-offish but she is the head teacher. Nice enough to me. I suppose it could have all been an act. I mean, I know she runs a tight ship – but that's the way things are these days in school. Like a business more than anything.'

Thelma nodded in agreement. Education seemed more and more like that these days. After the week's events with her husband Teddy, she should know better than anyone.

'It was the staffroom that got me yesterday.' Liz's voice brought her out of her unpleasant reverie. She was frowning up at the café's bathtub lampshades, also bedecked with orange leaves. 'The atmosphere in there.'

'What about it?'

'It was all *wrong*. Everyone was really quiet, just talking about school stuff . . . like there'd been a row. *No one was smiling . . .*'

Instantly Thelma's mind went back to that warm July night and the school summer fayre.

The staff on the stage. Smiles that didn't feel real. That ghastly look on Kayleigh Brittain's face . . .

'Could this be down to Mrs Brittain, do you think?'

'I told you what a state Jan's been in. She *has* been having a terrible time with her.' There was a hesitation, a slight catch in Liz's voice, and all at once Thelma knew with certainty there was something else about Jan that was troubling her friend, something she wasn't saying. What? She didn't really feel able to ask because the truth was, uncharitable though it might be, she'd always found Jan Starke a thoroughly tiresome woman. The sort who had the strongest opinions, voiced loudly and confidently, never tempered by the fact they could possibly be wrong. But she was Liz's friend, or rather Liz was Jan's friend, and furthermore she'd stuck by her through some decidedly thin times.

And because of all this, Thelma could think of no way of suggesting that whatever trials Jan had been enduring could well have been brought on by Jan herself. What was needed at this point in the conversation, she reflected, was a cheerful, irreverent comment about Jan and her shortcomings to make them all laugh and to encourage Liz to say whatever it was that was on her mind.

Pat.

Instinctively she glanced across to their favourite table, the round one in the corner where they didn't like to sit when it was just the two of them. Today it was occupied by a group of women knitting with bright colours – scarlets, crimsons, sunflower yellows. She looked at Liz and caught her doing exactly the same. Their eyes met and Jan, Kayleigh Brittain and nasty letters were momentarily forgotten.

'Have you heard from her?' asked Liz.

Thelma shook her head. 'You?'

'Not since I sorted her borders out, back end of the holiday.' Even though they were all retired, late July and August were still referred to by them as 'the holidays'. 'And even then, like I said – I sensed she didn't really want to talk. I hope everything's all right.'

'We'd have heard if there was a problem surely?'

Liz nodded, and the conversation drifted into a bit of a lull. She looked round the café and to the garden centre beyond. Despite the golden September light, you could tell autumn was coming. Yet more fabric leaves were strewn round the big mock fireplace, and outside in the shop they could glimpse the blacks and oranges of the first Halloween displays. Halloween, Christmas next. Another year fading. All so ordinary . . .

And now this . . .

The front door shaking under the blows . . . the figure on the stairs, hands over her ears . . .

The sudden snake of a memory took Liz by surprise. Rather shakily she said, 'I don't know what on earth's happening to our school.'

'Well, I'll maybe have the chance to find out tomorrow,' said Thelma quietly, in the understated way she used to make her big announcements. Liz looked at her friend, who stopped stirring her coffee and told her what had happened the day before.

It had been late the previous afternoon, gone three, when Thelma had arrived back from a stint at the charity shop to find her husband Teddy, not at the college teaching 'From Ezra to Lamentations', but in his study, on his knees surrounded by a plethora of files and folders. These he was arranging with the frowning concentration of a child laying out a model railway set. Watching him warily from the top of the filing cabinet was Snaffles, the cat they'd recently given home to, a thin black and white scrap with a permanently horrified expression.

'What's this?' she'd said.

Teddy had looked up at her; in the split second before nodding in welcome he'd looked vulnerable and tired. 'Now I don't want you to worry,' he'd said.

She'd felt her stomach contract. *That bad.* She would have liked to sit down, but pretty much every surface was covered with ring binders and cardboard wallets. All week she'd suspected that something had been worrying him . . . the way he'd taken to striding round the garden with his morning coffee . . . the way he'd stopped following the Yorkshire championship final . . . the way he'd stopped singing 'What's New, Pussycat?' to a terrified Snaffles.

'Baht'at?' she'd said.

'Yes,' he'd said. 'Baht'at'

Baht'at Academy Trust, an Ilkley-based company, had taken over the running of Ripon and St Bega's College the previous year.

'The Informal Catch-Up?' Thelma had asked. Teddy had told her about this impending event earlier in the week; there had been something about the bland innocuousness of the words Thelma had found distinctly on the sinister side.

Teddy had carefully lined up six sky-blue folders. Thelma remembered buying them from Osbaldistons, the stationer's. Now long gone. 'It seems like the college is in rather dire financial straits.'

Thelma had been aware of a prickle of relief. They'd been using the word 'dire' to describe college finances as long as Thelma could remember. 'I see,' she'd said neutrally.

'It's not looking good. This is what they were saying.'

'The Children of the Suits?' That was their name for the frighteningly young people who comprised the Baht'at Visioning Team.

'Apparently there's a need for us to "open the kimono" and if necessary "punch the puppy".' Teddy had shaken his head perplexedly; he and Thelma could never quite get used to the rather bewildering range of terminology the Children of the Suits used.

'Which means?'

'They want a rebranding.'

Thelma had looked at him, vague images of cowboys with red-hot irons in their hands.

Teddy had frowned at a wallet marked rather obscurely 'God and Fertilizer'. 'They want to look at what we're offering course-wise so they can consider how best to package that, in a way that's more appealing to the wider world. And to do that, they want an overview of the course content.' He'd gestured rather helplessly at the files and folders. From the filing cabinet Snaffles gave an appalled sneeze.

'They just want a couple of sheets – a bare overview,' he'd said.

Thelma had nodded as if this was an easy, doable request – which they both knew it wasn't. There must have been something in the order of sixty-plus files and folders. Thirty-plus years of course content. The syllabus of the theology course – the Vicar Factory, as they referred to it – was at best a sprawling beast, one that evolved and changed year on year, according to students, to theological trends, to words from God. Was it possible to summarize this in any meaningful way in just two sheets? And if it was – was it something the Children of the Suits with their iPads and bottles of natural spring water and Instagram accounts could really comprehend?

'I can help,' she'd said.

'I'm nearly done,' he'd said cheerfully. Too cheerfully.

And it was then the phone had rung, the landline not the mobile. Going to answer, Thelma had been aware of a blurriness in her eyes. There was something about seeing her husband surrounded by thirty years' worth of paper – his whole working life – that she found infinitely sad and pathetic. She'd picked up the receiver, ready to give any cold-caller her best blast of Judi-Dench-as-Lady-Bracknell.

But it wasn't a cold caller.

It was Nicole, ringing on behalf of Kayleigh Brittain.

'What? Kayleigh Brittain's asked you to go in and see her?' Liz's voice came out in a sort of surprised squawk. 'Why?'

'She didn't say,' said Thelma.

'Do you think it's something to do with the letters?'

Thelma shrugged. 'I'll find out tomorrow,' she said, reaching for her car keys. 'Anyway – time's winged chariot, and all that.'

'Of course,' said Liz, standing up. 'This *could* all just be something and nothing.'

'Absolutely,' said Thelma. She looked at her friend, knowing there was something she wasn't saying. She was right.

This week St B's super attendance award goes to Oak Class with a stonking 98.2% attendance! Way to go, Oak Class! Coming to school IS important!

Tiff Banstead (Year Three teacher) found the letter sent to her at the start of morning break. She came into the staffroom slightly before other staff, box of marking under one arm, deliberately averting her gaze from the plate of Kit-Kats on the staffroom table. She checked her messages. Nothing from Glen. Not that she expected there to be.

The white envelope was in her pigeonhole, neatly tucked amongst the sachets of protein shakes from her latest diet regime: Weigh to Go! When it came to weight loss regimes, Tiff was something of a veteran – Hip and Thigh, Eat Yourself Thin, Weight

Watchers, Slimming World, 5:2 – going all the way back to the F-Plan; all these had been tried and tried by Tiff with varying measures of success. Weight had gone, dress sizes dropped – there had been a few glorious months . . . But always, inevitably, it had come creeping back on. The shapeless black dresses were unearthed from the back of the wardrobe, newer, slimmer garments stuffed regretfully away in a drawer, accompanied by the creeping, gloomy conviction that actually this was how life was meant to be. No wonder Glen did what he did.

This latest diet had been subscribed to on an impulse that was simultaneously optimistic and despairing in response to an ad that had popped up on her phone whilst she was playing FreeCell. According to some stick-thin presenter, if certain protein shakes were drunk three times a day the fat literally *melted* away – this statement being graphically illustrated by a bubbling, dissipating animation. And although the cynical, seasoned part of Tiff's mind knew this was literally too good to be true, there was some small corner that still wanted to believe in magic and happy-ever-afters and Glen and her in Corfu like in the old days; it was that part that thought: well, it couldn't hurt to give it a try. The £50 a month (that was the soon-to-be-ended trial price!) – well, she probably spent about that on gingerbread lattes from the drive-through. She was debating which shake to have as she opened the envelope.

WANT TO LOSE WEIGHT? TRY EATING
A BIT LESS, YOU FAT BITCH! NO ONE
RESPECTS A WEAK-WILLED FATTY!

The bald words smacked aside thoughts of cherry and mango shakes with a brutality that felt almost casual. Numb, Tiff sank onto one of the staffroom chairs, the letter clamped tight in hands that trembled. She could think of nothing but the harsh, mocking words, seeping like black poison into her mind, biting into her stupid, foolish plans. A noise in the corridor outside made her stiffen, stare wildly, guiltily at the door. She sprang up, stuffed the letter back into her pigeonhole.

'Coffee o'clock!' Pesto, the IT support assistant, was sounding chipper that morning. 'If my stomach can stand it.' He flashed Tiff one of his easy, confident looks. 'I need something. Honestly, Willow Base IT lessons, I swear they get worse.' He caught sight of the Kit-Kats. 'Hey up,' he said. 'Is it someone's birthday?'

'Pam's, I think,' said Tiff. She felt her voice coming out as if from a long way away.

'Dare I risk it?' he said cheerfully, nevertheless unwrapping one. 'Are you having one?' he said. 'Or are you being good?'

'I'm fine thanks,' said Tiff in that calm, distant tone. She sat down again, realizing she neither craved a Kit-Kat nor could she face a cherry and mango shake.

Indeed, she could barely imagine herself eating ever again.

CHAPTER THREE

Pat envisions the light and receives motoring tips from an arrogant man.

As Pat slowed down to park the Yeti, she tensed. Was that a knocking sound she could hear? She stopped the car but let the engine continue running, listening intently. A stack of possibilities with their attendant scenarios began welling up in her mind . . . the AA . . . the garage in Ripon . . . Jed Archer shaking his head . . .

She realized her heart was knocking, more insistently than any engine noise. She turned off the engine, let her hands rest on the wheel at ten and two, breathing slowly, methodically, just as Hollie her hypnotherapist had taught her . . .

Breathe in the light, breathe out the dark, the inappropriate . . .

All was good.

She forced herself to focus not on her dark thoughts but the tranquil scene outside, the late afternoon sun low in the sky, streaming light from over the distant Pennines, illuminating the church, the churchyard, the closed school and the coppery trees. It also cast a merciless light over the dusty shelf above the dashboard, the screwed-up gum wrappers, the discarded hospital parking tickets . . .

Fix your attention on the light . . .

She turned on the engine again, letting it run, listening intently. Nothing.

'Get a grip, Patricia,' she said to herself, turning off the engine and scooping up her bag and Laura Ashley notebook.

Car locked, she checked her phone. No message from Doug, so she presumed her son Andrew's mess-up with the joists had been satisfactorily sorted. Nothing from her husband Rod, but then she didn't expect there to be. Crossing the playground of the former Baldersby St James Primary School, she saw someone waiting by the padlocked front door: Martin Baker, a local builder she mentally called 'Martin the Mekon' on account of his bald head and large ears. Her heart sank at the sight of him; presumably he was bidding for the same job. More than once in the past had Baker Renovations won contracts over R & D Builders.

Find that sweet place Pat – envisage the possibility, not the pitfall.

Martin the Mekon looked up from his phone as she approached. Maybe he was surprised to see her, maybe – like her – he was annoyed at the prospect of competition; being a Yorkshireman he showed neither emotion but merely nodded.

'Now then, Pat.'

'Martin.'

'How's Rod doing?'

'Brilliant thanks.' She crossed her fingers and pasted on the optimistic smile she'd perfected for these occasions. She didn't want to give any indication Rod wasn't up to work, and she really didn't want to get into the whole 'all clear' conversation, and subsequent congratulations as if cancer was some all sort of trial of skill and endurance. Plus, she wasn't yet daring to allow herself to trust the consultant's words . . .

Caught it in nice time . . . Of course, we'll need to keep an eye on you, Mr Taylor, but my advice to you is go and live your life.

'Give him my best,' said Martin the Mekon.

'I will,' said Pat. 'But you'll see him yourself – he's back at work now.' The fingers remained firmly crossed.

'And I hear your Andrew's been helping out?'

'Just for the short term.' She smiled brightly, a smile that gilded over a multitude of glitches and cock-ups. 'But he's off back to uni in a couple of weeks.' She made a mental note to get a date for driving him back to Loughborough set in stone.

The creak of the playground gate made them both look round. An absurdly young man in a sharp suit was bouncing across the leafy tarmac in flashy-looking shoes that were entirely unsuitable for a North Yorkshire autumn day, however sunny. Next to her she could hear Martin the Mekon sucking his teeth.

Again she hoisted on a bright smile, one she'd grown used to flashing these past nine months, which said R & D Builders were open for business and whatever problems R might be having, D was very much in action, as was R's wife.

The man smiled back. Somehow the smile fitted perfectly with the shoes.

'Hi!' His voice was bright, sunny and so very young. 'Jared Keen, Lodestone Academy Trust.' *Mr Keeny-Keen,* Pat christened him.

'You must be Martin Baker – we spoke on the phone? And you are?' He turned to Pat, the smile now holding a sunny question.

'Pat Taylor, R & D Builders. We also spoke on the phone. I'm married to the R.'

'Terrif!' said Mr Keeny-Keen, bouncing slightly, hands clasped. 'Shall we make a start? FYI, I have to be somewhere at six.'

He undid the padlock and the battered red wooden door opened, releasing both the sad smell of an unused building, but also that faint indelible aroma of the primary school: wax crayons, coats, paper, thick custard.

Pat followed the bouncy figure inside. Despite the streaming sun it was dim and shadowy; Mr Keeny-Keen turned on the lights revealing in sad harshness the empty lobby, bare of chairs, notices, the inevitable rack of leaflets. On the wall by the sliding glass windows to the office a solitary notice: *All visitors to please sign in.*

'So, the plan is, as you know, a conversion to three high-end luxury dwellings.' Mr Keeny-Keen's voice sounded brightly insensitive. 'All planning, permissions, all of that good stuff is oven-ready to go.' He smiled. 'It's going to be a lovely, lovely use for the old place.'

Both Pat and Martin were silent at this; the truth was that there were plenty who thought that the old place had already *had* a lovely use, and that there had been no need to close what had been a thriving but admittedly small school. Indeed, for the past eighteen months or so the issue had been the subject of a vociferous campaign, which had been seldom absent from the pages of both the *Ripon Gazette* and the *Thirsk Advertiser*. To close a village school that boasted nearly thirty children was nothing less than an act of educational vandalism.

But Lodestone Academy Trust had been, regretfully, adamant. Though it saddened them greatly to see the end of over 150 years of tradition, such a small school was, in this day and age, simply not viable, so at the end of the previous July, Baldersby St James School had closed its doors for the last time.

Crossing the empty school hall, feet echoing on the scuffed parquet, Pat was aware of a feeling of melancholy. This was, after all, a school, the sort of place she'd spent thirty-odd years of her life in, and to see it denuded of its lifeblood – its plastic hoops and reading books and desks and, above all, its children – was undeniably sad.

Get a grip, Patricia. She was *not* here to be sad; she was here to land the contract to convert this building for R & D Builders. It would in so many ways be the perfect job to get Rod nicely back into the swing of working – good money, contained site, not too far away, not too taxing.

Get life back to something approaching normal.

You go and live your life, Mr Taylor.

Grimly energized by this thought she began asking Mr Keeny-Keen a series of bright, enthusiastic questions, ones she knew Doug (and Rod) would need the answers to in order to provide a quote – timescales, architects, materials. And Mr Keeny-Keen responded well, very well, to her cheerful, almost flirty barrage of questions and suggestions; he virtually squeaked in excitement when she floated the idea of a mezzanine floor in the old school hall. By contrast Martin the Mekon remained almost totally silent. Taciturn even. Didn't he even *want* this job?

In one of the classrooms Mr Keeny-Keen's phone rang, the confident, corporate tone incongruous in the empty room with its high arched windows.

'So sorry.' His face was a study of regret. 'I *ought* to take this!'

Pat opened the notebook to review the notes she'd written in her confident, loopy handwriting. She thought she had enough information, though Rod or Doug was bound to ask her a question she couldn't answer. But never mind, she felt quietly confident she'd made a good enough impression to land R & D Builders the contract. A sudden scenario flashed before her of herself and Mr Keeny-Keen swapping cheeky texts as work progressed.

In the bag, Patricia.

As she bent her head to replace the notebook, a flash of bright green on the floor caught her eye. A single, plastic unifix cube, the sort she herself had used in maths lessons countless times. She picked it up, hand closing round the smooth plastic shape. It brought a far-off sense of classroom buzz: tens and units, leaf prints, Chapter Three of *Stig of the Dump*.

'You needn't bother.' It was Martin the Mekon; he'd walked up

43

to her as Mr Keeny-Keen assured someone that something was 'totes no probs'.

'What do you mean?' There was something about Martin's tone that made Pat feel suddenly naïve, foolish even.

'I reckon this is all sewn up.'

Pat was going to ask more, but at that moment Mr Keeny-Keen ended his call and came bouncing across the room, all smiles and regret with the news he really had to be Exiting Stage Left.

Sat in the Yeti, Pat transcribed the email address from the card he'd given her into the Laura Ashley notebook, allowing herself a smile of satisfaction. She looked at the dark, unlit school, envisioning the R & D Builders board propped up by the railings. At *last* things could get back to normal. Looking up, she saw Mr Keeny-Keen get into what she had correctly guessed was his car, a long, low red jobbie. Even the roar sounded expensive, throaty and confident – with no trace of any sort of knock. The lane was now empty; Martin must have already gone. What on earth had he been getting at? Sewn up? More like sour grapes because he realized Pat was making a better impression? Well, he didn't deserve to get the job, not with an attitude like that!

She fired off a quick text to Doug and Rod – *GOT THE GEN WILL TYPE UP.* She considered cc-ing Andrew in, but decided against. She didn't want to do anything to give the impression he was going to be part of something he wasn't.

Time to go home.

Except she found herself not turning on the ignition. A sudden image of Rod ensconced in front of the flat-screen, the kitchen in goodness knows only what state and the utility room liberally draped with Andrew's drying pants, gave her the most profound feeling of weariness.

Without really thinking about it, she found herself getting out of the car and crossing the road to the church. Walking under the lychgate and up the cracked, mossy path, she had absolutely no idea where she was going and why she was going wherever it was. There was just a sense of *something* that kept her going.

Looking into the porch, with its notices for service rotas and parish council meetings, she remembered the last time she'd been inside, the church bedecked in flowers for Topsy's funeral. She paused, remembering that day, all that had happened . . . She smiled ruefully remembering the wake . . . all those spilt drinks and broken glasses! And then all that happened subsequently: the tears, the confront-ations – and of course the arrests. She walked round the side to the back, to where the newest graves lay drowsing in the last few fingers of fading sun. A few more had been added since Topsy had been laid to rest . . . how long ago was it now?

There was the headstone, plain, slightly grim, like Topsy herself. She smiled as unbidden the trademark sound of Topsy's click of disapproval sounded in her mind. It was a peaceful spot. She remembered at the funeral people saying how nice it was that Topsy was laid within earshot of a school playground.

No more, thanks to Lodestone Academy Trust.

She walked closer towards the grave. It was beautifully and meticulously kept, grass trimmed, stone cleaned. A bunch of late dahlias made an orange splash in the dimming light. Liz's work. Or Thelma's. At the thought of her two friends, her mind gave a weary sag as it does when one thinks of something that should be done and has been put off for far too long. She stood a moment, looking at the grave, letting her thoughts run.

You go and live your life, Mr Taylor.

And now, after months of Rod watching *Ice Road Truckers*, was the time to do exactly that: get him up off the sofa, back to work and converting Baldersby School into luxury accommodation with a mezzanine floor that made grown men squeak with excitement.

And getting his son back to Loughborough for the final year of his forensic science degree.

We need to get back on track.

She wasn't sure whether she said the words out loud but whether she did or not, the only answer was the wind soughing in the fir trees and the lowing of cattle being driven in for milking somewhere.

And then there was that other lurking darkness. The one she would not think about, certainly not in a graveyard. The one that would hopefully soon be buried under a blizzard of materials and hired machinery and trips to the wholesalers.

Envision the light not the dark, Patricia.

Time to go home, to tell Rod the good news, though maybe best be a tad muted until she knew one hundred per cent the contract was in the bag.

Emerging from the lychgate she stopped. Lights were on in the school. Had Mr Kenny-Keen left and forgotten to turn them off? But she was sure he had. She remembered how dark the building had looked in the fading afternoon light. Crossing to the Yeti, she noticed that once again a long red car was parked outside the school. Mr Keeny-Keen must have forgotten something. Hadn't he said he had an appointment at six? It must be nearly that now – he was going to be late.

She turned the engine on, and let it run for a few seconds. No, she was sure whatever it was, it wasn't knocking. She was just pulling out, when all of a sudden, another expensive throaty roar swelled up behind her and another long, sleek car – this one black – nipped swiftly into the space in front of her with the dexterity and assurance of a child pushing into a queue. Panicking, she jammed a foot onto the brake, stalling the engine, the movement jerking her handbag off the seat to fall in the footwell, where it scattered its contents liberally. Angry, heart thudding, she slammed

46

the heel of her hand onto the horn. Stupid idiot! What was he playing at?

And then, just as suddenly, outrage melted into embarrassment as he levered himself out of the low seat and walked towards the Yeti with confident, even arrogant, purpose. Pat saw a short, stocky man who appeared to be wearing working clothes – donkey jacket, jeans, sweatshirt – but she noted were actually designer equivalents.

He rapped assertively on the window. Wishing she didn't have to, she wound down the window, and caught a whiff of a rather aggressive aftershave.

'Have you got a problem, love?' The voice had a nasal Yorkshire twang; there was something bullish, challenging about it that made Pat shrink back slightly.

'I could've gone into you!' Her voice sounded shrill, defensive.

'You should've used your mirror – that's what it's there for.' She noticed his face was roasted an engrained sunbed-brown, his teeth were improbably white and round his neck he wore a thick gold chain.

'I did, that's why I stopped!'

'You want to take care, love.' There was something about the certainty in his voice, the way he held her gaze, that was deeply unnerving, making her shrink back, palms tightly clutching the wheel. Then he shrugged, turned and walked away with a dismissive air that made her cheeks burn. Angrily she turned on and revved the engine. He looked over his shoulder.

'You want to get that engine seen to,' he said. 'I can hear knocking.' Pat watched him go, scared, and flamingly angry, a very uncomfortable mix of feelings. *Hang on!* He was opening the gate of the playground! Why was he going into the school? She watched, astonished, as he walked across the playground with a barrelling, entitled gait, and through the door where Mr Keeny-Keen could be seen waiting.

CHAPTER FOUR

The virtues of academization are extolled, and a school tour is unexpectedly interrupted.

It was another gloriously sunny morning, though there had been traces of chill mist lacing the fields and allotments across from the school and the lime trees outside the front bore a distinct coppery hue. It was under one of these that Thelma parked the mussel-blue Corsair, but before getting out she sent up a quick prayer for Teddy followed by a text. She'd left him sitting at his desk, surrounded by towers of files and ring binders, staring at a piece of A4 paper that had been, as far as she could see, totally blank.

Getting out of the car, she stood for a moment, allowing the early autumn sun to warm her face. Just why did Kayleigh Brittain want to see her? It surely had to be, as Liz had said, something to do with the two letters? It'd be a huge coincidence if not. Of course, coincidences *did* happen – but in Thelma's experience more often they *didn't*. All too often, careful planning and concrete motives were to be found behind many seemingly 'coincidental' events. And whatever the truth of the matter, still the question that had worried her all night remained: should she tell Mrs Brittain about the letter Liz had found?

Walking inside she was immediately struck by a blast of warm air, plus the peaceful yet insistent tones of panpipe muzak. The lobby had been freshly painted, new bright blue chairs were ranged up against the walls where the display cabinets used to be and a large flat-screen dominated the wall where in her day there had been a display of children's work. At the sliding window to the office, Nicole popped up, putting Thelma in mind of something from a puppet show. Once again, she was wearing the grey jacket with another scarf, this one a lush shade of aquamarine. Behind her in the office, Thelma could see Linda Barley rattling away on her keyboard. She fully expected her to turn, smile and wave; any encounter with Linda Barley in school or out was invariably accompanied by at least five minutes of cheerful chit-chat – but now Linda kept her eyes firmly fixed on her keyboard. Concentrating perhaps?

'Mrs Cooper, good morning. Would you just like to sign in for me.' Nicole's voice, though perfectly pleasant, still held that 'actually I carry the world on my shoulders' quality, making Thelma, think of Joan Crawford in some of her more glacial roles.

Sitting down on one of the brilliant blue chairs, Thelma again registered the temperature – it was hot, almost unpleasantly so. Reaching out a hand she felt the radiator was full on. *Why?* When it was such a lovely day outside?

Again her thoughts turned to the letter, and she sent up a quick, reflexive prayer for guidance. *Should* she mention it? At first it had seemed a no-brainer – if an anonymous letter writer were targeting Kayleigh she had every right to know. But could Thelma be *sure*? Suppose that other letter had been dropped in the corridor by someone who had second thoughts about actually sending it? With a flush of embarrassment, she remembered her mistake about Donna Chivers – slandering an innocent woman! She decided to wait and see what Kayleigh Brittain had to say before deciding what to do.

Another trilling burst of panpipe music drew her attention to the video screen where a balding man in his forties sat in some featureless office looking earnestly into the camera.

'I'm Chris Canne,' he said, 'and I'm in the privileged position of being able to realize my vision for children's education through Lodestone Academy Trust.' The image changed to that of children running across the school playground, accompanied by yet more swelling panpipe music. 'Strive for success and reach for your dreams,' said a rich, trustworthy voice, 'at Lodestone Academy Trust!'

When St Barnabus's had become an academy more than one person said to Thelma that she must be glad she was Out Of It, as though the school had turned into some sort of war zone. Indeed, many had assumed that the impending academization was the reason Thelma retired, but in truth it was nothing to do with academization and everything to do with her IKEA boxes of history resources.

For the latter decade of her teaching life, Thelma had been history coordinator, a role that involved overseeing the curriculum, and organizing its attendant resources. Vikings, monasteries, World War Two, the Brontës – each had their blue IKEA box full of lessons, books and pictures meticulously maintained by Thelma, who also organized the various class trips to Rievaulx, Whitby, Jorvik and Haworth.

Then the history curriculum had been changed.

She remembered watching the then Minister for Education on television earnestly explaining how children learning topics out of chronological order gave them a confused, flawed concept of history . . . and from now on it was *imperative* that history was taught in *strict* chronological order, to prevent young people getting what he sorrowfully described as 'a pub quiz knowledge of historical facts'. Thelma (who numbered amongst her alumni several history teachers, two Oxbridge scholars and a moderately successful historical novelist) knew this to be absolute tosh. But the minister was the minister, and she was a primary school teacher approaching retirement. She remembered looking at her beloved IKEA boxes stacked neatly in the resource cupboard and realizing that under this revised curriculum a good three-quarters of them were redundant.

The next day she gave in her notice.

Not long after, she'd seen the same minister explaining the benefits of academization with an air that was equally earnest. It was ALL about freeing schools from the confused, flawed shackles of the local education authorities. It was imperative that the money was targeted DIRECTLY at the children! Ever since then she'd regarded the whole notion of academization with a jaded scepticism, and sitting in this overheated, expensively decorated lobby with its trilling soundtrack was doing nothing to dispel that feeling.

'If you'd like to come through . . .' Nicole broke into her reflections with the air of someone who had managed to save the world from chaos, just. As she used her lanyard to buzz open the electronic lock of Kayleigh Brittain's office, Thelma glimpsed a discolouration on the woman's neck, imperfectly concealed by her scarf. Some ongoing allergy perhaps?

Kayleigh Brittain's office was much as Thelma remembered – the desk, the chairs, the crimson carpet. The only difference was that the vivid seascape had gone; in its place was a decidedly bland view of the bridge at Mukor, a view familiar to Thelma from countless calendars and tea towels. Perhaps Kayleigh Brittain had felt the need to make the office even more corporate and conformist? More in keeping with the ethos of Chris Canne and his panpipes?

'Mrs Cooper, how lovely to see you again! Thank you so much for coming.' Kayleigh's voice was warm and engaging, her broad smile displaying improbably straight white teeth. 'Please take a seat. May I call you Thelma?'

51

As before, her face was discreetly and exquisitely made up; the abundant chestnut hair crisply waved. Sitting down, Thelma wondered just what it was about this woman that had led to someone writing to her anonymously in such graphic and bitter terms. Mrs Brittain looked so poised, so in control – could Thelma have somehow imagined or even misinterpreted that frozen, stricken look at the summer fayre?

As they chatted about the weather (glorious!), Nicole brought them in coffee (excellent colour), in what appeared to be exquisite bone china cups. Kayleigh pushed a coaster (bearing the ubiquitous Lodestone logo) across the polished surface of the desk to Thelma. Her own cup, however, she rested on a torn-open white envelope; this struck Thelma as rather incongruous. Surely the trust could run to more than one coaster?

'I want to thank you again for your support on the night of the fayre,' said Kayleigh. 'Really I don't know what we would have done had you not been on hand.'

'I hope there have been no more . . .' Thelma paused choosing her word carefully '. . . occurrences.' She looked at Mrs Brittain intently. Should she speak out?

'You know a primary school! Always something kicking off!' Was it her imagination or was Kayleigh's voice too light, her laugh too easy? 'But we have a new PTA and they seem to be shaping up well, touch wood.' With a light smile she rapped an exquisitely manicured nail against the rosewood desk. No mention of any letters. Now of course was the obvious time to say something about the letter, but Thelma felt reluctant. There was something about this composed, confident woman that made the thought of repeating those ugly, spiteful words a deeply uncomfortable one.

'Anyway . . .' Kayleigh took a business-like sip of coffee in a way that signalled the nitty-gritty of this meeting was upon them. 'The reason I called you in. Cutting to the chase as t'were.' She leant slightly forward. 'A vacancy has occurred on our school governing body, and I'd like to sound you out on the possibly of being co-opted on board. I know you did it for many years; I've heard very good things about the work you did.' She looked at Thelma with an earnest gaze. 'Not forgetting the help you gave us with that unpleasantness at the summer fayre. I thought to myself then: "This is a lady I want to have on my team!"'

Thelma stared. Go on the governors? This was totally unexpected. Immediately and instinctively she could feel in her mind a big, black, uncompromising 'no' forming. Governors, with all that entailed? The long evening meetings? All that paperwork to read? Quite simply it wasn't something she felt equal to taking on – certainly not with whatever was going on with Teddy at the college. She was trying to process these thoughts and frame a tactful negative, when Kayleigh began speaking again. She explained – with smooth, warm, well-chosen words – how she needed someone who *wasn't* a parent, someone who had some experience, someone who was an outside pair of eyes. She was one of those people who have the ability to speak on, politician-like, fluently, eloquently, framing and presenting points, before seamlessly flowing on to the next, leaving the other person unable to get their bit in.

Finally, she paused, but it was a dramatic pause; obviously something else was coming. Once again, Thelma was put in mind of Dame Helen Mirren.

'. . . You see, Thelma, I need people who I can *trust*.' There was a very definite emphasis on the word. 'And I need people who are on the *outside* of the school setting and . . .' here Kayleigh dropped her voice, again giving that sense of words being very carefully and deliberately chosen '. . . who can give impartial support in potentially difficult situations.' She met Thelma's eyes with a limpid gaze. *Had* she received another letter after all? But before

Thelma could even think further, let alone speak, Kayleigh held up one exquisitely manicured hand and said, 'Before you make your mind up – let me show you my school.'

Seeing her old school through the prism that was Kayleigh Brittain, Thelma began to feel something she had not expected to feel: impressed.

No two ways about it, the smart (and expensive) makeover the place had undergone did generate a strong impression, but actually it was much more to do with the school's head teacher. Everything – every detail about the place, every innovation, removed wall, flat-screen, maths scheme and data system – was subject to an intelligent and enthusiastic commentary from Kayleigh. *All* of it targeted, as she repeatedly said, directly at children to enable them to reach their *maximum potential*. Because that, at the end of the day, was what it was all about!

Whatever her doubts about academization, Thelma could not but help contrast all she saw and heard with how the school had been in her day – Feay's pleasant day-on-day vagueness, the muddle of battered reading books, the dumping ground of mats and PE equipment in the corner of the hall. Sid Dunn with his unmarked work and frequent absences; she couldn't imagine *him* lasting more than five minutes under Kayleigh Brittain's beady gaze.

Indeed the whole place gave off an air of pleasant order and efficiency – the children were all on task, the smiles of the staff bright and unforced . . . And yet, Thelma reminded herself, someone had written that letter – those *two* letters . . .

Jan Starke jumped to her feet as they entered Elm Base. 'I hope you like the room, Mrs Brittain!' she announced proudly. 'Welcome to our phonic-rich environment!' Thelma looked round. What on earth had she been doing? Every single surface seemed to have some bright, dayglo label bearing some phonic or other. 'Remember, boys and girls!' carolled Jan.

'Phonics is fun and funky,' chanted the children tonelessly.

Kayleigh's smile was rather mechanical, Thelma thought.

Out of all the teachers they saw, Sam Bowker seemed to have the strongest connection to his class. He was talking to the class about improving their writing and didn't even notice their entrance. In a quick, eager voice he exhorted the children to delve deep into that vocabulary treasure chest – find those pearly adjectives, those diamond nouns . . . Thelma could see he had thirty-two Year Six children in the palm of his biro-smudged hand.

'Sam's one of our strongest teachers,' said Kayleigh warmly. 'It was his writing results last summer that got us our Beacon School status.'

At this moment Sam caught sight of them and paused, smiled, looking decidedly flustered, fingering his collar – but then was it any wonder with his head teacher and one-time class teacher watching him?

'Of course, Sam actually came here once upon a time,' said Kayleigh as they walked away from the room.

'I know,' said Thelma. 'I taught him.'

For a moment Kayleigh looked surprised. 'Of course,' she said. 'I never thought of that. I suppose there's a few staff you know as well, like Jan.'

'A few,' said Thelma with a pang of sadness. 'Less every year of course.' A thought suddenly struck her. 'How's Bunty Carter?' she said. She tried to put a warmth into her tone, conveying the fact they were old friends – which was not even slightly true.

'She's not here at the moment.' Was it her imagination or was there a sudden restraint in Kayleigh's tone? 'She's off sick.'

'Oh dear,' said Thelma. 'Nothing serious I hope?'

'Some bug or other.' Yes, there was a definite deliberate element to the vagueness of the answer, and Thelma was opening her mouth to ask more when Kayleigh stopped in the middle of the Key Stage One corridor.

'It must be strange being back?' She smiled a warm, slightly ironical smile, one that invited confidences.

Thelma felt a sudden, unexpected desire to win the approval of this richly dressed, successful woman who was so passionate about her school. 'There's been a lot of changes,' said Thelma.

Kayleigh's smile widened, now with an air of comical self-deprecation. 'Oh Lordy!' she said. 'I hope you don't hate what I've done to the place.'

'No, not at all.' Thelma spoke quickly to avoid any misunderstanding. 'Change is a necessary part of life – nowhere more than in a school. The school I started teaching in was a very different place by the time I retired. And as we all know, education exists in a culture of change.'

Kayleigh smiled, nodding admiringly. 'You know, Thelma, that's such a wise thing you're saying.' Thelma felt a pulse of pleasure at having won the approval of this designer-clad lady but at the same moment she suddenly she felt tired. Old and tired and out of place in this modern, successful environment with its targets and phonics and iPads, which seemed to bear little relation to the place she'd worked all those years. *I've had my day,* she thought. *Coming back here was a mistake.*

She realized Kayleigh was looking at her shrewdly. 'I daresay,' she said, 'you've heard a lot about the changes here. And you've probably heard a lot about yours truly!'

Thelma was about to disavow this, despite it being against her principles to lie so roundly, but Kayleigh was still speaking. 'I wouldn't expect anything less,' she said. 'But the way I see it – I've a job to do. And that means making changes. I'm not here to make friends with people, I don't want to know about their private lives – I'm here to make the best job I can of running this school.'

It was then they became aware of the noise coming from Rowan Base.

It was loud – loud and with an edge that Thelma recognized instantly as verging on the out-of-control, followed by a sudden shout and crash. Thelma followed Kayleigh to the classroom. Standing at the front was Margo Benson, glasses madly winking, looking decidedly flustered. 'Children,' she said. 'Children, settle *down*! Ms Clegg will be back *any* moment!'

Thelma fully expected Kayleigh to walk in, take control (as she herself was itching to do), but Kayleigh stood in the doorway, almost indecisive. Margo fairly sprinted across the room to them. 'Becky – Ms Clegg – I think she's in the you-know-where.' There was something very significant – almost pleading – in her tone; it seemed like she was about to say a lot more but Kayleigh cut her off with a firm 'Thank you, Margo,' and closed the door. Turning on her expensive heel she hurried off down the corridor, Thelma trotting after her.

'Thank you so much for your time,' Kayleigh said rather breathlessly. 'I hope you enjoyed seeing the school.'

What on earth was going on?

They rounded the corner to a scene of crisis. Stood outside the door to the ladies' toilet were no less than four people: Linda, Nicole and two women Thelma recognized as dinner ladies, arms folded in that instantly recognizable posture of people witnessing trouble.

Linda was knocking on the toilet door. 'Becky love,' she was saying. 'Becky, is everything all right in there?'

One of the dinner ladies looked at Kayleigh. 'Oh, Mrs Brittain,' she said. 'Ms Clegg just pushes right past me. Ever so upset she is. Fair slammed the door.'

'Becky love!' said Linda knocking again. 'Are you okay in there?'

'All right, ladies.' Kayleigh's voice held a crisp tone of command. 'I'm sure whatever it is, Ms Clegg doesn't want the whole school gawping outside.'

She paused, and in that second an awful sound of sobbing was heard by everyone.

'She's in a right state,' said one of the dinner ladies somewhat redundantly.

'Pushed right past me,' said the other again.

'If you just want to leave Nicole to deal with this . . .' There was an even sharper tone in Kayleigh's voice, and the others reluctantly moved away. Nicole, looking somewhat nonplussed, took Linda's place by the toilet and Kayleigh firmly steered Thelma to the main entrance.

'Sorry about all this.' She held out a trembling hand. 'Thank you for your time. And if you could let me know about the governors, there is a meeting next week, which I know is ridiculously short notice—' She smiled, whilst at the same time looking back over her shoulder towards the toilets.

'Actually, I've already decided,' said Thelma, slightly out of breath. She was about to open her mouth to say 'regretfully, no', but at that second, the door from the main corridor fairly flew open and Margo appeared.

'Mrs Brittain,' she said, 'I'm sorry, but I couldn't say. Not in front of the kids . . . But, Mrs Brittain . . . It's Becky . . . in her handbag . . . *There's been another*!'

There was a fresh burst of decidedly angry sobbing from behind the closed lavatory door.

CHAPTER FIVE

There is consternation in the staffroom, and some prominent scratches in an unusual place give pause for thought.

In the morning, if his wife were to leave the house before him, Derek Newsome would invariably tell her to 'take care' in serious tones, as if she were some Captain-Oates-type figure who had decided against all the odds to venture into an Antarctic wilderness. Most of the time Liz found this both touching and reassuring. Most of the time, it was fine and exactly what she wanted.

Most of the time.

Sometimes – *sometimes* – it frankly got a bit much. Sometimes she wanted her husband of thirty-three years to clap her cheerfully on the back and say words to the effect of: *My darling – knock the world dead! Stuff caution! Go tango across Thirsk market place with a rose between your teeth!*

And now walking up the path to St Barnabus's in her Matalan fleece, shoulders hunched against a decidedly fresh breeze, was definitely one of those times.

Again, she thought back to her conversation with Thelma the night before. Derek had been out on his run, so she had been able to talk freely.

'Margo *must* have meant another letter.'

'Maybe.' Thelma had sounded cautious.

'Well what else could it have been? Another *what*?'

'I'm not sure.'

'Why didn't you tell her about the letter I found?'

'She didn't give me a chance,' said Thelma and explained the way she'd been bundled out of the school. 'But in any case, whatever is going on, she's aware of it and I think we need to be careful.'

'Careful' was Thelma's verbal equivalent of the yellow card, and Liz had detected a definite note of 'let's back off' in her words. After their conversation Liz had sat there, looking out of the conservatory at the inky skies.

First Kayleigh Brittain, and now Becky . . .

Jan picked up at the second ring.

'Liz, I'm right in the middle of something.' As was usual with Jan, there was the implication that Liz had not only known this but had deliberately chosen that moment to ring.

'I was just wondering how you are.'

'I'm fine.' There was an exaggeratedly puzzled and at the same time combative quality to Jan's voice.

'And I was just wondering how Becky Clegg was.'

'What do you mean?' Now she sounded guarded and suspicious. 'Why are you asking about Becky?'

'It's just something Thelma said—' Liz began.

'Thelma!' Jan broke in with a laugh. 'I might have known! Honestly, you and Thelma Cooper!' She sounded cheerfully exasperated, as if Thelma and Liz were two lovable but slightly irritating old biddies with nothing better to do than gossip their days away.

'She just said Becky had had to leave the class and seemed upset.'

'Becky's fine.' Jan firmly cut in using that irritating tone – that

'*I know more than you do, but I can't say, but I still know*' tone. 'She's absolutely fine. More than fine.'

'And is Bunty Carter still off ill?' Liz decided she might as well go for it.

'Liz – what *is* this?'

'I heard Bunty was ill, and I wondered how she was.'

'I suppose this is also from Thelma?' Liz said nothing. 'To the best of my knowledge she's off with some sort of bug, but to be honest I've more important things to do than check up on Bunty Carter!'

Liz knew when she was beaten. 'I'll let you get on,' she said.

'Liz.' Jan's tone definitely held a warning. 'Liz, you need to be keeping shtum on this one.' She spoke as if the usual occurrence was for Liz not to keep shtum, and indeed broadcast what she knew on Radio York. Liz frowned out into the strengthening twilight; at the end of the drive, she could see Derek standing in the driveway, one hand on his knee, the other doing whatever it was he did with his watch when he finished a run. She needed to end the conversation . . .

A huddled figure . . . fingers in her ears. 'Tell him to go away!'

On an impulse she blurted, 'Tomorrow when I come in, maybe we can talk?'

There was a pause. Then: 'What about?'

'Are you okay?'

'Of course I'm okay. And now if you don't mind, I need to get on.'

Putting down her phone Liz exhaled, feeling distinctly battered.

Becky wasn't fine. She knew that as clearly as if Jan had told her outright.

And more importantly that snake of a thought had gone nowhere; if anything it had got bigger and stronger.

'Who were you chatting to?' She hadn't heard Derek come in. He stood now, head round the door en route to the shower.

'Just Jan,' she said.

He stopped, came into the room. 'Oh?' he said.

'Just chatting,' she said in airy tones that fooled neither of them.

In the overheated lobby, tapping her name into the intimidating sign-in screen, she could hear coming from the school hall the timeless, reassuring sound of the children singing. Harvest assembly this week. She thought of all those harvest hats hanging up in Jan's classroom and made a mental note to take a stapler into the assembly to deal with the inevitable mishaps.

'Here you are, Mrs Newsome.' Once again, Nicole was swathed in a scarf, this one a jaunty shade of cobalt. Was it even bigger? It seemed to shroud her whole neck. With a pleasant smile she held out the name label – but just out of reach, preventing Liz from taking it. 'We were wondering this morning whether you could go through to Year Five – Sycamore, that's Mr Berryman's class – if that's okay.' Something about the pleasant but empty tone told Liz it mattered little whether it was okay or not.

'But Mrs Starke's expecting me.' Liz could feel herself getting flustered. How on earth could she put her worries about Jan to rest if she was working with Year Five? In her mind was an image of Derek sadly shaking his head, his face one big 'What did I tell you?'

'Mrs Starke said to say she's fine this morning. But Mr Berryman does need some help and Mrs Brittain thought you might like a change of scene.'

Kayleigh Brittain? She tried and failed to imagine Kayleigh Brittain caring two straws about whether Liz would like a change of scene . . . Unless . . . *Jan*. Her mind flew back to that conversation the night before . . . What if Jan had requested she be sent elsewhere? For a moment Liz felt manipulated, outmanoeuvred. She was very tempted to walk out, but something stopped her.

She needed to see Jan more than ever and she couldn't do that out of school.

She stretched out her hand. 'That's fine,' she said brightly.

Twenty minutes later and Liz was aware of the beginnings of a headache pulsing behind her eyes. Ian Berryman's maths lesson – Pineapple Maths as it was called – was like no other maths lesson Liz had ever seen (or indeed taught).

The heart of it seemed to consist of a lot of slides – PowerPoints as they were called these days – projected onto the vast flat-screen that dominated the front of the room (where dear old Maggie Backhouse had had her flags of the world and times table posters). The succession of mathematical images – glaringly bright – were presented with a lot of enthusiastically shouted instructions from Ian – 'and now it's time to partition up the number, guys!' – more like an aerobics class than any maths lesson. From time to time there were pauses to 'hit the thinking space' and the whole of this shebang was accompanied by frequent rolls of fists on the desks and shouts of: 'Pineapple One! Pineapple Two! Pineapple Three – and GO!'

The purpose of this latter exercise was totally lost on Liz.

Of course, it didn't help that it was so very hot in the room despite all the windows being wide open. Ian Berryman was yet again wearing PE kit: trackie bottoms and T-shirt (stained under the arms). And those trackie bottoms were really almost *offensively* tight. Liz tried to avert her eyes but again and again found her gaze wandering back with morbid fascination to the Lycra sculpture between his legs. It reminded her of a gerbil she had had when she was a girl; when it was on heat it had a habit of hanging from the ceiling bars of its cage, swollen genitalia on full view. It always seemed to happen when Great-Auntie Doris was coming round for tea.

'Okay, guys . . . let's use that thinking space!'

Liz mentally sighed; for all this shouting about thinking spaces, there didn't seem to be that much actual thinking going on. She was feeling decidedly redundant. She wasn't even needed for the three children at the side whom her expert eye had identified as 'the plodders' – two boys and a girl sat with that classroom assistant, the one selling raffle tickets the night of the summer fayre. What was her name? Claire? Plump, rather spotty and watching Ian with sparkling eyes and the widest of grins.

'Okay, guys.' Ian punched the air; the lesson seemed to be reaching some sort of climax. 'What do we do now?' Silence. 'We . . .' Silence. 'We round up to the nearest ten, don't we?'

Energetic nods of agreement from round the room, none more energetic than from the plodders, Liz noticed, who obviously hadn't a clue what was going on. Her heart went out to them, as it always went out to those who struggled, who were lost, who generally fell by the wayside in a primary classroom. She fanned herself discreetly with a Pineapple Thinking Slate, wondering how much more of this she could stand.

The classroom phone trilled into the melee; Ian sprinted across the room and scooped it up. Really someone needed to have a word with him about that tracksuit.

'Hola, Willow Base!' he said cheerfully. A pause. 'Okay.' His voice was suddenly almost deliberately casual. His glance at the class was furtive – almost shifty. 'Five.' He replaced the phone and turned to the class.

'Okay, guys,' he said. 'Pineapple try time! I want you to try challenges one through five using those thinking brains.' (What other sort of brains were there? Liz wondered). 'Miss Donnelly will help you if you get stuck. Which you won't because you're going to Pineapple Try!' He turned to Claire. 'Got to see a man about a harvest assembly,' he said. Again, that casual tone in his voice. 'Back in five.'

'That's fine,' said Claire, but he was gone.

But it didn't look as if it was fine, not one little bit. Indeed, Claire look as dejected and lacklustre as she'd been pink and animated not five minutes previously. 'Okay, guys.' She moved to the class. 'Pineapple try time.' But the words were bleak and had none of Ian Berryman's energy. Maybe she didn't like being left in charge?

'I can sit with your group if you'd like?' offered Liz. Claire nodded miserably and all at once it struck her that tears were not far away. What on earth could be the matter? Liz moved over to the plodders who greeted her bright smile with impassive looks. 'Now,' she said cheerfully. 'You're going to have to help me here.'

After twenty minutes Liz felt they were getting somewhere. The children (Jacey, Blair and Amos) seemed to be growing confident with what they were doing. Once she'd abandoned any attempt to follow Pineapple Maths, a few basic questions had revealed a very fundamental problem: they didn't know their number bonds to ten. And without that very basic knowledge all the shouting in the world wouldn't help them understand maths, Pineapple or otherwise.

With the help of the whiteboards plus a tray of rather dusty dear old unifix retrieved from somewhere by Jacey, they were making some headway. Plus, they were relaxing a bit. Jacey was talking about her sister's boyfriend's motorbike, whilst Blair and Amos were solemnly informing her about the mysteries of a new level of Minecraft – a subject she knew something about thanks to her grandson Jacob. Claire had largely ignored them, hands full as they were with the rest of the class (some of whom seemed to need a lot of Pineapple thinking space). She had at one point said a quick 'thanks' to Liz, but she still had that overwhelming sense of misery. *Why*? Could *she* . . . could she have had a letter? But that didn't make sense. The girl had seemed fine – more than fine – until Ian had been called away.

'Okay, guys!' Ian Berryman burst back into the room, even more sweaty and slightly red in the face. Indeed, he rather looked as if he'd been running. But then it really was absurdly hot. 'How are we all getting on?' But without waiting for any sort of answer he burst into a shout of 'Pineapple One, Pineapple Two, Pineapple Three!'

Liz felt she ought to talk to him about the work her group had done, but something told her he wouldn't be interested. She looked over at Claire. You'd have thought she'd be pleased at Ian's return, but she was looking out of the window with such an expression of dumb misery that Liz felt a sudden impulse to hug her. At that moment she said, 'Excuse me a moment,' and rushed out of the classroom.

Ian seemed totally oblivious to both her misery and her absence. He was now energetically writing on the flat-screen with some sort of stylus, right arm pumping up and down across the lit surface. As he did, his T-shirt rucked up slightly at the back – and there on the bare flesh . . . Liz looked, frowned . . . but before she could look further the bell went, and he turned to dismiss the class. As they cheerfully made their way outside, he turned to Liz, looking at her properly for the first time that morning. 'Right!' he said. 'Coffee o'clock!'

Time to find Jan.

Pausing on the threshold of the staffroom, Liz saw at once she wasn't there.

Hiding in her classroom no doubt. Very well, if she wasn't there, she'd just have to go and find her. It'd be better to talk in private anyway.

She turned and stopped. Just down the corridor from the staffroom, Kayleigh Brittain had appeared and was standing there smiling pleasantly at the children making their way past her. Although she wasn't looking at her directly, Liz was seized by the sudden conviction that she was watching out for her. She took one tentative step forward and immediately that pleasant gaze was upon her.

'Mrs Newsome! Helping us out again! We're coming to rely on you! How are you getting on in Sycamore Base?' There was something about her bright tone and smile that Liz found frankly terrifying.

'I was looking for Jan,' she said.

'I'm afraid she's on duty.' The smile did not waver one jot. 'Why don't you go and grab a coffee? I'm sure you've earned one!'

There was no way Liz was ever going to do anything other than back down; cravenly she retreated into the staffroom, convinced more than ever that Jan had asked to be kept away from her.

If anything, the room was even quieter today than it had been the previous week. Again, staff were gazing into their drinks or having those quiet, muttered conversations. That good-looking support assistant with the strange name – Pasta? Pesto? – was talking about some ongoing stomach problem. 'The slightest whiff of anything spicy sets if off,' he was saying earnestly. On the whiteboard Margo was putting the finishing touches to a notice she had been writing. *Staff Xmas Do! The Lamb, Rainton. Buffet and Rod Stewart Tribute Act, £15 deposit to Margo by October 10th.*

It was just a staffroom, like a thousand thousand school staffrooms up and down the country. *Get a grip, Liz.* Just because people were being quiet . . . *And yet* . . . there was a something about the atmosphere she found deeply disturbing. She allowed her eyes to roam round the room – the people, the mugs, the pigeonholes . . .

The pigeonhole.

Her eyes stopped, drawn to a blue bag wedged in one of the

rectangular spaces. She stood up, walked across. Yes, she hadn't been mistaken. Bunty Carter's pigeonhole – and there was her Knowbody order wedged in.

She turned to where Margo was drawing little Christmas trees around the notice she'd written.

'Bunty Carter's order.'

'What about it?' Margo's fluty tones were decidedly on the sour side.

'Doesn't she get her daughter to come in and collect if she's off?'

'Normally she does,' said Margo. 'And bring the money! I tell you something – if Milady thinks I'm taking any more orders from her she is in for one rude awakening!' She seemed set to say a good deal more when the crash of a mug made them both look round. That large teacher – Tiff? – was standing by the water heater, frowning abstractedly down as if she'd forgotten something. On the floor by her feet was a shattered Lodestone Trust mug. Was she all right?

Liz took half a step forward, but even as she did so, the girl's eyes rolled ghoulishly up in her head, affording a sudden, nightmarish flash of milky white as the large body in the shapeless black dress convulsed and folded gently onto the floor. There was an instant's farcical stillness and then the room erupted into gasps, movements and cries of 'Tiff?' The only person who seemed to know what to do was Ian Berryman; with a confident, practised movement he was kneeling by her side, expertly tipping her into the recovery position whilst massaging her hand with a gentle, almost sensual touch. 'Tiff,' he said softly, insistently, repeatedly.

'It's that diet she's on,' said Margo, rather dismissively Liz thought.

'Is it still the five:two?' said someone else.

Margo snorted. 'More like the zero:zero!' she said. 'I swear, she's been starving herself, silly thing.'

'Poor love,' said Liz.

'That's what comes from marital discord,' said Margo. Liz looked at her. 'My lips are sealed,' she said. 'Let's just say some gentlemen need to learn to keep it in their trousers.'

Tiff started to stir, and this was everyone's general cue to leave the staffroom, apart from Ian and Margo. Liz's last view of Ian was him squatting beside the girl, still talking gently, insistently, as Tiff began to stir blearily back into life. Again, his T-shirt had become rucked up, and Liz had a clear view of what she'd only glimpsed before. Those nasty scratches on both sides of his lower back. They looked quite raw, and moreover Liz was perfectly sure they were fresh.

What on earth was there about a harvest assembly meeting that entailed one getting scratches just above the buttocks?

CHAPTER SIX

There is no sign of Big Mama; moreover, her garden is in a state of disarray.

'It was awful,' said Liz. 'She was spark out. I thought she'd had a heart attack. The turning's just down here.' It was shaping up to be another glorious sunny September day, though the early morning had been a chilly one, jewelled cobwebs in the hedgerows and even the first white tracings of frost.

'You're sure it's this one?' Thelma might have added 'this time'; they'd already gone wrong twice, entailing two rather tricky three-point turns in the narrow lanes. She wasn't at all convinced about the wisdom of this trip. After finding Bunty's uncollected order at school, Liz had made several unsuccessful attempts to ring her. After each attempt she'd sent a worried text to Thelma. In the end it had seemed simplest to suggest driving out and seeing her, delivering her order and hopefully putting her friend's mind at rest.

'Yes.' Liz didn't sound at all sure. She also sounded distinctly preoccupied, neither of which boded well for their successfully finding their way to Bunty Carter's. 'And you say Tiff's been starving herself?' Thelma manoeuvred the mussel-blue Corsair down the narrowing lane. 'I wonder why.'

'She was dieting. But then Margo told me her husband likes playing away. Hence these diets.' She shook her head. 'Silly, silly girl.'

'Even so.' Thelma frowned. 'As a rule most people dieting generally don't go starving themselves.'

'Do you think there's more to it?' Liz looked at her friend.

Thelma didn't answer immediately, a tractor was approaching, and it was going to take all her concentration to tuck the Corsair into the side to let it pass.

'There could be.' Thelma raised her voice as the vast machine lumbered past in a cacophony of dusty and wisps of straw. 'If this Tiff received a letter herself, maybe saying something about her husband?'

Liz stared at her friend. Obviously the thought had not occurred to her. '*Another* letter,' she said.

'From what Margo said, it does seem like there's been more than one,' said Thelma, setting off.

Liz frowned. 'Of course it could all be something and nothing,' she said. It was the fifth time she'd said this since Thelma had picked her up, and Thelma recognized the signs only too well. Liz was worried, and she suspected it was nothing to do with navigating the lanes or what to say to Bunty Carter.

Thelma sighed to herself. She simply didn't have the time or energy for this. Whoever was sending out nasty letters – if indeed that *was* what was happening – Kayleigh was obviously aware of it and much better placed to deal with it. She quelled the guilty pang at not having told her about the letter found by Liz – but then she had worries of her own. Teddy's plethora of files and folders had been duly reduced to the required two sides of A4, and now a 'Heads-Up' meeting (whatever that was) had been scheduled by the Children of the Suits. She'd watched Teddy that morning, pacing the garden, coffee in hand, and had wanted to be able do so much more than bang on the window and tell him to put a jumper on.

A blast of urgent music (which Liz recognized to be from that bit in *Titanic* when the ship sank) startled them both. 'I wish Jacob would stop beggaring about with my ringtone,' she said apologetically. She glanced at the screen: No caller ID. Well, she wouldn't be answering that! She had a policy of never answering such calls, certainly not after what had happened last year when a caller posing as a bank official had successfully frauded her friend and colleague Topsy out of an eye-wateringly large sum of money.

Replacing her phone in her handbag she frowned out of the window, not really seeing the workaday beauty of the beige and gold fields with their enormous shredded wheat biscuits of rolled hay. Kayleigh and Becky – and now *Tiff*?

'I know you're in there . . . !' 'Tell him I'm busy . . . tell him to go away . . .' But all that had been *years* ago . . .

She checked herself, as she did each time the thought slithered into her mind.

'It's all probably something and nothing,' she said.

Six times, thought Thelma. Aloud she said, 'Have you noticed anything about the temperature in school?'

'Hot,' said Liz immediately. 'Very hot.'

'I wondered if it was just the other day,' said Thelma. 'The radiators all seemed to be full on.'

'I know about that,' said Liz. 'Jan told me. They've got this new green boiler.'

'Green?'

'Biomatic? Runs on wood pellets.'

'Bio*mass*.'

'That's the one.'

'Well, it certainly does the job; really, it was almost unbearable.'

Liz felt slight feelings of impatience – what had this all to do with the price of fish?

'I just keep thinking about Bunty.' She spoke rather pointedly, as if reminding Thelma about the real nature of their errand.

Thelma glanced at her friend. 'You know if Bunty *is* having one of her "dos" . . . she might not thank us for going round.'

There was a moment's silence as they remembered the various 'dos' that had occurred since the tragic death of Bunty's son and her marriage break-up. That incident at sports day. And yet every time, with Feay's patient support, she'd somehow managed to scramble back on track. But now Feay had gone . . .

Liz nodded. 'I know,' she said. 'It's just with her not having collected her order . . . I want to see her with my own eyes. Turn right here.'

Now the lane was definitely petering out, as if it could no longer be bothered keeping up the pretence of being any sort of highway. To the left suddenly appeared a low, brick-built bungalow, seemingly half smothered by the waving fields around it; directly beyond were the ruled steel wires and lines of the East Coast Main Line.

'Here,' said Liz triumphantly. As they got out of the car, a sleek red and silver train blasted past with a shock of air and noise. 'It wouldn't suit me,' Liz said. 'Being stuck out here all on my own.' To those who didn't know her history, it had always been a bit of a mystery why Bunty had chosen to relocate to this remote bungalow after her divorce. 'I like peace and quiet me,' was all she'd said at the time. Those who knew her understood a little better but, all the same, the general consensus was whatever peace and quiet one needed could be found without sticking yourself at the end of a remote cart track next to a main railway line.

The front gate was broken, propped up wearily against the gate post. Liz cast a critical gardener's eye over the tangled plants. 'You do the talking,' she said.

Thelma, who had no intention of doing anything else, approached the door, panels of wood and frosted grass, and knocked firmly.

Liz took a step back. 'Be careful,' she said. 'I mean if she *has* got some sort of bug. It's the allotments fuddle at the weekend and I'm on puddings.'

But there was no answer.

'Maybe she's asleep,' said Liz doubtfully. She cautiously peered in through the living room window. Thelma was coming to her own conclusions. There was, she recognized, a very distinct quality to a knock that wasn't going to be answered and something was telling her Bunty Carter wouldn't be answering any time soon.

She knocked again.

'Maybe she's gone out?' said Liz. 'To the chemist perhaps?'

Thelma shaded her eyes and stood down, looking through the frosted glass panel. 'There's post on the floor,' she said. 'And more than one day's worth.'

'She could've gone away.'

'During term time?'

They walked round the bungalow, peering through windows, tense at the worst-case scenarios playing through their minds. The glimpses they saw – the latest *Radio Times*, a paperback book splayed face down on the arm of a chair – did not speak of someone who had gone away. In one room two large, full bags for life adorned with enormous garish rainbows stood near the door, as if ready for a trip to the charity shop. Thelma stared at these, trying to make out the contents.

'Maybe she's fallen,' said Liz worriedly.

'But where?' said Thelma, still peering into the gloom, eyes shaded against the sun. 'We can see into every room.'

'Maybe she's in the you know where,' said Liz. 'That's what happened to Joyce's mother. Fell against the door. They had to get the fire brigade.'

'I looked,' said Thelma briefly, not mentioning the precarious, undignified way she'd perched on a rusty, unused watering can, nearly coming to grief in the process. 'One thing . . .' She paused significantly. 'There's no bottles in the recycling.'

Liz frowned. 'Are you sure?' Thelma nodded and the two women looked at each other. Standing there, in the drowsing afternoon sun, amidst the waving fields of late barley, it seemed impossible to think anything untoward could have happened . . .

And yet Bunty Carter was not there and apparently had not been there for a couple of days at least.

'Do you think we should call the police?' asked Liz.

'I think maybe try her daughter first,' said Thelma.

'But do you even have her number?' There was a descant of panic in Liz's voice. 'Because I don't.'

'Yoo-hoo!' The cheerful voice made them clutch each other's arms again. 'Did I make you jump?' asked the voice. 'Soz! I parked up round the corner. It's a beggar with the four by four on these narrow lanes.'

The owner of the voice, a rotund figure with a basin cut of iron-grey hair, advanced towards the bungalow. 'Bunty?' she said, looking at Liz and Thelma. 'No Bunty. Blast and damnation.'

'I don't think she's in,' said Liz. 'We were also looking for her.'

'I should've realized,' said the woman, 'when she didn't message me back. Normally she's spot on when it comes to getting back to me. Unlike some sharks who shall remain nameless.'

They both looked blankly at her. The woman gave a shout of laughter. 'eBay!' she said. 'Or rather blessed, blessed eBay. Big Mama's one of the main people I buy from. I was hoping she could help me out with pencil crayons. Brownie bash this weekend and after all this sunshine it's threatening rain – law of Sod and all that. So, a plan B is most definitely needed.' She sighed, and again looked at the house. 'I have to say,' she said, 'this is most unlike her. She's normally one of my rock solids. And with me only being in Ainderby it is but a hop, skip and a jump away to click and collect. Oh well.' She sighed and looked at the house one last time. 'I suppose the Yorkshire Pound Warehouse beckons. Only their crayons splinter as soon as you look at them.' With a good-natured shrug, she turned and walked away.

Thelma and Liz looked at each other. Prickles of alarm were now definite pangs.

Where was Bunty Carter? Liz's phone gave an abrupt beep, as if giving electronic confirmation of their alarm. 'A message,' said Liz. She remembered the call she'd not taken. 'Probably our Jacob beggaring about.' But it was not Jacob.

'Hello, this is a message for Liz Newsome.' The voice sounded rather nasal and unsubstantial. 'It's Candice Burton-Carter. Bunty Carter's daughter.' Immediately Liz flipped the phone onto speaker mode and gestured Thelma closer. 'I understand from Mum you've been trying to get in touch with her. She's staying with me. She put her back out. She'd been working in the garden and it went, all around her shoulder and spine – she's in absolute agony, barely able to move.' There was something, some edge to the voice that both listeners picked up, but neither were able to fully identify. 'She's sending a sick note into school and will be in touch when she feels a bit better.'

Message ended, they both looked at each other.

'I thought you said she had a bug,' said Liz.

Thelma nodded. 'That's what Kayleigh Brittain told me.'

'I tell you something else – Candice said she did it gardening.' Liz nodded at the front garden, a waving mass of pink and yellow wildflowers. 'That garden's not been touched for months.'

With a thud and a blast, another train belted by.

CHAPTER SEVEN

A temporary escape is made from the world and a glittery option plumped for.

Pat slammed the back door. There was no one inside to hear it (except Larson) but it made her feel better. Her copper-bottomed pan! The one from the late, much-missed Cathedral Cook Shop! Her jaw tightened as she climbed into the Yeti. It was what Rod had said, and the casual way he had said it, as if it was no big deal – *Just getting himself a bit of breakfast* . . . It looked more like Andrew had been putting out a fire with it.

She paused, hands on the steering wheel, forcing deep breathes into herself . . . pushing out long exhalations . . .

And breathe . . . Experience the present moment, not the emotions from events past . . .

It wasn't that she didn't love her middle son. Of course she did . . . It was just at the moment she found him irritating beyond words. Growing up at home, his amiable meandering through life hadn't been a problem. It was part of the deal of motherhood, and also a peaceful contrast to Justin's confident charge and Liam's stressful trawl through childhood and adolescence. But now – he'd moved out! Left the nest! Off to be a forensic scientist in Loughborough, doing something that for once wasn't because his brother was doing it, or his parents had organized it for him. And he needed to be back there. Not ruining her pans – and festooning her kitchen with his pants.

And breathe. View the bigger landscape, not the immediate pitfall.

Again, she forced herself to breathe slowly . . . Only it didn't make her feel that much better as this particular landscape was as bleak, if not more so, than her ruined pan.

The rejection from Lodestone Academy Trust for the Baldersby quote had come yesterday afternoon. There had been something about the bland chirpiness of its tone (*Hi Pat, sorry, we've decided not to go with R & D Builders this time*) that had wounded her profoundly, as if Mr Keeny-Keen himself had been laughing at her for her naïve enthusiasm and eagerness. It blithely made mock of the hours she'd spent putting the bid together, the consultations with Doug (and briefer ones with Rod), collating the figures, going over and over, making sure it was as competitive as it could possibly be.

In the bag indeed. *Patricia, you fool . . .*

We've decided not to go with R & D Builders this time.

And why put it like that – as if at some unspecified point in the future they *would* go with them? And who *did* they go with? In answer, a stocky, tanned man in a designer donkey jacket came barrelling arrogantly across her mind, as he had been doing off and on since she heard the news. She remembered with shame her panicky feelings as he'd banged on her window, stared her down . . . Almost as if, as ridiculous as it seemed, that the bid had been a competition which she'd lost in the lane outside the school.

Face reality, Pat . . .

But, yet again, reality brought no perspective – rather the reverse.

Because the truth was, it wasn't so much the loss of the job; it wasn't a major disaster for the business. As Doug said, there were plenty of bits and pieces to keep them going.

It was Rod.

His almost total indifference to the news.

They'd been sitting in the living room the previous afternoon – something that in what Pat nostalgically termed 'normal times' would be almost unheard of. She'd been semi-reading her 'trashy magazine' (and feeling annoyed she couldn't catch up on *The Real Housewives of Tampa Bay*). Rod had been channel-hopping between some game show and some obscure basketball match. And then her phone had pinged with Mr Keeney-Keen's frankly insulting text.

'Bloody hell!' Her exclamation had been forceful and angry.

'What?'

'We haven't got the Baldersby job.'

'Okay.' His eyes never left the image of some overweight man frowning at a neon pink scoreboard.

'Just okay?'

'What do you want me to say?'

'I really thought we had a good chance.' She'd looked crossly and unseeingly at her magazine.

'You never know with these things.' Pat had looked across at him. What had happened to that driven, wiry lad who swept her off her feet with his restless energy and red sports car?

He'd become aware of her gaze and realized more of a response was called for.

'Like I say, it's the way these things go.'

'It would have been ideal. A big project, nearby, twelve months' work—'

And so much more than that. Without consciously realizing, she'd built up this whole scenario: Andrew safely back at uni, Rod and Dougie working away on site, herself zipping back and forth between Borrowby and Baldersby St James.

He'd shrugged and returned his gaze to the screen. 'I don't see what you want me to do about it,' he'd said listlessly.

79

Pat hadn't answered, not out loud. But in her head, she'd shouted, *I want you to care! I want you to shift your backside off that sofa and shout and scream and then ring Dougie and tell him you'll be in tomorrow. And tell our Andrew: 'Thank you for your help, son, but you can go back to Loughborough now.'*

Her jangling thoughts had reduced the words in her magazine to meaningless shapes. Rod had been focused on the TV, so she'd gone to the kitchen and began assembling ingredients for an Angela Hartnett midweek supper: braised artichokes. Vegetarian because of some vague nod towards being healthy though in her darker moments Pat felt that that ship had sailed.

Chopping the vegetables, her mind had run darkly on. *Why* was Rod being so apathetic? Surely it couldn't *still* be the effects of that last lot of chemo? That had been – she did some rapid calculations – six, seven weeks ago.

What if . . . what if . . . he was ill again? She was still timing his peeing, ear jammed to the en-suite door, and everything *seemed* fine . . . but you never knew, not really . . . One read these stories . . . For a moment the kitchen was subsumed in black possibilities; her hands were white as they clutched the frozen artichokes—

Breathe . . . breathe in the light. Envisage what is, not what you fear . . .

Remember – *remember* what it was the oncologist had said. *We've caught it in nice time.*

Maybe they had caught it in nice time but—

No! No, she would not go there.

Not today, when she felt so tired, so grey, so very alone.

And certainly not this afternoon, she thought, steering the Yeti out of the drive.

This afternoon she was getting her nails done.

You Glow Girl was tucked discreetly away down an alley off Millgate, taking over the premises of what had been a somewhat nondescript boutique. From the outside it looked rather quaint, a narrow stone frontage, recessed windows with wide lintels. Inside, however, well, 'quaint' was certainly not a word to be used. Faith, the proprietor, had relocated to Thirsk from South London some three years previously, bringing with her a metropolitan energy and zest, plus very decided views regarding décor. The salon was white, discreetly lit, with gleaming metal chairs and state-of-the-art (for Thirsk) nail stations. On its main wall an almost bewildering collage of nail varnishes – a kaleidoscope of pinks and blues and yellows and reds and oranges, which always brought to Pat's mind echoes of childish pleasures: Spangles, Cindy dolls, platform shoes and pick'n'mix. And there, in this world of scented colour and softly playing Classic FM, like three modern-day Disney princesses were Faith, and her two assistants, Hope and Simone.

Crossing the threshold on an afternoon that was darkening, with the first leaves blowing across Marage car park, Pat felt a definite sense of coming into a haven. She let the intoxicating smell of acetone fill her nostrils and the strains of Ravel soothe and dissipate her tired thoughts.

There were two clients already in place, arms outstretched as if in supplication like latter-day saints. One was a woman Pat recognized from the Skipton Building Society. The other . . . ? She looked familiar; Pat was sure she'd seen her before but for the moment couldn't place her. A rather hard-looking woman, not that old but trying to look younger, tan and hair colour welded on like armour. 'Mrs Nails' she christened her, partly because of the hard look and partly due to the rather startling shade of scarlet Faith was currently applying.

Faith looked up and smiled a welcoming smile. 'Pat my love, have a seat. Simone's looking after you today.' Pat especially liked

Simone, the youngest of the three, and definitely the sweetest-natured. She was the niece of Matt and Linda Barley; Pat remembered her as a bonny little thing, always with an armful of dolls and hairbrushes.

Simone smiled as she replaced a couple of bottles of candy-coloured polish on the rack. 'I'll just take your coat, Mrs Taylor, if you just want to sit down for me.'

Pat sat down, luxuriating in the feeling of switching off from her worries. Coming here during these past eighteen months had been a lifesaver for Pat: a space to relax, to listen and to have her gels swabbed away and replaced by these three tanned, gossipy angels. In a world of chemo, blood counts, rewritten wills and insurance claims it had been immensely soothing to come to a world where the only decision to make was between 'Hawaii 5 Oh!' or 'You make me blush'.

'So how are you, Mrs Taylor?' said Simone, reverently rolling back Pat's sleeves.

'Oh, you know,' said Pat brightly. 'Getting there.' Simone nodded and smiled and didn't ask any more. The lovely thing about these three was, like all good beauty technicians, they sensed when someone want to talk and when someone didn't. And this afternoon Pat didn't; she wanted to listen.

The chat was one of the things she came for, listening to staff and clients talking about everything and anything. It gave Pat the infinitely comforting sense of a world beyond her own immediate concerns, a world of which one was only a small part, and in which nothing escaped the attention of the employees of You Glow Girl. For when something scandalous *did* occur, you could bet your shirt that Faith, Hope and Simone would know the whos, the whys, the whens, wheres and hows with a forensic detail that made the combined forces of WikiLeaks and MI5 seem patchy and uncoordinated.

This afternoon the chat seemed to be about Hope's failing washing machine.

'So, the woman on the line says to me, "Okay, so they don't make the parts no more, not for your model." And I says, "It's only a year old." And she says, "I can't help that." And I said, "Excuse me but that's disgusting."'

There was a general mutter of support and disapproval.

'We're getting one of them LG machines,' said Mrs Nails. 'In us new kitchen we're having done.'

Pat had no idea what an LG machine was, but from the reaction realized it was something quite impressive.

'I'd love one of them,' said Simone wistfully.

'I tell you; it is absolutely amazing. It's on the Wi-Fi. So, I can start it remotely. I can be like in Booths and start the drying going for when I get home.'

Pat couldn't quite see the point of this, but from the reaction of those around her divined it must be a Good Thing.

'We're getting all us appliances on the remote, not just the heating . . . I tell you, it's going to be a godsend.' There was more than a slight air of boastfulness in Mrs Nails' tone. It was by no means deliberate, more as if the woman was speaking it aloud to prove something to herself. Nevertheless, Pat could tell that Hope, who couldn't even afford a new machine, and Simone who was frantically saving with her boyfriend to get a place of their own, were finding this all a bit hard to take. As ever Faith charged cheerfully in, covering any slight tinge of atmosphere, a skill Pat had noticed her use on more than one occasion in the past.

'My mum had this twin tub that lasted years,' she said. There then followed an account of how a twin tub worked, something Hope and Simone seemed to equate with beating clothes on rocks in the river. (*What, stand over it? It'd do me head in.*) Pat was happy to sit peacefully with her memories of her own twin tub, a hand-me-down from Rod's mum. Standing over it in the kitchen at Manfield Terrace, filling it with a bucket, Justin crawling round her feet. Happy, uncomplicated days when it all lay in front of her. The mention of a familiar name plucked her attention back to the conversation.

'Just after our Shanice started at St Barney's, that was when I got the machine,' Hope was saying. 'Like I say, only a year.'

'How's she getting on now?' asked the lady from the building society. Shanice's trials in Acorn Class were a regular topic for discussion in You Glow Girl. According to Hope the teachers didn't understand her; having heard accounts of Shanice's exploits, Pat's sympathies lay largely with the teachers.

'Did you manage to see that Mrs Brittain?' asked Faith.

'Did I heck.' Hope shook her head. 'Four times I've tried since term started. Four! And each time, she's never available. Reckons she "too busy".' The vocal inverted commas implied Hope believed her 'too busy' to mean being sat in her office under a tanning lamp with a magazine and a mocktail.

'It's a full-on job being head teacher,' said Mrs Nails. Pat noticed a certain amount of defensive restraint in her voice. Then it came to her exactly who Mrs Nails was. *Of course!* The woman married to that teacher in the tight tracksuit. Ian? Ian Berryman. Started the term she left. And now she came to think about it – hadn't there been some sort of scandal with Mr and Mrs Berryman? Something that happened in his previous school – him leaving his wife and taking up with Mrs Nails? And hadn't she been someone who had actually worked with him in the school? She must remember to ask Linda Barley.

'Busy or not, I've got a kid in her school, and she needs to make time for parents,' said Hope, applying a lurid orange to the lady from the building society's nails. 'No one's been able to get hold of her lately.'

'There's a reason for that.' Now Mrs Nails sounded superior, like she was relishing some secret knowledge. The ladies in the nail bar looked at her with interest, but instead of hinting more, she closed her mouth and looked superior.

Pat was reminded of a schoolgirl chanting: 'I know something you don't know!' What could she be referring to? Looking at her, she suddenly felt there was something about the tan and the hair that gave her a curiously vulnerable air. Almost as if she'd realized what her best features were and set about pouring into them industrial amounts of care and energy, giving a sense of parody to what had once been natural and spontaneous.

'I tell you something interesting.' Once again Faith's confident, cheerful voice cut through and dispelled any lingering trace of awkwardness. 'I tried looking her up on Facebook.'

'Mrs Brittain?' said Hope.

'Why?' asked Simone.

'I wanted to see this famous hairstyle I've heard so much about.'

'What did you think of it?' asked the woman from the building society.

'No idea,' said Faith. 'She's not on Facebook.'

'She must be,' said Hope.

'I couldn't find her,' said Faith, her tone definitive. 'Or Instagram, Snapchat – you name it. No social media whatsoever.' There was a moment's awed silence as the staff and clientele of You Glow Girl considered someone not on social media.

'She has to be careful, being a head,' said Mrs Nails knowledgably. 'It's the parents. I know Ian's just on private settings. There was someone in Doncaster got the sack because of something they posted.'

The conversation moved on to social media and all its pitfalls. Pat was silent, remembering Liam and his own bruising brush with Facebook. How was he getting on in Durham? she wondered. It was a few days since they'd spoken. The panic hit her like a sudden punch. How on earth were they going to afford to support the boys if Rod couldn't or wouldn't get back to work?

'Now,' said Simone. Her voice was brisk. 'What shade do you want, Mrs Taylor?'

'Something purple,' said Pat.

'That's a bit dark, just when the weather's getting bad,' said Simone in mild concern, going to the varnishes.

I feel dark, Pat wanted to say. *I feel dark and worried and a failure.*

'Okay.' Simone's voice was brisk and business-like. It seemed to imply that whatever may or may not be going on, here in You Glow Girl life went on. 'I've two shades for you, Mrs Taylor. "Jamaica me Happy" – that's this one. Or "Damson in De-stress".'

Pat considered them. 'Damson in De-stress' was a lovely rich colour, more formal – it'd go well with that new scarf she'd picked up from the outlet mall. 'Jamaica me Happy' was something else altogether lighter and brighter, shot through with glitter. It didn't at all match her current mood.

Meanwhile Hope was back on with the shortcomings of St Barnabus's Lodestone Academy. 'I tell you something else about that school,' she said putting the second of Mrs Nails' tanned hands under the UV drying lamp. 'They must have money to burn. When we went for "Meet the Teacher", the heating were full on. Red hot it were.'

'It's this new boiler they've had fitted,' said Mrs Nails, again with that air of superior knowledge. 'Green energy, dead important.'

'I don't care what it were,' said Hope censoriously. 'One woman nearly passed out.'

As Simone bent in to work to clear her last nails, Pat said, 'I imagine as site manager it'll be your Uncle Matt who gets it in the neck.'

'Don't get me started,' said Simone. 'Auntie Linda says he's getting ever so stressed with it.'

86

'It'll all settle down in time,' said Pat comfortably.

'The problem is . . .' Simone lowered her voice confidentially. 'The problem is, Mrs Taylor, it's not so much the boiler as the bloke who has the contract to maintain it. It's contracted out to a firm see, not just the boiler, but all the maintenance round the school.'

'So much is these days,' said Pat, thinking of the various bits of schools work R & D Builders had lost recently.

'The man who runs the firm . . .' Simone's voice dropped still further as she scrubbed off the polish on her little finger. 'He does all the work for the academy schools. He's a real crook, Uncle Matt reckons.'

'He's responsible for the boiler?'

'The boiler, the odd jobs – any building work . . .'

Like Pat's natural nail, a glimmer of something began to appear in her mind.

'And he's not good, this man?'

'Arrogant, Uncle Matt says. Acts like he owns the place. Drives this expensive black car—'

Pat's mind did one of those quantum leaps that lady primary school teachers are particularly gifted at, adding two and two and producing considerably more than four.

'Wears a designer donkey jacket?' she said.

'Uncle Matt says he wears these posh work clothes, but he looks like he never actually does any work.'

Pat's mind was racing. Someone Matt Barley reckoned to be a crook had won the contract over R & D Builders. *Right.*

'Anyway,' Simone's voice became louder, brisker. 'Which is it to be?' She held the two bottles out in front of her.

'Glitter,' said Pat with confidence. 'Glitter every time.'

CHAPTER EIGHT

Care is advocated, and there is indignation about social conditions aboard the **Titanic**.

With one eye on the grill, Liz watched Derek as he set whatever it was he set on his phone prior to going for his run; some app that flashed up a map on her own phone with a moving, pulsing dot that represented his progress. Since Rod's illness her husband had started performing this ritual three times a week; what had started out as a rather panicky reaction had developed into a fully fledged hobby, complete with expensive running shoes, a subscription to *Run Run* magazine and inordinate amounts of Deep Heat cream.

Device set, Derek opened the back door and peered suspiciously out into the deepening September twilight. 'Right, I'm off,' he said in grave tones.

She had twenty minutes. Twenty-seven if he did that extended loop round by the allotments.

'Okay,' she said, not taking her eyes off the fish fingers. One shade too dark and Jacob wouldn't touch them.

Plus, she didn't want Derek to guess what was in her mind.

When she'd found that awful anonymous letter, it had been an inexpressible relief to blurt out the shock she was feeling to her husband. However, even as she did so, part of her was aware that by doing this, something was being set in stone, i.e. Derek's opinion of her having any further dealings with Jan Starke and St Barnabus's Lodestone Academy. Jan herself had always been someone he'd viewed with a certain amount of caution after that business all those years ago.

Sure enough, on the evening after her return from Bunty Carter's, she'd been gathering up the ironing when Derek muted Paul the *Look North* weatherman and said, 'Can I have a word?' (In thirty-three years of marriage she'd observed that these 'words' invariably seemed to come when she was right in the middle of doing something else.) She'd put the ironing down and sat next to him. He'd taken her hand, something he only reserved for the really serious 'words'.

He hadn't been *really* happy about her going into St Barnabus's, but he understood how Liz had wanted to help out a friend. But now that friend was managing better, surely Liz could step back? He wanted her to enjoy her life – not be lying awake half the night worrying about some anonymous letter that had nothing to do with her. So please, *please* leave St Barnabus's, nasty letters, Jan Starke and everything concerned well alone.

She'd nodded. What else could she do? He said he loved her, stroked her wrist with his thumb and unmuted Paul the weatherman. She'd rung Jan (knowing full well she'd be at Boogie Chakra), and left a rather craven message on her voicemail saying she wouldn't be able to come in that week, and was planning a series of further excuses that would enable her to step back from her sessions in Elm Base.

But that didn't stop her thinking. About a tall Raggedy Ann figure sobbing in the toilets. About Tiff, eyes rolling back into her head as she collapsed onto the staffroom floor. An empty house with a tangled garden by the railway line.

And always that snake of a memory . . . *Are you in there, you mad bitch? You'll pay for the damage!*

She sighed. The thoughts were showing no signs of fading; if anything they were growing stronger. An image of Pat came into her mind. Derek had said to step back and Thelma had urged her to tread carefully. Pat never ever trod carefully – cheerfully, flamboyantly, recklessly even – but never carefully.

'Grandma.' Jacob's gravelly voice brought her attention back to the fish fingers in the nick of time. He was regarding her from the doorway. 'Grandma, did you know that there were only two bathtubs available for all the second-class passengers on board the *Titanic*?'

'Really?' She pursed her lips in an automatic expression of sympathy and disapproval, flipping the fish fingers onto a plate. 'Which one are you on with?'

'Glimpses from a lost world,' he intoned, mournfully inspecting his plate – three fish fingers, two spoonfuls of peas, two slices of wholemeal bread (unbuttered) and a glass of water – each item totally separate. Liz knew far better than to suggest any embellishments to this rather spartan meal – oven chips, ketchup. ('*Do you know how much sugar and fat you get in heavily processed food, Grandma?*')

'If you were in third class you stood a fifty per cent higher chance of drowning than first-class passengers,' he said in outraged tones.

Liz put the plate on a tray and looked at him. Her grandson's face was sombre with the social injustice of it all.

'You carry that through,' she said. 'I need to make a quick phone call.'

At about the same time, Thelma was standing six steps down the stone stairs to the cellar under St Catherine's peering down into the gloom, eyes fixed on the dancing lights from Sheila's phone.

'It's not coming on,' called Sheila. Her distorted voice sounded remarkably steady for someone who liked neither the dark nor enclosed spaces.

In the doorway above Thelma, Contralto Kate appeared. 'He says it's the red button,' she carolled.

'Try the red button,' called down Thelma.

'I *am* trying the red button,' said another voice, this one decidedly tetchy. Dot, the church warden, had been called out of Pilates and was not best pleased.

'What we need is a hive,' said Contralto Kate with authority. 'Not a beehive. It's a gizmo that lets you turn on the boiler remotely. That way James can turn it on without even taking his foot off the footstool.' James, the other church warden – the one with the boiler know-how – was currently laid up at home on account of a recent toe amputation. There was general agreement among the group behind Kate that a hive would be a good thing, providing of course the Wi-Fi could penetrate the stone walls of the church.

Thelma drew her coat round herself. Despite the warmth of the day, it was chilly in the church and even chillier on the stairs. She'd arrived early for choir practice only to find the building cold, and a gaggle of choristers gathered worriedly round the door to the boiler room – just when she'd hoped for a few peaceful minutes for some much-needed reflection.

The Heads-Up meeting had been scheduled for the following week and, according to Teddy, people were tense. 'Please may all be well at college,' she said into the darkness but even as she spoke, she found herself wondering whether her idea of 'well' coincided with the Almighty's. Really what she wanted was for things to go on as they always had at Ripon and St Bega's. But increasingly over the past few days she had been wondering if that was a realistic, or even fair wish? She thought of the college: the wood-panelled walls; the card index files; the library with its prehistoric microfiche; the scuffed, scruffy tutorial rooms. Perhaps she was praying for something outdated, quaint, something with no place in the modern world?

Kayleigh Brittain kept coming into her mind. Confident, controlled Kayleigh and her passion for the school she ran; that manicured finger on the many efficiently throbbing pulses that beat round that smart building. Wasn't that the way a place of education *should* look in this day and age?

The school. She had to let them know she wasn't going to be a governor – hadn't Kayleigh said something about there being a meeting in the next day or so? She quelled the memory of that angry sobbing – that spiteful letter Liz had found. At the end of the day, it was no concern of hers. Kayleigh was more than capable of sorting out whatever was going on. So why then this reluctance to ring and fully extricate herself from the school? An image of Pat popped into her mind, as it often did when she was feeling indecisive. *Just do what you want to do* – that's what she'd say. But what did she want to do?

There was slight snapping noise and a scream from below.

'Hold the light steady,' snapped Dot.

'I *am* holding it steady,' protested Sheila. 'My hands are shaking.' *Shaking hands.*

Thelma gripped the cold iron rail, a sudden image in her mind. Kayleigh seeing her out of school. *Her hand had been shaking . . .*

A frozen look, in a stuffy school hall on a warm July night.

Thelma suddenly knew that whatever else she might be, Kayleigh Brittain was a frightened lady.

'We're in business,' said Dot grimly, mounting the steps.

'Hallelujah!' cried Contralto Kate. 'You know I knew something was going to happen tonight. I always get a feeling when something's going to go wrong. I think it must be a word from the Lord.'

'I wish he'd had a word with me before I forked out fourteen quid on a Pilates class,' said Dot. Behind her appeared *not* Sheila but Soprano Kate.

'I thought you were Sheila,' said Thelma, surprised.

'You'd not get Sheila down there!' said Soprano Kate. She had the triumphant air of someone who had just been through an ordeal on behalf of someone else. Thelma felt rather foolish. She'd heard the voice down there and assumed it was Sheila because Sheila was in charge of the choir.

Hang on . . .

Liz looked at her phone. The pulsating dot was now by the race-course – she had ten minutes left at most. Without giving herself time to think, she picked up her phone and dialled.

'Liz! Hello stranger!' Margo's tones held delighted surprise, as if it had been a good deal longer than just two days since she'd seen her, and somewhere a sight more genteel than a school staffroom. Margo was one of those people who portrayed their world in the best possible light; her job in school she would refer to as 'educational professional' – as opposed to classroom assistant (chief duties: hearing readers and photocopying worksheets). 'What can I do for you, my love? I was just in the middle of preparing a spot of supper!' Her voice conjured up images of farmhouse kitchens, gingham cloths and dewy pats of butter.

'I won't keep you,' said Liz. 'I was wondering if you could help me.'

'I'll do my very best.' Another note had crept into her voice. Something wary.

'Gardener's hand gel,' said Liz. 'I'm right out.'

'Ah!' The voice ramped back to full-on sunny. 'Of course. Let me dig out my little blue book. How many?'

'Just the one.'

'Oh.' The tone dimmed. If she didn't know better, Liz would have said Margo was disappointed. Suddenly she knew for whatever reason this sale was important to her. 'On second thoughts,' she said, 'make it three.'

'That's more like it! It's such refreshing stuff!'

Margo's tones implied the gel was created in a flagged workplace with bunches of dried herbs hung from beams, as opposed to churned out by the vatful in a Chinese factory. Oh well, she could always give them as raffle prizes to the allotments club.

'I tried calling round to see Bunty Carter,' she said.

'Oh?' Margo was obviously focused on filling in the order.

'I understand she's at her daughter's?'

'Very probably.'

'It's good she's got Candice looking out for her.'

'As long as she doesn't start selling her stuff on eBay!' There was a sour note of humour in Margo's voice. What did she mean by that? 'There, that's all done for you, my love. I'll give you a tinkle when it arrives.'

'You don't happen to know where her daughter lives? I was thinking I could drop the order round.'

'Somewhere in Boroughbridge,' said Margo vaguely. 'You could try there.' There was a definite 'end of conversation' note in her voice.

Liz dismissed a picture of herself tramping the streets of Boroughbridge, a blue Know-body bag brandished before her. 'How are things at school?' she asked.

She hadn't meant the question to come out so abruptly, but Margo sounded on the point of going, and the pulsating red dot was getting ever nearer.

The portcullis dropped. 'Fine.' How was it that word 'fine' so often implied just the opposite? Nonplussed Liz floundered on. 'And Tiff? Is she all right?'

'To the best of my knowledge. Liz my love, I really must love you and leave you! I've something about to boil over!' And with that she rang off.

Liz frowned, her mind as far from at rest as it was possible to be.

Later on, as she was filling the dishwasher and Derek was testing Jacob from his *Titanic Significant Facts* album, Thelma rang.

'I've decided I'm going to join the board of governors after all,' she said. Her voice was firm. 'But that *doesn't* mean I'm going to be finding things out. I still think there's a need to tread carefully.'

'And I'm going to keep helping in school,' said Liz, a shade defiantly. *If Jan lets me in the classroom,* she thought.

There was a pause. 'Well take care,' said Thelma. 'Listen, I've been thinking. When Bunty Carter's daughter rang you yesterday . . .'

'What about it?'

'Have you ever spoken to her before?'

'No,' said Liz. 'No, I haven't.'

'Neither have I.' Thelma paused, but Liz knew she'd not finished speaking.

'What?' she said.

'I just wondered,' said Thelma. 'I mean we are sure that *was* Candice who was calling you?'

There are still some tickets left for Thursday's Super Duper St B's Academy harvest festival, at 9.30 a.m. and 2 p.m.! Any donations of tins, dried goods and pasta, please bring to the office! Please note, due to health and safety we are UNABLE to accept ANY fresh produce or home-baked goods.

Margo Benson found the letter sent to her in the box containing that month's 'Know-body' orders, in amongst sachets of face masks and foot rub. She'd come to the staffroom before the start of school, both to put people's orders in their pigeonholes and also to help herself to someone's coffee. The most obvious choice was Ian Berryman's plain, straightforward Arabica Gold Blend, but today she was feeling particularly low and wanted something to perk her up a bit, something to take her beyond Thirsk and the grey morning and mentally closer to that lovely property in St Ives she'd seen on *Relocation, Relocation* the previous night.

There was Becky Clegg's hazelnut blend, which looked very inviting in its sage green tin, but she wasn't convinced she'd like the taste. Of course, her favourite was Nicole's Americano roast – but she'd already helped herself to that twice that week and it wouldn't do for her to become aware of the rate her coffee was going down. Margo didn't even look at the plain orange label of the Kostkwik premium roast with her name inscribed on in felt-tip pen. She only used it if other people were there; 49p a jar and it tasted it, every mouthful. And it wasn't just the taste, it was all the other dragging sensations it conjured up – the worry about turning on the heat, the bleakness at yet another pasta-based meal and of course that awful, horrible feeling when faced by the day's post.

Footsteps sounding down the corridor spurred her on into the safe, dreary choice; with the practice of an expert she furtively spooned some of Ian Berryman's Gold Blend into a mug and, by the time Becky Clegg entered the room, was putting the pale blue bags with their creams and gels and powders into the various pigeonholes.

'Morning!' trilled Margo. 'I'm putting orders in pigeonholes!'

Becky looked in her jar of hazelnut blend. The level seemed to be the same. She wondered whose coffee Margo had taken that morning. Coffee made, she was about to walk out when something stopped her.

'Look, Margo,' she said, 'if you ever want a coffee, just help yourself.' Her voice whilst not exactly soft held a certain unaccustomed gruffness.

There was no answer.

She saw Margo was standing stock-still by the Know-Body box of orders, looking at something she held in her hands.

'Everything okay?' said Becky.

'Yes, fine,' said Margo quickly. She walked out, leaving her cup of coffee on the side.

In the ladies' toilet she looked at the sheet of white paper again, the stark print blurring as she blinked back the tears.

BRING YOUR OWN COFFEE, YOU THIEVING
BITCH. YOU REALIZE EVERYONE KNOWS
WHAT YOU'RE DOING? WE'RE ALL FED
UP WITH YOU! STEALING IS STEALING.

CHAPTER NINE

A Green Miracle is called into question, and a late-night meeting comes to a dramatic conclusion.

'So, drilling down, this is what the data's telling us!' Jared Keen refreshed the screen to show yet another purple-and-green pie chart. Kayleigh Brittain, the head of the table of governors, gave a warm nod. 'Thank you so much, Jared,' she said. 'It's brilliant to see just how much Pineapple Maths is moving us forward!'

There was a cough from Josie Gribben, sat across from Thelma. 'There are three sorts of lies,' she said clearly. 'Lies, damn lies and statistics.'

Josie Gribben was the community governor. Thelma had known – or rather more accurately known of – Josie of old. She was the sort of person you referred to by their full name in a certain tone of voice . . . Josie Gribben. 'Passionate' was one of the more charitable terms used to describe her. 'Pain in the jacksie' was another. She was the sort of person who lived and breathed various committees and groups; looking at her now, sitting to the left of Kayleigh, with her straggly grey curls and sage green Allotment Society sweatshirt, Thelma felt certain it was her Kayleigh had been referring to when she'd talked about governors not knowing their roles.

The contretemps had happened about half an hour into the meeting.

They'd been fairly zipping through the agenda with a speed that Thelma, with her previous experience, had found surprising – but was apparently a feature of how governor meetings ran in academy trusts. Most items on the agenda were covered by 'supporting papers' – which governors were supposed to have read in advance; each time a new item came up, Nicole claimed that 'no questions had been submitted'. It all felt rather superficial. Like the finance report; when Thelma was on governors in the past this was something that was good for a twenty-minute discussion. (That time with all the hoo-ha about toilet rolls!) But now: 'no questions submitted'. That was, Thelma supposed, how things were run in this new age of trusts and academies. As for the finance report itself – the very brief finance report – Thelma had been able to glean little except that the school was in a financially stable position.

Throughout all of this Josie Gribben had been silent.

Biding her time, Thelma thought later.

Then had come the buildings report.

'So, we're having Nursery painted this half-term, fingers crossed, and we're hopefully getting a report on the wiring in KS1,' said Kayleigh. 'We're on it, are we not, Terry?'

'Aye, we are,' said Terry. 'Are there any questions?'

'One's been submitted by Mrs Gribben,' said Nicole blandly.

'Yes.' Josie sat up. 'This biomass boiler,' she said, knotting her fingers together.

'What about it?' said Kayleigh evenly. There was a studied control in her voice.

'My question is quite a simple one,' said Josie. 'How long are staff and pupils going to have to put up with this incessant, stifling heat?'

There was a pause. Thelma was put in mind of that bit in

westerns when the barman takes down all the bottles before the shooting starts. Terry Meadows exhaled and shrank back in his chair, Nicole stared down fixedly at the laptop and Sam began rolling his biro even more furiously.

'I'm not exactly sure what you're referring to.' Kayleigh smiled, a sweetly quizzical smile; at the same time there was a distinct timbre of 'here we go again folks!' in her voice.

'It's red hot by all accounts,' said Josie. 'An absolute disgrace.'

Again, that calm, controlled voice. 'I'm not saying there haven't been issues, but Mr Hewson – he's our maintenance guy – he's on it.'

'Not very effectively,' said Josie.

'No one wants a hot school,' said Kayleigh reasonably. 'I prefer my heat on a beach.' She smiled, inviting everyone into the joke. Thelma found herself smiling uneasily along with everyone else. But Josie wasn't done yet.

'This is meant to be a biomass boiler,' she said. 'Save the climate and all that. I don't see how pumping out heat 24/7 can be very good for the environment. I don't just see why you can't turn the damned thing off.'

Thelma thought if Sam rolled the biro any faster, he'd be in danger of friction burns.

Now Nicole spoke, her voice pleasant and clear. 'The trouble is, Josie, we don't actually own the boiler. There's a company who owns it, and they deal directly with the trust. And there's another company responsible for the engineering, and another that supplies the pellets.' It all sounded very complicated to Thelma, who could remember the old days and the big heap of coke that would appear periodically in the corner of the car park.

'It sounds like a case of Uncle Tom Cobley and all,' said Josie. 'Maybe one of these companies can come here and sort this out because it can't go on like this.'

Kayleigh was obviously angry now. She stared at Josie, her eyes wide. 'Let me just make one thing clear,' said Kayleigh. 'This biomass boiler is brilliant – it's efficient, it's environmentally friendly—'

'And it can't be turned off,' said Josie Gribben.

'Okay,' said Kayleigh '*Right.*' She stood up.

Thelma had wondered if she was either going to walk out or possibly fetch Josie one with her iPad. What had happened was the entire meeting had been marched across the darkened playground, led by Matt and his torch, to see the boiler. Quite what this was going to achieve Thelma wasn't very sure, but it wasn't a thought she dared give voice to. And so, it was for the second time in a week she found herself looking at a boiler. In distinct contrast to the faithful old gas boiler at St Catherine's, this was a rather sinister squat metallic cuboid sprouting numerous foil-clad pipes, humming rather menacingly, Thelma thought.

'It's fed by pellets,' said Matt. Everyone looked as indicated in what had been Bob Perlman's old storeroom. Where there had been buckets, mops and vast quantities of Izal toilet paper there was now a dusty void, with an enormous beige valley of what looked like breakfast cereal. 'Wood pellets,' said Matt. 'They get fed in through there.' He indicated a ridged plastic tube that went from the base of the void into the boiler; his voice seemed cracked and slightly husky, Thelma thought. No wonder in this stuffy heat.

'Our carbon footprint is negligible,' said Kayleigh Brittain rather challengingly. The governors nodded politely, wanting to be back in the fresh air.

'So, what are all these notices in aid of?' Josie, totally unperturbed, indicated a series of hazard warning signs.

'Purely health and safety,' said Kayleigh frostily. People looked uneasily at the yellow and black signs; the atmosphere really was very dusty.

As people began filing back out, there was a dull whoomph as the boiler fired up into life.

'Why is it coming on now?' said Josie. 'It doesn't need to be on now, surely?'

'Some technical reason,' said Kayleigh. 'Believe it or not, boilers aren't my strong point!' She laughed dismissively and stalked out, the others following, grateful to be outside in the cool, damp night. The breeze was getting up and, as they crossed the playground, Thelma could hear the wind stirring in the lime trees with a sound that made her think of waves on the beach at Filey. She thought back to the sleek metal beast in the boiler room. Why had it chosen to come on now, for nine o'clock at night?

'Enjoying your first governors'?' Kayleigh asked and fell into step beside her.

'It's certainly interesting,' said Thelma, suddenly shy.

Kayleigh laughed in a way that made Thelma feel they were allied together; yet again she felt a sense of pleasure at having the approval of this designer-clad manager. Was now the time to ask about the letters? But Kayleigh was already speaking.

'FYI,' she said, 'Bunty Carter. You were asking about her. She phoned in today, with a sick note for three weeks. She's hurt her back.'

'And was it actually her who phoned?' asked Thelma.

Kayleigh frowned, puzzled. 'I think so,' she said. 'Why?' But before Thelma could answer, Kayleigh paused abruptly, clutching Thelma's arm and staring into the gusty darkness.

'What is it?' asked Thelma.

'Nothing. I just thought for a second I saw something.' She released her arm. 'I must be tired.'

And now it was nearly half past nine. At long last the meeting seemed to be winding down.

'Any other business?' said Terry Meadows, stretching out his arms, revealing another twist of a tattoo.

Yet again there was a sudden tension. Terry looked warily at Josie Gribben, who looked serenely back at him, but it was Sam and Nicole who Thelma noticed. Nicole had stopped typing and looked up, a curiously watchful expression on her face. And Sam had stopped rolling the biro and was staring fixedly at the table. It reminded Thelma of wedding services, the moment when the vicar asks if anyone knows any just cause or impediment. The letters? *It had to be.* But then who else knew about them?

'Right,' said Terry, unaware. 'That's a wrap.'

'Thank you,' said Kayleigh. 'And don't forget, folks, it's our harvest festival tomorrow, ten thirty – you're all very welcome!'

More than one person thought the shrill gasp she made was somehow part of this announcement – but the fact she was standing bolt upright, pointing at the window, told them otherwise.

'Someone's looking in,' she said, trembling finger pointing at the dark glass.

For a moment everyone was still, looking towards the window.

In the sudden silence the night looked very black indeed.

Then Terry Meadows strode across. Eyes shaded against the reflection from the lights, he peered out into the night. 'I can't see anyone,' he said.

'Well, they were there, just outside.' There was a quaver in that normally controlled voice and Thelma found herself remembering that stricken look at the summer fayre.

Terry crossed to the door. 'Matt,' he called out. 'Reckon there's someone playing silly buggers outside.'

Matt appeared looking totally unfazed. 'Best take a look,' he said.

'Just what I was thinking,' said Terry. 'Come on, lads.'

There was a moment of slightly comic confusion as it dawned on Jared Keen that a) he was classed as a lad and b) he was expected to go out into the night and look round the exterior of the building for someone playing silly buggers.

After they had gone Nicole began stacking the coffee cups onto a tray.

'I really must apologize,' said Kayleigh, her voice shaky. 'Calling out like that. I don't know what you must think of me.'

'Kiddies most likely,' said Josie.

'They were too tall for a kid,' said Kayleigh definitely.

Thelma went to the window and looked out. It was hard to make out much in the darkness. The window, she knew, gave out onto a grassed area; to the left was the school car park and to the right the playground, giving onto the allotments. 'Did you see which direction they went?' she asked.

'It was too dark to see much, just a figure. They were there – and then they were gone.'

'Earlier on,' said Thelma, 'when we were crossing the playground, you thought you saw someone?'

'I really don't know,' said Kayleigh. 'I thought I was just imagining it.'

'Did you see their face?' asked Thelma.

Kayleigh shook her head. 'It was covered by some sort of scarf – oh, it was *horrid* . . . They were just stood there.'

'I really think we should call the police,' said Nicole. 'They might still be around.'

'It was just someone being silly,' said Kayleigh, but her voice was still shaky.

'I wonder . . .' said Thelma. '*Why*.' The others looked at her. '*Why* would someone be looking in?'

'Curiosity?' said Josie.

'But it wasn't like someone would just be passing,' said Thelma. 'Not round the back.'

'Don't,' said Kayleigh, voice cracking slightly. 'I don't want to think about it.'

A noise outside made them all pause; Thelma went to the window. Outside she could see the bobbing lights and mobile phone torches and hear the voices of Matt and Terry. Another thought came to her: CCTV – or the lack of it. She remembered when the cameras were put in, and how they only covered the front and side round the school. It was perfectly possible to approach the library window from the playground *without* being picked up on the cameras.

But *why*? Why would someone be looking in? It wasn't as though they could hear anything. Her mind went back to that letter . . . YOU'RE NOT WANTED HERE . . . No two ways about it, she needed to speak to Kayleigh. She looked round, but saw her leaving the room with Nicole, carrying the dirty cups. Maybe now wasn't the time.

'So how did you enjoy your first Lodestone governors' meeting?' It was Josie who had joined her by the window. 'Sadly they're not always this interesting.'

'Hardly my first,' said Thelma. 'But yes, very . . . informative.'

'Really?' Josie gave a slight bark of laughter. 'I tend to find information can be somewhat thin on the ground at these meetings.'

'I imagine you manage to ask the questions you want answers to.'

Josie gave another bark of laughter. 'You mean I'm an awkward old fossil.' She sighed and looked suddenly tired. 'I certainly feel like it. I'm out of my time, I reckon.'

Thelma felt an unexpected pang of sympathy at these words. 'It certainly has changed,' she said.

Josie sighed. 'This whole academy trust set-up . . . It all seems to be about *money*. Everything paying its way and making a profit. They bang on about progress, but all it seems to come down to is pounds, shillings and pence. Like with Ripon College.' She shook her head. 'How's your chappie doing with it all?'

Thelma had a very unpleasant feeling growing from her stomach outwards. 'I'm not sure what you mean,' she said.

'This crazy scheme to close the place down.'

Thelma stared at her. 'As far as I'm aware,' she said, 'they're just having some sort of review.'

'I must be wrong,' said Josie easily.

'What have you heard?' Thelma fought to keep her voice calm.

'I must have the wrong end of the stick,' said Josie. 'Do it all the time these days.'

At that moment the door opened, and Kayleigh and Nicole walked back in, closely followed by Terry and Matt, trailed by Sam and Jared. Thelma noticed with amusement that a large sycamore leaf had attached itself to Jared's shoe.

'There's no one about now,' said Terry.

'I suppose I could always have imagined it,' said Kayleigh slowly. The three men looked solemn.

'What is it?' asked Thelma.

'There was someone there all right,' said Terry. 'I'm afraid some-one's keyed your car, Kayleigh love.'

CHAPTER TEN

*Anger leads to fact-finding at Back Bagby Farm,
where more is learnt about a shifty so-and-so.*

Driving up the muddy rutted lane to Matt Barley's farm, Pat still
felt angry – blazingly, burningly angry.

Just stop nosying will you!

Her face was tingling, her breathing rapid. Her heart's knocks
matched the bumping of the car up the rutted track to Matt's farm.
Nosying! When what she was trying to do was make sure the
business stayed on track. There was plainly something dodgy about
this Steve Hewson – the man who'd whisked the Baldersby job
away from them – and all she was doing was pointing that out!

And breathe . . .

Let go of what cannot be changed and focus on the now . . .

And the now was finding a space to park. As always, with Matt's
farmyard, this was something of an issue. There was Matt's battered
grey tractor, beyond that the forklift jutting a couple of haybales
aggressively out in front. Against the barn wall sat a skipful of
what looked like scrap metal, beyond that an immense log stack
dwarfing various bundles of wire. From one of the sheds a brown-
eyed cow eyed the chaos balefully as if to remind the world what
a farm *should* be about.

As she got out of the car there was an eruption of raucous barking as Matt's dogs came pelting round the corner of the barn towards her. Nervously Pat tried to remember their names . . . Scary and Sporty? She stood stock-still, hands gripping her bag and the papier-mâché egg boxes as they came haring towards her, a breed away from her placid Larson. A stern wordless shout stopped them in their tracks; at a whistle they reluctantly retraced their steps, looking resentfully back over their shoulders. Matt, ponytail clipped back, looking more than ever as if he'd just emerged from some muddy rock festival, regarded her with his trademark lack of emotion.

'Eggs.' She waved the boxes.

'If you're wanting a paint job for your car, I believe Mrs Brittain knows a chap.' There was something significantly humorous in his voice; he was obviously making reference to something – but what? 'Up at school,' he said as if that explained everything.

'Just eggs,' she said, walking towards him.

'Our lass would've dropped them off.' This referred to the ritual that had been going on since Pat had retired; how every Thursday night she would leave two egg boxes and a fiver under a slate by the gate, and by Friday lunchtime they'd have been replaced by two full ones.

'I was just passing,' said Pat. 'Thought I'd save Linda a trip.'

This was a total lie.

Like all serious arguments it had come, if not out of nowhere, at a time when neither of them expected it, or was prepared. The bones of the problem were all there in place, had been for some weeks now, the escalation of issues into something more volatile was something neither she nor Rod would have chosen at the start of an evening, just as Pat was starting to assemble supper (minty chicken and bacon).

Andrew had been out somewhere, and Rod had been not

108

exactly admiring but commenting on her nails, glittering with Jamaica me Happy, and Pat had been reporting on the conversations in You Glow Girl. That had been when she'd mentioned Simone's words about the boiler and the crook who maintained it, the same crook who probably got the Baldersby contract and seemingly worked across all the Lodestone Trust schools.

'So?'

'So – Matt Barley thinks there's something dodgy about this Steve Hewson.'

'So, what if there is?'

'Well, it shows it wasn't fair how the Baldersby contract was awarded and maybe if someone said something to these academy people – who knows?'

'I wish you'd just leave it.' The sudden snap in his voice had surprised her. She'd looked at him to check; yes, he'd had that half-smile he wore when he was really riled up about something. She'd taken a mental step back.

'I was just saying what Simone told me,' she'd said.

'Pat, we lost the bid – that's all there is to it.' The exasperation in his voice had driven her on to explain.

'I'm not even talking about that; I'm saying how there's something dodgy about—'

'This Steve bloke – I get it.' Rod had stood up, chair noisily scraping the flags. 'Look, we lost the bid – end of. The last thing anyone needs is you nosying around.'

That had been it. The flashpoint. *Nosying around* . . . after the months, *months* of hand-holding, driving, taking calls, running to the wholesalers, supervising deliveries, the long bleak nights sat staring out into the dark not wanting him to know how lost and afraid and inadequate she had felt.

Of course, it hadn't come out like that. What had come out had been a series of statements (increasingly incoherent) from Pat about the business needing to get back on track, countered by a series of statements (clipped and very coherent) from Rod about everything being fine and he'd go back to work when he was good and ready. Neither gave in; in fact as the row went on and got louder (Pat) and brisker (Rod) it could be said they more or less stopped listening to each other – Rod interrupting Pat, Pat shaking her head and closing her eyes at Rod, until a climax of sorts had been reached by Rod walking out and Pat throwing a tea towel at the window and bursting into noisy sobs.

Supper hadn't happened. Pat had retreated upstairs with a glass of red and a bowl of leftover curry. Rod, she deduced later, had worked his way through a box of Pringles and half a pack of garden centre Melmerby crunches. And then . . . then there had been the sort of freezing coexistence that you can so easily get with long-standing couples.

Pat had spent much of the evening sat on Liam's bed, staring out of the window, Larson unconcernedly asleep on the pillow. She had half thought of retreating to her favourite lay-by on Borrowby Hill but had not wanted to risk another confrontation downstairs, and besides, she'd had at least a glass and a half of red (which had tasted like mouthwash, as is usually the way with alcohol and emotional upsets).

Leave it, Rod had said. That was all very well – but what about the business? The next job – and the job after that? The boys' university fees? The time left on the mortgage?

Nosying . . . It was so unfair!

In bed Rod seemed, as he always did, to lose himself in immediate, blissful childlike slumber (a good foot away from Pat with no goodnight nose bump). And Pat? She'd replayed and replayed the argument, morbidly picking and repicking at the comments that had hurt her the most. It felt like all the worries, all her struggles of the past twelve months, instead of propelling her to some kind of vindication had instead smacked her very hard around the head.

She'd eventually dropped off, and on waking (blearily) was prepared to concede, as one often was in the grey light of day that it might, just *might* be a case of six of one, half a dozen of another. That was the attitude she'd come down with, and to put this into practice was in the process of putting rashers of Farm Shop bacon into the grill pan when Rod came into the kitchen.

'I'm doing bacon sandwiches,' she'd announced in a tone of voice that said 'okay, I'm sorry I overreacted but that's not to say I haven't got a point'.

'Not for me.' He'd got his jacket, scooped up his car keys without breaking stride, before Pat realized what had happened.

'Where are you going?' she'd called. No way was she going to go out into the yard after him.

'A few places,' he'd said, and was gone.

She'd looked at the bacon under the grill. It had already begun to pale and pucker. She'd have to finished cooking it, maybe save it for a risotto. She'd felt the anger again starting to build, like toothache, and knew she would have to do something about it. Nosying around indeed!

'So, how's Rod doing?' Matt spoke over his shoulder as she followed him across the yard. The dogs (Ginger and Baby? She definitely remembered it was Posh who had died) sniffed her coat but dared do no more.

'You'll have to ask him,' she said and instantly regretted the snappy edge to her words; for a taciturn Yorkshire man Matt could be one heck of a gossip. 'You heard he'd been given the all clear,' she said, deliberately softening her tone.

Matt nodded. 'It's a good do,' he said, but he was still looking at her questioningly.

111

'It's just a question of getting back on track,' said Pat.

'Tell him if he fancies a go of golf,' said Matt.

She smiled and nodded, not saying that the last thing she wanted was Rod beggaring around Asenby Links when he needed to be getting back to work.

Matt opened the outhouse and she followed him in and stood by the big chest freezer she knew would be full of joints of meat, which in the past had served them for many a Sunday lunch. The shelves were full of eggs; stacked outside were sawn logs and bundles of firewood. Matt and Linda's was one of the last small farms in the district and they had to slog unremittently to make all their various ends meet. Pat could just about remember a time when the whole area had been a patchwork of farms like this – Tom Harrowby's place, Mucky Miller's twenty acres. Now there was more or less just Matt and Linda's land, hemmed in to the north by swathes of land belonging to the Duchy of Rievaulx and to the south by the property of a business consortium (including, it was rumoured, an Arab sheikh and their local MP). And squashed between them were Matt and Linda, with their bits of farming, bits of contracting, bits of produce – all supplemented by their work at the school.

The school. She suddenly remembered something that puzzled her. What was that he'd been saying before?

'What was that you were saying just now, about a paint job?'

'Have you not heard?' He coughed, face suddenly flushing, hand reaching out to the freezer to steady himself. Pat took half a step forward. 'I'm reet,' he said dismissively, waving her back.

'Have I not heard about what?' she said as he recovered.

'I thought you were bound to have heard on account of Mrs Cooper being a governor these days.' His voice was still hoarse, though recovering rapidly.

Pat frowned. Thelma? *A governor*? Her mind gave a guilty stab. 'I've not seen her for a while,' she said.

'Well,' he said, 'there was a governors' meeting last night . . .'

One of Matt's notable qualities was his ability to tell a tale. Many was the lock-in at the Borrowby Arms that had been enlivened by his stories; now, such was the power of his narration, Pat felt her upset from the argument beginning to recede.

'So did anyone see who made this scratch on her car?' she said when he'd finished.

'Rule Britannia had parked off up the side, not in the head teacher's space where she usually parks. If she'd been there she'd have been fine – as it was she was just off the CCTV.'

'So, whoever it was looked in the windows and then keyed Kayleigh Brittain's car?'

'The other way round more like. Me and Terry Meadows, we were out there sharpish and there was no sign of anyone.'

'So, who would want to do something like that?'

Matt cleared his throat, counting eggs into the boxes. 'Reckon there'd be something of a queue forming on that one.'

Pat nodded, remembering the various tales she'd heard about the doings of Kayleigh Brittain. 'Why look in the window anyway?' she wondered. 'I mean why risk getting caught? Why not just key her car and leg it?'

'Put the wind up her maybe. She's not what I'd call a popular lady.' He coughed again – a nasty, rattling affair. Now she looked closely at him he didn't look too well. Under his ruddy skin his face looked sallow; beads of sweat were on his forehead. Pat hoped he wasn't going to pass anything on to her. He handed her the eggs.

'How does Linda get on with her?'

He snorted, gave the door an expressive kick shut and wedged it with a brick.

'Put it this way: if she gets to the end of the week I'll be surprised.' He spoke in the slightly dramatic tones of doom that

Pat had learnt, over the years, to take with a more than a slight pinch of salt. 'Mind you, with our lass, it's not so much Mrs Brittain as t'other one.'

'What other one?'

'The one in the office. Madame Iceberg-up-her-arse. You know our Linda, she gets on with the job, but likes a bit of a chat along the way.'

This was putting it mildly. Pat had many memories of many chats with Linda, and not so many of her getting on with the job. She felt the smallest prickle of sympathy for this Madame Iceberg, whoever she was.

'It's not so much what she says,' said Matt, 'as what she doesn't say. Like blumin' Siberia, Linda reckons. I can't see her putting up with it much longer.'

Another beat of scepticism from Pat, she knew how much both Matt and Linda relied on their work from the school. 'It can't be much fun,' she said neutrally.

'You don't know the half of it.' Matt once again leant back against the freezer in storytelling mode. Pat was half tempted to cut him short; after all, she'd come here for a purpose, not to hear the latest tales from Matt Barley.

Listening to him, she was very glad she hadn't.

Matt talked for twenty minutes; what he said was so astonishing that Pat almost forgot about Rod, Steve Hewson and the Baldersby job.

'I can't believe it,' she said. 'Poison pen letters! At *St Barney's*!'

'It's a bad do,' said Matt – the Yorkshireman's ultimate condemnation.

'And does anyone have any idea who's sending these letters?'

Matt shook his head. 'Remember,' he said, 'keep this to yourself.'

'Of course.' Pat nodded, just as if she wasn't planning to ring Liz and Thelma the first chance she got.

'Anyway . . .' He shifted his weight from the freezer. 'I've a couple of ewes to see to.'

'Yes of course.' Pat came to herself; she'd come here to find something out and as gob-smacking as this all was, she had not yet found it out. 'One thing,' she said trying to sound casual. 'Do you know someone called Steve Hewson?'

Matt breathed out through his nose, looking as if he'd like to spit, which brought on another cough. 'That bastard,' he said indistinctly. 'Him and his bloody boiler.'

On her way back Pat pulled into the Shell garage for an emergency wee, and to jot down what Matt had said before she forgot. The repeatable bits. Her first impulse to call Thelma and Liz was fading – there was too much stuff to explain to them about why she'd been avoiding them. Pushing the awkward thoughts from her mind, she opened her mindfulness journal and frowned, trying to remember the gist of what Matt had told her.

Steve Hewson ran a firm called Joe Public. (Slogan: 'It does what it says on the tin!') They'd started off as builders, but had, as so many things did these days, diversified into plumbing, electronics and boiler maintenance. As such they held a contract with St Barnabus's to be in charge of all the general maintenance at the school – including the biomass boiler. This boiler seemed to have developed a habit of coming on by itself at irregular intervals, heating the school beyond the limits of endurance, but whenever Matt made any attempts to turn the boiler off or down, he'd invariably earn a reprimand from Steve Hewson, who insisted only qualified people touched it. And since Joe Public seemed to have only one accredited boiler engineer – who was, according to Matt, elusive to say the least – the school remained overheated.

None of this was made any simpler by the fact that there seemed to be two businesses involved with this biomass boiler – the ones who owned it – some finance firm apparently – and the ones who had the contract for maintaining it – Joe Public. Pat frowned, looking at her notes – it all seemed very complicated. The question of Steve Hewson, however, had seemed a lot more straightforward.

'Cocky little shit,' Matt had said. 'Very thick with Mrs Brittain. A load of fingers in a load of different pies. All sorts of shady stuff he's been mixed up in. There was all that business over in Bradford. Argy-bargy with that academy.'

Pat had been about to disown any knowledge of any argy-bargy in Bradford when she stopped, frowned. An academy trust – Heaton Royds? Some scandal with the money? Not being paid or money being pilfered or both, and the schools suffering? Sipping her coffee, she remembered more – didn't her friend Victoria work in one of the schools affected? She recalled a couple of successive Christmas cards with 'don't even ask' written in Victoria's firm green scrawl.

She reviewed her notes. There was definitely *something* there – what, she wasn't sure. She hadn't dared mention the Baldersby job to Matt. Neither he nor Linda were known for their discretion and the last thing she wanted was to inflame the situation with Rod any further. What should she do? She tried breathing and envisioning tranquillity, but it was hard to envision anything except a stocky arrogant figure in tan cowboy boots trampling all over her peace of mind. She needed to find out more about him.

The thought that came into her head was as clear and direct as any spoken answer.

Hadn't Matt said that Thelma was now a governor at St Barnabus's Lodestone Academy?

CHAPTER ELEVEN

At an unusual harvest assembly, a hat breaks and another letter is received.

The school hall was packed – packed and fiercely overheated.

With arms akimbo and bright showbiz smiles, the girls of Rowan Class kicked out their legs in time to explosive, pumping music accompanied by discreet miming directions from a bony woman in a bright turquoise leotard, presumably the choreographer. In their yellow and orange T-shirts, the girls were, thought Thelma, more like Pan's People than any part of a primary school harvest assembly. Even so . . . She regarded the girls who were now doing a series of leapfrog – it was hard to work out just *how* all this was connected with harvest.

Suddenly she was assailed by a sharp, sweet memory: Topsy grimly bashing out 'Look for signs that summer's done' on the old North Riding County Council piano, various PE benches stacked with produce from allotments and back gardens and, centre stage, mounted on the old vaulting horse, a magnificent varnished brown loaf in the shape of a wheatsheaf. Tommy Wheatcroft, who'd had the bakery down Kirkgate, had done it for them year on year. Then all the produce would be lovingly divvied up by Topsy and taken round by the Year Six class to the local sheltered housing.

Now, so Thelma understood, it all went straight to the Foodbank.

She looked to the back of the hall. No sign, as yet, of Kayleigh Brittain. She'd arrived early at school specifically to speak to her, only to be informed she wasn't available – whatever that meant. How was she feeling after last night's events? A few people – Terry, Nicole, herself – had wanted Kayleigh to call the police, but she'd been adamant her insurance would sort it and she just wanted to get home. Thelma again pictured that scratch in the caramel-coloured paintwork – bright, shiny, *malicious* . . . Despite the warmth of the hall, she shivered. It had been in this very hall she'd seen that look on Kayleigh Brittain's face. *What* had she seen? Or who?

Sitting next to her, Liz was also thinking about damage to a car.

'Go away!!! I don't want to talk to you!' A face distorted in anger . . . 'I'm not surprised after what you've done, you mad bitch!'

Come on, Liz, get a grip. Paint stripper was *not* the same as a scratch, not at all. She looked across to where Jan was crouched with Elm Class, a fixed, almost manic grin on her face. One or two of the class waved at her, making the leaves on their hats shake, but Jan was definitely avoiding meeting her eyes. Probably annoyed with her for not coming in. As she looked, Elijah held up his hat, which had yet again come unstapled. With an almost furtive glance round, Jan got up and left the hall.

The thought hit her like a brick to the head.

Whoever was leaving letters needed to do so at a time when everyone was otherwise occupied. *Like assemblies!*

Another crescendo of pulsing music exploded to one last climax, and the hall erupted into whoops and cheers from the parents, who had been filming everything on their mobile phones.

'Way to go, Kelsey!'

The voice sounded familiar to Thelma, yet she couldn't quite place it. Turning, she saw the woman she'd been on the stall with at the summer fayre. Izzy, wasn't it? Izzy Trewin. She was sitting two seats down from her – well, not exactly sitting, she was stood waving energetically. Thelma wished she would sit down; she was sure she could feel heat radiating off her. More than one person in the hall was fanning themselves with the leaflets that had been put out on the chairs.

'Thank you, Year Six girls!' It was Ian Berryman, thankfully in flannel trousers, not trackie bottoms. 'Thank you for "Strictly come harvest!" More cheers. Both Liz and Thelma noted the dark stains under the arms of his Lodestone Academy polo shirt. 'And also, a big thank you to Roz from Dance-tastic Academy for her hard work with the group.'

The bony woman sprung up, a freakishly Botoxed mouth smiling a frankly terrifying grin. 'I teach several children's classes,' she announced. 'All the details can be found on the leaflets on your seats.' Which explained the origin of said glossy leaflets. Thelma skimmed the print, eyebrows raising slightly at the price.

'Now before we go on to Year One . . .' Ian's voice rose ineffectively above the murmur in the hall. 'Before we go on, I've an announcement to make . . . I've a message from Mrs Brittain. She's very sorry but she's been "unavoidably detained"!' His heavily humorous inverted commas drew no reaction, except from Claire, who giggled. 'But she wants all you guys to know—' he inclined his head at the children '—you've all done a brilliant job!' His voice went up again, obviously hoping to provoke a supportive cheer but there was only a subdued murmur.

'How can she know they were brilliant if she's not here?' Thelma heard one parent say.

'Never here that one,' said another.

'I've not seen her since the summer fayre,' said Izzy Trewin.

Thelma frowned, concerned. In her experience it was one of the

119

unwritten rules of a primary school that the head needed to be on display, beaming and smiling at each and every event: Christmas, harvest, sports day, parent evenings and assorted fundraisers.

Had what had happened shaken Kayleigh more than any of them realized? Maybe she should call her?

'Now,' said Ian. 'We come to Year One and "Once Upon a Time in the Cabbage Patch". Over to you, Mrs Starke!' Without waiting to see what happened, he ducked out of the hall.

There was a faint but growing mutter as it dawned on everyone present that Mrs Starke was nowhere to be seen. Liz and Thelma exchanged glances.

'I thought she was going out to mend Elijah's hat,' said Liz.

They both looked over to where the green and orange hats were beginning to stir and the Year One children knowing this was their time and that something was expected of them. Elijah stood, hatless, eyes wide with uncertainty. The staff were also stirring uneasily, unsure what to do.

Liz rose, looking anxiously at the door. Thelma put her hand on her arm. 'I'll go,' she said. 'You're needed here.'

Liz nodded. There are some situations where a primary school teacher's instincts kick in as powerfully as adrenalin, when uncertainty and embarrassment are replaced by iron-calm conviction and decisive action. This was one of them.

'Now, boys and girls,' said Liz in a quiet voice that could nevertheless be heard by everyone in the noisy hall. 'Boys and girls, stand up and take your places, just like you did the other day for me and Mrs Stark.' She sat (gingerly) down on the parquet floor in front of them, praying that when the time came, she'd be able to get back up again.

Thelma meanwhile negotiated her way out of the side door to the hall, into the (slightly) cooler corridor. As she headed down to the Key Stage One corridor, she was slightly surprised to see

Ian Berryman walking in front of her. Was he too looking for Jan? Hearing her footsteps he turned, his expression surprised, almost shifty. 'Is everything okay?' he said.

'I was just looking for Mrs Starke,' said Thelma. 'She's not in the hall, and they're ready to start.'

'Isn't she?' He looked uncertainly back. 'Right,' he said, appearing to come to a decision. 'I better just go . . .' His words trailed away as he headed back towards the hall. He really needed to change his shirt.

Hurrying down towards Jan's classroom, Thelma wondered just where he'd been going, but before she could consider the question, the stock cupboard door opposite the cloakrooms opened, and there stood Nicole, framed in front of the racks of paper and tubs of power paint. 'Oh,' she said in an affronted tone. 'Aren't you in the assembly?'

'I'm looking for Mrs Starke,' said Thelma again. 'They're waiting for her.'

'Well, I was just checking the cupboard.' Nicole sounded almost accusing. 'I just wish people would clear up after themselves.' She was sounding distinctly huffy. She locked the door and headed back up the corridor; Thelma looked after her.

Interesting.

From what she'd seen, the stock cupboard looked perfectly tidy.

Jan was in her classroom, sat in her teacher's chair by the carpeted area, staring out of the window to where the coppery trees shifted in the sunny breeze. There was something utterly defeated and weary about her posture and tears glistened dully on her face, which was blotchy and puffy.

'Jan,' said Thelma. 'Whatever is the matter?'

'It's all right, Thelma.' Jan's voice was harsh. 'Now I finally know what people here really think of me.' She flung a finger towards something lying on the carpet.

Typically dramatic, thought Thelma, and was immediately ashamed of the thought. She looked where Jan was pointing. On the carpet in front of her lay a torn-open white envelope and a folded rectangle of white paper. With a sinking feeling Thelma picked it up; the printed words leered out offensively.

*CALL YOURSELF A TEACHER? DON'T MAKE
ME LAUGH! ALWAYS SHOUTING YOUR MOUTH
OFF! WHY DON'T YOU SHUT THE FUCK UP
FOR A CHANGE, YOU GOBBY COW, AND LET
THE REST OF US GET ON WITH THE JOB?*

CHAPTER TWELVE

Friends are reunited and letters discussed, but still secrets are withheld.

Liz looked out across the garden centre car park. A gusty wind was strengthening, swirling up the leaves and rattling the plastic pumpkins and skeletons that were hanging in the entrance. Since they'd arrived, the sky had darkened; today there were noticeably more coats on the backs of the chairs. She shivered slightly and looked around the café, its blessed mundane normality, barely half full, as it generally was on a Thursday morning. At the round table in the corner were a group of ladies knitting, but today there was something Liz found jarring about them, the bright colours of their wool: crimson, custard yellow, lime green. As they knitted, the women chatted, cheerfully, inconsequentially. Everyone *seemed* pleasant enough – but underneath? Could anyone ever tell what was going on inside people's heads?

Again, she thought of those hateful, spiteful words . . . the lonely figure of Jan crossing the car park, having been sent home by Becky. As she'd reached her car she'd stopped, looked over her shoulder . . . there was something almost furtive in the glance she'd given . . . Liz sighed to herself. She'd need to ring her later on – either that or go round herself.

'They're out of the chicken and vegetable soup, so I ordered the red pepper and Wensleydale, as I seem to remember you quite liked it.' Thelma placed the tray of coffee on the table, an angel in an M&S jumper. She sat down and looked at her friend. 'Are you all right?' she said.

'I'm not the one who's been sent an anonymous letter,' said Liz flatly.

Thelma nodded.

'I thought it might be Jan doing it,' Liz said. 'Sending out the letters.'

'I know,' said Thelma gently.

Liz reached for her coffee. Outside in the car park someone was wrestling sacks of potting compost into the boot of their car. 'I was hoping it might all just stop,' she said eventually.

'What might stop?' They both looked up at the bright voice, a voice that seemed to take the greyer bits of the day and treat them as some sort of huge joke. Pat was standing there, her hair a vivid shade of auburn, set off by her favourite autumn wrap of russet and dark green. Glittery purple nails caught the light and winked from where they held the tray containing coffee and a Melmerby slice.

'Now, ladies,' she said, 'I have a bit of a problem.' She looked over to the round table in the corner where the last of the knitting women was gathering up an enormous ball of pink fluffy wool. 'But first,' she said. 'Shall we relocate?'

'So be honest with me. Am I going nuts? Trekking all the way over to Bradford to see Victoria?' Pat smiled in that self-mocking way of hers but they both had noticed the lines around her eyes and mouth. 'So what if this Steve Hewson is the biggest crook going? I mean, we've lost the Baldersby contract – end of. Am I just being a nosy old bat?'

It was an hour later; the lunchtime rush was well under way. A good three-quarters of the tables were full, and the café had just run out of Helmsley three-cheese quiche.

'If you think there's something not quite right, then yes definitely, you need to find out more,' said Liz.

'What harm is there in going over to see an old friend?' asked Thelma.

'It's just, what would Rod say if he knew I was nosying around?' Her friends both noted her choice of words. Pat looked down at her crumb-strewn plate and empty coffee cup. 'We've only just nicely smoothed things over.' She looked at her friends – Liz frowning, worrying about Jan Starke, and Thelma stirring her coffee, thinking goodness knows what.

It was good to see them again.

'So, you say this Steve Hewson is connected to the boiler at school?' said Thelma thoughtfully.

'Amongst other things,' said Pat. 'His company has the contract to service it. But I rather gather he's a man with many fingers in many pies.'

'We'll need to be pulling one of them out, and smartish,' said Liz. 'It was like a furnace at the Harvest.'

'That'll be what's behind all these anonymous letters,' said Pat. The others looked, still surprised she'd been told about them by Matt Barley. 'It'll be the mad boiler man taking his revenge.'

But Liz wasn't in a mood to joke. 'It's awful,' she said. 'The whole thing. Horrid. If you'd seen that letter to Jan . . . Why on earth would someone do something like send nasty letters?'

'To Jan Starke?' Pat was on the point of saying something along the lines of there being a queue outside WHSmith of people stocking up on stationery to do just that – but a look from Thelma made her think better of it. 'There could be all sorts of reasons,' she said. 'Someone pisses you off, you want to get back at them. But then to send so *many* – it seems to me someone might have a screw loose.'

Liz and Thelma frowned at this comment but Pat was pursuing the thought. 'I don't know,' she said, shaking her head.

'What?' asked Thelma.

'Poison pen letters,' she said slowly. 'I don't know . . . it all just feels a bit . . .'

'Nasty,' supplied Liz.

'Outdated.' Pat chased the last crumbs round her plate with a finger. 'Miss Marple and Enid Blyton.'

'The trouble is we just don't know anything,' said Liz in frustration.

'That's not quite true,' said Thelma. 'Apart from the letter you picked up, the letters we know of were found by the victims.'

Liz shrugged. 'I'd have thought that was fairly obvious,' she said.

'Except it means whoever left the letters *knew where to put them* so they'd be found by the recipients. Jan's diary, Becky's handbag. Which indicates a certain amount of local knowledge.'

'You mean a teacher?' said Pat with interest.

Liz stiffened, uneasy at a sudden thought.

'Any member of staff really,' said Thelma. 'Someone who's able to walk freely round the school without attracting attention.'

. . . a figure slipping out of the school hall . . . Liz looked worriedly out at the car park.

'I wonder,' said Pat. 'If Kayleigh Brittain has gone to the police?'

'I don't think it's likely,' said Thelma.

'Not for two or three nasty letters,' agreed Liz. She sounded snippy, a sure sign she was worried.

Now it was Pat's turn to frown. She opened her mouth to speak but Thelma was talking.

'What I mean,' said Thelma, 'is that I don't think Jan and Becky and whoever would *want* her to go to the police. That's even if they'd told her in the first place.'

'Why on earth not?' said Liz.

'Think about it,' said Thelma patiently. 'You get a letter, saying how awful you are . . .' She paused briefly, gathering her thoughts.

'Maybe, *maybe* even alluding to something you might have done . . . would you really want people to know?'

'But everyone must realize whoever's doing this is unstable.' Liz looked distressed.

'They might well be. *But that doesn't mean what they're saying isn't true.* Or even partially true,' said Thelma.

Thinking about Jan Starke, Pat found herself nodding. She could have called her a lot worse things than a gobby cow over the years.

Thelma stirred her coffee again. 'There was a case – a good few years ago – in a parish where one of Teddy's students was a curate. Similar thing – people started getting nasty letters dropped through their letterboxes, in the post, hand delivered. No one had any idea who it could be . . . Lots of people were suspected – but nothing was *known*. There was plenty of *talk* – but nothing that could be *done*. Over two years this went on for.'

Liz stared. 'Did they eventually catch this person?'

'Eventually. It turned out to be some elderly gentleman, member of the parish council. A retired lecturer I think he was. Someone everyone got on with – the last person anyone expected. And of course, by the time he was caught – well, the damage was done. There's still a funny atmosphere in the place so I hear.'

'Damage?' Pat looked puzzled. 'I mean if the person was caught?'

Thelma shook her head. 'It's not that simple. You see everyone at some point more or less suspected someone else. Asked themselves that question – *could* it be them sending these letters? Could it be so and so? It's hard to be neighbourly when you've been having thoughts like that. It drives people apart . . . it fragmented the community.'

Liz thought of that quiet, uneasy staffroom, muted conversations, sidelong looks.

'Kayleigh Brittain needs to *do* something,' she said decisively.

From the look in her eye, both Thelma and Pat judged their friend to be quite capable of marching down to the school herself and demanding action.

'Talking of Kayleigh Brittain,' said Pat, 'do you think the letter writer, whoever they are, *was* the one who keyed her car – or was that someone else?'

Thelma suddenly frowned and stiffened; something Liz and Pat recognized of old.

'What?' said Pat.

'I suppose I was just wondering *why* someone should key her car?'

'Someone obviously had it in for her.'

'But then why look through the window of the meeting? Assuming it was the same person? It's not like they could know for sure Kayleigh would be the one facing the window.' She shook her head. Vandalizing a car, looking in through a window . . . they didn't *fit* with writing nasty letters. Yet somehow – they felt as though they *should*.

'Anyway,' said Pat, 'at least it's hardly likely to be Mrs Brittain writing the letters. From what you say, it sounds like she can make people stressed enough without fannying around writing nasty notes. In fact—' she held up her hand as a thought struck her '—does she even know about all the other letters?'

'She knows about the one Becky got,' said Liz, 'but she won't have heard about Jan yet, not if she wasn't in school.'

'I mean about all the others?' Liz and Thelma looked at her. 'What others?' said Liz. 'There's only been a few, surely?' said Thelma.

Pat was shaking her head. 'I thought we had some crossed wires going on,' she said. 'According to Matt Barley there's been more than one or two. At least twelve. Maybe as many as fifteen.'

★

128

When Thelma nipped to the ladies' Liz said to Pat: 'How are things?'

'Okay thanks.' Pat smiled a bright smile. 'Getting there.'

Whilst Liz was fumbling for her loyalty card at the checkout, Thelma said to Pat: 'Is everything well with you?'

'You know,' said Pat cheerfully. 'Plodding on.'

That night found Liz sat in her conservatory staring at her phone and wondering at what point her frequent and fruitless attempts to call would be deemed a nuisance by Jan. And also, at what point should she do something? Plus – what exactly should she do?

Derek – thank goodness – was safely immersed in a hot bath and likely to be there for at least the next forty minutes. On his return from his run, he'd pronounced he'd felt Something Go at the allotments and had taken himself upstairs with the *Yorkshire Post* and a new tube of Deep Heat cream. Liz's guilt at the relief she felt at this turn of events was just another disquieting feeling she'd shoved in amongst all the other disquieting feelings that the day had produced.

Fifteen letters. That was just about half the staff. *Fifteen.* Including Jan.

The furtive glance over her shoulder in the car park . . . *What have you done?*

One more attempt to get through, then she'd need to go round. As if reading her mind, her phone juddered, and a text appeared: *JUST NEED TO SLEEP. AM OK Jxxx*

And that seemed to be that.

CHAPTER THIRTEEN

Various untruths are bandied about, and there is Sunday sadness in a canal-side flat.

Thelma lit the tealight, which flickered uncertainly into life, faded, flared and then burnt unsteadily, joining all the other tealights flickering uncertainly on the iron stand by the altar steps.

She sat down for the five minutes' reflection she always allowed herself at the end of Sunday service, left-hand side, towards the back. 'Please God,' she began as she always did. And then stopped. She realized she had absolutely no idea what to say next.

There was so much on her mind – St Barnabus's, the college, Teddy, Jan Starke, Bunty Carter and of course the letters . . . but what should she be asking *for* exactly?

Your Father knows what you need before you ask him.

Thelma looked at the flickering flame. She was glad someone did.

Since the day of the harvest, part of her mind had been dominated by thoughts of those letters – those *fifteen* letters. If they were anything like the few she'd seen . . . what on earth was going on in her old school? In one respect, however, it slightly eased her conscience about not telling Kayleigh about the letter Liz had found. It was obviously part of a much *much* bigger picture.

After their previous conversations, she wondered if Kayleigh might call her but Friday and Saturday had come and gone without any communication. Looking at the flame, she admitted to herself she had been feeling slightly *hurt*. She had thought she was maybe someone Kayleigh might choose to confide in.

The call, when it did come, on the Sunday morning, was a surprise in more ways than one. For a start, Kayleigh's voice had been upbeat, sunny even, giving no indication of any such thing as fifteen anonymous letters sent to her staff. She realized it was short notice, but would Thelma be able to take part in the book scrutiny next week? They could really use her expertise as a former teacher! The call been both brief and very one-sided. Thelma had barely been able to say 'yes' before Kayleigh had rung off, let alone mention the letter Liz found or ask how she was. After the call she sat for a while wondering – *was* it simply an invitation to take part in a book scrutiny? Or was there more to it?

And then of course she had been just as preoccupied by that other issue – that glossy, sinister document sitting at home on the kitchen counter. 'Ripon and St Bega's College, a way forward'. The flowery phrases: *vibrant college . . . charming cathedral city . . . a vital part of this Yorkshire community* . . . And amongst all those flowers, those thorns: *increasingly financially unviable . . . tough decisions . . . Suggestion: could the best way to preserve this college potentially be relocating operations to another Baht'at campus?*

It's only a discussion document – that's what the Children of the Suits had said in their 'way-forward' meeting and that was what Thelma and Teddy had been saying to each other repeatedly since he came home with it on Friday. But what if Josie Gribben had been right? What if the college *was* earmarked for closure? Looking at the guttering candle, she remembered the conversation with Teddy about the curriculum summary he'd shared at the meeting.

He'd been standing in the garden, coffee in hand, deep in thought, when she'd asked about how things had gone.

'Well enough,' he'd said.

'But?'

'There they all were . . . smiling, nodding . . .' He'd paused as though seeing the words written in the tracery of the clematis spidering up the wall. 'All the suits, the PowerPoints . . . I can't escape this feeling . . . *that's* what felt important. Not what we were doing – are doing – with the course. It's that whole *business* element to education.'

Thelma had remembered Josie's words . . . *pounds, shillings and pence* . . .

'But surely the course content is what the whole thing stands or falls by?' she'd said.

'Times change,' Teddy had said. 'And one has to accept that.'

'But not basic training in ordination, surely?'

He's shrugged. 'Everything has its day.'

Everything has its day.

Outside the church breaths of chill autumn wind were stirring the yew trees round the graveyard with unsettling sea-like sounds that matched her mood. God, she had long accepted, moved in mysterious ways but actually – right now on this gusty autumn day – she didn't want him to move at all, or if he had to, in gentle easy steps that didn't leave her with these great clutches of fear.

'And how's our friend Fluffypaws getting on?' Maureen's cheerful voice broke into her thoughts.

Thelma looked at her blankly for an instant, before remembering. 'He's fine,' she said. 'Settling.'

When Frankie Miller had been taken into the Friarage that final time, her worries had been all about her cat Fluffypaws.

Visiting her, it had only seemed natural for Thelma to offer to take him in until something could be sorted out. Even though it had been some years since Artaxerxes had died, they still had the various accoutrements of cat care stowed away at 32 College Gardens, and the cat had become a rather nervous addition to their household with very little difficulty.

Except for one thing. His name.

'Fluffypaws' had sat well with neither Thelma nor Teddy; still, as his stay was only temporary, it hadn't seemed much of an issue. But as the days went by, they both began to realize they couldn't refer to the wide-eyed black scrap as 'Frankie's cat' forever. Then, on the day when they heard she'd died, the cat had been caught in the act of making off with one of Teddy's mid-morning custard creams; it was then the name Snaffles had been applied and stuck.

To the general congregation of St Catherine's, however, honouring Frankie's memory, he was still Fluffypaws. It was such a trivial thing – one of those social lies that arise in life from time to time. But sitting there that morning, Thelma found it irritating. Not, she reflected, because of the lie itself – but because of a sudden, insistent feeling it was one untruth amongst many. What these untruths were Thelma wasn't sure, but she suddenly felt surrounded by them, as opaque and vague as her unfocused prayers.

As Derek retreated upstairs for his post-run shower, Liz looked at the laptop she'd slammed guiltily shut. Another silly complication.

It wasn't that she was *worried* about Bunty Carter, but at the same time, she was on her mind. She'd started thinking about it more as a way of diverting her annoyance away from that awful phone call with Jan earlier that morning . . . She was sure Bunty *was* at her daughter's, but even so, short of tramping the streets of Boroughbridge there seemed to be no way of knowing. Then she'd remembered that cryptic comment of Margo's about eBay. And that jolly Brownie leader looking for pencil crayons. And all at once Liz had realized there was a way she could track her down.

Of course, it hadn't been that simple. There were, eBay informed her, over 57,000 people selling pencil crayons – even when she narrowed it down to sellers within a five-mile radius there still seemed to be an inordinately large number, as if Thirsk were some Pencil Crayon Capital of the north. And none of them had seemed to be Bunty. Then she had remembered the username she traded under – Big Mama . . . There had been a few sellers with that name. The nearest had been in Pickering . . .

The display of basques had come as a fascinating shock. So many! All colours and textures! And the models – all so heartbreakingly young – standing with one leg on a stool or chair of some description.

And that had been when Derek came in. Just what she didn't need after their earlier confrontation . . .

From upstairs came the sound of the shower starting and she shook her head. She sighed. She hoped she hadn't broken the laptop, slamming it shut like that.

Such a mess.

All thanks to Jan Starke.

After all she'd worried and fretted about the wretched woman. She felt her annoyance swelling back into anger. Her perverse relief at knowing Jan hadn't been behind the letters had been tempered by a much bigger worry of how her friend would be coping with being on the receiving end of one of them. Again and again, she'd tried to call her, again and again the call had gone straight to voicemail. (*Hi it's Jan! Leave a message!*)

'She knows where you are,' Thelma had said.

'She'll be fine,' said Pat. 'You know old Starke-Staring.'

But that was just it – Liz *did* know Jan. She was one of the few people who had seen beyond that loud brittle façade and Liz knew her friend would have been desperately hurt and upset. And when Jan was upset, you never knew what she might do (though at 3 a.m. two nights running she'd had some pretty nasty ideas).

The call had come earlier, as Derek had been plotting that day's run on the iPad with the concentration of a NASA scientist planning the trajectory of an *Apollo* launch. Liz had been clearing up lunch, biting back the yawns after another restless night of imaginings (LOCAL WOMAN FOUND DROWNED IN RIPON CANAL), when her phone had shrilled. Derek had looked up questioningly. From the display she could see it was Jan.

'Better just take this,' she said in airy, dismissive tones that she hoped would fool him and took herself off to the relative privacy of the conservatory.

'Jan!' She tried not to sound too relieved. 'How are you?'

'I'm fine.' The voice bounced out loud and confident.

'I've been worried about you,' said Liz.

'I knew you would have been.' Jan's voice sounded amused. 'I said to Kayleigh, I bet Liz's in a right old stress, bless her!'

Remembering those two sleepless nights, Liz felt the first prickles of irritation.

'You just seemed so upset after – you know – getting that horrible letter.'

Jan gave a cheerful laugh. 'That,' she said dismissively. 'I think shocked was the word. Now I just find it rather amusing.'

'Really?'

'Liz, if someone wants to say something to me, and that's the only way they can find to say it – well I rather think it's their problem. It's like I was saying to Kayleigh: you just pick yourself up and you put one foot in front of the other. There's absolutely no need to fuss.'

'You've been talking to Kayleigh Brittain?'

'She's been brilliant, Liz. Ringing me every day, checking to see how I was.'

Liz felt those prickles of irritation becoming a pronounced flush. So, Jan picked up for Kayleigh Brittain, the woman who had been making her life so difficult, but not her friend who had been there for her so many times before?

'As long as you're okay,' she said in an end-of-conversation tone.

'Now, the reason I'm ringing you, Liz—' Jan cut across her, suddenly brisk and business-like. 'I know you've been concerned for me, which is very sweet and lovely of you, but it's very *very* important that nobody talks about this.' The tone was deliberate and calm, the sort of tone Liz had heard her use with her Bumblebees group. 'All in all it's probably just as well you've decided not to come in.'

'I wouldn't—' began Liz but Jan was on something of a roll.

'You'll appreciate what a delicate situation this is. Not for me. Hey! All water off a duck's back—' (here Liz came very close to hanging up) '—but some people, bless them, have really been taking this to heart. Kayleigh's been super, ringing them up, offering them support – but the one thing nobody wants is for this being spread all around Thirsk. I know what it's like when you and Thelma and Pat get together.' She gave an arch laugh. 'But, Liz, people talking about this business is going to make the whole thing ten times worse . . .'

After she had hung up, Liz had expected Derek to have already left on his run, but he was waiting in the kitchen. He looked at her. 'What did Jan want?'

'Just to catch up.'

'You did say you weren't getting involved.'

'I'm not!'

She truly hadn't meant to sound so tetchy. Watching the

Lycra-clad figure disappear down the road, she had hated herself for the craven, casual way she was lying to him.

Upstairs the hum of the shower stopped and she could hear the muffled yelps as Derek bent down to dry between his toes. She put the laptop into its satchel. She should just leave it all alone. Leave Jan alone – she was so obviously fine. More than fine—

Screams in the distance . . . Smoke . . . What have you done? Jan surely wouldn't send *herself* a letter? Almost angrily she shook her head at the thought.

Jacob was lying on his front on the lounge rug, utterly absorbed.

'How are you getting on?'

'I'm on Joseph Ellison Lidster,' he said. He was currently creating a set of memoriam pages for each passenger who had perished on the *Titanic*.

'You're still on third class?'

'Grandma, I'm not even halfway through.' His voice held a gloomy relish.

Looking at him, so absorbed, so resolute, she felt something inside her twist and strengthen. 'I got you more black ribbon,' she said. 'It's in a bag on the side next to the Swiss box. And when you see Grandad, just tell him I've popped out to the garden centre.'

'I was just passing,' said Liz. 'On my way back from the garden centre.'

It wasn't a total lie she told herself; she *had* been to the garden centre. She placed the bulb catalogue down firmly on the over-crowded coffee table.

Finding Becky Clegg's canal-side flat in Ripon had been rela-tively straightforward to locate. It had just been a case of finding her red Fiat and scanning all the doorbells until she found the right one.

'I hope I'm not interrupting anything.' Liz raised her voice, though she hardly needed to. The kitchen where Becky was making tea was barely a tiny recess off the small lounge-cum-dining-room-cum-everything else.

'Not at all,' said Becky.

The answer was obviously not true. So dominated was the space by Becky's schoolwork that it was hard to make any real judgements about the taste and décor. On the pocket-sized dining table was a pile of exercise books and a couple of magazine boxes of documentation; there was another pile of books in a plastic crate on the floor. Precariously stacked on the sofa were no less than six ring binders. Next to them were three more magazine boxes marked 'Autumn data predictions'.

The only real sign of any life beyond the schoolwork was a framed photo on the side, partially obscured by yet another magazine box. It showed Becky, with a man her own age, heads touching as they laughed into the camera. Both were wearing ski hats, the man was wearing goggles and Becky's eyes were screwed up against a brilliant blue sky; no amount of sun and ski apparel could disguise the couple's sheer joy at life. Presumably this was the other half of the train-wreck split.

'You look hard at it,' said Liz as Becky came with the tea. She recalled bygone days, her own strewn dining room table, the books, the tick sheets, her beloved green mark book.

Becky looked vaguely round, as if surprised by her comment. 'I'm just sorting out one or two bits and pieces for next week.'

Liz smiled; now it had come to it, she was feeling decidedly uncomfortable about asking any questions. 'Have you heard how Bunty is?' she asked.

Becky frowned vaguely. 'Still off with her back I think,' she said.

Liz sighed, maybe she'd just leave the bulb catalogue and go. Sipping her tea she looked out of the window, at the end of the canal basin, brightly painted barges and disdainful swans. 'I do like the view,' she said. 'How long have you been here?'

'A week short of six months.' Becky spoke matter-of-factly but there was a sudden sadness in those hazel eyes as they strayed instinctively to the partially hidden photo. 'Of course, I was planning on buying with someone. But it didn't work out.'

'I'm sorry to hear that,' said Liz and looking at that cluttered, lonely room, she genuinely was.

'Oh well,' said Becky. 'One of those things.'

'And I was so sorry to hear about what happened to you.' The words came out in a rush of genuine emotion; Liz hadn't been exactly sure she was going to say the words until she actually did. 'About the anonymous letter.' Jolted out of her reverie, Becky looked fixedly at her. There was something distinctly unnerving about that calm, direct gaze. 'I realize it's none of my business,' said Liz flustered. 'It's just Thelma happened to mention it, after what happened with Jan.'

'We've been told not to talk about all that,' said Becky firmly.

'Of course,' said Liz hastily, thinking that actually she'd much rather be talking about Cherry Sorbet and Madame Butterfly bulbs. 'As long as you're getting the support you need.'

Becky gave a short, harsh laugh. 'Someone asked me a couple of times if I was okay, if that's what you mean,' she said. 'Asking me in a way that implied I probably was.' She shook her head and began stroking the end of one of the ring binders. 'Ignore me,' she said. 'I just can't seem to get my head round it somehow.'

'It's a vile and nasty thing,' said Liz with conviction. Becky looked at her for a brief moment and crossed to one of the magazine boxes from which she extracted a plastic wallet that contained a sheet of A4 white paper.

'It's a copy,' she said. 'Kayleigh has the original. I don't even know why I'm keeping it. I hate it, but I can't quite bring myself to get rid of it.' She laughed mirthlessly and handed the sheet to Liz.

YOU THINK YOU WORK SO HARD! YOU'RE THE ONLY ONE WHO DOES! YOU SHOULD HEAR SOME OF THE THINGS PEOPLE ARE SAYING BEHIND YOUR BACK, YOU BOSSY COW.

Liz handed the sheet back, feeling rather nauseated at the sheer ill will of the letter. But at the same time, she felt something else, a feeling she couldn't quite pin down. There was *something* about the letter that struck her as . . . *off-key*.

'I've only seen you in school a little bit,' said Liz. 'But I do know you work very, very hard.'

Becky briefly closed her eyes. 'Of course, I'm not the only one who's had one.'

'That doesn't make it any easier,' said Liz.

'Some people have really taken it badly,' said Becky with a sigh. She frowned slightly, as if deciding whether to speak. 'Keep this to yourself,' she said, 'but you know Margo Benson?'

'I do,' said Liz, thinking of those jars of gardener's hand gel.

'No one knows this, but she and her husband are in pretty dire financial straits. Something about his job going. She *desperately* doesn't want people knowing this – I mean of course a load of people do, you know what it's like in a school.'

Liz nodded. She knew exactly what it was like in a school.

'Anyway.' Becky dropped her voice. 'She's started nicking people's coffee. I keep telling her to use mine, but anyway, she doesn't – and then she gets this letter calling her a thieving bitch. She was in a terrible state about it.'

140

'Does the letter mention her finances?'

Becky shook her head. 'Just the coffee. But it doesn't stop her thinking everyone knows about the money.' She sighed. 'I just worry someone's going to get a letter who *really* can't cope with it. I just keep thinking something awful's going to happen.'

Who was doing this?

The spiteful, stark words of Becky's letter played and replayed through Liz's mind as she drove up Sharow Hill. She felt nothing but compassion for lonely Raggedy Ann Becky in her bleak tiny flat of books and ring binders. Indeed, she felt a pang of sorrow for all the Beckys of this world, with their Sunday afternoons and chairs and sofas full of spreadsheets and exercise books. Right now, Becky should be with the man in ski goggles, trailing round IKEA or simply sprawled across a clutter-free sofa watching a box set.

She remembered Jan's rather dismissive tones. *Her relationship was a bit of a car crash, reading between the lines. She's not the easiest person in the world to live with.* Liz shook her head at yet another instance of Jan's breath-taking lack of self-awareness. She wondered how many other people in school knew about Becky's break-up. Like Margo's financial woes – probably a fair number.

Hang on. Driving up Sharow Hill she almost braked as a thought suddenly struck her. If the letter writer was so intent on upsetting people, *why hadn't they mentioned Becky's car-crash relationship in what they had written?*

CHAPTER FOURTEEN

A bittersweet trip into the past leads to speculation about events in the present.

Despite her obvious problems, the country and western singer sounded cheerfully perky. 'I lo-ove him but I cannot change him,' she purred. 'He's mah man and I ne-ee-ed him.'

'Piss off, you smug cow,' said Pat. She thumped the car radio off, realized the lights ahead had changed to red and braked abruptly, kangarooing to a stop. The man in the next car gave her a knowing and reproving smile. In normal times Pat would have been tempted to wind down her window and tell him where to stick his National Trust bumper sticker, but today she felt a familiar clutch of cold inadequacy – fear even. She gripped the wheel tightly, staring rigidly ahead.

Get a grip. Breathe . . . Face the truth – it's a landscape not a threat.

Only, she thought as the lights changed and National Trust man sped off, only it was a landscape she wasn't familiar with and had no map for. Nothing of any import had been said at their reconciliation (an awkward hug plus a trip to the Wheatsheaf for 'Two-4-Wednesday'). Rod was still showing no signs of going back to work and there had been, she knew, more conversations with Nazil, their finance guy, fuelling those 3 a.m. worries that the business was in trouble. But she just hadn't felt like she could ask.

'Are you putting off that necessary conversation?' one of Pat's trashy magazines had asked in a nagging pink font, and Pat was forced to admit yes, she very much was. Not that she could see how this journey over to Bradford would help improve things, not if she was honest. A possibly dodgy man was unfairly awarded a building contract. So what? It wasn't as if the confirmation of the news would galvanize Rod into any sort of action. But then Victoria had sounded so pleased and enthusiastic on the phone, and after all it had been a few years (Five? More like ten) since she'd seen her.

Driving down Hollins Hill and seeing Bradford spread out over its eight hills (like Rome she used to tell her class) brought a sweet painful pang. Not so much for the place, but for that time in her life, the Manningham bedsit, pints of Saltaire blond in the Beehive, incense sticks and CND mugs, the Love Apple, the Java, Mr B's. And Rod. Reeking of Old Spice, in the red sports car, fretting about the possibility of it getting stolen.

She took the slower route to the city centre, down Manningham Lane and past Lister Park. The turning trees were now starting to shed leaves in earnest, and she found herself remembering long-ago gusty days, leaves clattering round her crimson pixie boots as she walked laden across the park to catch the bus to that first job at Atlas Street. And then in the springtime, how the grass would be a starscape of yolk and purple crocuses. It had been by the boating lake one Sunday when the sun was battering at her hangover that Rod had said diffidently: 'How about you and me getting wed then?' in the same way he'd propose grabbing a curry at the Kashmir.

She had been going to turn off and drive by Sunderland Avenue, but suddenly she didn't want to face the sadness of happy times lost forever in the past, and after all what would there be to see?

Just another shabby Victorian villa. From the street you couldn't even see the dormer window of her former residence. A sudden image came to her of the view from the bedsit, the sweep of huddled slate rooftops and the stern sentinel of Lister's Mill chimney, and she realized she was blinking back tears.

'Get a grip,' she said to herself, hoping her new mascara was all it was cracked up to be.

Turning off Wakefield Road and trying to remember the way to Hedley Primary Academy, Pat reviewed what she'd found out about Heaton Royd Academies Trust, via various online news stories and a *Look North* documentary on YouTube. The trust had started well enough, with a number of schools across Leeds and Bradford (mostly struggling) taken in under the trust umbrella, which was led by an ex-head teacher with a bit of a vision. Not long after that, this vision had been substantially altered when the trust board, led by local businessman Barry Peel, had ousted the ex-head teacher – leaving Mr Peel as CEO.

Mr Peel was not an educationalist in any recognized sense of the word. 'I've been to the school of life, me,' was one of his favourite quotes. And what Mr Peel seemed to have learnt at the School of Life was how to make money, lots of it, for himself and those close to him. These included his wife (appointed as clerk of the trust) and his 'Very Good Friend', a lady appointed as his office manager (there had been a number of fascinating accounts of blazing rows at the trust headquarters). Mr Peel, on top of his not insubstantial salary, claimed extra hours (up to four a day, ten at weekends), petrol, at a rate of over a pound a mile (even on days when he was working from home), plus the very best in laptops, phones, iPads, cars – even a specially enclosed area at the trust HQ for Sheba the Cockapoo.

All of this funded by government money meant for the trust schools.

Things had all come crashing down in a rather spectacular fashion when (according to the tabloids) Mrs Peel had literally come to blows with the office manager. Mrs P had sued for divorce, the Very Good Friend had gone to the papers and the whole sorry story had hit social media and news feeds like several lorry-loads of the proverbial hitting many, many fans.

All that was clear. What seemed less clear was how exactly Steve Hewson fitted into all of this. And even if he did, how on earth was that relevant to anonymous letters and threats to Kayleigh Brittain?

Hedley Primary School, like a number of Bradford schools, had been built in a flush of optimism back in the 1980s, a cluster of sandy breeze-block pods containing open spaces, linked by open areas, an energetic reaction against the Victorian structures they replaced. Pat remembered coming here as a probationary teacher; how impressive, how space age, the structure had looked amongst all the brick and stone terraces. Now, some thirty-five years later, on a greying autumn day, it looked decidedly tired. Scaffolding clung to one of the pods; on others Pat, with her builder's wife's eye, noted signs of rot, of rust, and decay. Nothing ages so quickly as visions of the future.

Victoria came out into the lobby to greet her before Pat had even finished signing in. The wide smile, the smooth black skin, the surprised eyes – her face had hardly aged since they were young teachers together. Her hair though was now silvery and closely cropped to her head. Pat remembered the vibrant mass of plaits and beads that had flung themselves about with a life of their own when she got excited or laughed – which had been often.

'Oh my God, Pat, how long has it been?' That rich, rolling laugh hadn't changed either; neither had her taste for purple and green floaty skirts, magenta lipstick and emerald nails that only

Victoria could carry off. She enveloped her in a warm, scented hug and then looked closely at her. 'Coffee,' she said.

'We're still picking up the pieces here.' As if to emphasize Victoria's words, somewhere not far off a drill added a bizarre descant to her words.

They were sat in her office, walls ablaze with children's artwork, with a mug of blissfully strong coffee ('I can't be pissing about with decaf, not at my age.')

'You mean the work that was done on the school?'

'I mean the work that *wasn't* done. I kid you not, for three years the place was left to fall to pieces. Oh my God, Pat, you would not have wanted my job! I went from being a head teacher to a building inspector like that!' She chopped the air with a flash of the emerald nails. 'Hours every day I'd be on that phone about leaking pipes or knackered fire doors. And then when I finally got through to someone – nothing.'

'They refused to do the work?'

'Not even that. They just did nothing. You'd get Mrs Peel all la-di-dah: "Your concerns are noted" – and that was it, you'd hear nothing more.'

'So, they didn't do the work?'

'Didn't do the work, didn't provide the books and pencils, didn't supply new teachers . . .' She laughed again. 'You know, little things like that.' She shook her head, the smile suddenly replaced by something much grimmer. 'It was disgusting and never should have happened. At one point I had nearly half supply staff, a hole in the Year Three roof and fire doors that wouldn't shut! Then – the cherry on the cake – the sewer backed up. Right in the middle of the Nursery Bear Hunt.' Again, that rich, life-affirming laugh. 'Can't go round it, can't go under it, gotta go through it! That was me and Cash, my site manager, going to rescue the kids.'

'And Steve Hewson?'

The smiled vanished. 'What about him?'

'What's he like?'

'Ah'm from Castleford and ah'm proud of it,' she said in broad Yorkshire. She shook her head sombrely. 'He was Brian Peel's Mr Fix-it-man.'

'No good I take it?'

'He was fine – when he was here. But he was always being "re-prioritized" by Mr Peel. I'd hear his voicemail more than I heard him. But then when he did show up . . .' Her voice trailed away.

'Yes?'

'Put it this way – I never liked being alone with him. I'd always leave the office door open and have Meera on standby.'

'Why?'

Again, Victoria shook her head. 'Nothing he ever did or said,' she said. 'There was just *something* about the man.'

Pat remembered that arrogant rapping on her car window. It wasn't just her then.

There was a knock, and the office manager stuck her head round the door. 'Mrs Dolby says to say have you forgotten Nursery stickers?'

A beringed hand clamped to the magenta mouth. 'Oh my God! Meera, tell Mrs Dolby I am on my way!'

Crossing the school hall, Victoria's heels clicked authoritatively on the parquet floor.

'My pride and joy, this,' she said, gesturing downwards. 'That was my Friday job for a while, with the electric buffer thing. I'd say, "Cash, fire that bad boy up, here comes Buffy the Parquet Slayer!"'

'You had to clean the hall floor?'

'No cleaners. The company contracted to clean wasn't paid, so it was me, Cash and Meera.'

She whirled into the nursery class like a fragrant, bright tornado.

'Oh, my goodness me!' she exclaimed. 'Just look at all you super sitters!' Twenty-six pairs of legs scissored shut, twenty-six spines straightened. 'Well, hello there!' she said. 'I hope I get to give out some of my "well done" stickers today.'

On the way back to the office, Pat noted again how every wall was alive with children's work, bright, happy and colourful. Very, very Victoria.

There was a distant burst of angry shouting.

'Our exclusion unit,' said Victoria. 'We have our problems, God knows we do. It's never been a good area round here – shit housing, tick; TB, tick. The go-to place for crack cocaine, so I'm led to believe.' She shook her head as she opened her office door. 'And they say to us "why can't schools be run like a business?" Because schools are about people – and people aren't businesses.'

'So, who runs the school now?' asked Pat, sitting down.

'Oh, another trust,' said Victoria airily, before bursting out laughing. 'No, to be fair, these Lodestone people are way, way better.'

'*Lodestone*?'

'You know them?'

'They run my old school,' said Pat.

'St Barney-bums?'

Pat nodded. 'My friend's a governor there now,' she said.

'I worked with Chris Canne.' Victoria sank into her chair. 'The CEO. He was my deputy for a couple of terms.'

'What was he like?'

Victoria smiled. 'A man on an upward trajectory, our Chris. Very focused.' She gave a comic furtive look round the office and hissed. 'VPL.'

Pat hadn't laughed so spontaneously in ages. VPL, their all-purpose male-description from thirty years ago: Visible Pantie

Lines. That ed-psych with the sandy beard who used to drive a Lada, with a squashed coat hanger for an aerial.

'But he's been a teacher, has our Chris, and to be fair he hasn't totally forgotten what it's like for us on the chalk face,' said Victoria. 'He's lost no time cracking on with our buildings.' As if on cue, another electrical whine started up somewhere. 'And he's a bit of a vision going on. Whether he can make it work here – that's another matter. He's big on something called Pineapple Maths, which he reckons will revolutionize kids' learning. I don't know.' She smiled and they both grimaced, the shared sigh of people who have heard it all before, many, many times.

'So, you reckon everything at your St Barney-bums is okay?'

Pat nodded neutrally. It didn't feel right to start going into the ins and outs of poison pen letters; love Victoria though she did, she could well imagine the news being all round Bradford south by the weekend. 'Mrs Brittain seems to run a very tight ship,' was all she said.

Victoria stiffened. 'Not *Kayleigh* Brittain?' she said.

'You know her?'

'Big hair? Charm bracelets you could use as spike strips.'

'That sounds like her.' Pat realized she didn't know what Kayleigh Brittain actually *did* look like. 'Have you met her?'

'She was here – under Barry Peel. Kayleigh Bling we used to call her; I swear, Pat, when that woman raised her arms you could hear those bracelets clashing two streets away.'

'So, was she dodgy?'

Victoria frowned. 'Not so much dodgy as one tough cookie. You say she runs a tight ship – I'd say she made Mussolini look benevolent. I had one girl went to work for her, lovely girl – she had a terrible time I heard. Gave up in the end, works in Morrisons now.' She shook her head, her eyes sorrowful. 'No one should be made to feel like that. And Anji, she was lovely – the kids loved her.'

This all sounded like Kayleigh Brittain. And it was perfectly possible to imagine someone dashing off a quick poison pen letter to her. But to fifteen other staff?

'More importantly . . .' Victoria dropped her voice and looked round shiftily even though there was no one else in the room '. . . the word was – she liked a bit of the old rough did our Kayleigh. Not averse to the odd fling. And always with, shall we say, an artisan?'

'A what?'

'The site manager. The man who came to fix the broadband. At least two electricians. And . . .'

Pat looked, understanding dawning. 'And Steve Hewson?'

'You did not hear *any* of this from me. But put it this way – her gutters were always in a much better state than anyone else's . . .'

'Is there a Mr Brittain on the scene?'

'Somewhere. But he never seemed to figure very largely. And Stevie Wonder did very well out of all the work that came his way. Paid for a fair few trips to the sunbed.'

'So do you think . . .' Pat frowned. 'You think there was something shady going on?'

'Nothing wrong.' Victoria shook her head. 'But then not what you'd call *right* necessarily.' She sighed. 'That's the trouble with the academy system . . . it's not so much about what's right and wrong as how much you can play the system. Your school. Your St Barney-bums. It might be worth telling your friend the governor to cast an eye over the accounts.'

In the lobby Pat found herself once again enveloped in a glittery hug and felt her eyes suddenly smarting with tears. Victoria held her at arm's length and looked at her searchingly. 'Rod *is* okay?' she said.

Pat nodded. 'Like I say, he's been given the all clear.'

'And what about you?' said Victoria 'Are *you* okay, my love?'

She cupped Pat's cheek in her hand and Pat could smell the coconut oil and another sweet, sweet scent. 'You've got to look after *you*.'

'Rod doesn't seem to want to go back to work,' said Pat abruptly.

Victoria smiled. 'There's more to life than work!' she said. 'Though these days the idea is we work till we drop so it seems.'

'Have you not thought of retiring?'

That rich chuckle. 'Me? I'm a fixture and fitting, me. Mind you . . .' She sighed. 'Some trust directive, another half-arsed government dictate and I'm like, Victoria, you are so out of here! But then I do an assembly or walk round the nursery or have a barney in the exclusion unit with some lost soul we're trying to reel back in . . . and I think, maybe a while longer.' Another laugh. 'Reckon they'll be carrying me out in my box!'

All at once she looked sombre, the brown eyes sad. 'But if I go . . . who's left?' She looked out of the window at the ranks of Wakefield Hill, visible beyond the green security railings. 'Oh, I know I sound like Mrs Big-Head . . . but since Doctor Chaudry and Doctor Vaz retired, there's an ever-changing cast of unknowns at the surgery. The church is a carpet warehouse and don't even get me started on all those lovely community outreach schemes given the governmental heave-ho. There's only us and the mosque that's left pretty much. Us, the mosque and a load of struggling people.'

Victoria's laugh was still in Pat's ears as she drove home through the darkening afternoon. It was impossible to imagine poison pen letters in any sort of school run by Victoria. Something about her bright, forceful presence chased away the mere thought of such darkness.

It had been a lovely day – but reviewing it, despite everything she'd learnt, it was hard to see how it had got her any further. Steve Hewson had been involved with a dodgy trust manager. She pretty much knew that already. And he maybe had a thing going with Kayleigh Brittain. Maybe they had a history – maybe still had something going on – but what did that have to do with anything? There seemed little doubt that Steve had got the Baldersby job on the strength of who he knew – but so what? And yet it all felt significant. Like *something* was going on. But what? She remembered Victoria's words – *maybe check the accounts at St Barnabus's*. She thought of the office with that Madame Iceberg in residence. How on earth would that be possible?

These thoughts were still buzzing wearily round her mind when she walked into her kitchen, busting for a wee. The smell of (slightly singed) pasta sauce surprised her; the pile of utensils by the sink told their own story. Rod had been cooking.

'Where's our Andrew then?' she asked. He'd obviously gone to some trouble, so she deliberately stood with her back to the unwashed pans.

'At a mate's,' said Rod in a vague way, handing her a glass of Merlot in a way that immediately made her think there must be more to it than that. She could see he'd used the Farm Shop mince she'd earmarked for meatballs and had probably been too liberal with the pesto. 'This is a nice surprise,' she said. At least the Merlot tasted as it should.

'Thing is,' said Rod in that same evasive tone. 'Thing is, I've been thinking.'

Pat took a larger sip of her wine, suddenly on red alert. 'Oh?' she said noncommittally. A pause. 'What about?'

'Packing it all in.'

For a moment, for a heart-dropping moment, she thought he meant their marriage, but sense prevailed. In her experience men didn't, as a rule, make spaghetti Bolognese as a prelude to ending a relationship.

'Packing what in?' she asked finally.

'The business,' he said. 'I want to retire.'

★

Huge congrats to our St Barney's Beacon writers who wowed the Northern Literacy Conference with their Hopeful Haikus! A special thanks to Mr Bowker for all his hard work!

The seventeenth letter was received by Pesto Johnson (IT and Year Four support). His name wasn't actually Pesto, it was Dean. He'd received his nickname at Venture Scouts due to his Italianate wavy black hair and white teeth; like many quirky nicknames people have, it had stuck.

The letter had been placed inside his IT Troubleshooting Book, sticking out from a page with yet another long-winded comment from Jan Starke about the unreliability of her interactive whiteboard. Pesto knew exactly what the significance of the envelope was. He had some pretty good ideas about what the letter within would say; however, the main thought in his mind was that whatever it was, it could not be allowed to divert him from his planned course of action that morning.

EVERYONE'S SICK OF YOUR SKIVING! YOU DON'T THINK ANYONE BELIEVES YOUR LIES FOR ONE SECOND? DO US ALL A FAVOUR, AND EITHER DO THE JOB PROPERLY OR PISS OFF.

Reading the words, his hand instinctively strayed to the bump on the back of his head, reminding himself there were bigger things to worry about than anonymous letters. The washing machine repairman was coming any time after ten and he had no choice, he simply had to be there. Three days without a machine and Stace was at her wits' end. Again, he fingered that bump. Again, he ran through his mind the words he'd planned and rehearsed – the listless voice he'd use – *I need to tell you; I've just been throwing up . . . I'm feeling really rough to be honest.*

He mentally shrugged; it wasn't like he had a choice. It was his own fault; he should have phoned someone last night and not come in at all. But he *had* to get those one or two jobs done before the IT audit tomorrow.

What to do?

He pressed the bump, trying to find resolve and motivation from the spurt of pain. Say something else maybe? A bad back? Or he'd forgotten something? Or the burglar alarm was going off?

No. Better stick with the tried and tested. Anyway, it was half true – since that do last night, he'd been feeling more than a little churned up.

He looked sadly at his reflection in the glass front of the IT cabinet. Since when had his life become all about treading on eggshells?

He stood up. He needed to find Becky or better still Ian, tell them how rough he was feeling. With any luck he could be out of the building before Rule Britannia put in an appearance.

CHAPTER FIFTEEN

Higher level punctuation is exhorted and a warning given.

'Creeping mischievously, the translucent, shimmering phantom apparated decisively through the mossy, damp stone edifice.'

As Jared Keen read the words, with one hand he tapped notes onto an iPad, whilst tracing the text with the other. 'This is?' he asked, glasses flashing.

'Melanie-Jade Hargreaves,' said Sam, with a sort of enthusiastic flourish, like a compere announcing an act at a talent competition.

'So, what this little lady is needing to tip her over into that greater depth,' said Jared, 'is *more* of that advanced punctuation . . . ellipses, brackets – how about some semicolons to link together these fabbo phrases!'

What Melanie-Jade Hargreaves needed, thought Thelma wearily, was to stop writing such overblown twaddle and be allowed to write as – well, as a nine-year-old writes. She was faintly surprised at Sam, going along so enthusiastically with all this tyrannical emphasis on grammar, especially having seen him teaching writing that day. Was this what being a Beacon of Writing Excellence entailed? She looked at Jared Keen tapping away at his iPad with a fervour that was making the coffee cups jingle and wondered just what he'd make of the fabbo phrases in those fifteen or so anonymous letters.

She chided herself. Kayleigh Brittain had asked for her help, not her carping criticism. Mind you, it was hard to see how she *could* help – she'd managed to say barely six words since this book scrutiny had started. And just where was Kayleigh? Any thoughts of talking with her had long since faded – she wasn't even sure if she was in the building. Plus, there was that other looming issue – college. Today was the day of the way-forward meeting. Everyone was sounding optimistic, but merely being with Jared Keen was giving Thelma an unpleasant feeling about the future of Ripon and St Bega's College. The jargon, the lurid graphics, the spreadsheets were combining to make Teddy's ring binders seem as outdated as the Dead Sea Scrolls he taught his students about.

Sam bit off a yawn as Jared finally looked up from the iPad. 'Okay, folks!' he said. 'Going forward and drilling down, I'm seeing the need for targeted bespoke intervention to push these guys forward. Bam! Semicolons! Bam! Ellipses!'

As he spoke, he struck the table with his palm, again making the cups rattle.

At this moment his phone shrilled into life with what sounded like an electronic piano being hit by a sledgehammer. 'I'm so sorry, folks,' he said regretfully. 'I have *got* to take this.' He strode into the corner of the library and began speaking in terms of great enthusiasm about something that was apparently Totes Amazeballs.

Thelma fanned herself.

'I'm sorry about the heat,' said Sam apologetically. Another yawn. 'Excuse me, Mrs Cooper,' he said. 'I just can't seem to wake up.'

Thelma thought of the bright rosy cheeks on the photo of baby Robyn she'd been shown earlier. 'Teething, I'm thinking?' she said, pushing aside the sad thoughts that instinctively rose whenever she saw a baby.

Sam nodded. 'At least we think it's that,' he said. 'She just won't seem to settle.'

'I wouldn't worry,' said Thelma soothingly. 'Madam's just found a good game. Yell and watch Mummy and Daddy run.'

'You think?' said Sam, looking at her with a sudden need for reassurance that Thelma remembered from years gone by. He'd been one of those children who was always worrying about something or other: PE, spelling tests, whether the great Fire of London could happen in Thirsk. Billy Blackside, Topsy used to call him.

'Sam, if I had a pound for every time I've heard stories of sleepless nights with babies – well, I'd be wintering in the Seychelles,' she said.

Sam smiled, and for a fleeting moment the ghost of his seven-year-old self looked at her. Again, the smile turned into a yawn; again the hand went over the mouth.

His nails were bitten.

Just as they used to be at times of extreme stress – SATs, country dancing with Mrs Lowther, that time his bike was stolen. Thelma looked at him more closely. *Was* it simply the engrained exhaustion of a new father?

'So how are things, anyway?' she asked neutrally.

'You know,' he said. 'Getting there.'

Now she looked, she could detect a distinct air about him. More than just tiredness. She hadn't planned to say anything but seeing those bitten nails, Thelma knew without a shadow of a doubt that whatever was worrying him was something more than a few sleepless nights and a book scrutiny.

'I've been hearing about these dreadful letters some people have been receiving,' she said in a low voice as Jared chattered away by the window.

157

The effect was palpable. It wasn't so much that Sam moved or reacted, as the tension spread across him like frost, stiffening his neck, splaying his fingers against the table so the knuckles went white.

'Yes,' he said, eyes sliding uneasily in any direction but Thelma's.

'I can't imagine how upsetting it must be for people,' she said.

'Yes,' he said again. 'I know.' He fingered his collar, and now she looked she could see a livid mark where it had been rubbing. 'We've been told not to talk about it,' he said.

'I can understand why not,' said Thelma quietly. 'It must be awful.'

'I haven't had one.' He blurted out the words abruptly, almost rudely. 'A letter.'

He was lying of course. He hadn't been able to lie convincingly in 1997, and he couldn't now. He looked exactly as he had when he dropped Rosie Thwaite's Boyzone rubber in the class tadpole tank.

'Sam,' said Thelma, making her voice calm and gentle. 'Sam, you know if you ever want someone to talk to, in the strictest confidence, you could always talk to me.'

Finally, those troubled grey eyes slid round to meet hers. There were definitely tears there – but tears of what? Sadness? Fear?

At that moment the library door opened, and Nicole appeared.

'I'm so sorry to interrupt,' she said in a polite but careless tone that said: actually, she wasn't at all. 'Mrs Brittain was just wondering if she could have a quick word with you, Jared. And you, Mrs Cooper.'

'Will it take long?' asked Jared, casting a distracted glance at the pile of books.

'I've no idea,' she said. She smiled pleasantly enough, but there was a distinct air of 'I don't give a toss' about her manner. Thelma looked at her curiously. It was again the aquamarine scarf today, but the bruise on her neck had gone. No, hang on – it was now on the *other* side . . .

And it wasn't a bruise – it was a love bite.

'I'm speaking to you, Jared, in your capacity as trust representative – and you, Thelma, as a governor. Thelma knows some of this already.' Kayleigh Brittain looked at her significantly. It was the first time Thelma had seen her since the night of the governors' and she was slightly shocked at the woman's appearance. She was still nothing less than immaculately turned out, but there was a palpable tension showing in the lines around her eyes. On the desk in front of her lay a red cardboard folder.

'I hate to have to tell you this,' she continued, 'but something rather unpleasant has been happening here.' Her tone was grave and formal, matching her charcoal jacket and white blouse. Even the clouds massed over Mukor Bridge in the picture behind Kayleigh's desk seemed grey and reserved.

'Your car?' Jared said.

'I don't know if that's connected,' she said. 'It could well be. It's enough to make me feel I needed to talk to the trust.' She paused, clasping her hands together on top of the folder. The gesture felt very deliberate, as if giving herself time to marshal her words. 'In this folder,' she said, 'are a number of letters. Anonymous letters, received by staff members. Letters saying some pretty nasty things.'

'Letters?' said Jared in puzzled tones. 'Who are they from?'

'We don't know,' said Kayleigh patiently. 'They're anonymous.'

'I see.' Jared shook his head with incomprehension. It seemed that with his reliance on electronic devices, he found the concept of physical letters somewhat difficult to take in.

'The first one turned up the night of the summer fayre – at first we thought it was just an angry parent.' Kayleigh looked again at Thelma, who felt a pang at the memory of her mistake. 'But since the start of term more have appeared, left all around school, so it looks like it has to be a member of staff.'

She sighed and looked down at the folder, looking tired and drawn. 'I don't mind admitting I'm at my wits' end.'

'Isn't this all covered in one of your policies?' said Jared. The two women's eyes met in a moment of shared irritation.

'Policy?' said Kayleigh with incomprehension in her voice.

'Staff well-being,' said Jared vaguely.

Thelma shook her head. Data whizz kid he might be (though she had her doubts) but when it came to life's darker problems, Jared Keen was a total washout.

'I wonder,' Thelma said, 'if you've noticed any *pattern* to these letters.'

'Pattern?' Kayleigh frowned at her.

'Any *commonality* to them. Places they were found, days they were found on – that sort of thing.'

Kayleigh looked at the folder considering. 'I don't think so,' she said thoughtfully. 'They were all white paper, white envelopes . . . found in different places . . . different days . . . Unless . . .' She stopped herself.

'How about the recipients?' asked Thelma. 'Were they teachers, support staff, auxiliary staff – a mix? Those you know about, of course.'

Kayleigh glanced at her sharply. 'What do you mean?' she said.

'I imagine not everyone would be keen to admit they've had one,' explained Thelma.

'No.' Kayleigh looked thoughtful. 'Well, there have been seven teachers.' (*Eight,* thought Thelma, picturing Sam's worried face). 'Eight members of support staff – and . . .' she took a breath. 'And of course myself.'

'You got one?' Jared's voice came out as a startled yelp.

'I got the first one, the night of the summer fayre.' Thelma stirred guiltily, remembering the letter Kayleigh had not even seen.

'I wonder . . .' she said. 'I wonder if I could possibly see them?'

'Why?' Kayleigh's voice suddenly held a note of caution.

'Because,' said Thelma, 'they might tell us something.'

'What?' asked Jared.

'That's just it,' said Thelma. 'I don't know.' Even before she'd finished the sentence, Kayleigh was shaking her head.

'I'm sorry,' she said. 'Really I am, but I've staff confidentiality to think of. But trust me, I've been over those letters thoroughly. Like I say, there's nothing. Same font, same size of font, all obviously done on the school copier.' She picked up the folder and put it in her desk drawer, closing it firmly.

Thelma was thinking. She had this growing feeling she badly needed to read the other letters, but she wasn't sure why. Thinking about all the letters she'd read, there had been this growing but obscure little niggle in her mind, something that might become clearer if she could see all the other letters.

'Maybe there's a risk assessment that could help?' said Jared. At that moment his phone rang. 'I'm so sorry,' he said for the second time that morning. 'I really have to take this.'

Kayleigh nodded wearily. As Jared jabbered brightly away in the corner to someone who seemed to be called Carpool, Thelma said, 'I need to apologize.'

'Apologize?' Kayleigh looked puzzled. 'Whatever for?'

'Getting it so wrong, for one thing. I was sure it was Donna Chivers.'

'Thelma.' Kayleigh pressed her fingers to her temples. 'You've nothing to apologize for.'

Thelma took a deep breath. Now was the time to tell her about the letter Liz had found. But before she could open her mouth, Kayleigh was speaking again.

'I just keep thinking: who could be doing this? Sending these vile things. And *why*?' There was a tremor around her mouth and eyes. 'I can't just get away from the fact that someone's out to get *me* in some way.' She suddenly looked lost, a little girl behind that big cold expanse of desk. There was frank appeal in her eyes and Thelma felt a swell of guilt at not having told her.

'Surely,' she said, 'whoever is doing this is trying to hurt lots of people, not just you.'

'But then why key my car like that? And . . .' Kayleigh paused as if making the decision to speak. 'And there's been other things.'

'What other things?'

'I can't be sure – that's why I haven't said anything. But I'm sure someone's been in this room. When I've come in, things have been disturbed. Not how I left them.'

'There's an electronic lock isn't there?'

Kayleigh nodded, showing the fob that hung round her neck on a tasteful scarlet cord. 'There's only myself and Nicole who could get in, and I know she wouldn't . . . And something else. A couple of times, when I've been working late . . . I've had the feeling *there's been someone watching me.*' There was a pause.

'Actually,' said Thelma, 'there's something else I need to apologize for. It's something I should have told you before now, and for that I'm truly sorry.'

Kayleigh looked surprised. Her face became watchful. As Jared continue to jabber away in the corner, Thelma told her about the letter Liz had found, and how she'd put off telling Kayleigh about it. 'I can't remember the exact wording,' she lied. 'But it said . . .' She paused. 'It said you should leave the school.' There was a pause that felt distinctly on the icy side.

'I see.' Once again Kayleigh interlaced her fingernails. 'Well, thank you for telling me now.' Her voice was grim, and Thelma wondered if she was angry with her.

'Do you think,' Thelma asked tentatively, 'you should maybe talk to the police? In view of what the letter was saying?'

Kayleigh shook her head. Something had happened. The frightened girl had been replaced by a woman, and a determined woman at that. 'No I do not,' she said, and there was resolve in her voice. 'I can tell you something for nothing, Thelma – it's going to take more than some nutty letter writer to frighten me away from my school.'

Liz hacked back browning fronds that had once been flourishing cotoneasters and thumped them down in the wheelbarrow, sending crumbs of soil skittering across the grass. There was energy in the hacking and the thumps. Frustrated energy. What she was doing felt like one of the few things she could do these days without drawing some sort of censure from someone – Derek, Thelma . . . Jan . . .

But fifteen letters! Fifteen messages of spite and ill will. At least! Margo, Becky, Jan, Kayleigh Brittain, maybe Tiff. If her own restless nights were anything to go by, none of them would be sleeping.

But then people seemed to want to let it go. Not tell anyone . . . Keep that toxic pain to themselves. And really . . . who was she to go against their wishes? It wasn't as though she'd received one herself.

Cotoneaster cut back, she paused, panting slightly, hot despite the cool overcast afternoon. Normally her garden was where she felt most at peace . . . Not today.

She wheeled the barrow across to the plant-waste wheelie bin. It was virtually full, which meant a trip to the tip; it wasn't due to be emptied until the week after next.

She suddenly felt a longing to make a bonfire, a great, big autumn day bonfire . . . vegetation smouldering with blue and grey curling smoke, making her clothes and hair smell, a proper autumn smell. But bonfires, like so much else these days, were frowned on, and she certainly had no wish to provoke a lecture from Jacob on carbon emissions.

A reek of smoke on the grubby cardigan . . . in the distance misty fronds climbing above the fences . . . a shout – 'Get back!' A scream . . .

The phone startled her from the memory. It was her old gardening one, which she kept in her apron pocket.

'Liz?' At first, she didn't recognize the hoarse low voice. 'I understand you've been trying to ring me.'

'Bunty?' she said.

'Sorry not to be in touch, but I've been suffering from stress.'

'Stress? Not your back?'

'Stress. I've been terrible. I've sorted a sick note for three weeks.'

'I'm sorry to hear that,' said Liz. The voice didn't sound particularly stressed . . . but having said that, there was *something* in the tone. 'Are you with your Candice?'

'Yes, but I'm all right. Or at least I am now I'm away from that place.'

'Your bungalow?'

'School!' The word came out with a dour release of energy.

'You mean the nasty letters?' said Liz.

'It won't stop at letters, Mrs Newsome, I'd lay money on it.'

'What do you mean?' Despite all her activity, Liz could feel herself growing suddenly cold.

'Bad things are going on in that place, Mrs Newsome. Bad things. *People are going to get hurt* . . .' Had she been drinking? But her words didn't sound in any way slurred; in fact her voice was the opposite: focused and urgent. 'I'm telling you, Mrs Newsome, stay away from that school. There's a nutter on the loose in that place and I'm not setting foot there until whoever it is has been caught.'

CHAPTER SIXTEEN

In a converted church, there is mathematical stress along with impassioned assurances.

The headquarters of Lodestone Academy Trust was in a converted greystone Victorian church, at the bottom of the hill just down from the University of Leeds. So complete, so thorough was the internal remodelling of the old building that, sitting in the reception area, Pat was hard put to identify where within the old church she was actually sitting. From beyond a smoked glass partition, she could hear the sounds of the soft rattle of keyboards, the trill of phones and melodic carolling of 'Lodestone Academy Trust, good afternoon!' Despite the spaciously arranged leatherette chairs, the waiting area felt rather cluttered owing to piles of glossy turquoise cartons, each about the size and shape of a shoe box and bearing a bright yellow pineapple logo, stacked up on the table, the dove-grey carpet, even some of the chairs.

Pat shifted in her leatherette chair, trying to avoid making any raspberry noises. *Breathe and focus . . . breathe and feel purpose . . .* What on earth was she doing here?

The answer, tinselled with embarrassment, came singing into her mind all too readily.

After Rod had made his big announcement, his intention had

been for her to see this was nothing but a great idea. He'd produced a bottle of (cheap) champagne and talked her through his plans; plans he'd typically got all worked out after several meetings with Nazil. These plans involved activating Rod's private pension, cashing in something somewhere, then drawing down on something else – somewhere in all this was Andrew buying out their part of the business as and when time allowed. They couldn't go wild, but they should be financially okay – just about.

Pat (who hadn't felt in the least like going wild) had zoned out after about thirty seconds of all this, sipping her frankly nasty champagne, staring darkly into the middle distance. She'd found herself remembering a time at Harrogate Station, many years ago, pre-Liam, when Justin and Andrew were at the buggy stage. The train had come in, and she'd just succeeded in loading Andrew aboard, before going back out for Justin and the baby bag. At that point the train doors had slid shut.

'Noooo!' The cry she had let loose had come from somewhere down amidst the depth her lungs and her soul. It had certainly been loud enough to stop the train in its tracks.

Listening to Rod, that was how she'd felt.

Of course, it explained so much. Rod's reluctance to go back to work, his indifference at the failure to get the Baldersby job, all those calls from Nazil, those abruptly terminated conversations – with Dougie, with Andrew. Plus, Andrew's amiable vagueness whenever the question of his return to Loughborough had come up.

Andrew, she grasped, had spoken to the university; here another set of deals been worked out. Apparently, he'd never really felt like the course had suited him. (This was the first she'd heard of it.)

The whole thing, apparently, made total, no-brainer sense. It certainly did the way Rod explained it and, as had often been the

166

case during their marriage, it hadn't seemed to occur to him that Pat would feel anything other than the same way. He'd been so enthusiastic – once again that wiry young man with the red sports car – more alive than she'd seen him in a long, long time. Certainly, since he'd been ill and, thinking about it, maybe before that.

'I wish you'd said something,' she'd said at one point.

'I didn't want to worry you.' This Pat had rightly taken to mean: *I didn't want you to kick off.*

Part of her had felt she should be angry at all this planning behind her back, but a much bigger part of her felt too weary to be bothered, indeed, to do anything other than sip her deflating champagne and say, 'It's a lot to take in,' at periodic intervals.

After Rod had finished, she'd excused herself, poured herself another large glass and taken herself, her champagne and iPad upstairs and fired off an irrational but eloquent email to Chris Canne, saying how disappointed she was that R & D Builders had been passed over in favour of someone who had a dubious reputation through his involvement with Barry Peel and the Heaton Royd Trust. Although she knew that Rod must have been planning this for some time, part of her thought if they *had* landed the Baldersby job . . . well, it may have in some way altered or softened his plans. Then she'd sat on the window seat in Liam's room, staring out at the darkening fields, brooding on what 'just about financially okay' actually meant.

It was later the next morning, cradling a coffee and nursing a thick head, scrolling through the iPad for money-saving tips, that she saw that Chris Canne had replied.

'What did he say?' Thelma's voice over the phone had sounded typically and blessedly calm.

'Not much at all. Just if I'd like to make an appointment to discuss my concerns, Chris Canne would be happy to see me. He's the head honcho, used to work with my friend Victoria.' She hadn't mentioned VPL; there were some jokes you didn't share with Thelma.

'Kayleigh did say yesterday that she was going to let him know about the letters.' Thelma had sounded thoughtful. 'Are you planning on going?'

'Do you think I should?'

'That's entirely up to you.'

Pat knew that tone of old. 'But?'

'Well, it occurs to me, it might just put your mind at rest.'

Pat had opened her mouth to say that her mind *was* at rest, but of course it wasn't, hadn't been for a long, long time, and moreover she knew from her tone Thelma was well aware of that fact. Were they still talking about her email to Chris Canne? With Thelma you could never be sure. One thing she *was* certain of was that she didn't want to get into the whole Rod retiring business – and certainly not that other blackness, which had been given a worrying new perspective by Rod's news. Not on the phone, not with Thelma – not with anybody come to that.

'You have concerns; here's a way to maybe address those concerns,' Thelma had said.

'Or a way of being fobbed off by Lodestone Trust,' Pat had responded firmly, making it clear what they *were* talking about.

'I don't think so,' Thelma had said matter-of-factly. 'After all, why would Chris Canne go to all the trouble of inviting you in? If he wanted to fob you off, it'd much easier just to ignore any emails. And . . .' she'd paused significantly '. . . he may have another reason altogether for wanting to see you.'

'Making ten-tastic. Fraction fan . . . Number bond bonanza.' A rather manic voice disrupted her thoughts. A thin, besuited man of Asian origin (whose name tag rather breathlessly proclaimed him to be Tony Lee PhD Maths Consultant Lodestone Academy)

168

was checking the stacked boxes. There was a slight frown on his face, the light glinting off his expensive-looking John Lennon spectacles as he ticked off the boxes against a list and loaded them into plastic crates. 'Division Dinosaurs? Where are you, Division Dinosaurs?' he said, voice singsong with stress. Pat noticed a faint transatlantic twang. He frantically scanned the seats and coffee table. At that moment the door opened and a balding, earnest-looking man who could only be Mr VPL himself was frowning round the room.

'Mrs Taylor?' he said tentatively. 'Pat?'

She smiled, stood up. 'Hello,' she said. 'Thank you for seeing me.'

'I can't find Division Dinosaurs!' said Tony Lee plaintively, reminding Pat of a boy who'd lost his football cards.

'There's a box under the chair by your foot,' she said helpfully.

'Ah!' Tony barely looked at her as he seized the offending Division Dinosaurs. 'You can tell Hamad to start loading up.' The comment was addressed at Chris. 'Tell him – Ryanair, the Belfast flight.'

Chris smiled uneasily. 'Pat,' he said. 'Would you like to come on through?'

'Chris.' Tony's voice was nasal with warning. 'We need to be leaving in twenty at the latest!'

'We've loads of time. Check-in doesn't even start for over an hour.' Mr VPL's voice was calming, placating even. Something about his voice gave Pat the impression that this wasn't the first time he'd spoken to Tony like this; surely an odd dynamic for CEO and employee?

'You know the traffic at Leeds Bradford,' said Tony. 'Rush hour. We could miss the flight.'

'Pat.' Chris turned to her with a smile. 'Why don't you go on through? Second door on the left.' As Pat left the waiting area, she could hear him talking in that same placating voice but could only make out some of the words '. . . important I see her. Especially after . . .' After what? What was he referring to?

Beyond the door was a corridor; again, it offered no clues as to what part of the original church it married up to, but what was interesting was a display showing photographs of the church being converted into the Lodestone building, gaping roofs, cement mixers and stacks of timber in the old chancel, Chris himself in pristine hard hat and a hi-vis jacket – *and standing next to him . . .*

But before she could look more closely, Mr VPL appeared, all earnest smiles, Tony Lee obviously placated, and he ushered her (or hustled her?) through a door that bore a plum-coloured plaque announcing 'Christopher Canne MEd PhD' in an ivory serif font.

The large, sparsely furnished office was adorned with portraits of children working in classrooms – counting towers, drawing, writing. As they did so their faces were alight, animated; in Pat's thirty-plus years of experience they bore very little relation to how children actually looked when working in a classroom. She wondered how long it had taken the photographer to achieve the effect. Yet despite all of the pictures, the room felt curiously impersonal – bleak even. The PC seemed a bit lost on the large desk; way over by the door huddled a bag and laptop. The only item of any personal note was a framed snapshot on the desk, Chris and Tony in bright summery T-shirts, heads huddled together sharing a fluorescent pink cocktail.

Ah, thought Pat. *Aaah.*

'So, Pat.' Chris Canne regarded her frankly, from behind his desk, the light glinting off his head. 'First thing – thank you. Thank you for coming all this way to see us here at Lodestone.'

'Not at all,' said Pat. 'Thank you for asking me. I know how busy you must be.'

'Education conference in Belfast.' Chris Canne smiled dismiss-ively. 'All very dull and boring.'

Pat smiled and thought, actually, an education conference in Belfast sounded a bit of a hoot. For reasons she didn't fully under-stand, she felt a sudden sensation of sadness, and it was with some effort she had to force her attention back to Chris.

'Tony – Tony Lee, our maths guy. He's developed this new maths scheme. Pineapple Maths. Absolutely brilliant. We're using it across all the trust schools with some excellent results; it's really taking off. People are queuing up for us to do presentations here, there and everywhere.'

'How exciting,' said Pat. She reflected on the odd fact that despite the pink cocktail picture, Chris seemed at pains to stress the professional nature of their relationship.

'Now,' he said. 'Baldersly—'

'Baldersby,' corrected Pat.

He smiled briefly, tapping up a file on his iPad. This he angled round, revealing to Pat a table that seemed to contain the three itemized quotes for the work.

'I was, naturally, very concerned to read your email,' he said. 'Not because of what you were saying, I hasten to add.' He flashed a rather nervous grin at her. 'No skeletons to hide there! No, what worried me was how we'd communicated with you. "Chris, you've got some explaining to do," I said to myself.' He smiled another nervous smile and in spite of everything, Pat felt herself starting to warm to Mr VPL, his energy and earnestness.

'As a trust, it is really important – nay, vital – that we seek out prices that are competitive. That's one of the fundamental philos-ophies of the academy system. The three-quotes way of doing things is pretty much sacrosanct. Now I don't know you – or rather R & D Builders – but I've no doubt whatsoever you would do a corking job for us. I have to say up front, I don't know Steve

Hewson so well – he does work for us at Lodestone schools – but after the whole Heaton Royd business . . . well, one can't be too cautious. Which is why, when his quote came through, I got my guys to go through it with the proverbial fine-tooth comb.' He sat back, hands held out with a helpless smile. 'And there were several areas in which Steve just had that edge – though I have to say to you hand on heart, Mrs Taylor, it was a close-run thing.' He laughed nervously, as if commenting on *Strictly Come Dancing*. He began running a stubby finger down the list, itemizing some of the price differences; as with Rod previously, Pat felt herself very quickly switching off.

'I know you know about Heaton Royd; that's presumably why you shared your concerns about Steve.' She was aware his voice had suddenly become serious. Looking at him she saw the grey eyes were now firmly fixed on hers. 'A total mess, the whole thing. How that bar-steward Barry Peel can sleep at nights – well, it's beyond me.' He shook his head. 'But I was there on the inside – and *because* I was there on the inside, well, let's just say I saw more than most. Stuff the papers didn't even get hold of. And I said to myself at the time: "Chris, if you're ever fortunate enough to run an academy, it will be *nothing* whatsoever like this."' His voice was strong, passionate almost, and Pat found herself believing every word.

'I've a few staff here who were part of the Heaton Royd team and I've said to each and every one of them, any sign, *any* sign of anything dodgy and it's "sayonara, chum". And that includes Steve Hewson.'

A peremptory knock and the door opened. 'Babe.' Tony Lee's agitated head popped round. 'Babe, it's nearly five to.'

'I know.' There was a distinct trace of impatience in Chris's voice. 'I'm nearly done.'

'I'll let you get on,' said Pat, standing up.

'Hang on.' There was something in Chris's voice that made her sit back down. 'I understand from Jared Keen you have some connection with St Barnabus's in Thirsk?'

'I used to work there,' said Pat, surprised at this change in the conversation. 'But I've been retired a few years now.'

'But you still have dealings with the place?' His voice was light and casual. Too light, too casual. Thelma's voice sounded in her mind – *he may have another reason altogether for asking to see you.*

'One of my friends is a governor there,' said Pat carefully. 'And another does voluntary work.'

'So, you hear what's going on there?'

'A fair bit.'

'Have you heard anything about any malicious letters?' The question was rapped out, quick and direct.

'Something,' said Pat cautiously. 'Why do you ask?'

'I was just wondering whether you could shed any light on what's going on,' he said.

Pat frowned, completely thrown by this turn in the conversation. Surely he wasn't suspecting her? 'What sort of light?' she said feebly.

'I don't know. Why it could be happening? Has anything like this ever happened before?' His voice was hopeful, and Pat suddenly realized how worried he was.

'I've never heard of anyone sending letters before,' she said eventually. 'And I can't think why anyone would be sending them.'

He sighed, the hope fading in his eyes. 'That's what Kayleigh, the head teacher there, said to me. She's pretty much beside herself, poor love. She's enough on, running the school, without all this see are ay pee, pardon my French.' He sighed. 'Still, it'll probably all blow over.'

It hasn't yet, thought Pat. She wondered if he'd been told about Mrs Brittain's car. Aloud she said: 'I'm sorry not to be more helpful.'

173

'It's just the sort of thing the papers would have a field day with,' he said, almost to himself, and Pat detected an emphatic timbre of worry in Mr VPL's voice.

Pat had hoped he'd let her see herself out. She badly wanted another look at those pictures in the corridor, to check what she thought she'd seen. But Chris had almost whisked her out into the waiting area, somehow deftly managing to keep his body between Pat and the photos, whilst simultaneously placating Tony who was yapping on about the rush-hour traffic and his need – his absolute gasping need, babe! – for a G and T in the airport bar.

But sitting in the Yeti, collecting her thoughts, Pat was pretty sure what it was she'd caught a glimpse of in those pictures of the renovation. Or rather *who* it was. The person standing next to Chris, in equally pristine hard hat and hi-vis vest; the same person she'd seen barrelling across Baldersby playground and had been so often in her thoughts. The man, who according to the caption, was in charge of the building work: Steve Hewson.

The man Chris implied that he barely knew. But that picture of them stood smiling side by side during the renovation of the building argued a rather different state of affairs.

CHAPTER SEVENTEEN

Differences are aired over coffee and an entirely inaccurate prediction is made.

'Look at the school accounts?' Thelma frowned uneasily, stirring her coffee.

'That's what Victoria said I should do.' Pat laughed in an effort to make the notion seem ridiculous. She looked out of the window, as if distancing herself from the whole idea. Instead of classic brown or red, the leaves in the trees round the garden centre seemed mostly to have gone a washed-out yellow, and were now blowing listlessly round the car park, gathering in soggy drifts against the piles of oven-dried logs and plastic pumpkins.

'Did your friend say exactly *why* you should look at the accounts?' asked Thelma, still looking uneasy.

'I think it was more a general comment,' said Pat. 'Something that might be worth doing. Chris Canne obviously knows Steve Hewson, and just as obviously doesn't want people to know. Why else have him look round Baldersby School separately from me and Martin? And if there is something going on between Steve Hewson and Kayleigh Bling, Chris Canne will be wanting to keep it quiet. He was worried enough at the thought of these letters making it into the papers.' She shook her head.

'There's something really wrong in that place,' said Liz. Her friends looked at her, knowing there was more than accounts on her mind. 'Someone needs to do *something*.'

'Anyway, how on earth would I go about it?' Pat sounded slightly defensive.

'You'd need to be able to log onto the system,' said Thelma. 'And do it at a time when no one is in the office.' She was trying her best to sound off-putting, but only succeeded in sounding as though she was considering the plan carefully.

'Despite always fancying myself in *Mission Impossible*,' said Pat, 'I think I'll give it a miss.' She looked at her friends. 'Why, do you think I should?'

'I think you need to be careful,' said Thelma.

Pat considered her response. 'Being careful' was Thelma's verbal yellow card.

'Well, I think you should,' said Liz with some energy. 'And whilst you're at it, you should ask Kayleigh Brittain exactly what action she's taking about these letters.'

Thelma silently shook her head at this.

'I don't see what she actually can do,' said Pat. 'Short of searching everyone's handbags.'

'There'll be *something*,' said Liz. 'She's paid enough.'

'She is supporting people,' put in Thelma.

'Not according to Becky Clegg.' Liz looked defiant. 'She said she didn't get much support at all after her letter. It was more a case of "oh dear, never mind, now get on with it".'

'So, what do you suggest?' said Pat.

'The person who's sending these letters needs *help*,' said Liz. 'The longer it's allowed to go on, the worse it's going to get.'

'Or it could all just die down,' said Thelma quietly.

Pat wondered what to say; there seemed to be more than a bit of tension brewing between her two friends. Both seemed preoccupied; Liz was obviously worrying about Jan Starke and as for Thelma . . . She'd asked her about the college closing only to receive a classic Thelma non-answer about it going to consultation, whatever that meant, but she was obviously worried. Pat sighed to herself – they all seemed to be keeping so much from each other these days.

'I was thinking,' Thelma had a distinct tone of changing the subject in her voice. 'A while back I was reading in the *Yorkshire Post* about biomass boilers. Some sort of scam. Nothing to do with the school,' she added hastily as Liz's eyes widened.

'What sort of scam?' asked Pat.

'That's just it, I've been trying to remember. Something to do with some sort of payment. Not RNLI—'

'That's lifeboats,' said Liz dismissively.

'*Not* RNLI,' repeated Thelma patiently. 'Something like that. I wish I'd kept it. But something to do with biomass boilers and payments.'

'I keep thinking of what Victoria said,' said Pat. 'Schools being run as businesses. It just feels all wrong.'

'I agree one hundred per cent,' said Liz emphatically.

'But there has always been that element to it,' said Thelma. The others looked at her; this wasn't how she traditionally spoke about academies. 'We were always being told there was no money.'

'Yes, I remember,' said Pat, thinking of those end-of-financial-year trips down to Poundland at Monks Cross to buy crayons and glue sticks. 'But now it seems *all* about money. You should have seen that Lodestone headquarters.'

'The thing about the academy system,' said Thelma, 'is that it's here to stay. Like it or loathe it, it's the way things are, and we have to live with that. And there's a great many principled, genuine people involved in the running of them.'

Pat looked at her friend in surprise, remembering many indignant

177

comments on this subject, made here at this very table. Liz, she noted, looked increasingly frosty.

'So, that's the view on Kayleigh Bling then?' Pat said quickly. 'Principled and genuine?'

'She *seems* as nice as pie,' said Liz. 'But she gave Jan a terrible time, remember.'

Thelma considered this for a moment before giving her answer. 'She's got a strong personality and a clear vision – and of course she represents the new order.'

'A bossy cow?' said Pat.

But Thelma didn't smile. 'It's natural for people to resent her,' she said, 'but that doesn't mean she's without her vulnerabilities.'

'Victoria called her Mussolini,' reminded Pat.

Thelma stirred her coffee. 'I know there's an understandable tendency to think of her as this big, bad ogre. But notwithstanding, I think this business has upset her.'

'I suppose it'd upset anyone,' said Pat. 'Getting threatening letters and having their very expensive car keyed. Not to mention having half the staff upset.'

'She should do something then,' muttered Liz in a mutinous undertone.

'There's something else to consider,' said Thelma. She told Pat about the raffle draw, the ghastly look she'd seen on Kayleigh's face. 'And this had to be a good hour after she'd first seen the letter.'

'Maybe it was delayed shock?' suggested Pat.

'I said that at the time,' said Liz dismissively. 'It'd been a long, hot night. We were all tired.'

'I mean if you think about it, it could have been almost anything,' put in Pat. 'Maybe she suddenly remembered she'd left the gas on or remembered she'd forgotten to pay her credit card or even her bra had suddenly started digging into her.'

Thelma shook her head. 'Kayleigh Brittain was shocked by

something she saw *there and then*.' She looked at Liz. 'And I know for a fact she's very concerned about the letters, and of course the people who got them.'

'Not according to Becky,' said Liz flintily.

'So, what did this Becky's letter say?' Pat spoke quickly.

'Nasty stuff.' Liz pursed her lips in disapproval.

'What nasty stuff?' persisted Pat.

Liz shook her head. '"You–think–you–work–so–hard. You're–the–only–one–who–does!"' she recited tonelessly.

'Does she work hard?' asked Pat.

'Like smoke,' said Liz emphatically. 'Everyone knows so.'

Pat shook her head. 'It seems a bit of a waste of a poison pen letter,' she said, 'to say something everyone knows isn't true.'

'True or not, it's horrible and upsetting.' Liz spoke firmly. 'And remember – Bunty Carter doesn't think it'll stop with letters. She thinks someone's going to get hurt.' She gave an ominous nod. 'Anyway.' She took out her Trebah Garden notebook, which she put on the table with a crisp slap. 'I've been making a list,' she said. 'Of who got them. Jan, Becky – Kayleigh – these are the ones we know who have received letters.' She looked defiantly at Thelma. 'And I'm writing the names of people who might have sent them.' Her emphasis on the words indicated at least somebody was doing something.

'Like who?' asked Pat with interest.

'Well, not Donna Chivers,' said Liz (rather pointedly, Pat thought). 'It's a bit tricky seeing as I don't know so many of the staff any more.'

'There's that woman in the office, Nicole,' said Pat thoughtfully. 'Madame Iceberg, Matt Barley calls her.'

'And of course there's Margo,' said Liz. 'She always did have a bit of a funny side to her. And . . .' She took a deep breath. 'And Jan.' There was a pregnant pause. 'I mean I don't think for one moment it *is*,' she said unconvincingly.

'What? Old Starke-Staring sent *herself* a letter?' Pat looked at her friend incredulously.

'Before you go any further.' There was a note they did not often hear in Thelma's voice. If you didn't know her you might almost call it flustered. 'Kayleigh asked particularly that this matter *not* be discussed.'

'Did she now?' said Liz combatively.

'Yes,' said Thelma firmly with a crisp tone of authority. 'For very good reasons.' In her mind was an image of Sam, that awful expression on his face. 'People don't want their private affairs gone through left, right and centre.'

'Neither do they want to be getting nasty letters.'

'There is a lot of hurt and upset in school.'

'I know!' The colour was rising in Liz's face. 'There's someone causing that hurt and upset. And they're not just going to stop.'

'We have to be careful,' said Thelma firmly.

'What do you suggest we do? Sit back and let people like Becky suffer?'

'It's not a question of sitting back. Kayleigh Brittain, as head of the school, is dealing with it.'

'Is she though?'

'Yes, she is.' Thelma's diction was deadly. 'In her own way.'

There was the most awful silence. Liz looked frostily out of the window as Thelma briskly stirred her coffee again. Both sets of bosoms were high in the air, a sure sign of a Yorkshire lady's high dudgeon. Pat felt sure any second now one or the other would get up and walk off, which would be disastrous.

'I dunno,' she said as brightly and cheerfully and quickly as only she could. 'These blumin' letters. They all just feel so . . .'

'Spiteful,' supplied Liz tartly.

'No, I was going to say *outdated*,' Pat said.

Her friends both looked at her.

'You said something like that before,' said Thelma. 'What do you mean?'

Pat considered. She'd said it primarily as an attempt to head off a crisis. Now she wondered . . . what *did* she mean? 'Nowadays,' she said slowly, 'if people get a monk on with someone . . . they send texts. Or emails. A few clicks and done. I mean why go to all the trouble of fannying around sending anonymous letters?'

Thelma folded her serviette into neat triangles. There was something in that. And then of course there were the letters themselves – Jan's and Kayleigh's, and now Becky's. Plus, all those they didn't know of. Sam's. What *was* it about them that struck her as off-key?

Pat looked at her two friends.

'Come on, ladies,' she said. 'Let's not fall out over a few nasty letters.'

Liz said nothing.

'The thing we have to remember,' said Thelma earnestly, 'is no matter how horrible all this is – it could just stop. And then it really and truly is a case of "least said, soonest mended".'

There was a grudging acceptance of her words, not because any of them actually thought that, but because it seemed like the only way to leave things that morning without having a more serious disagreement.

'You know what,' said Pat as they stacked their coffee cups onto the tray, 'maybe whoever's doing it has got tired of it. Maybe this is the last we're going to hear of these here poison pen letters.'

But here she was wrong, totally wrong.

The very next day the news was all round Thirsk and Ripon. Natalie Berryman – the woman from the salon christened Mrs Nails by Pat – had received a letter about her husband Ian. And because of this letter, she had bagged up all his clothes, distributing them round various local charity shops.

All except for his tracksuit bottoms.

These she had cut the crotch from and thrown in the skip outside their house, the one holding the remains of their old kitchen.

CHAPTER EIGHTEEN

News of a scandal spreads far and wide, and an envelope is found in the trousers of an adulterer.

YOU NEED TO ASK YOUR HUSBAND ABOUT HIS RELATIONSHIP WITH NICOLE KIRK AS WORKS IN THE SCHOOL OFFICE. SORRY BUT YOU NEED TO. YOU DESEVE THE TRUTH. A WELL-WISHER.

A screen shot of this note had been posted on Natalie Berryman's Facebook page at 9.23 p.m., captioned: *That's just about made my Friday night*, and then, half an hour later: *The bastard's admitted everything.* This latter post was made after Natalie had confronted Ian, stormed out of the house and decamped, weeping, to the home of her best friend Trace, where the two of them proceeded to polish off three bottles of Prosecco. This information Pat gleaned from Olga at Mums, Bums and Tums, whose son worked with Trace at the Farm Shop. Some thirty minutes later Natalie's sister Jules blasted in, having abandoned a girls' night out in York, made everyone strong coffee and persuaded Natalie to take the picture down. This Thelma heard via Polly from the charity shop, who knew Jules through Beavers.

However, despite the relative lateness of the hour and the brief time the screenshot had been posted, it had been seen by many, copied and forwarded by many more and accrued a plethora of emoji-strewn comments, all along the lines of unfettered sympathy for Natalie and articulate condemnation for both Ian and Nicole. Indeed, Nicole came in for particular ire from those St Barnabus parents who had experienced her icy take-no-prisoners approach to dinner money arrears and term-time absences. *Always reckoned on she were so superior and all along she had her knickers round her knees wrecking someone's marriage,* was one of the more repeatable comments.

The image of the letter was forwarded to Thelma by Polly, Pat and Maureen from church. It was forwarded to Pat by Olga, by Linda Barley and, bizarrely, by Liam up in Durham. (*Hey up, Mother! It's all kicking off in Thirsk!*) Liz wasn't forwarded the image at all but heard about it in word-perfect detail from daughter-in-law Leoni who heard the whole tale thread-to-needle via her Used School Uniforms WhatsApp group.

'They've both been given "time off" by Rule Britannia,' Linda said, speaking through the open window of the rather muddy Barley landrover, her voice slightly raised above the strains of 'Wannabe'. 'She had no choice. Not with all the argy-bargy on social media.'

Pat nodded, clutching the egg box whilst fishing for money from her purse; she had happened to be in the yard as Linda was dropping off the eggs. Actually, there was no 'happened' about it – Pat had spent a good forty minutes with the leaf blower for the express purpose of grabbing this conversation.

'Of course,' Linda went on, 'with Ian Berryman it's a case of history repeating itself.'

'Yes,' said Pat, remembering how she'd meant to ask about this. 'Didn't he meet his current wife in a school as well?'

'When he was in Preston. She was working in his class. It seems some people just can't keep their bits in their trackie bottoms.'

'Did you have any idea what was going on?' asked Pat, passing money through the jeep window.

Linda shook her head. 'I mean it makes sense, looking back,' she said. 'But then most things do. Everyone reckons they knew something was going on, but honest to God I didn't, and I share an office with the woman. But no more, praise the Lord and pass the biscuits!' She punched the air with a triumphant fist.

'And they've both gone?'

Linda nodded. 'There's a supply in Year Five and Little Miss Muggins here is holding the fort in the office.' She sounded remarkably cheerful at the prospect of the extra workload, but then remembering Matt's comments about working with Nicole, perhaps it wasn't too surprising.

'Before I forget,' she said. 'Message to Captain Chemo from Matt.'

Pat smiled, but the casual, irreverent reference to Rod's cancer made her want to simultaneously touch wood, cross fingers and drop to her knees in prayer. 'Tell him Matt says if he's interested, they're shooting up Blakey Coppice on Thursday if he's around.'

Pat nodded; inside she felt a cold clutch at the use of the term 'around'. From now on, 'around' would be Rod's permanent state. Unless . . . unless the Baldersby job *did* somehow end up coming their way after all . . . A thought struck her.

'But presumably there'll always someone with you in the office?'

'I wish! I can see I'm going to be crossing my legs good and proper!'

'So, it'll be just you? Running all the systems?'

'Systems?' Linda looked at her.

Pat nodded vaguely. She always found it difficult, mentioning something specific in a casual way. 'You know,' she said. 'Registers, attendance . . .' She smiled vaguely. 'Accounts.'

'A lot of that stuff I do anyway,' said Linda. 'And I think they're getting a trust person in to look at the accounts at some point. But until then it's just moi – and on Tuesday, when el-shitto is still going to be hitting the fan in a major way, Rule Britannia's taking herself off on a nice little jolly, sorry, professional development course.'

Pat smiled, her mind racing. So, if she *did* want to take a look at the accounts – and she was still not at all sure about this – it would need to be whilst Linda was still on her own in the office. And on a day when Kayleigh Brittain wasn't in. Like Tuesday next week.

You got a problem, love?

Yes, you, you dishonest git!

With an effort she forced her attention back to Linda, who was revving the Land Rover as a prelude to going.

'So, you've not seen them then? Nicole or Ian?' she asked.

'Ian's been in for his stuff,' said Linda. 'Looking like see are ay pee – but there's been no sign of Madame Iceberg.'

'Too embarrassed to show her face?' ventured Pat.

Linda snorted explosively and expressively, quite drowning out the chorus of 'Holler'.

'Not her!' she said. 'She's got everything she wants!'

What 'everything' boiled down to was a rented flat by the ring road in Acomb. This Nicole had calmly produced in a rabbit-in-hat-like way, apparently having had it all lined up ready to go. She briskly left husband and house in Northallerton and moved in with (according to social media) nary a backward glance. To this flat Ian had decamped after a day or so, with such clothes as he had left. The two were spotted in the car park of York outlet mall with a trolley full of bedding and men's clothes, kissing full on outside Dunelm Mills.

'What you need to remember, Liz,' said Jan in airy, world-wise tones that made Liz want to put the phone down, 'is that these are two people who've found each other and found happiness. As both you and I once did.'

Liz reflected that happiness could hardly be said to be the defining characteristic of Jan's eight-year marriage to Dave Starke – and that whatever she and Derek had once found had never extended to snogging outside Dunelm Mills (or any store for that matter). She remembered Ian's hasty exit from the classroom that day – those tell-tale scratches on his back. Her lips compressed grimly – in a school! She brought herself firmly back to the present and her concerns about Jan. She wasn't *aware* of any fall-out between Jan and Ian – or Jan and Nicole – but even so . . .

'You're sounding well,' she said tentatively.

'Yes,' said Jan in puzzled tones, as if to say: *Why would I sound any other way?* 'Anyway, I'm calling to ask if you're okay to come in for Year Five on Wednesday.'

This was the very last thing Liz expected. After all the upset, she was sure the school wouldn't be wanting visitors of any kind, and after that last lecture from Jan, keeping away from the place seemed the only way forward. And besides, she'd only been in the Year Five class that one time.

'I'm not asking for me,' said Jan. 'It was Kayleigh who specifically mentioned it.'

Kayleigh Brittain? Asking for her to come into school? If it were not for the fact that Jan was temperamentally rubbish at telling any sort of lie, Liz would have suspected her of making it up.

'She said,' continued Jan blithely, 'how good it would be for the kids in Year Five to see a familiar face, and she's quite right.'

Liz considered. If the class *were* struggling in the sudden and enforced absence of Ian Berryman . . . She had been saying how

187

Kayleigh Brittain should be doing something – and asking her in would certainly qualify as that.

'Who was that?' asked Derek as she rejoined him on the sofa. They were in the middle of catching up with *Bake Off* and a paused Prue Leith regarded her, a piece of something or other held halfway to her lips.

'Just Jan,' she said, in the deliberately casual voice she was growing so sick of.

Derek looked at her. 'Is this to do with that business up at the school?' he asked.

Liz didn't bother to ask how Derek knew – Norman at the allotments at a guess. In a town like Thirsk the wonder would be if he *hadn't* somehow heard. She nodded again hoping he'd press play; however, both he and Prue Leith continued looking steadily at her.

'I'm really glad you're out of all that,' he said. It was a question, not a statement.

Liz nodded for a third time. 'Yes,' she said, feeling the guilt prickle at her cheeks and the back of her neck. Still, she hadn't actually said she *would* go in, just allowed Jan to cheerfully assume she would.

'So, it was all due to a letter someone sent this chap's wife?' asked Derek.

'An anonymous letter. There's been a few,' said Liz. 'A nasty business, a lot of people upset.'

'Anonymous letters?' Derek puffed out his cheeks and shook his head, his standard reaction to anything that was beyond his comprehension, from Brexit to the British Gas helpline.

Still Prue Leith remained frozen.

'I saw Sam today,' he said. 'Up at the allotments.'

'Sam Bowker?'

Derek nodded. 'When I was out on my run.'

Liz waited patiently; she knew there was some point to this story. She also knew that Derek needed to tell it his own way.

'He was just sat there. On Billy's bench.'

Liz nodded, thinking of the bench the allotment holders had clubbed together to buy Sam's grandad for his eightieth. It had been put on a rough triangle of waste ground where three allotments conjoined, and people tended to gather for a natter and the occasional bonfire. And though Billy had been gone some seven years, his bench still remained.

'He was just sitting there,' Derek said. 'He didn't look right.'

'Did he say anything?'

Derek shook his head. 'I was running see. I sort of said "hello" or something and he sort of smiled . . . but he didn't look right.' He looked at Liz again. 'And you say there's been some argy-bargy up at the school? Anonymous letters?'

Liz nodded once more. Again, Derek puffed out his cheeks.

'I'm glad you're out of it,' he said for a third time and this time it wasn't a question.

As Prue Leith unfroze, Liz entwined her fingers with his, hating herself for not saying actually she *wasn't* out of it; indeed it seemed she was very much in it.

She looked at the screen, but it wasn't someone's disastrous attempt at focaccia she was seeing but faces . . . Those children in Year Five . . . Raggedy Ann Becky alone in her flat . . . And now Sam, sat alone on Billy's bench at the allotments. Bunty's scared face as she looked over her shoulder . . . Jan, her face red and ugly from crying.

And someone deliberately setting out to cause damage and hurt.

Approaching sirens . . . a face twisted . . . A scream – 'My things!' Red fire blackening . . .

Derek took the tightening of her fingers as a sign of affection and absently he squeezed back, totally unaware that the squeeze meant something quite different, a reflexive grip as Liz realized with a sinking feeling that she would be going into school on Wednesday after all.

Thelma heard even more of the story, in so far as it related to the hospice charity shop.

'It was just after eleven when she came in,' said Verna, eyes and perm glinting with animation. 'I'd just come back off my break. And in she walks.' A dramatic pause. 'I can't say as I'd ever seen her before, but you don't miss a person like that.'

Thelma nodded. What was it had Pat christened Ian Berryman's wife? Mrs Nails . . .

'And she's carrying two great big carrier bags. "Men's clothes," she said, and there's something in the way she said it. I thought, *You're not happy, missy.* "That's a lot you've brought," I said, and she dumps them down. "I won't be needing them," she said and there was something in the way she said it made me go funny, right in the small of my back. I thought, *Hey up, Verna, there's a story here.*'

Thelma, who had heard many instances of Verna Going Funny in various places over the years, continued sorting the carrier of paperback books in front of her.

'And you know what, somehow I couldn't bring myself to touch them. They're there.' An orange fingernail pointed dramatically to where two Urban Outfitter carriers stood huddled together in the corner, as if shunned by the other carriers and bin bags. Thelma wondered momentarily if Verna was considering fixing labels to them: *Clothes of an Adulterer.*

When Verna had gone on 'her five-min breather' (at least forty minutes, which would invariably include an extended spell in Oliver's Pantry with the *Ripon Gazette*) Thelma upended the bags, tumbling the contents on the floor. Christmas jumpers and polo shirts, jokey ties and tank tops, the worn, the saggy, the almost new. Clothes bought online, on Saturday shopping trips, unpacked, held up against one with a 'how does this look?'

The wreckage of a relationship.

She recalled Pat's description of Mrs Nails, the effort and energy that had so obviously gone into creating an impression, and how an excess of emotion (and Prosecco) plus easy access to the internet had in a few seconds created another, far more memorable and indelible image. She thought of the man whose clothes she was now sorting into three piles (wash, recycle, you've got to be joking), his feeble attempts at jokes, his good-humoured (but sweaty) energy. *Mr Berryman, he's a real laugh.*

Only now he was, and always would be, Mr Berryman who carried on with that woman in the office and eventually ran off with her.

And she'd been the one to say it would all probably all die down.

So much mess, so much pain. All because of some letters . . . She checked herself. No, not because of some letters – it was just the one letter, the one sent to Natalie, which had caused all this furore. It seemed ironic – in a single night social media had caused a cataclysmic scandal of a scale that a month of anonymous letters had failed to achieve.

She paused in her sorting of the clothes. There was something significant in that thought, though for the life of her she couldn't work out what.

Picking and sorting the garments, a piece of paper fell out, an envelope. Unfolding it, she saw it had been torn in two, before being screwed up. Putting the two halves together she saw it was addressed to Natalie; the date on the postmark was from a few days previously. She looked carefully, there was just an envelope, no accompanying missive. Could this be the envelope that the fateful letter had come in? The date certainly fitted. The tearing, the scrunching, spoke of some strong emotion; it was easy to imagine it, torn up by or perhaps thrown at Ian Berryman, before being stuffed in a pocket, and scooped up with the rest of his clothes.

She smoothed the envelope out, joined the ragged halves together. The address had been printed on a sticky label of the sort so prevalent in primary schools. She remembered the envelope of Jan's letter, which had also had a label, with just the name 'Mrs J Starke' printed on it. The one to Natalie would need an address because it had been posted. She looked closely . . .

The noise of the door signalled Verna's return. She needed to put it out of sight.

She thought about police shows she'd seen and considered finding some plastic bag to drop the envelope in; however, looking round, the only thing available were plastic refuse sacks, which seemed like overkill, so she dropped it in her handbag as it was.

CHAPTER NINETEEN

Parental opinions are shared, and an unconvincing excuse is seen right through.

During the first part of the following week, all three friends visited the school. Each went at a different time, for different reasons, but following their tense exchange in the garden centre, neither told the others that they were planning to go.

It was the Tuesday morning when Pat went, a dark gusty morning with the wind sweeping chill from across the moors, and (according to the *Look North* weatherman) directly from the Ural Mountains. She'd aimed to arrive about ten minutes after school had started but owing to a row that morning, she'd made an angry exit earlier than planned and nine o'clock found her parked up on the York Road amongst the four by fours and family hatchbacks, watching parents disperse from the school gates having dropped their children off.

Pat placed both hands on the steering wheel and took a deep and hopefully calming breath. She tried to let it out slowly and evenly as she'd practised but only succeeded in making herself hiccup. She realized her hands were trembling.

Align your emotions with the facts not the fears. The past can navigate us, if only we choose to allow it to.

Only it was hard to see how this particular episode of flung pants and slammed doors could navigate her, Rod and Andrew anywhere – other than separate rooms.

It had been over the daftest thing. The previous day, feeling a bit flat, she'd decided to give Monday morning Mums, Bums and Tums a miss in favour of a bit of retail therapy in Cathedral Girl, that new boutique in Ripon. It had not been a successful session. The one jacket she had tried on had put her so much in mind of Dame Edna Everage that she'd fairly charged out of the shop in a state of full-on angst about her weight, hair and age.

All the rest of the day she'd regretted missing that exercise class, with a feeling that somehow forty-five minutes of buttock clenching under the supervision of Craig could have King Canute-like turned the tide of her self-image woes. That morning she'd been bemoaning this fact to Rod and Andrew; Rod had (as always these days) stayed focused on his iPad but Andrew had looked up mildly and said, 'It was on in the afternoon. It got moved. You could have gone.'

It wasn't so much the fact she'd missed a session she'd planned to miss anyway, or even that Andrew had seen Olga in the village and totally failed to pass on the message.

It was his shrug. *Why didn't you tell me?* Shrug.

The same helpless, 'so-what' shrug that accompanied each and every one of his domestic irritations from strewn pants to burnt pans to the clouding of her favourite Tuscan drinking glasses from energy shakes.

Sitting in the Yeti she couldn't now remember exactly what she'd said to him. Probably, were the words to be written down, nothing much – something about consideration, something about it not being his house, certainly something about his pants . . . No, it was the steadily escalating tone, the increasingly incoherent repetition of the words that had Andrew stock-still, eyes wide, Rod hovering nervously by the dishwasher and Larson hastily legging it upstairs. The upshot of all this was she'd slammed out of the house a good fifteen minutes before she planned, in the wrong coat and without having had a security wee – a fact she was increasingly starting to regret.

She sighed. The stream of parents was starting to falter. Give it another five minutes (if her bladder would stand it). She didn't want to meet anyone who might know her; in light of what she was planning, the fewer people who saw her at the school the better. They were nearly all gone now, just a stubborn knot chattering animatedly next to the school gate. No mystery as to what they were talking about. Her experiences as a mum had taught her a deep and abiding respect for the information and rumour afforded by the school drop-off. They were still showing no signs of moving and Pat (or rather her bladder) decided she'd just have to risk it.

Like her friends, the first thing that Pat noticed on entering school was the heat. It slapped her round the face the second she walked in through the doors, reminding her of entering the butterfly house at Leeds Tropical World. She remembered Thelma talking about some scam involving boilers. It was hard to imagine what sort of scam that could be – but really this heat was crazy. What exactly was it Thelma had said? Something that sounded like the RNLI but wasn't the RNLI . . . ? She must remember to ask Liam.

Despite Linda having proclaimed herself Little Miss Muggins running the office single-handed, she didn't seem to be showing any undue signs of stress. Nor did she display much curiosity about the reason for Pat's visit, ushering her through without question first to the ladies', and then the office. The first thing that struck Pat on entering the room was the bewildering blizzard of fluorescent green, pink and yellow Post-it Notes covered in Linda's firm scrawl adorning every flat and vertical surface round her workstation.

The second was that she wasn't on her own.

The IT technician lad was there – that one who'd been in Venture Scouts with Justin, the one who had all that bother with his girlfriend. Had some Italian nickname she could never remember – Pablo? He was busily doing something to Linda's monitor screen.

'That should do it, Linda,' he was saying. 'Just go easy on the webcam lap dance.'

'Behave, you,' said Linda, with a snort of laughter. She jiggled the mouse and the screen flared drably into life with a vista of spreadsheets. 'Praise the Lord and pass the biscuits,' she said. 'If that packs up, we might all as well go home. Ta, Pesto love.'

'Hi, Justin's mum.' Pesto's words and smile were easy but despite this and despite the teeth and wavy black hair, Pat noticed a lack of confidence lurking behind the eyes that took the edge off his attractiveness. 'How's Justin doing?'

'Fine,' said Pat. She presumed he was. Certainly, his sporadic WhatsApp and Instagram posts seemed to suggest so.

'Loved his latest podcast,' said Pesto. 'I found it really motivational.'

'Good,' said Pat, who had never managed to make it all the way through one.

'Anyway!' said Pesto. 'No rest for the wicked. Go easy on that monitor, Linda.'

As he turned to go, Pat saw the lad's profile. 'Your face!' she said before she could stop herself.

The easy smile didn't slip as he touched the livid bruise around the eye. 'The kitchen cupboard,' he said. Like the smile, the lie was easy. 'My own fault for not fixing the latch. Wham!'

When he'd gone Pat said, 'His girlfriend still up to her tricks then?'

'I tell you, Pat.' Linda's face was grim. 'Why he stays with that slap-happy madam I do not know. Poor lad. Three times she's had him take time out of work to sort out something or other at home, and there's him having to tell us it's a sickness bug.' She shook her head. 'Forcing the poor lad to lie through his teeth. Now I must just write this down before I forget.'

Pat watched as she scrawled, *Mrs Briggs-Buchanan – CALL!!!* on a lime-green Post-it Note, which joined all the other Post-it Notes. 'So have you had many parents ring in?' she asked.

'Just the usual subjects.' Linda affected a nasal whining voice. 'I don't want my child affected by what's gone on.' She took a noisy sip of her coffee. 'I want to tell them: unless they both dressed up as Transformers or summat, no way would anyone have been affected – because no way did anyone know. *I* certainly didn't and I shared an office with the bee eye tee sea aitch.'

'I wonder how his wife's doing?' mused Pat, thinking again of that lonely figure in the nail salon. What would become of that new kitchen with all its much-vaunted appliances?

'Not good.' Linda shook her head. 'Kicking off good and proper so I hear. Though not like his first wife, thank God.'

'Oh?'

'According to Ian she was always a bit, shall we say, "loop the loop". And apparently when he got together with Natalie – well, all sorts went off. Turning up at the school shouting the odds, slashing tyres in the car park.' She waggled a finger next to her right temple and whistled. 'I reckon people like Ian Berryman bring that out in people, you know.'

Fascinating though this all was, Pat had an objective to achieve. And despite knowing Kayleigh Brittain was not in the building, it was an objective she wanted to achieve as quickly as possible. 'Steve Hewson,' she said.

Linda looked at her puzzled. 'Him?' she said. 'Matt said you were asking about him.'

'Not so much him,' said Pat hastily. No way did she want such suspicions as she had broadcast round the Thirsk farming community. 'It's the prices he charges.'

Linda looked at her quizzically.

'I know he does quite a bit in school,' Pat continued. 'It's something Rod and I were thinking of getting into and I was wondering what the going rate was.' She knew her words sounded just as lame now as they had when she'd recited them to herself sat outside in the car, but it had been the best excuse she'd been able to think of.

'I think he's quite reasonable.' Linda frowned vaguely. 'I can't remember off the top of my head.'

'Would it maybe be on your accounts?' said Pat, trying to sound as bland and casual as possible.

Linda shrugged. 'Maybe,' she said. 'I can always get the system up.'

'Only if you've got time.' Again, Pat forced herself to sound blasé. If she could somehow get a print-off of the accounts to take away . . .

There then followed what could only be described as a palaver. First off Linda had to find a ring binder, where some operating procedures were set out – then she had to locate the system password. This was no easy task as the password was on a Post-it Note, somewhere amongst the many, many Post-it Notes that comprised Linda's filing system. 'It's definitely a green one. A green one or a yellow one. Not pink,' Linda kept saying as she and Pat searched. Twice Linda had to break off to answer the phone, and once to admit Byron Harper back from the dentist's. By the time the password was found (on an orange note) and the system laboriously logged onto, Pat was suffering twin agonies from needing another wee and fear that someone from the staff would come in and catch them at it.

Finally, simultaneously, Linda grunted and the computer beeped, indicating they were into the school accounts. Pat leant in towards the screen; quite what she hoped she'd see she wasn't sure, but with only her driving glasses all she could make out was a series of annotated columns. She was just about the ask for a printout – when the office door opened.

The noise made them both turn; in that second, with the pair of them both staring and open-mouthed, they must – Pat thought – have presented the very image of guilt.

'Nicole!' Linda's voice held that totally unconvincing cheery note people used when unexpectedly caught out doing something. 'I didn't expect to see you.'

Despite the agony of her embarrassment, Pat regarded the Femme Fatale of St Barnabus's Lodestone Academy with intense interest. She'd heard her appearance described variously by different people: buttoned up, neat, Madame Iceberg. However, this person was displaying none of those qualities; her hair was casually held back by a scrunchy (and looked like it needed a wash), her bright red blouse was a striking contrast to Linda's corporate grey affair and the love bites round her neck looked the very opposite of ice and repression. Plus, there was an air about her – a confidence, almost an insolence. Mrs Cat-with-the-cream, Pat christened her.

'What's going on?' Nicole addressed her question to Linda; Pat she barely glanced at.

Rich, thought Pat. 'I'm sorry.' She smiled and spoke with disarming cheerful confidence. 'It's my fault. Pat Taylor – I used to work here many moons ago.'

Nicole still didn't look at Pat but continued to fix Linda with a gaze that shrivelled the normally cheerful countenance.

'Me and my husband, we run a local building company,' she

199

continued fighting back the urge to give Nicole a sharp shake to get her full attention. 'We're looking at upgrading out systems; Linda was saying what a terrific set-up you had here and very kindly agreed to talk me through it.' It was the most convincing thing she could think of to say under the circumstances. No way did she want to mention Steve Hewson by name to Mrs Cat-with-the-cream.

Linda didn't help matters. She was the sort of person who was incapable of joining in a spur-of-the-moment lie, no matter how necessary. She blushed and stared fixedly at her lap where her fingers were convulsively twining round each other. She might as well, Pat thought, have a flashing neon sign above her head reading 'Guilty as Sin'.

Nicole reached across Linda and shut down the system; it was as if Pat had not spoken, or even existed.

'May I remind you, Mrs Barley, school systems are confidential and should not be shared with just *anyone*.' Finally, a scornful glance thrown in Pat's direction.

'I would have asked you of course,' said Pat. 'But I understood you'd left.'

Nicole stared back, fearlessly, brazenly, the trace of a 'so-what' smile playing round her lips. Pat realized whatever the community thought of her, Nicole had no problems at all with what she'd done.

'I called in to collect some things,' she said. 'And a good job I did.'

'Anyway,' said Pat brightly, 'I must be making tracks. Thanks so much, Linda, it looks just the sort of system we're after.'

At the office door she turned back and faced Nicole. 'By the way, love,' she said, 'that's a nasty rash on your neck. You want to get some Savlon on that.'

The next fifteen minutes were all about a frantic dash to the garden centre toilets. Washing her hands and inhaling the calming smell of the potpourri, Pat thought about Linda, with not a little guilt. She hoped she wasn't in too much trouble, and that her lie had at least in some way deflected Nicole's suspicions. Anyway, what exactly had she found out? 'Diddly squat,' she said aloud into the mirror.

Again, a picture of that blushing downcast face and those twining fingers came into her mind. And Linda had been so cheerful when Pat first arrived. She sighed. Maybe she'd drop a bottle of pink Prosecco round later by way of an apology. She could only hope that the whole saga would not get back, via Matt, to Rod. Crossing the road to the Yeti, another thought struck her. Never mind Mrs Cat-with-the-cream having everything she wanted with her love bites in Acomb, all because of an anonymous letter. With Nicole's enforced absence, Linda must also have been thanking whoever it was who sent it.

CHAPTER TWENTY

There is breakfast-time conflict, plus love and
heartbreak play cruel tricks in the staffroom.

It was on the Wednesday morning, the day after Pat, when Liz made her visit to St Barnabus's. Another unpromising morning with inky sullen skies, with wind whipping up the leaves into crackling swirls as Liz walked up the path to the school. Yet again she sighed at the memory of what had happened that morning. She wouldn't have been at all surprised if Derek had stepped out from behind the yellow grit bin, his face a mask of reproach.

It had been a stressful breakfast time; Derek had a team meeting in Northallerton, a sure-fire source of gloom and tension. He was running late and in danger of that apocalyptic event of Not Getting A Parking Space, when crisis of crises he couldn't find his council lanyard (despite his many cries of knowing *exactly* where he had put it down the night before). And of course, his lateness was in danger of making Liz late for her morning in Year Five – not that she could say so. Any signs of her preparing to go out would prompt questions from Derek, and she simply could not face one more evasion of the truth. So, she had no choice but to stay sitting at the table with Wordle, listening to him banging around upstairs with plaintive shouts of exasperation.

Eventually he'd entered the kitchen holding the offending item grimly aloft as if it were dead vermin. 'Right,' he said, 'I've got to go. I'll not get a parking space.'

'Where was it?' said Liz as mildly as she knew how.

'It had fallen down the back of the bedside table.' He shook his head, as if bewildered by the unfairness of the universe, and began donning his coat.

It was then her phone went. Thanks to Jacob her current text alert was a rather penetrating ship's siren. It was Bunty Carter giving her daughter's address – *not* in Boroughbridge but Tadcaster. Could she possibly drop the order off there today?

'Hell,' she said loudly and involuntarily.

'What is it?' cried Derek in a panic. 'I've got to go!'

'Nothing – you go.'

'What?' He stood, a study of fraught tension in the doorway and Liz knew he wouldn't shift until she'd explained herself.

'I've got to go over to Tadcaster.'

'Tadcaster? Why?'

'To drop Bunty's off – her cosmetics order.'

Derek looked at her as if she'd said she needed to run an undercover reconnaissance mission into occupied territory. 'Why you?' he said, his voice accusing.

And it was then the tirade had come.

She was dropping the order off because Bunty didn't dare go into school, Bunty didn't dare go into school because someone was sending anonymous letters, which no one seemed to be doing anything about, least of all the very highly paid head teacher.

She's spoke quickly, angrily, her voice fuelled by all the stress of the last fifteen minutes, and the guilt she felt at having voiced her suspicion about Jan.

There was a pause. The lanyard hung from Derek's finger, twisting slightly.

'I meant,' he said quietly, 'why does it have to be *you* who takes the order?'

There was a silence as Liz realized what she'd given away.

'I thought,' he said, 'you weren't having anything to do with school anymore.'

He said nothing else; he never did on these occasions, just turned and walked away.

Linda was a whirling presence in the office; phone jammed under her chin as she simultaneously opened mail and counted dinner numbers, but today Liz noticed she had none of the trademark bounce and cheer that usually characterized her actions. She looked pale, subdued; as she handed Liz her identity sticker, she barely met her eyes. Was she perhaps ill? Or had she too, God forbid, been a recipient of one of those awful letters? Liz tried the muddled beginnings of a conversation, something about the wind and the weather forecast, but Linda just nodded, turned away and released the electronic door. Had she been *crying*?

Liz was seriously considering going in and seeing if she was all right but even as the thought coalesced in her mind, the door to Kayleigh Brittain's office opened and there was the woman herself. In spite of Jan's message Liz felt herself tensing up – but Kayleigh was smiling.

'Mrs Newsome. Thank you SO much for coming in! I know that Mr Shah will welcome you with open arms!' Today she was wearing a charcoal-grey suit and sober navy scarf, the glossy hair was subdued back into a severe French plait; under one arm was a sheaf of canary-yellow paper. 'As you can imagine we're somewhat at sixes and seven.' She allowed a wry smile and a short but significant pause. 'And on top of everything else we've the school photographer in!' Her tone was humorously ironic, but Liz could see that under the make-up and hairdo Kayleigh looked *tired*.

There were lines round the eyes, a slight tremor playing in the left temple. *Fifty if she's a day,* thought Liz, surprising herself with a sudden pang of pity.

'But work goes on! I've two reports and a policy to write by lunchtime. Not to mention a couple of rather tricky phone calls!' Kayleigh held out the paper. 'I wonder – could you just drop this into the staffroom on your way past? Claire Donnelly's in there putting together the PTA newsletter.'

By the hall door was a large A-board, bearing the emblem 'Class Act Photography' and a selection of school photos. Gone were the traditional head and shoulders studio portraits – instead children were posed lying face down on some sort of rug, legs kicking the air. In the class photos, instead of three sober rows, the children were a whole mishmash, lying down, standing in groups, laughing, arms round each other. Liz remembered Ernie Bostock and his annual trips to the school, the unimaginative but somehow reassuring shots that had appeared year on year.

Sam's class were awaiting their turn. Jan, in some sort of organizational role, was shepherding the children to line up outside the hall. To Liz, she shot a vague 'I'm too busy to acknowledge you' look that made Liz briefly think of fetching her one with the A-board.

'Now, guys!' she carolled. 'Have you all got your very bestest "oh wow" grins ready for your mums and dads?' Her voice was bright. Too bright?

A voice hoarse with anger . . . You're as sane as me!

'Hi there, Mrs Newsome. Are you okay?' Sam's voice and smile were so chirpy that Liz felt slightly foolish for her concerns about him. She looked at him closely, but he seemed fine. Surely there could have been any number of reasons for him sitting alone on Billy's bench at the allotment.

★

205

It was as she was approaching the staffroom door that Liz heard the noise: a low, bubbling moan, hastily and breathlessly suppressed. Claire Donnelly was sitting to the side of the room, out of sight of the doorway, surrounded by sheets exhorting people to join the friendly and thriving St Barnabus PTA. As Liz came into the room, Claire ducked her head, her fingers whitening around the fistful of tissues she had in each hand. Like Jan she was not an easy crier, her face grown pinker and somehow larger, all except for her eyes, which were shrunken and wet.

'Oh, lovey,' said Liz. She came in, closed the door and sat down next to her.

'I'm all right,' said Claire. 'I'm fine.'

Why, wondered Liz, did people say they were fine when they so patently weren't? But long experience of such occasions had taught her to keep quiet, certainly to say nothing along the lines of 'what's the matter?' She simply sat there and swapped the balls of sodden tissues for two of her own balsam-impregnated ones.

'Thank you,' said Claire. 'I'm so sorry.'

'You've nothing to be sorry about,' said Liz automatically.

Claire's response took her by surprise: a swift, almost sly sideways glance at Liz followed by a fresh bout of sobbing.

'I just feel so bad for them,' she said between gasps.

'Mr Berryman?' guessed Liz.

'And his wife,' said Claire quickly, almost defensively. 'Both of them.'

'I understand he's going to another school,' she said.

Claire nodded, her expression dejected, defeated and infinitely bleak.

'Maybe it's for the best,' said Liz gently.

Claire's face didn't change; instead she looked out of the window at the darkening skies, her face pinker and larger than ever. Love, thought Liz, plays the cruellest of physical tricks.

'It's when you know something's a secret and it's what's best to do about it.'

'You knew what was going on?' said Liz, remembering the girl's upset in class that day.

Claire nodded. 'It wasn't like Nicole was discreet.' Now there was shard-like anger in her voice. 'She wanted him and that were that.'

Stumbling and sniffing, the story came out: how Nicole had been forever turning up in the classroom on some excuse or other; how Ian, bless him, well he hadn't really had a chance, poor man (Liz had her own opinions on that one but naturally said nothing). Things had come to a head that previous summer at the Year Five residential. It had been her and Ian with the class, staying at some outdoor centre in Lancashire. And on the last night Nicole had suddenly turned up – supposedly there'd been some plan for her to help the girls with their make-up for the last night disco. (Make-up? On a school residential? Times certainly did change!)

Only it had got later and later, and Nicole had shown no signs of going. Eventually Claire had gone to bed, leaving her talking with Ian – and the next morning her car had still been there.

Liz said nothing, for what was there to say? All she could do was press another balsam tissue into the trembling hand.

'And now she's got what she wanted.' Claire's words were spat out with real venom; venom and something else . . . Sadness? Regret? But before Liz could identify what it was, the door opened and Kayleigh Brittain walked in.

Despite the fact she'd been delivering papers at Kayleigh's request, Liz's first reaction was a strong feeling she'd been caught in the wrong place at the wrong time.

But when Kayleigh spoke, it was to Claire and her voice was both calm and kind.

'Claire,' she said. 'You need to go home.'

'I'm fine,' said Claire, sounding anything but.

'You're not.' Now firmness was winning out over kindness, but the kindness was still palpable. 'You're not; I don't think any of us are, not with what's been going on. I'm telling you: go. We're fine, we can manage.'

As she watched Kayleigh calmly despatching Claire – with many sobs and sniffs and protestations of being fine – Liz found herself warming to her, the firm but kind way she was dealing with the girl. She felt ashamed about her previous harsh thoughts. It was as Thelma had said: she was obviously under a lot of pressure. No two ways about it, it must be horrendous dealing with all that was going on. She expected Kayleigh to follow Claire out of the staffroom but instead the woman sat down and sighed a deep, weary sigh.

'What's happening to us all?' she said.

It didn't feel like a question that required any sort of answer – which was fortunate, as Liz didn't have a clue how to respond to this, beyond wondering fleetingly whether to offer her last balsam tissue.

'It must be very difficult,' she said.

'It is.' Kayleigh looked almost lost. 'The latest thing is the Christmas do.' She gestured at the whiteboard; Liz saw that under Margo's notice was one stark word – CANCELLED.

'What a shame,' she said.

Kayleigh shrugged. 'To be honest, it doesn't bother me unduly. But it shows how people are feeling . . . They just don't want to be spending time pulling crackers with each other, and who can blame them?' She sighed, stood up.

Liz fully expected her to leave the room but instead Kayleigh closed the staffroom door, sat back down and drew herself forward on her chair, looking intently at Liz. 'Did Claire say anything to you?' she asked.

'About what?' said Liz cautiously. She wasn't sure that the story about the school residential was one that should be repeated.

'About the letters,' said Kayleigh, holding her gaze.

'The one sent to Ian's wife?'

'That, and the others.'

'No,' said Liz.

'So, she said nothing? Nothing whatsoever?' There was something almost pressing in her tone.

'Not about the letters, no.' Why all this interest in Claire and the letters? 'Is there something Claire knows?' Liz ventured.

'No.' Kayleigh sat up. 'No, no more than the rest of us. And of course, the only one who knows anything is the person who's sending them.' She stood, shaking her head, as if trying to inject some energy into herself. 'No, it's nothing,' she said firmly. 'I'm probably just tired and imagining things.' She smiled at Liz, another weary smile.' I just hope that whoever it is can live with themselves.' She seemed on the point of saying more but at that moment the door opened, and Jan appeared. She seemed surprised at seeing Liz in there, giving her a brief, questioning smile.

'Staff photograph,' she said with her customary breezy energy. Whatever else was going on in school, Jan, it seemed, was back on full form. 'I've had a word and the photographer wants to do staff after break.'

Kayleigh's face changed suddenly, with an impassive blank look that made Liz prickle with unease. Had Jan somehow said or done the wrong thing?

Jan, however, carried blithely on. 'He should be able to do siblings and Key Stage Two this afternoon, so he reckons he can squeeze staff in before they set up for dinners.'

Kayleigh stared, nodded briefly and without comment exited the staffroom.

Liz felt puzzled; there had been something distinctly odd about her manner. Could it be something to do with Claire Donnelly?

Immediately Jan turned to Liz. 'I thought you were meant to be in Year Five?' Her tone was accusing.

'I am,' said Liz. 'At least, I'm on my way there.'

'So, what are you doing in here?'

Liz could feel herself growing flustered in the face of Jan's forthright tones. 'I was just talking to Kayleigh, and before that Claire.'

'Claire? Why?' Again, that almost angry accusation in her voice.

'Well, she was a bit upset and—'

'Didn't I say, Liz?' Jan seized on her words. 'Didn't I *say* to you about not getting involved? And now I hear Pat Taylor's been in, trying to access confidential school systems, why goodness only knows—'

'Pat?' Liz looked at her friend. '*Pat's* been in?'

'Don't pretend you don't know.' Jan looked sorrowfully at her friend. 'Liz, it's horrid what's going on. I know you're concerned, which is sweet and lovely, but people nosying is only going to make everything fifty times worse.'

That was it. Liz had had enough of being accused for one morning.

'Now hang on!' The strength of her tone startled them both. Jan opened her mouth but closed it promptly as Liz, eyes flashing with what Pat called her Boadicea look, raised a hand to ward off any further comments.

'First off, lady, I only came in here at the request of Mrs Brittain, so if you've any sort of problem with that I suggest you take it up with her, and secondly – no, let me finish.' Again Jan's mouth closed. 'Secondly I've no idea *at all* about anything Pat has done. Listen, I don't know if you've ANY idea how worried and upset I've been about this – about *you* – but if you think I'd do one single thing to make matters any worse than they already are then you don't know me very well at all. No.' As Jan's mouth opened a third time, 'No, I do *not* want to hear any more from you.'

She exited the staffroom with a great sweep of angry energy, heels rapping on the floor as she made her way to Year Five. She paused by the stock cupboard, trying to breathe away some of the anger. Much as she hated any sort of confrontation, she had to admit she felt rather good. She briefly considered going back – but only briefly. Points had been made, as they periodically had to be with Jan Starke. And now she felt nothing but an over-whelming desire to step all the way back from her friend, no matter what she'd been up to.

She only wished things could be so straightforward with Derek.

The noise of a revving car broke into Liz's thoughts. The caramel sports car was reversing quickly and noisily out of the staff car park. At the same moment the Sainsbury's delivery van turned into the driveway and began attempting to reverse up to the door of the school kitchen. The natural thing to do would be for Kayleigh to wait, but the sports car continued reversing, bumping over the grass, narrowly missing the Key Stage One nature garden. Why this sudden exit? Hadn't she said she was writing reports all morning?

That afternoon Liz had intended to have a further go in the garden, but the wind hadn't dropped, just the reverse; listening to it gusting against the glass, she could see there was little point in attempting any sort of raking. Sitting in the conservatory with her after-lunch cup of tea she tried to rake her thoughts in the same way as she'd planned to rake leaves, but whenever she gathered ideas from one thought, along came a gust of another idea, scattering them again . . . Jan . . . Kayleigh . . . Claire. And she felt so tired, no two ways about it; the morning in school had left her physically and mentally drained. Plus there was whatever was in store when Derek came home . . .

Without planning it, cooling cup of tea at her side, she slipped into a drowse – not exactly awake, but not properly asleep. She sat there in the sort of dreaming doze you get, where at some level you realize you're dreaming, but are still a prey to the concerns and worries those dreams throw at you.

. . . there was Kayleigh Brittain, looking directly at her. 'Who is it, Liz?' she was saying. 'Who's doing these awful things?'

There was Bunty, face a picture of doom. *There's a nutter loose in school you know* . . . And then there was Jacob, lying in his favourite prone position in front of the TV, pad of paper in front of him. Only he wasn't drawing memorials or even the *Titanic*, but writing letters, nasty anonymous letters. 'Someone has to do it, Grandma,' he was saying.

'This is a dream,' she said to herself, but the words failed to dispel the unease, instead shifting it onto someone else . . . Becky Clegg, smiling abstractedly, stapling canary-yellow sheets together in the staffroom, only they weren't PTA notices but anonymous letters . . . Jan, writing confidently on a whiteboard. 'This is how you write a letter!' she was saying brightly. 'With a cursive flick!' And then Liz was looking through the office door. Nicole was smiling to herself, bent over something she was writing. 'I only wanted one thing,' she was saying—

Then in the way dreams do, time and place shifted. She was on a school trip to the seaside – Filey? And Topsy was there, organizing the class, lining them up . . . She was saying something, something important – what was it? *There's one missing* . . .

With a dropping feeling she scanned the shore – and there, out

212

at sea was a lone figure. Sam. Waving cheerfully . . . *Hi, Mrs Newsome!* No, not waving . . . *drowning.*

Sam?

She sat up, wide awake, realizing she'd said the name out loud, and that her phone was ringing. It was Thelma. What could she be wanting?

CHAPTER TWENTY-ONE

In a forgotten space, actions are challenged
and an olive branch extended.

Thelma's visit to St Barnabus's, on the Monday morning, before either of her friends, had been the briefest of the three, lasting as it did barely five minutes. Her first instinct on hearing the news about Nicole and Ian had been to ring Kayleigh Brittain and reach out with her support; after their conversation the previous week, it had seemed the natural thing to do. With it being the weekend, there had been no point in trying to make contact through school and she didn't have Kayleigh's mobile number, so any reaching would need to be done by Mrs Brittain herself.

Just as before, when she'd first learnt of the extent of the letters, Thelma was thinking Kayleigh might ring her – and as before it was the Sunday, late on the Sunday night, when her phone trilled with 'number withheld' showing.

'Thelma.' The normally measured voice sounded flustered. 'Kayleigh Brittain here. I'm sorry to ring so late.'

'That's not a problem; I've been half expecting you to call.'

'No prizes for guessing why.' Kayleigh gave a grim half-laugh. 'I imagine half of Thirsk knows what's been going on.'

And Ripon, plus all points between, Thelma wanted to add.

Unsurprisingly Kayleigh had had a Full-On weekend, speaking with Ian, with Nicole, at length to Chris Canne. She detailed the actions she'd taken, giving both Ian and Nicole 'gardening leave', sorting cover for Year Five and having repeated conversations with Chris Canne, who seemed to believe that it was only a matter of time before the whole sorry saga hit the press. 'Honestly, Thelma, it's been a complete nightmare,' she said. 'Chris seems to think I should've somehow stopped it. I said to him: "How could I stop it when I didn't know it was going on? You pay me to run a school, not get involved with the private lives of the staff . . ."'

After the call, Thelma sat in her favourite wing chair by the fire, deep in thought. Something, she felt, had been missing from the conversation. Whereas there had been plenty of talk about what had been done to manage to the situation, and plenty of speculation about the mentality of who must have sent the letter, there had been no real mention of the situation *itself*. What had been *done* by Ian and Nicole, clandestinely, regularly on school premises during school time. She thought of the neat figure looking out of the stock cupboard on the day of the harvest assembly. The scratches Liz had seen on Ian's back. Of course, she couldn't assume Kayleigh hadn't spoken to the pair of them . . . And how was Kayleigh? She had sounded strong enough, but she remembered the image of the frightened girl behind the huge desk . . . How was she really doing? After some further thought she decided to go and see her the next day.

Like Pat would, she timed her visit to avoid the parental presence at the start of the school day, but even though it was gone nine fifteen when she parked up the mussel-blue Corsair there were still at least half a dozen women gathered by the school gate, deep in conversation. The body language of gossip is as distinctive as that of love or anger or grief. The darting eyes, the discreetly dropped heads, the very proximity of the women, all told an obvious story. Like Pat the following day, Thelma had no difficulty in guessing what they were talking about.

The office was a scene of cheerful chaos, with Linda and Margo Benson both on phones, both scribbling messages as Thelma looked in through the hatch.

'All I can say is Mr Berryman is not in school, and that the class is being taught by a supply teacher for now.' Linda, her voice calm and reasonable, winked at Thelma and mimed sticking two fingers down her throat. 'I'm so sorry but Mrs Brittain isn't available. I can get someone to give you a call later back if that's any good?' This seemed to satisfy whoever was calling and Linda was able to firmly replace the handset with a cheerful cry of 'Plonker'. Immediately it burst into trilling life. 'Give me strength,' she said, opening the glass hatch.

'You look to have your work cut out,' said Thelma.

Linda laughed. 'You should have been here half an hour since,' she said. 'All this AND a lobby full of angry parents all shouting the odds. All I can say is a certain Ms Iceberg had better give this place a wide berth for a while.' She nodded significantly and Thelma got the distinct sense that despite the ringing phone, Linda wouldn't have been averse to a quick chat about recent events. Thelma, however, had no wish to further fan the flames of gossip she'd seen burning so strongly outside.

'I was wondering,' she said, 'if I might have a quick word with Mrs Brittain.'

'She's not in I'm afraid,' said Linda, with even more significance. From behind her, Margo fired off an eloquent grimace.

'She's gone out you mean?' said Thelma.

'Never came in, in the first place,' said Linda. 'Not well. She rang in first thing. Up all night, head down the toilet apparently.'

Thelma frowned. No mention of feeling ill had been made the

night before – though of course Kayleigh may have been hoping any feelings of illness would pass over. Or maybe she only started feeling ill later on? It was perfectly possible stress could have brought on some stomach upset. And yet she felt faintly surprised at the head teacher's absence on a day of such obvious crisis. She recalled times when Feay had literally dragged herself in at times of importance – herself too for that matter. That awful Nativity play where she'd nearly passed out in church.

'Linda.' Margo sounded imploring. 'Mrs White. She's awfully upset.'

'I better take that,' said Linda. 'I'll tell Mrs Brittain you came in, Thelma.'

On the Tuesday after lunch Thelma had called again, to be informed by Linda that Kayleigh was out all day on a course; she had spoken to her and passed on Thelma's message. No cheery claim of being little Miss Muggins; in fact Linda sounded remarkably subdued. Had she, Thelma wondered, received one of the letters?

Late on the Wednesday afternoon Thelma found herself at the college sitting in a room she'd never spent time in before, looking at a vase of rather bedraggled orange chrysanthemums. Outside the wind tugged at the trees on the edge of the college playing fields, recalling to mind something from the *Poetry Pathways* book that she used to use with her class:

The autumn winds bestir the trees
And make the sound of distant seas

She looked around the dusty room. The student chapel of Ripon and St Bega's College was a grand title that was much bigger than the room it described, a side room on the main corridor just down from the lecture hall. She was there, having called in at Teddy's request, bringing in a ring binder he needed.

She thought about the conversation they'd just had. He'd not yet properly replaced all the various folders and files in his study at home and it had been gone three when she'd arrived at his study with the dusty, slightly forlorn item. The voice that had answered her knock had been the voice of the Reverend Edward Cooper, senior lecturer and chaplain of Ripon and St Bega's College, deliverer of sermons and lectures, marker of essays and occasional comforter of stressed trainee vicars. When he saw it was her he'd relaxed, morphing into the man she'd shared her life with all these years. But tired. And yes – old. No – *older.*

'I'm sorry it took longer than I thought,' she'd said, handing him the file. He'd nodded, smiling his thanks. 'Before you ask, there's no further news.'

'I presumed not.' She'd sat down next to him. No further news, but plenty of speculation, some of which she'd heard in indignant detail from Brummie Maureen in the office. She took his hand. 'I've been thinking.'

'Oh?' He turned his eyes to her. Was it her, or had they become a bit faded in their blueness?

'As you say, there's a good chance things are – well, going to change.'

'That college could well close.'

She nodded. 'Of course things may be fine. But if not, I was wondering – maybe this is something to look on as an opportunity.' She took out the folder she'd been preparing over the past couple of days – pamphlets she'd picked up from the library or downloaded at home: Dementia Forward, Age UK, Friends of Foundations Abbey. She'd spoken earnestly, at length outlining various projects and options. Teddy had let her speak without interruption, as he always did, even during those dark times when they were trying for a child and everyone else seemed to want to quieten her with platitudes.

'There's a lot of work that needs doing,' she'd concluded.

He'd nodded, smiled at her and for just a second there was the blond rugby player she'd met all those years before. 'I rather thought,' he said, 'I was already doing a lot of work.' He gestured at the shelves of books and files and folders.

Thelma had said nothing, for what was there to say? Instead they sat in a companionable silence until the first students arriving for 'God and Conflict' in the shabby, panelled lecture room could be heard.

Now, sitting in the student chapel thinking about her husband, about the folder, she sighed; why, she wasn't exactly sure. She looked round the room. Those orange chrysanthemums were definitely past their best. She wasn't sure who, if anyone, ever used this room but she couldn't remember a time when it hadn't been here. There had been, she seemed to recall, some feeling that students being taught to help others find God needed a space to find God themselves. As spaces went it really wasn't very much, barely big enough for a dozen chairs, two inwards-facing rows against each side, with a Bible on each alternate chair. On one wall was an open-faced cupboard crammed with texts that Thelma suspected hadn't been opened for years. And below the single leaded window, a simple table with a cross. And the flowers. Did anyone ever try and find God in this dusty, forgotten space?

The trill of her phone cut sharply into her thoughts. The number was withheld, but a sudden intuition told her who the caller was likely to be.

She was right.

'Thelma, Kayleigh Brittain here. I believe you've been trying to speak to me.'

Today there was different tone to her voice – not her usual easy charm – rather a formal, restrained quality. Had something else happened?

'Are you feeling better?' asked Thelma. 'I understand you were ill on Monday.'

'I'm much better thank you,' said Kayleigh. Now the tone was almost brusque.

There was a pause, almost as if she were challenging Thelma to speak.

'I was calling to see how things were.' Thelma spoke hesitantly. 'In school. How it's gone this week.'

'I rather thought you might know.' There was a definite spikiness to her tone.

'I'm sorry?'

'With both your friends being in. Liz Newsome was in at my request of course, but Pat Taylor — I understand she was caught trying to access confidential school systems.'

Thelma felt a guilty flush as she remembered her conversation in the café. Hadn't she been discouraging enough?

'I take it you knew she was coming in?' The sudden question was rapped out in a way designed to wrong-foot people into a confession of guilt.

Thelma took a calming breath. 'I had no idea Pat was coming into school this week,' she said. This at least was true.

'But you knew about what she was planning?' There was something expert about the way Kayleigh seized on this point that made Thelma instinctively want to confess or deny what was being implied. For the first time she fully appreciated Victoria's label of Mussolini.

'As I say,' she said, 'I had absolutely no idea Pat was coming into school.'

'Then I've no choice but to accept your word, Thelma.' Hanging unspoken in the air was the coda: *You didn't tell me about that letter — what else aren't you telling me about?*

'Is everything else all right?' asked Thelma, chastened.

'You mean have there been any more letters? Like the one sent to me this afternoon?'

'You've received another letter?'

'Tucked under the windscreen wiper of my car,' said Kayleigh. 'I found it just now when I went out to get something. But this time please, *please* keep it to yourself.'

Thelma ignored this. 'Your car, you say? Could you look on the CCTV?'

'I could, but the system's been playing up. Someone techno from the trust is supposed to be coming out to sort it, but no one's appeared yet.'

'I see.' Thelma looked at the chrysanthemums. This was all a lot to take in. 'And are you all right?'

'I was a bit teazy at first, but I've got far more important things to worry about.' Kayleigh sounded defiant. 'Anyway, whoever it is has changed their tune a bit.' There was a gallows cheerfulness in her voice. 'They must be getting bored of the same old schtick.'

'And are you able to say what said it said?' Thelma spoke tentatively.

'Sweet and to the point. *YOU'RE NOT WANTED HERE! GET OUT, YOU BITCH, OR ELSE – THIS IS YOUR FIRST AND LAST WARNING.*'

'Do you not maybe think,' said Thelma, 'now might be the time to involve the police?'

'No I do not!' The answer was rapped out with something very like anger. 'What would you suggest I say? We've had some letters but have no idea who might be sending them? 'Her voice changed, becoming patient in an almost exaggeratedly strained way. 'Thelma, you've got to remember people have been to me repeatedly and said they do not want this getting out. I know everyone knows about Ian and Nicole, but at least, thank God, that's as far as it goes.'

'But that letter you received today – and the other one—'

'There's nothing the police can *do*, Thelma. Besides, if someone wants to play silly beggars, that's fine – they can send me as many notes as they want. I've got a school to run.'

After the call ended, Thelma sat thinking. Kayleigh's displeasure was a powerful thing, no two ways about it. She felt a spurt of her own anger towards Pat – she could only guess how cheerfully and carelessly she'd gone about trying to see the school accounts. But then, she reminded herself, she had known full well what Pat had been thinking of doing.

She looked sombrely at the altar cross. *THIS IS YOUR FIRST AND LAST WARNING* . . . The sheer spite and nastiness of that last note somehow made everything a notch more serious. It felt like the bad feeling was increasing, blowing around in ever more relentless gusts and waves, like the strengthening wind outside. What was the phrase from John's gospel? *The wind blows where it pleases, you hear its sound, but you cannot tell where it comes from* . . . Something like that. Only that was referring to the Holy Spirit, not nasty letters?

She thought of Kayleigh's voice – accusing, patient, weary . . . the voice of someone at their wits' end . . . Until now, she'd felt Kayleigh Brittain had a handle on what was going on . . . but now?

And outside the wind still soughed in the trees . . . *the sound of distant seas* . . .

Liz answered her phone on the second ring.

'I'm truly sorry,' said Thelma. 'You were absolutely right about this business, something does need to be done.'

After the call she was gathering herself up to go home, when her phone rang for the second time in twenty minutes. Her first thought was it would be Liz, saying something about their plans to meet tomorrow; hard on its heels came the more worrying notion that it was maybe Kayleigh Brittain with news of even more trouble?

But it was neither of them. It was a number unknown to her, a Bradford number, and for the second time that afternoon she had a strong instinct that this was a call she needed to take.

CHAPTER TWENTY-TWO

The timetables of psychotic people are considered, and thoughts are shared about the nature of dreams.

'I'm so sorry! I feel just awful!' Pat, upset, pushed aside her plate, with its piece of Melmerby slice from which she'd only taken a single bite.

'You weren't to know,' said Thelma mildly. There was absolutely no point in there being any more bad feeling than there already was.

'That's two people I've landed in Kayleigh Brittain's bad books,' lamented Pat. 'You and Linda.'

'I think that one's bad books must run to more volumes than the mobile library,' said Liz. 'I wouldn't worry about it.'

'But I do.' Pat was genuinely distressed. A bottle of pink Prosecco felt woefully inadequate. After what she'd heard from both her friends, she was not even sure a whole case would make it up to Linda Barley.

'In my case, Kayleigh did have a point,' said Thelma.

'I don't see how,' said Liz. 'You've done nothing but try and help the woman.'

'Look at it from her point of view,' said Thelma patiently. 'Someone's attacking her school by sending out these poison pen letters. Every single day she must be asking herself who it could be. Imagine how that must feel – looking at everyone you meet and trying to imagine if it could be them . . . And then she hears of the one person she thinks she can trust, possibly being part of a plan to sneak a look at the school accounts.' She held a hand up as both Pat and Liz opened their mouths to speak.

'I'm not saying she's right – I'm saying how she might see it.'

'I suppose you're going to say we need to leave well alone,' said Liz a trifle sulkily.

'No,' said Thelma. 'Quite the opposite.'

'Why?' said Pat. 'Did she say something else?'

'It wasn't what she said,' answered Thelma. 'But how she sounded.'

'And how was that?' asked Liz.

Thelma paused and looked directly at her two friends. 'Afraid,' she said simply.

'So,' said Thelma eventually. 'What are the facts?' They had now been sitting at the round table in the corner for a good half an hour and it rather felt like they were getting nowhere fast. There seemed to be so much to consider and discuss; as soon as one of them offered an idea or thought, another would interrupt with their own viewpoint, or a bit of information they'd forgotten to say. To the other people in the garden centre, that raw foggy morning, they merely looked like three ladies of a certain age, discussing nothing more innocuous than family or friends or the increasingly stormy autumn weather.

'What is it we actually *know*?' said Thelma.

'Lots,' said Liz. 'Someone's sending out nasty anonymous letters, which are upsetting a lot of people and causing real harm.' She spoke rapidly and firmly, in the tone of someone expressing the blindingly obvious.

225

'And,' said Pat through a mouthful of the now reclaimed Melmerby slice, 'Kayleigh Brittain's had three, and the last couple seem to be threatening her.'

'And you think she's scared,' added Liz. 'Also, don't forget you thought for some reason she looked all funny at the summer fayre.'

Thelma nodded, remembering that stricken look. *What* had made Kayleigh look like that?

'Plus,' said Pat, 'somewhere in all the mix is Steve Hewson and his overheating boiler. And he may or may not be overheating our Ms Bling. And there might be something dodgy with the accounts – which we're not now likely to get a look at thanks to me.'

'Whoa!' Thelma raised a hand as if staving off the flurry of comments. 'We need to take all these things one at a time. *Organize* our ideas.'

Pat smiled. 'Who, where, what, why, don't forget when,' she sang. 'I've got a story, I can't wait to begin.'

In spite of all that was happening, the other two joined in with her smile; it was a jingle they'd all used so many times over the years as a way of ordering ideas when they were teaching story-writing. It was also a remarkably effective technique when planning some of the school's more complex events: school trips, stay-and-read sessions, turning the role-play area into the Gruffalo's castle.

'So,' said Thelma, taking out her notebook. 'Let's start with the "what".'

'That one's easy,' said Liz. She sounded slightly impatient. 'Anonymous letters.'

'All written on a computer, all sent in the same type of white envelope,' said Pat.

'All saying nasty, wicked things,' said Liz.

Thelma frowned at this. She was becoming increasingly aware

that there was something off-key about those letters, something that was lurking somewhere just beyond her conscious thoughts. What was it? Whatever it was, she needed time and peace to fathom, two things she didn't have at this present moment. She mentally shelved the thought and merely said: 'How many?'

'A lot,' said Pat. 'Maybe fifteen according to Matt Barley. And there's been more since.'

'Becky, Natalie Berryman.' Liz counted the names off on her fingers. 'Margo.'

'Jan,' said Pat.

Liz didn't react but said, 'Then there's those people we *think* had one – Bunty, Tiff.'

'Sam, we think,' said Thelma.

'And not forgetting Kayleigh Brittain,' said Pat. 'Who's had three now.'

'And had her car keyed.' said Thelma. 'Plus she thinks someone's been in her office.' She stirred her coffee. 'The question we have to ask ourselves is this: is there any *connection* between all the recipients? Other than that they work at St Barnabus's?'

'Natalie Berryman doesn't remember,' said Liz.

'No.' Thelma's stirring slowed. 'No, she doesn't does she.' The spoon stopped, the words hung on the air, and she gazed, abstracted, out across the windy car park.

Liz and Pat looked at each other, with a hint of exasperation.

'How about "where"?' said Pat a trifle impatiently.

'In school,' said Liz, again with slight exasperation. 'Left somewhere where they'll be found by the victim.'

'Again, apart from Natalie Berryman,' said Pat.

Thelma continued looking out across the car park, and the metal sign for kiln-dried logs that squeaked and tilted in the window. Natalie Berryman. Once again, the odd man out. 'Hers was posted,' she pronounced.

Pat shrugged. 'The writer, whoever they are, could hardly go up to Ian and say, "Oh, Ian, I've this anonymous letter. Can you see that your Natalie gets it?"'

'No,' said Thelma. 'No, they couldn't.' Again, her attention seemed to wander; again, Liz and Pat exchanged impatient glances.

'When?' said Pat firmly.

'Since the night of the summer fayre,' said Liz. 'At least that's the first one. I don't think any more were sent until the start of term.'

'When you think about it, it's all been a bit rapid,' said Thelma thoughtfully.

'Rapid?' said Pat. 'How so?'

'Say fifteen letters have been sent at least. That's maybe three or even four a week – *that we know of.*'

'What of it?' said Liz.

'In the case I was telling you about, the letters went on over two years. Weeks – *months* could go by between letters being received.'

'So,' said Pat. 'We have an anonymous letter writer who wants to get a shift on.'

'Which begs the question *why*,' said Thelma.

'Because,' said Liz sombrely, 'they're someone with problems who needs help.'

'Or,' said Pat, 'they're a twisted individual getting their kicks from all the upset they're causing.'

'I'm no expert,' said Thelma, 'but if it was someone like that – wouldn't whoever it was get more enjoyment from spreading the letters out? Savouring the power so to speak? Let everyone think it's all died away – and then send another one?'

'I don't think,' said Pat. 'Psychotic letter writers necessarily fall into set patterns of behaviour.'

'Which,' said Thelma, 'brings us onto our "who".'

The three looked at each other. 'If we knew that,' said Pat, 'we wouldn't need to be going all round the houses and back.'

'It could be someone we know,' said Liz quietly. Her friends looked at her.

'I can't see how it *isn't* someone we know,' said Pat as tactfully as she could.

'What I mean,' said Liz, 'is whoever it is, yes, they need to be stopped. But they need *help*. For their sake as much as anyone else's.'

'I wonder . . .' said Pat suddenly. 'I mean this is only a thought – but do you think Kayleigh Brittain *knows* who's sending the letters? And is trying to protect them? Maybe that's why she looked so odd at the summer fayre?'

Thelma frowned. That was certainly a new idea.

There was a pause. A natural break seemed to have been reached. Liz suddenly gave a huge yawn. 'Excuse me,' she said.

'Are we keeping you up, Liz Newsome?' asked Pat.

'I'm fine.' Liz's words glided easily over the truth that was the arctic atmosphere at home between her and Derek. Again, her friends looked at her, both knowing something was the matter. She shook her head, as if pushing off their unspoken concerns. 'I don't know,' she said. 'These blumin' letters. I was even dreaming about them yesterday.'

'Did you see who was writing them?' asked Pat. 'It'd save us a heck of a lot of hoo-ha.'

'All sorts of people.' Liz took a sip of her coffee. 'And for all sorts of reasons.'

'Different reasons?' There was something in Thelma's voice that stopped Pat from changing the subject.

'Daft things,' said Liz dismissively.

'Such as?'

'I don't know . . . Like Becky sending them out to spite the

229

PTA – and Nicole to get her claws into Ian . . . even Jan to teach Year One handwriting!' She smiled to show how foolish it all was. For reasons she was unsure of, she didn't want to share her disturbing vision of Sam. 'Stuff like you get in dreams,' she said, her tone signalling the subject was closed.

'Well, try as I might, I can't see how any of this can have any which way to do with Steve Hewson and that biomass boiler,' said Pat.

'It was like a furnace again on Tuesday,' said Liz.

'Did you get any further finding out about that scam I mentioned?' asked Thelma.

'A little bit,' said Pat dismissively in airy tones that belied the frustrating hour she'd spent on the iPad. 'I was going to ask Matt, but I don't like to, not after having landed Linda in the do-do.' She sighed, the guilt returning. 'I just can't see how any who, where, why, what could link some twisted letter writer with a boiler.' She made a helpless gesture with her pastry fork. 'You tell me how the things are connected.'

'They may not be,' Thelma admitted. 'But if you look at the *facts* – Lodestone is the trust that runs St Barnabus's . . . This Steve Hewson is connected with Lodestone Academy in a number of ways, all of which benefit him financially. And then Chris Canne, head of the academy, plays down the fact he works with him. *Why?* Unless there was something about the connection he wanted to cover up.'

'Plus, he might be having fun times with Kayleigh Brittain,' reminded Liz.

'It's funny,' reflected Pat. 'I hear so much about this woman and yet I don't even know what she looks like.'

'We don't even know that much about her,' said Liz. 'Not like we do with the other teachers.'

'I might find out a bit more tomorrow,' said Thelma quietly in a way that made them both look at her.

She's going to make one of her dramatic announcements, thought Pat.

'You see, I had a phone call yesterday,' continued Thelma. 'From a Mike Brittain.'

'Brittain, as in Kayleigh Brittain?' said Liz taken aback.

'He's rather worried about his wife,' said Thelma. 'And he wonders if I could drive over and see him tomorrow and have a confidential word with him.'

Later on, as they waited for Liz whilst she nipped into the ladies', Pat said, 'Is everything all right with Boadicea d'you think?'

Thelma shook her head. 'Reading between the lines, I think she might have had words with Derek about this.'

'You think?'

'She hasn't said anything to me as such.'

Pat sighed. Thelma was also looking worried and no wonder. News about the closure of the college had been all across the news.

'And of course,' said Thelma, 'Liz is worried about Jan.'

Pat snorted. 'Why she didn't tell her to go years ago is beyond me.'

Thelma nodded, a private 'I-know-more-but-am-not-saying' sort of nod.

Pat knew better than to ask. Instead she said: 'Liz's dream?'

'What about it?' said Thelma.

'You obviously thought it was significant in some ways.'

'I might just be jumping to conclusions—'

'But?'

Thelma frowned, choosing her words. 'I often find dreams can be the mind's way of working out the problems of the day. Not always of course, but sometimes if you recall a dream, you can get some . . . insight.'

'And what insight did you get?' asked Pat. 'That Becky doodah's in cahoots with the PTA?'

Thelma smiled. 'We've always assumed that whoever was sending the letters out was some twisted individual – a nutter, Bunty Carter said . . . But what was common with all the people in the dream Liz had is *they were all sending out the letters for very practical reasons.*'

CHAPTER TWENTY-THREE

At Badger's Fold there is an unexpected and unsettling encounter by a stack of breeze blocks.

Kayleigh Brittain lived over towards Bradford, on the hills to the north of the city. Driving slowly along the narrow road between Baildon and Bingley, Thelma frowned, scanning the tangled hedge-rows for the turn-off to 'Badger's Fold', the Brittains' home. Not being a satnav person, she had little more to go on in the way of specific directions other than the name, plus cheerful but vague assertions from Mike Brittain that she 'couldn't miss the place'.

In fact, she could; indeed she missed it twice, necessitating a couple of tricky three-point turns on the narrow road, before she finally located the uncertain-looking track indicated by the mossy, obscure sign.

There were neither badgers nor any particular folds in the land in evidence as the mussel-blue Corsair breasted the top of a rise, jolting on the uneven track. What there was, was a rather bleak expanse of drizzly hillside, in the middle of which some trees and a house were plonked down in a seemingly random way. It was a barn conversion, of course it was – so many places were these days. To the left of the building was the former arched doorway, now glassed in with a panelled door suspended in the glass. The rest of the house spread out to the right – a long, Yorkshire jumble of stones and windows.

To the left of the door some sort of building work was evidently in progress. The ground had been levelled, raw and muddy, and an ugly breeze-block wall had been started. A cement mixer grumbled away in front of this, next to stacked piles of more breeze blocks; three men in grubby hi-vis jackets were working. Why, wondered Thelma, have an extension built onto somewhere that was already pretty substantial? Especially if it was just Kayleigh and the cheerfully vague Mr Brittain?

Driving up to the house, Thelma wondered again about possible reasons for her summons. Mike Brittain had been as vague about why he wanted to talk as he had been about directions. All he'd really said was that he wanted to speak to her in her capacity as school governor. He'd be grateful if she would call in at her earliest convenience and oh, perhaps *not* mention this to his wife – something that after that last phone call, Thelma was only too happy to concur with. There had been, she thought – in the airy, well-spoken words – something of the air of a summons; an assumption that Thelma would come over as soon as possible and that the sixty-mile round trip was a trifling detail that hadn't occurred to him.

There were a fair number of vehicles parked up in front of Badger's Fold (no caramel-coloured sports car, Thelma noted with considerable relief). Aside from a hefty pair of four by fours, there was a sleek, expensive-looking black car and beyond that, a grubby white van, obviously belonging to the workman, and it was behind this that Thelma squeezed the mussel-blue Corsair. Looking at the general state of the driveway she wondered whether walking boots might not have been a better bet than her regular M&S flats.

She failed to see the young man with the wheelbarrow until he was more or less upon her, rounding the corner of a stack of breeze blocks. Similarly, he didn't see her, certainly not in time to stop the muddy wheelbarrow bumping into her shins and running onto her left foot.

'Sorry!' The word was almost a primal bark; he tore out his earphones from under his curly black hair and stuffed them into the pocket of the hi-vis jacket. 'I so sorry!' His voice was accented by shock, but even so Thelma caught the distinct tenor of some European accent.

'I'm fine,' she said, more to counter his obvious shock and fear than anything else. Those tights were way past their best anyway, and it had really only been a small knock to her left shin. She looked more closely at the young face, the stubble, the wide brown eyes, the curly hair under the battered helmet. 'Please don't worry.' She smiled reassuringly; she could smell cigarettes and sweat. Why was he looking so alarmed?

'Everything okay here?'

Thelma looked round at the man who confronted them; both his hi-vis jacket and helmet were far superior in quality and cleanliness to the young man's, as were the designer jeans and sweatshirt visible underneath. He regarded Thelma with implausibly blue eyes set in a broad, deeply tanned face. The combination of face and chunky gold chain round the thickset neck put her in mind of some breed of pit bull.

If the young man had looked nervous of Thelma, this was as nothing compared with his reaction to the man now facing them. He stood stock-still, head lowered, arms dangling by his sides, staring fixedly at the ground.

'Everything's fine,' said Thelma pleasantly. 'We just had a slight collision.' Surely this couldn't be Mr Brittain? She did not like the arrogant way he was staring at her one bit and sent up a quick prayer for protection and guidance, fingers instinctively feeling for the rape alarm in her left pocket.

'Dimitri, you get on,' commanded the man. 'Axl needs the blocks supporting.' Without looking up, Dimitri reversed the barrow back round the breeze blocks and was gone. The man turned to Thelma who caught a distinct whiff of some overpowering and no doubt expensive aftershave; on reflection, she rather preferred the young man's cigarette and body odour. 'Can I help you, love?' he asked. His tone, whilst reasonable enough, held a distinct element of challenge.

Thelma paused deliberately before answering. She usually found one of the many plus points of being a lady of a certain age was not engendering the same levels of suspicion and confrontation that a younger person or a man would. Having said that, there was something both confrontational and suspicious in the way the man regarded her.

'Mr Brittain?' she asked, smiling pleasantly.

'Who wants him?' The man was, she noted, standing directly between her and the house.

'I do.'

'Why?'

'That's between me and him,' she said, her smile not slipping. If he'd been someone in her class, she'd have had him sat right at the front where she could keep a strict eye on him.

'He's busy right now.'

'I'll let him tell me that.' She kept her voice light but now her fingers were curling round the rape alarm. The words *resist the devil and he will flee* came into her mind, but this devil was showing no particular signs of fleeing anywhere.

'Steve?' The call came from an elderly man who had appeared, framed in the front door, wearing a thick, almost gaudy multi-coloured cardigan.

Steve.

At that moment several pennies dropped with what Thelma

thought must have been an audible clatter. The builders. That expensive black car with the personalized number plates . . . Steve . . .

'Steve Hewson,' said Thelma, and instantly regretted her words. The effect on Steve Hewson was marked; a tensing, a confirmation of suspicion, his hackles so to speak rising like the pit bull he reminded her of.

'Okay, missus,' he said. 'Just who are you and what do you want?'

'Is everything all right?' The elderly man — presumably Mike Brittain — was approaching them, picking his way through the puddles in his slippers. He was a good bit older than his wife, which came as something of a shock to Thelma.

'Mr Brittain?' said Thelma. 'You asked me here to see you.' The gentle emphasis inflected in the sentence was her equivalent of sticking two fingers up at Mr Hewson.

'So, you found us all right,' he said genially though he didn't seem particularly bothered whether she'd found Badger's Fold or not. 'This lady's come to see me, Steve.'

'Why's that then?' Steve sounded less aggressive, but only slightly.

'There was something I wanted to talk to her about. The arts centre.' Mike Brittain still had the same easy, vague tone. 'And she was good enough to say she'd come over.'

Thelma mustered up her bounciest, most jovial tone, the one she'd used to such strong effect as Mrs Malaprop in that very successful production of *The Rivals*, a few years ago.

'I hope this is not an inconvenient time, Mr Brittain!'

Steve Hewson looked as though he'd like to question her further, but his phone bleeped and as he turned away to look at it, Mike gestured Thelma to follow him to the house. Crossing the gravel sweep, Thelma's mind was racing — why had Mike told such a deliberate lie? And he was showing no signs whatsoever of referring to the untruth . . . Of course, from her point of view it worked out very well . . . But even so . . . And then there was the way Steve Hewson had spoken to Mike . . . Surely that wasn't how builders generally spoke to their employers?

At the front door Thelma turned to see he was talking to one of the workmen. Even at this distance the subservient worker–boss relationship was glaringly apparent. No, not a nice man at all.

'Good fellow, Steve.' Mike obviously felt the man's behaviour needed some sort of explanation. 'Can be a bit suspicious of strangers, but that's as well, stuck out here. You get all sorts turning up. But he's a heart of gold.'

Thelma smiled politely, thinking of all the nasty pieces of work she'd encountered over the years who'd been described in exactly that way.

'He's building us a hot tub room,' said Mike. 'Hence all the rumpus.'

As Thelma followed him through the house, she noted he had a vague, disinterested air about him, rather like that of an elderly hotel porter. He must be, Thelma thought, at least in his seventies, a good bit older than his wife. Looking at the stooped figure, the thin hair and uncertain gait, she suspected maybe a bit more than that. She felt a certain amount of surprise, realizing that she'd subconsciously pictured Mr Brittain to be like every other element of Kayleigh's life – her car, her office, her outfits – in pristine condition.

That there was money in the Brittain household was obvious as they progressed through the house, from Mike's cardigan (Valentino?) to the designer rugs, antique furniture and opulent drapes. On a credence cupboard they passed stood a vast designer bouquet of avalanche roses and lilies, a bright glow of colour in the dim room. Yet for all the money that was evident, Badger's Fold didn't feel like a homely house. Everything was too poised, too polished, too . . . perfect. One could never imagine muddy boots tumbled around that oak front door, nor chip butties being eaten off the gate-legged table. The vast plum-coloured sofa did not look like the sort of place one could curl up with the *Yorkshire Post* crossword. On the walls the pictures were the blandest of bland local landscapes – Bolton Abbey, Haworth Parsonage, Linton Falls. Thelma remembered that wild seascape on the wall of Kayleigh's office back in the summer; who was the deciding voice on the décor and furnishings at Badger's Fold?

'Through here,' said Mike. 'We'll go into my man cave.'

This did feel more lived in. The walls were lined with shelves of books, prominent among these were several binders of magazines, plum and royal blue, the titles stamped in gold: *The World at War*, *Modern Conflict*, *Falklands and Beyond*. Also on the shelves and walls were numerous framed photographs, mainly of a blonde woman who Thelma thought was Kayleigh but whom she couldn't completely identify with only her driving glasses on. The oak desk was comfortably littered with torn-open envelopes and mail, a half-finished *Daily Telegraph* crossword and a cup of coffee (also half-finished). She noted a number of the letters were bills, which looked rather like they were headed red.

'I expect you'd like some coffee,' he said vaguely. 'I can get Yana to rustle some up if you want.' Thelma smiled and said that would be lovely, thank you. As it happened, she didn't really want a drink, not with the prospect of a thirty-mile drive back ahead of her, but what she did want was a closer uninterrupted look at those photographs on the bookshelves.

A closer look confirmed her suspicion; the photos were of Kayleigh, a younger, blonde Kayleigh, hair falling free and straight and uncoloured. Judging by the vivid sunsets and beach clothing, they were taken somewhere considerably warmer than Badger's Fold. The time span of them and the array of different outfits argued somewhere lived rather than visited. Outside the door she could hear Mike talking to a woman who spoke with broken, accented English, obviously Yana, so surreptitiously she took out her phone and photographed some of the images; why, she wasn't exactly sure, beyond some instinct they might come in handy.

And here was a picture of Mike, a younger Mike, hair thicker with more colour, arms tight around Kayleigh, smiling lovingly at her, whilst she smiled a brilliant smile out at the world. Behind them on a wall of spangly silver streamers could be read a notice: 'Happy New Year 2005 Emirates Golf Association'.

'Dubai.' She hadn't heard Mike return to the room; thank goodness her phone was now safely stowed back in her pocket. 'That's where we met. She was teaching out there.' There was a wistful, soft tone in his voice that Thelma had not heard before. *He really loves her,* she thought, and for some reason the revelation gave her a sad pang. As they sat down, she noticed for the first time a slight but definite tremor in his left hand.

'Thank you for coming,' he said.

'May I just clarify something,' said Thelma. 'Your wife is unaware of my visit?'

'That's correct.' Mike looked around, suddenly uneasy, even slightly sly. 'I didn't think it necessary to tell her. She's some sort of meeting after school tonight so she shouldn't be home until gone six.'

Thelma nodded, reassured that there was absolutely no prospect of the caramel-coloured sports car putting in a sudden appearance.

Mike sat at the desk smoothing and re-smoothing a red credit card bill. 'I don't know if you know anything about what's been happening at the school. Kayleigh has mentioned you once or twice and I rather get the impression she confides in you.'

'She's told me a certain amount,' said Thelma. She wondered if Kayleigh had mentioned her recent displeasure with her. She felt acutely aware of the many, many ways this conversation could blow up in her face.

'The letters?' said Mike. 'The scratch on her car?' Thelma nodded. 'And now this latest letter to her?'

'She read it to me over the phone,' she said.

Mike blew his cheeks out and shook his head uncomprehendingly. 'It beggars belief,' he said. 'I want her to go to the police, but she won't hear of it.' There was something defeated in his voice that gave Thelma an indication of the power dynamics in the Brittain household. 'I'm worried,' he said, and Thelma didn't doubt his words.

'It is a very worrying situation,' said Thelma. She couldn't quite think of what else to say. She realized he was looking directly at her.

'Do you have any indication who could be doing this?' he asked.

Thelma shook her head decisively. No way was she going to share such thoughts as she had. 'I don't think anyone does,' she said. 'It's causing a lot of pain and distress to a lot of people.'

Mike nodded distractedly. It was obvious that any pain and distress caused to others was not something he was overly concerned with.

'I'm just worried, Mrs Cooper. What if this lunatic decides to have a go at Kayleigh?'

'There are always people around at school,' she said. 'She never need be alone.'

As she spoke, Bunty Carter's words came into her mind: *Someone's going to get hurt.* What if someone really were out to harm Kayleigh?

Mike nodded, unconvinced. He carefully folded the credit card bill as if it was an exercise in origami.

'I wonder . . .' asked Thelma. 'I hope you don't mind me asking. Did your wife mention the school summer fayre?'

He looked up puzzled. 'The what fayre?'

'The school summer fayre. This would have been back in July, towards the end of term. It was held one evening after school.'

'I don't think so.' He frowned. 'Why?'

'I just wonder if she mentioned anything that happened that night.'

'What sort of thing?'

'I don't know. Something that might have upset her or annoyed her maybe? I realize this might seem an odd question to ask – but it's something I've been wondering.'

'Do you think it could be connected with these letters?'

'I honestly don't know. It could well be nothing.' Thelma tried to speak casually; she did not want to have to mention Kayleigh's shocked expression that night if she could help it.

He considered. 'No,' he said finally. 'All that happened in July, I seem to remember, was she insisted we had a meeting with our finance chappy. I thought,' he said, 'she was thinking of stopping work, but no such luck.'

'You want her to stop?'

Mike nodded. 'I do.'

'Being a head teacher, or working in Thirsk?'

'Both,' he said. 'I certainly want her out of that place.'

'And it is quite a drive,' agreed Thelma.

He looked at her uncomprehendingly. 'Is it?' he said. 'It's more she doesn't need to work all the hours God sends. Not if we pull our horns and downsize. There'd be my pension, and her pension, plus one or two bits and pieces we've got invested.' Thelma thought about the red bills and the hot tub room, wondering just how far those horns would need to be pulled in.

'What do you want me to do?' she asked.

'Keep an eye on her,' he said. 'Maybe talk to her if you get the chance. See if you can get her to talk to the police. Or better still, leave. Be a friend to her.' He was completely unaware he was talking to Thelma in exactly the same tone of casual command as he'd just used with Yana.

It was some twenty minutes later when Mike Brittain saw her to the front door.

'Perhaps it would be better if you didn't say we had spoken,' he said.

Thelma nodded whilst mentally shouting 'you bet'.

As she put her coat on, he looked out of the glassed front entrance, something rather sad in his eyes. He reminded her of a lion she'd once seen sadly pacing an enclosure at Flamingo Land. 'I'd be quite happy to downsize,' he said. 'One does rather rattle round this house. But Kayleigh does love it.'

'Home is very important,' she said, thinking with affection of 32 College Gardens.

'Look out for my wife.' Suddenly the voice was low and urgent. 'I really am most dreadfully worried about her.'

Outside the workmen had knocked off for lunch. To Thelma's relief there was no sign of the expensive black car. The men were sat in the back of the white van rather glumly devouring shop-bought sandwiches; Thelma noticed on each discarded packet were those bright yellow reduction stickers. She wondered just who these European workmen were and why it was they were so horribly scared of Steve Hewson.

CHAPTER TWENTY-FOUR

Filial opinion is given on career choices, and a surprise visit brings no peace of mind.

At the same time Thelma was setting off back from Badger's Fold, Pat was sitting at her kitchen table talking on the phone. In front of her was an open laptop; on an open page of her mindfulness journal was written: *Biomass boiler – RNLI?* – and nothing else. Despite extensive trawls on Google, she'd NOT found anything that she could readily make head or tail of. She really needed to talk to Matt Barley (and indeed had a text ready to send to him), but thoughts of how upset Linda apparently was stopped her. So instead, she was doing what she usually did when faced with something she didn't quite understand – ringing her youngest son Liam.

'Like RNLI,' she said above the whine of the washing machine. Once again Andrew's pants, plus two shirts and a pair of socks that had been found lying on the utility room floor.

'That's lifeboats,' said Liam.

'I said *like* RNLI, *not* RNLI.' She spoke loudly and clearly with a hint of exasperation. 'It's to do with biomass boilers.'

'Mother, I'm unfamiliar – not deaf.' He was using his patient, sardonic voice, which meant that life was going well for him in some way. Perhaps it was this Bern she'd heard him mention a couple of times recently?

'I thought you might know about it,' she said.

'Why would that be?'

'Because you're doing engineering,' she said patiently. There was a silence. 'And it's to do with boilers, and boilers are engineering.'

'We haven't done boilers yet,' said Liam. 'That's next week. We've only done tin-openers and staplers so far.'

'Oh, ha ha.' Yes, her son was definitely in a good mood.

'Anyway, what's with all this interest in biomass boilers?'

She wondered if she could face unravelling the whole Baldersby-Joe Public-Steve Hewson saga at this particular moment. On the whole she felt not. At that moment the back door opened, and Andrew marched in with an air of casual confidence. He smiled amiably and kicked his work boots off, leaving them just anyhow by the back door.

'I'm just on the phone to your brother,' said Pat brightly. Over-brightly.

Andrew nodded and ambled over to the bread bin.

'Hey, bro,' said Liam down the phone.

'Liam says "hi",' said Pat. 'I'm just going through to the living room.'

'So how are things?' said Liam as she settled onto the sofa.

'Fine.'

'Fine, are they? Things are *fine*. Oh dear, oh dear.'

'What are you talking about?'

'On the Pat Taylor Shittometer "fine" ranks just a smidge below "bloody awful".'

'I haven't a clue what you're going on about,' she said.

'So, is throwing our Andrew's pants at his head what you do when things are fine?'

She felt her cheeks warming. 'He's rung you, has he?'

'It was Dad actually. And then I rang Andrew.'

She paused, not quite sure what to say. *Rod had rung Liam.* That was a first.

'Dad still planning to retire, I take it?' asked Liam.

'He pretty much already has.' The words slipped out, hotter and more dismissive than she'd intended.

'And Boy Wonder still planning on dropping out from Loughborough.'

'You'd have to ask him,' said Pat. 'They seem to talk to you more than they do to me. I'm obviously the last one to find out anything that goes on in this house.'

'Mother,' said Liam in that way sons have of speaking to their mothers. 'No way is our Andrew ever going to be a forensic scientist.'

'He certainly won't be if he jacks it all in,' said Pat tartly.

'You've seen how he is when Larson gets sick. How on earth d'you think he'd be with a bona fide corpse?' Pat had often wondered this herself, but it would not do to concede this fact at this point in the conversation. 'He just doesn't seem to have thought this through,' she said lamely.

'Mother, have you not been looking at his Facebook page? He's been loving working with Dougie.'

Pat fell silent. The truth was she'd skipped over all this because it had irritated her. There was a pause. Then Liam said: 'It's Dad retiring, isn't it?'

Another pause.

'I just don't know if he's ready for it.' The words sounded lame even to herself.

'He obviously thinks he is.'

'It's just – if he's here all day—'

'—in his own home, yes?'

'He'll get in the way.' There, she'd said it. Some of it.

246

'Then tell him to get out of the way.' Another silence. *If only it were that simple.*

'The thing is, Mother,' said Liam, 'you can't have the poor old bugger going on working till he drops just so you can have the kitchen to yourself.'

'I don't mean that at all,' she said protestingly. Though of course she did. Partly.

'Is that all there is?'

'I just need to get used to the idea.' Not even to Liam could she face giving voice to that other, lurking blackness.

When she returned to the kitchen, Andrew was peaceably chewing a sandwich and staring into space. From by his feet Larson regarded him with all the concentration of someone watching the Wimbledon semi-finals. On the side were two dirty knives, the sunflower spread, a loaf, the bread board and a packet of Farm Shop ham trim that she'd mentally earmarked for a carbonara.

'Have you seen your father?' She crossed to the side and pointedly began clearing away the detritus.

'No.' Andrew seemed to realize slightly more was required and frowned. 'I think he said something about going down the golf range.'

'Did he,' said Pat grimly. The news gave her an overwhelming sense of bleakness. This was how life was going to be. She checked herself – Liam was right, of course he should be able to retire . . . Only . . .

As she shut the fridge, she desperately tried to think of something to say to her middle son. Maybe a question about his morning or if he was eating with them tonight. But all she wanted to do was scream: *Why can't you clear up after yourself?* That and fling those wet pants at his head.

Suddenly she realized Andrew was looking at her, an expression

247

she recognized. He had something to say to her. She watched him, feeling a sudden flutter of panic. Had he guessed how she felt?

What he did say was the last thing she expected.

'RHI payments,' he said.

'What about them?'

'On your notepad. I presume you mean RHI. Standing for Renewable Heat Incentive.' He shook his head. 'A right old scam if ever there was one.'

Later on, as dusk was falling, Liz was driving into the new estate where Sam Bowker lived, a pristine collection of small houses to the south of the town arranged in looping closes, avenues and ways. The sign at the entrance to Herriot's Meet stridently proclaimed a stunning development of luxury houses! Looking at the small, somehow forlorn dwellings Liz briefly wondered whether any of its residents ever thought, *How luxurious! How stunning!* Somehow, she thought not. Her phone gave an apologetic little buzz. Another missed call from Jan. And another message. *RING ME.* With a sigh, she turned the phone off. She did not want to speak to Jan Starke.

Walking up the paved path to number 18 Pumphrey Gardens, she felt not a little apprehension, so much so she found herself paused and indecisive at the plastic-wood front door. *What to say? I had a sort of dream about you and was wondering if you were all right?* Clutched in her hands was a box of flapjacks, one of the few things she could successfully bake and at times like this her all-purpose excuse for dropping in on someone.

As the melodic chimes faded, she found herself hoping that Sam would appear, relaxed and smiling as he'd been in school, and that in five minutes she'd be driving off and reflecting on how foolish she had been.

It wasn't Sam who opened the door.

The pale, sulky-looking girl with the baby scooped in her arms looked tired, her lank straight hair scrunched back in a lifeless ponytail. She had, Liz noticed, the loveliest, clear hazel eyes.

'Yes,' she said. Her voice wasn't welcoming and neither was it hostile, it was merely flat. The baby, who had obviously been crying, stared at Liz, obviously making up its mind whether to start again. Liz smiled brightly and brandished the flapjacks, which the girl and the baby both regarded uncomprehendingly. 'I'm so sorry to bother you,' said Liz. 'I wonder, could I have a quick word with Sam d'you think?'

'Sam? He's still at work.' A slightly guarded tone matched the wary look. On a corner of the muted flat-screen, Liz could tell it was approaching seven o'clock.

'I'm so sorry,' said Liz again. 'I thought he'd be back by now.'

There must have been a note of something in her voice because the girl blurted out, somewhat unguardedly, 'He tries to get all his work done at school. So he doesn't have to work at evenings and weekends.'

Liz nodded. 'Could you please tell him Liz Newsome called?'

'Mrs Newsome who used to teach him? Who comes into school?' Something dropped from the girl's face and a range of emotions flitted awkwardly across: relief, worry, a kind of welcome. 'He's talked about you.'

'Good things I hope.'

The girl nodded. 'I'm Macy – Sam's wife. Would you like to come in? It's a bit of a tip.' She looked worriedly over her shoulder at the living room, which seemed tidy enough aside from the detritus of infancy.

'I won't bother you,' said Liz. 'I just came to see Sam – and of course to bring you this.' Once again, she brandished the Tupperware box, which once again they all looked at, the baby

249

with the suspicion of a tremor in its bottom lip. 'I only wanted a very quick word with him.'

'I wish you would. Talk to him.' Despite the gruffness of the words, there was a real note of worry. 'Is he . . . is he, do you know, in some trouble at school?'

'I really don't know,' said Liz. 'Do you think he is?'

'I don't know – that's just it.' The words blurted out, sad and urgent. 'Normally he talks to me when there's something bothering him.'

'And you think there's something bothering him?'

At this point the baby had obviously decided enough was enough; her face screwed up and she emitted a startlingly loud bellow.

'Look, I can see you've got your hands full,' said Liz. 'I'll let you get on.'

'Can I give him a message?' asked Macy, fruitlessly jogging the wailing infant.

'No.' She was about to smile and turn away, say she'd see him in school – only something stopped her. 'You could give him this,' she said, fishing in her bag. She produced one of the last of her cards she'd had printed at that machine at the outlet mall some time ago.

Macy looked at it blankly.

'Tell him if he ever wants to talk . . . just to call me,' said Liz.

The girl nodded, took the card and the baby wailed helplessly and hopelessly.

So young, was Liz's thought as she walked back to her car, and it wasn't the baby she was thinking of.

Driving away down something or other close, she reflected it was pretty much five minutes later, but she had none of the feelings of reassurance about Sam she had been hoping for.

★

Thelma was sitting in her favourite wing chair by the gas fire, tired after her sixty-mile round trip, too tired to do anything but let the thoughts drift round her mind. Mike's words kept playing in her mind:

Keep an eye on her for me . . .

Outside she could hear the unsettling noise of the autumn wind rising in the poplar trees by the recreation ground. *The autumn winds bestir the trees and make the sound of distant seas . . .* For some reason that poem had kept coming into her mind lately.

On the coffee table she could see the folder of pamphlets she'd given Teddy. She knew for a fact he'd not yet looked at them. Indeed, they had somehow acquired the air of certain Christmas presents Teddy received – that coffee table book about the Cairngorms, the collection of *Giles* cartoons – items she knew would at some point find their way, unread, to the Baldersby St James book fair.

Why hadn't he looked at them? Could he not face the prospect of college closing? Or was it that at sixty-two, the end of his job would signify an end to his working life?

Another gust of wind made the curtains billow out slightly. Snaffles, body tense, eyes wide in distrust, regarded them from under the coffee table. She knew exactly how he was feeling.

She reached for her Grandma Spilman's psalter as she often did at times of stress, let the soft-backed red book open where it would. It fell open at Paul's letter to Timothy.

The love of money is the root of all kinds of evil.

Her first reaction was a pang of disappointment. The phrase seemed to have no direct bearing on all her current upset . . . yet at the same time it felt somehow relevant. Of course, there was money involved with both those educational organizations, Lodestone and Baht'at – lots of money . . . the expensive suits, those laptops and iPads, Kayleigh Brittain's caramel-coloured sports car. Education and money seemed to go hand in hand these days. What was it Pat's friend had said? Education run as a business.

When her phone rang, she felt sure it must be Kayleigh Brittain ringing to tell her of yet another anonymous letter, but it wasn't.

'Thelma.' The voice was slightly too loud, slightly too stilted; Thelma recognized that Josie Gribben was one of those people who hated using the phone. 'Thelma, I'm ringing to see if you've heard the news.'

Thelma's thoughts went back to their last conversation, the night of that fateful governors' meeting. 'You mean the possibility of the college closing?' she said. 'Yes I have.'

'I mean,' said Josie, 'the nasty little plot *behind* the college closing.'

Thelma frowned. 'What nasty little plot?' she said.

'Thelma!' There was grim relish in Josie's voice. 'It's time to man the barricades!'

CHAPTER TWENTY-FIVE

*Business with an envelope is witnessed
and there's a shocking discovery beginning
with 's' in the Nursery playground.*

As the rain started to fall from darkening teatime skies, the lights
of St Barnabus's shone out yellow, oblong, reassuring, even though
it had now gone six. As she parked up, Pat noted the drops beginning to speck and spatter on the windscreen; should she have
brought her umbrella? She checked in her bag for her notebook
and tried to remember again everything that Andrew had said to
her that morning about RHI payments.

'It's a grant given out by the government to try and encourage
more people to use biomass boilers.' Her son had spoken in measured, careful tones, a slight frown on his face. Unlike Liam there
was no sarcasm, no humour – just plain, straightforward facts. 'The
intention is sound – the more renewable energy you use, the more
money you get. The only problem is, like all these things, it's open
to the rip-off merchants. Basically, the more boilers you have, the
more money you get from the government, whether you actually
need the boilers or not.'

She wasn't sure if any of this related to Steve Hewson or the
boiler at St Barnabus's. Surely the school needed the boiler? In

which case how could there be any ripping off going on? Eventually, plucking up courage, and having reached another dead end, she'd sent a text to Matt: *COUPLE OF BOILER QUESTIONS IF THAT'S OK*. The reply had come whizzing back almost immediately: *COME TO BOILER HOUSE AFT 5 WILL XPLAIN*. Which was why she was here now, cold, needing a wee, with two bottles of pink Prosecco on the back seat. Pat noted there were only a few vehicles left in the staff car park, including Matt's pick-up (MOO 376G).

No sign of the caramel-coloured sports car, thank goodness.

Walking round the side of the school to where the boiler house still presumably was, Pat had an impulse to duck beneath the classroom windows. Even though she was there by Matt's invitation, after the trouble in the office she very much didn't want to be seen by anyone. She ducked under another lit window, checking if anyone was in the room – and with something of a start she realized it was her old classroom.

It looked different, of course it did . . . different paint, new furniture . . . everything arranged differently. She paused, momentarily back in the past, remembering how the morning sun would slant in across the carpet when she'd walk in first thing laden with bags and holding a coffee.

Times change, she told herself firmly. *Times certainly change.*

She was about to move on when the door opened, stopping her in her tracks. Sam walked into the room; a sheaf of photocopying clutched to his chest. As she watched, he placed it carefully down on a table and started sorting it, retrieving a single sheet of paper. This he took and sitting down read carefully. There was something weary and sad about the way he did this, with a fixed, almost glassy stare for the longest time . . . Even from this distance Pat guessed that whatever it was that was written on the sheet, it was something he was not happy about.

Could it be he'd received another anonymous letter? But even as she watched him, he took the sheet – *and put it inside a plain white envelope.* This he sealed and put carefully in his bag, suddenly glancing at the door as if he was afraid of being seen.

Surely not . . . *Surely not Sam . . .*

Pat realized that she was saying the words aloud to herself as she crossed the darkening Nursery playground, hunched against the weather as she stepped over the various items of play equipment.

Sam? She remembered that driven little boy talking about tadpoles in the class assembly.

Her foot caught the plastic playhouse with a hollow thump, which made her start. *Come on, Patricia! Focus!* In the dim light she could make out a notice, presumably written by the Nursery teacher: *Phonics Hunt! How many objects can you find beginning with S?*

S for slide! S for sticks!

S for slightly nervous retired teacher.

The boiler-house door was ajar. 'Matt?' She pushed it open and put her head round. The space was dark – dark, hot and smelling so powerfully of sawdust that she took a step back. 'Matt?' But no reply, only a deep, almost sinister, thrumming.

She opened the door wider and looked in. In the dim light the biomass boiler was a dark, almost menacing shape. On the side was an illuminated panel. Squinting she could just read the words: *80% burn.* Eighty per cent? Did that mean the thing was on and heating the school? At gone six thirty at night?

She turned on the torch on her phone. Motes of dust swirled like the rain outside. She could feel them catching at the back of her throat.

'Matt?' She wasn't late, was she? Maybe he'd been called away? Maybe he was in school doing something?

To the side of the space was a wooden door, an open panel in the door made a dark space. Suddenly nervous, she looked through; the space was filled with what presumably were wood pellets, shifting, falling, like cake mix in a food processor.

All of a sudden, she realized she was feeling sick. Sick, dizzy, strangely light-headed. Stepping back, she felt herself stumbling slightly, catching the side of the door as she fell out into the playground. Hands on her knees, she took several lungfuls of cool evening air. What was the matter with her? And where was Matt?

She took her phone and dialled his number – and heard the familiar klaxon sounding not too far away, somewhere across the yard. Following the noise took her back to the Nursery playground. Underneath one of the rainbow notices she realized what she'd taken to be playground equipment was in fact a huddled shape . . . The torch on her phone picked out a pair of boots sticking straight up at the stormy skies. With an oddly detached, unreal feeling she brought the beam up to the grey face, the eyes half shut, the dribble of vomit on the chin.

S for site manager.

As the evening wore on, the weather rapidly deteriorated into what Derek called 'a full-blown wild one'; rain smattering violently on windows, wind breathing hollowly down chimneys, nudging wheelie bins and wrenching the trees from side to side. From time to time Liz's garden gate – which was in need of a new latch – would give an irritating clatter and she would look worriedly towards the window. Although the silence between Liz and Derek was still largely there, after a few days' chilly politeness where he'd spent a lot of time in his study with running magazines, tonight it had mellowed into something rather more companionable than frosty.

Once again, they were catching up with *Bake Off*; someone's breaded something was just collapsing spectacularly as it was taken out of the oven, when the shrill, unsettling ring came from the next room. 'That's your phone,' said Derek, pausing the scene of culinary carnage. Frostiness was suddenly back in full force.

'If it's Jan Starke,' said Liz, 'I'm not answering.'

'You better see,' said Derek reasonably. 'It might be something important.'

It was an unknown caller. Normally, well versed in horror stories of scams, Liz never took such calls, but like Thelma earlier in the week, some deeper instinct told her this was not a call to ignore.

The voice was abrupt, rude even. 'Have you seen Sam?'

'I'm sorry?' She sat at the kitchen table. Out here the wind and rain were even more noticeable.

'I don't know where Sam is,' said the voice, and a series of images came into Liz's mind: a cluttered room, an angry baby, a tired young girl.

'Macy,' she said.

'He's not picking up and he's never normally this late and I don't know where he could be.' The words blurted out in an awkward rush.

Liz looked round with some idea of finding a pen and paper, to feel like she had some sort of control more than anything as the words continued slamming out on a tide of growing panic. Sam hadn't come home – he was never normally late; his phone was going straight to voicemail . . . She'd tried the police and when she finally got through to someone all they basically said was to wait a bit and see.

Listening – and repeating the facts – Liz felt her own growing fears. To the facts she was hearing she added facts of her own – the uneasy darting eyes, the bitten nails, that awful sore mark on his neck where his shirt had rubbed. What on earth should she do? Ring the police? But then Macy had already done that.

She realized that Derek was standing in the kitchen doorway watching her. Any thoughts of playing down what was going on had vanished at Macy's first panicked words. 'It's Sam Bowker's wife,' she said. 'She doesn't know where he is.'

Even as she spoke, Derek was reaching for the car keys on the hook by the back door. 'Tell her we're coming round,' he said.

Driving across town, through the full-blown wild one to Sam and Macy's, Liz told Derek almost everything: about the letters, about school, about Becky and Jan, Nicole and Kayleigh Brittain and Sam. Only her suspicions about Jan she kept to herself because, after all, they were only suspicions and things were complicated enough as it was. Sometimes telling Derek things was difficult, owing to his insistence on understanding every single fact and nuance; sometimes it was easier as he let the facts pour out and made what sense of them he could. This was one of the easier times – he only interrupted Liz twice, once as he negotiated the mini roundabout by Tesco's, and once as he pulled round an awkwardly placed skip in Bridge Street.

Flinging open the front door, sleeping baby in her arms, Macy was a wide-eyed, frightened child. 'What shall I do if he's dead?' she said, her eyes staring into a bleak series of scenarios. Liz gently took the baby from her, and equally gently Derek sat her down on the sofa. Watching her, Liz felt her own panic rising. She made an effort to steady her breathing and not cling too tightly to the sleeping child, though she was sure the pounding of her heart must be disturbing the infant she held.

Derek was calm. That was the one thing everyone said about him: Derek Newsome kept his head in a crisis. Liz often thought that was because he was so busy processing the various facts of whatever it was he had to deal with – he had no other choice. Tonight, he was wonderful. He sat next to Macy on the sofa, and with a steadying hand on her shoulder made her talk the whole thing through, thread to needle.

Sam had been worried recently, as Macy had said to Liz. (Was it only the day before?) In the last twenty-four hours this had got much worse. The previous night he hadn't come to bed till gone three, and Macy was sure he'd been crying – though he vehemently denied the fact. He'd left as usual that morning but hadn't texted throughout the day as was his usual practice, not even to respond to a picture Macy had sent of Robyn, finally and blissfully asleep for an afternoon nap.

He was often late home these days, so it wasn't until gone six thirty that she'd tried texting him again. There then began a periodic series of texts which Macy showed them, seeing their progress from chirpy (*WHEN U HOME? CURRY?*) to panicked (*PLS PLS RING NOW*). Liz felt a pang to her heart and found herself again having to stop clinging too tightly to the baby.

The police – when Macy had finally got through – had said all sorts of unhelpful things, suggesting pubs or friends (both seldom visited by Sam), family (Spain, Goole and Weston-Super-Mare), or perhaps, and she needed to consider this, another woman (again, a total non-starter). Each prompt and question from Derek elicited the same panicky response, the same abrupt, blurting tones; periodically she'd lose the thread of what she was saying and convulsively wring her hands and insist that Sam must be dead.

Liz held the warm bundle in the pale-yellow cardigan and inhaled the sweet, life-affirming smell of warm baby and fabric conditioner. It calmed her and stilled her own cries of panic. What could have happened?

Looking at the lonely girl – a slight insubstantial figure on the big, grey sofa – Liz reflected bleakly that at this moment the room should have been full of concerned family and neighbours. But these days families were more often than not dispersed to the ends of texts and Facebook posts, and Stunning and Desirable developments like Herriot's Close didn't seem to lend themselves to community as such.

'Okay,' said Derek calmly, after what felt like ages but could only have been ten minutes. 'We better go and have a look for this husband of yours.'

'Where?' Both Liz and Macy spoke at the same time. Pubs? Not at all likely, Liz thought. And school would surely be locked up at this hour?

'There's one or two places I can think of,' said Derek easily. 'I'll have a look there, and if there's no joy, I'll drive into Northallerton and have a word with the police myself.' He spoke as casually as if he was planning a trip to pick up some fish and chips. Macy half rose, uncertain.

'The best thing you can do,' said Derek, 'is stay here in case he comes back.'

'Besides,' said Liz, 'there's a little lady here who needs you.' She gently handed over the baby who stirred slightly and yawned, a tiny, gummed-up but infinitely comforting noise.

CHAPTER TWENTY-SIX

*At the Friarage Hospital an invitation is issued,
and there are panicked moments at the allotment.*

When Matt came fully round in the Friarage Hospital and gained
some sense of consciousness, he found the whole thing intensely
embarrassing. Sitting up on the trolley in the cubicle at the Friarage
A&E, starkers apart from a hospital gown, his face was redder than
ever as he cracked a series of increasingly feeble jokes.

'Good hotel this,' he said to the nurse checking his temperature.
'What d'you have to do to get room service?' The nurse smiled
distractedly.

'You behave and let him get on with his job,' said Pat from her
chair.

'You might as well get off,' said Matt to her. 'No need for two
of us to be sitting round wasting us time.'

'Charming,' said Pat. 'You might give a girl five minutes. You're
my first body. Anyway, I need to recover from that ambulance
ride.' She spoke cheerfully enough but the truth was she was still
feeling very shaky inside . . . Those awful moments simultaneously
trying to take his pulse, turn him into the recovery position and
phone 999 . . . and that endless wait in the dark, stormy playground,
trying to shield him from the worst of the rain, Matt covered

inadequately in her coat, her shivering and wet, straining to hear the sound of sirens . . . She still felt damp now and dreaded to think what her hair must look like.

'There's nowt wrong with me,' said Matt.

'Other than carbon monoxide poisoning,' said Pat. 'I felt dodgy enough and I was only in there for a few seconds.'

'Aye, well.' He had the grace to look a bit abashed.

'And it was all caused by wood pellets?'

'It wouldn't be a problem if the place was well ventilated, but it was all put in in a hurry.'

'And you've mentioned this to Steve Hewson before?'

'Only about six million times. He always reckons he's onto it, but somehow nothing gets done.'

Pat nodded, remembering Victoria saying much the same thing.

'So why was the boiler on eighty per cent?' she asked.

Matt shrugged wearily. 'Sometimes it comes full on. Steve Hewson reckons it has to, in order to burn the pellets properly – ash burn he calls it – stops the ash building up, and the boiler going out.'

'And that's when you go and turn it down?'

'I'm forbidden to touch the bloody thing. But if it's come full on, yeah, I sometimes go and turn it down.' He coughed, a nasty hacking rattle, and lay back against the pillow. Pat remembered how under the weather he'd looked that day at the farm. He didn't look much better now, but then the guy had just passed out. She gave herself a mental shake. What was she doing asking him questions when he'd nearly died?

'You dozy sod!' At that moment Linda's strident voice cut across Pat's thoughts and indeed across the whole busy atmosphere of A&E. She walked into the cubicle, face flushed, tears spilling down her cheeks to Matt's obvious horror.

'Give over, woman,' he said. 'There's nothing wrong with me.'

'Which is why you passed out in the playground, I suppose.'

'The doctors seem to think he's okay,' said Pat soothingly. 'He wasn't in there long enough to do himself any real damage. But it'll have been affecting him for some time – that's what all the coughing's been about, the doctor was saying.'

'Er – I am here,' said Matt.

'That bloody boiler,' said Linda. 'It's going to kill you, Matt Barley.'

'I'll have a word with Rule Britannia.' Matt shut his eyes wearily, his comment obviously more wish than actual plan.

'No, you won't.' Linda's voice was shrill. 'Or rather you will, and she'll wrap you round her little finger as per. Because like me, like everyone in that place, you're shit-scared of her.'

'Not now,' said Matt uneasily.

'Yes now. How long are you going to let that woman and her mates call the shots when something's not right?'

At that moment another doctor appeared. After the past year of Rod's treatment, Pat was used to medics looking young, but really this one could easily have been of school age. Pat took Linda outside the cubicle. 'Trust me,' she said, 'no one here seems to be very alarmed.'

Linda nodded. 'Thank God you were there,' she said.

'He had the sense to get himself out into the fresh air,' said Pat. 'He'd have come round eventually.'

'That lot,' said Linda. 'Kayleigh Brittain and Steve Hewson. They're a law unto themselves. Ages Matt's been onto them about that boiler.'

'They'll have to do something now, surely,' said Pat.

'Don't hold your breath,' said Linda.

'Listen,' said Pat. 'Now is not the time or place but I'm truly, truly sorry about the trouble I got you into the other day.' Neither did it seem the time or place to mention bottles of pink Prosecco;

besides, they were on the back seat of the Yeti still parked up at school.

Linda looked at her, opened her mouth to speak – but at that moment Matt's voice floated from the cubicle. 'Are you going to take me home or what?'

'I'll leave you to it,' said Pat.

She hadn't gone five steps when Linda stopped her with a tug on the arm.

'Look,' she said, 'I don't know what's going on in that school and I don't want to. Above my pay grade and all that. But I do know that bloody boiler nearly killed my husband.'

Pat opened her mouth to say something, but Linda carried on.

'I'm on my own in that office thanks to Madame Iceberg bogging off. And on Wednesday Rule Britannia is taking herself off on yet another conference stroke jolly.'

Pat nodded. Where was this leading? 'Now I'm not supposed to access the accounts,' continued Linda, 'but I have been given certain passwords now there's just me. I'm under strict instructions to let nobody else see them. But if I had them up on screen on Wednesday, say about ten o'clock . . . and I had to go and spend a penny . . . and someone was in the office, and they printed off a set of accounts – well, I wouldn't know a thing about it.'

As Linda marched back to the cubicle, Pat's phone buzzed. It was a text from Andrew. *OUTSIDE*, it said, and there was something very comforting and secure in that one word. She was about to text back, when looking up she saw a familiar face.

'Derek,' she said in some alarm.

Derek drove straight to the allotments. 'You better stay in the car,' he said.

'No,' said Liz.

It was raining even harder now. The wind blew it straight into

264

their faces, screwed up against the wind and the light of Derek's emergency torch (kept at all times in the boot). White, buzzy flecks danced in the beam, and Liz's driving loafers were soaked within a few paces, as the ground squelched underfoot. In the dark and in the wind the allotments were a sinister place, the frantic harsh jangle of Sidrah's dreamcatchers were alarming, not soothing, and the shape of Mo's compost bin had Liz clutching Derek's arm in alarm.

The relief at seeing the figure slumped on Billy's bench was almost immediately slammed out by more panic. Was Sam even alive? What was in that plastic bag on the bench next to him? Tablets? *Pray God, no!* 'Oh, Sam,' said Liz, sad and wet and afraid and wanting to hold him, like she'd held his baby daughter. How on earth would she ever, ever find the words to tell Macy that her husband was not coming home?

Derek caught her arm and she checked herself.

'Now then, Sam,' he said, easily sitting next to him on the bench. 'It's a bit of a wet one to be sitting out, lad.'

It was in the waiting room of the Friarage A&E that Liz began to cry; quite why, she wasn't sure. The news about Sam was as encouraging as it could be. As far as anyone could tell, he hadn't taken many of the tranquillizers from the bag. He'd had his stomach pumped more as a precaution and he was being kept in overnight just to be on the safe side. Liz had been very measured, very calm when telling Macy all of this, and telling her that by far the best thing she could do for herself and for Sam was get a good night's sleep. It was when she was relaying all of this to Derek that something seemed to snap in her head and the tears began to roll helplessly down her face.

For the third time that night Derek sat next to someone, with a comforting hand on their shoulder.

'I am so sorry,' said Liz.

'Whatever have you got to be sorry for? Sam's going to be all right, thanks to you.'

'No, it's not that,' she said. 'It's not telling you what I was doing. I know you didn't want me to get involved, but I still went ahead and asked people things and found things out.'

Once again Derek let the words tumble out unchallenged. He sat there in silence and Liz wondered if he was annoyed; the hand, however, stayed on her shoulder, which had to be a good sign.

Eventually he spoke. 'You did what you thought was right,' he said. 'And at the end of the day, if you hadn't done what you did – well, it could have been a different story tonight.'

Liz sniffed. She was right out of balsam tissues but fortunately Derek always carried a packet; in his inside pocket they had been more or less protected from the rain.

'I don't always understand what you do,' he said, handing her a tissue. 'But what you do is who you are. And I love you.'

Liz retired to the ladies' with two more of Derek's tissues and her handbag to try and repair the worst ravages of weather and emotion. When she returned, she saw Derek was talking to someone. *Pat.* Her hair looking as ravaged as her own.

Once again, she felt her fears rising. What on earth was she doing here at this hour?

CHAPTER TWENTY-SEVEN

More scandalous news spreads, and challenging speculations are made in the garden centre café.

The Wakeman (or to give it its full title 'The Wakeman, God bless ye town of Ripon') was one of those online publications, author unclear, that had set itself up to inform the public about events that for whatever reason might not hit more regular news channels. Rumours, complaints, gripes – all of these were laid digitally before the populace of Ripon on a weekly basis. Mocked by some, decried by others, ignored by hardly any, it was by and large valued for its calling out of unchecked fly-tipping, mismanaged or clumsy roadworks and other items of local interest.

The story that had been shared that Wednesday night consisted of a leaked letter that seemed to imply some sort of done deal between Baht'at Academy Trust and a major planning developer, i.e. to develop the college buildings into a stunning complex of luxury apartments. Alongside this had been scanned extracts from 'Ripon College: A Way Forward', making it crystal clear the white-wash that had been the consultation process. And whereas the town had only been moderately miffed about the prospective loss of the college, and everyone agreed about the need for more housing; no one liked the sense of wool being pulled over their eyes. By the next morning the sense of outrage, shared by text and post and indeed face-to-face comment, was both indignant and growing.

This whole turn of events had left Thelma feeling rather breathless; the previous night she and Teddy had had little chance to discuss matters other than snatched updates between the many phone calls he'd taken. Brummie Maureen, with the ferocity of a tiger defending its young, had galvanized the faculty and a big meeting had been scheduled.

The next morning, standing up from emptying the dishwasher, Thelma saw her husband once again standing outside, coffee in hand, seemingly inspecting the clematis climbing the back wall.

She took her own coffee and joined him. It was a calm morning after yesterday's storm, a watery sun breaking through, catching the puddles on the flags with optimistic glints of light. 'That needs cutting back,' she said looking at the ascending tangle. 'I'll have a word with Ernest Crabtree.' Teddy nodded vaguely.

'What time has the meeting been called for?' said Thelma. She knew very well what time it was – this comment was to give him the opportunity to talk, should he so wish to.

'Ten.' He sat down on the garden seat, still wet from the night before. Not for the first time in their relationship, Thelma marvelled at his ability to sit down anywhere, regardless of damp, dirt or cold.

She stood next to him, not willing to risk the bench herself. 'Maureen's doing a good job.' He nodded. 'She cares very deeply,' he said.

Thelma looked at him, suddenly assailed by a question – *did he?*

'We've all received emails this morning,' he continued. 'From the Children of the Suits. Stressing we should not listen to any rumours, and under no circumstances speak to outside parties.' He stared at his coffee.

'So, the college could be reprieved, do you think?'

'It was never actually said it would close in the first place.'

Something was troubling him; exactly what, Thelma was unsure.

After she'd watched him walking off down College Gardens
– a heavy tread, not his customary springing step – she went up
to the bedroom to start stripping the bed. From the windowsill
Snaffles was staring with a look of deep suspicion at her phone
that was flashing on the bedside table. A missed call – no, *four*
missed calls. Kayleigh? But then she was half expecting to hear
from Verna, who had been revving up for one of her 'colds' –
which would mean covering for her at the charity shop. Still, a
stint sorting paperbacks would be a relief compared to recent
events.

But it wasn't Verna. Two calls were from Pat, and two from Liz. Plus,
a message: could she meet them at the garden centre that morning.

'There is absolutely no way it could have been Sam!' Liz's voice
rang out round the garden centre café; Pat and Thelma both
glanced round at the half-full tables in some concern.

'All I'm saying—' Pat deliberately lowered her voice in an effort
to de-escalate the conversation '—is I saw him putting a typed
letter into a white envelope.'

'The same sort as the anonymous letters came in?' asked Thelma.

'I'm pretty sure,' said Pat. 'I mean okay, a white envelope is a
white envelope but—' she raised her voice as Liz opened her
mouth once again '—but he was looking pretty miserable.'

'There!' Liz slapped the table and all their coffees rippled. 'That *proves*
it wasn't him!' They both looked at her for enlightenment. 'Why would
you be looking miserable if you were sending an anonymous letter?'

'We don't know how people look when they're doing such
things,' said Pat. 'I don't imagine they'd be sat there cackling and
rubbing their hands.'

'But Sam!' Liz shook her head, trying to dismiss the mental image of that huddled lonely figure slumped in the rain. 'If you'd seen him last night.'

There was a tactful pause. The news that morning from Pumphrey Gardens had been good, but Liz was still feeling distinctly wobbly.

'Maybe he couldn't cope with what he was doing,' said Pat. 'Like an addict.'

Seeing Liz's face, Thelma spoke hastily. 'We don't know why he was distressed last night,' she said. 'But we *have* noticed he's not been himself for a while.' This sudden turn of events hadn't been at all what she'd expected, but despite the awful news about Sam and Matt, and the fact passions were flaring between Liz and Pat, at least it was giving her something to think about other than college (a text from Teddy had informed her that Josie Gribben and a group of about a dozen people had turned up complete with placards, camping stools and thermos flasks).

'Sam had an anonymous letter sent to him, don't forget,' said Liz.

'We *think*,' qualified Thelma. 'He never actually *said*, remember. In fact, he categorically denied having received one.'

'He could always have sent one to himself,' said Pat.

Liz took a grim sip of her coffee, her face flinty. 'I refuse to believe he's been doing such wicked things. I taught the lad.'

'We all taught the lad,' said Pat, trying but failing to keep a tetchy note out of her voice. 'None of us wants to think badly of him. But, as we all know, kids have a way of growing up.' There was a slight pause as they considered the subsequent careers of some of their alumni. Robbery, fraud, drugs, prison, plus something dodgy and unnamed in Yarm.

Thelma looked at her friends – Pat flushed with her 'I'm only saying' look on her face and Liz with that Boadicea glint in her eye – and sent up a quick prayer for guidance.

'It's very difficult when speculating if someone has done wrong.' She spoke carefully. 'The easy thing is to suspect those you dislike – but when it's someone you like it's a whole different matter.'

'I know,' said Liz with some force. 'Better than anyone.'

'I like Sam,' said Pat quickly. 'Or rather I don't dislike him.'

Liz was shaking her head. 'Anyway,' she said, 'another reason I don't think it's Sam is because I think that it's *someone else*.'

Again, there was a pause and again they looked at her. Was she going to mention Jan? 'Who?' prompted Thelma eventually.

'Claire Thingy,' said Liz with an air of restrained triumph.

There then followed a brief, anti-climactic moment when it became clear that Pat had no idea who Claire Thingy was.

'You know,' insisted Liz. 'Support assistant. The one I found crying in the staffroom. Works in Ian Berryman's class – or did until . . .'

'Until he exited stage left for a life of debauchery in Acomb,' supplied Pat.

'Very much in love with him, poor lass,' said Liz. 'I'd see the way she looked at him.'

'So why do you think she sent the letters?' asked Pat.

'Something Kayleigh Brittain said to me in the staffroom got me thinking,' said Liz. 'Claire knew all about what was going on between Nicole and Ian.'

She spoke triumphantly as though this proved some kind of point.

'I'm being very thick here,' said Pat. 'But so what?'

'Claire wanted Natalie to know what was happening in the hope she'd put a stop to it. *So, she sent her the letter.*'

'Why not just tell her?' asked Pat.

'She couldn't do that,' said Liz. 'She didn't want Ian to know what she'd done.'

Thelma frowned, stirring her coffee. 'So, she sent out a load of letters to people to conceal what she was planning on doing,' she mused.

Liz looked distinctly miffed at having her thunder stolen. 'Yes,' she said, in a wounded tone. 'Yes, that.'

Thelma frowned. *Could* that be the answer? It somehow didn't feel right, but it did *fit* – at least the bit about Claire writing to Natalie Berryman.

'Okay,' said Pat, 'I get what you're saying. But you've no evidence for this.'

'There's the letter don't forget,' said Liz. '*It was posted.* None of the others were. Which makes it stand out.'

The noise of Thelma's spoon clinking round her cup made them both look across. She was sat looking into the distance somewhere, deep in thought.

'What?' said Pat.

'I'm just trying to remember,' said Thelma. 'What it was Natalie Berryman's letter actually *said?*'

'I've got it on my phone somewhere,' said Pat, fishing in her bag. 'As has half North Yorkshire no doubt.'

Eventually she handed across the phone to Liz and Thelma. Thelma squinted through her glasses, Liz looked above hers.

YOU NEED TO ASK YOUR HUSBAND ABOUT HIS RELATIONSHIP WITH NICOLE KIRK AS WORKS IN THE SCHOOL OFFICE. SORRY BUT YOU NEED TO. YOU DESEVE THE TRUTH. A WELL-WISHER.

'Well, for a start, that person can't spell,' said Liz.

'It doesn't sound nasty like the others,' said Pat.

'There's something else about it,' said Thelma.

The other two frowned, puzzled.

'I don't think any of the others said they were from a well-wisher,' said Liz eventually.

Thelma looked at them both encouragingly.

'Go on,' said Pat. 'You're obviously dying to tell us.'

'*It contains an apology*,' said Thelma. 'It says "sorry".'

There was a moment as they all looked at each other.

'You could imagine Claire writing that and saying sorry,' said Liz.

'But none of the other letters had any sort of apology,' said Pat.

'Not that we *know of*.' There was a quiet edge of frustration in Thelma's voice.

There was a pause whilst they all took a sip of their drinks.

'This what I hate,' said Liz in a deflated tone 'All this imagining who it *could* be.'

The smell of disinfectant and cooked food . . . the slumped figure, hair unwashed . . . stains on the cardigan front . . .

She sighed, and then realized her friends were looking at her.

'I know,' said Thelma.

'I even wondered if it might be Linda,' admitted Pat.

'How is Matt?' asked Thelma. 'I must send a card.'

'He says he's fine, though Linda says he's going to take at least a fortnight off,' said Pat. 'Apparently the school is swarming with engineers and health and safety people. The boiler's out of action and all the kids are having to wear coats. And Linda reckons as how the boiler company are going to try and wriggle out of it by blaming him for what happened.'

'How?' asked Thelma.

'Not following proper safety procedures, not updating risk assessments – that sort of thing.'

'The man ended up in hospital!' Once again Liz's indignant tones rang round the café; once again Thelma and Pat glanced round with nervous smiles.

'I don't know,' said Liz. 'I'd like to get this Lodestone Trust and sit them down and tell them a thing or two. Matt Barley could've died because of their blumin' boiler.'

'Lodestone Trust don't own the boiler remember,' said Pat. 'This finance firm, Grandass Solutions, own the boiler – and Steve Hewson's company Joe Public have the engineering contract – Lodestone just pay the bills.'

'The very high bills,' put in Thelma.

'I'll hopefully learn a bit more tomorrow,' said Pat. She looked at her friends. 'I'm going to do my commando raid on the Lodestone accounts,' she said. 'It's all arranged with Linda. I just need to iron the black cat suit.' She spoke lightly but they could tell she felt nervous.

'How will you get past Kayleigh Brittain?' asked Liz worriedly.

'With discretion, one imagines,' said Thelma.

'She's not going to be there,' said Pat. 'She's off to yet another meeting apparently.'

Liz pursed up her lips. 'The woman's never there,' she said.

There was a pause, the silence between them broken only by the sound of Thelma stirring her coffee again.

'Come on then,' said Pat. 'What are you thinking?'

'I don't really know,' said Thelma looking up. 'All sorts of things. I just wish I could get a *proper* look at those anonymous letters.'

CHAPTER TWENTY-EIGHT

Various suppers are planned, a confession is made and a frightened lady doubts the future.

Asleep in his bed, curled up in his claret and amber Bradford City top, Sam looked absurdly young. Liz adjusted the vast grey duvet slightly, taking care not to disturb him. She hadn't at all intended to perform what amounted to babysitting duties but when she'd called round at 18 Pumphrey Gardens to drop off some things and see how Sam was, baby Robyn had been bellowing with such determined force that the obvious solution had been for Macy to take her out in the pram for a couple of goes round the block. But of course, still very shaken from the night before, she hadn't wanted to leave Sam alone; hence Liz now sitting vigil in a chair at the end of the bed watching the sleeping man who didn't look so much older than his daughter.

Downstairs on the kitchen counter were the things Liz had brought for them: a Victoria sponge (the second of the things she could more or less successfully bake), a shepherd's pie (Quorn in case either were vegetarian) and a bunch of late burgundy dahlias that had survived the previous night's storm.

It was peaceful in the bedroom, the only sound Sam's even breathing and a slight ticking from the central heating. Maybe as her own reaction to the events of the past day, Liz felt herself beginning to drowse slightly.

'Mrs Newsome.' The flat, weary words woke her with a jolt. Sam was looking straight at her; how she wished she'd brought some calamine lotion for that mark on his neck.

'Sam.' She composed her face into a smile. 'Macy's just nipped out for a quick breath of air with Robyn. Try and get her settled, like.'

'Is she okay?' His voice was hoarse, probably from having his stomach pumped.

'She's absolutely fine. They both are.'

He nodded, and gingerly sat up. 'My coat,' he said. 'Do you know where my coat is?' He stared round the room, and out of the door. 'I need my coat.'

Liz cast around. In one corner was a big sodden heap of clothes obviously discarded from the night before.

'My coat,' said Sam again, and now there was a pang of panic in his voice.

'You're not to even think of going out,' said Liz firmly.

'There's something I need.'

Liz wanted to argue but something about that cracked, edgy tone made her think better of it. Dubiously she looked through the damp pile (would Macy object if she took it all home and ran it through the wash?) and located the cold, wet coat, really little more than a jacket.

Sam clutched it and feverishly felt in the pockets. With a sigh he retrieved a sodden white mass that, with a sinking feeling, Liz identified as an envelope.

'It's not been opened,' stated Sam, and sank back against the pillow.

Liz looked at the object held in his hands, suddenly afraid. 'Is it important?' she said.

Sam looked at her. 'Macy must never ever see this,' he said.

'What is it?' asked Liz, heart hammering. Somewhere in her mind was an image of Pat, arms folded, saying, *I told you so.*

'Macy mustn't see this,' he repeated. And then, surprisingly, he held it out to Liz. 'Mrs Newsome, could you take this and get rid of it?'

Liz nodded and gingerly took the wet paper. Wrapping it in an empty tissue packet she put it in her handbag. Did this make her some sort of accessory after some sort of fact?

Sam leant back against the pillow, obviously relieved. 'Thank you,' he said and all of a sudden, fat tears began coursing down his face.

'Sam,' said Liz, handing him a balsam tissue.

'I'm sorry,' he said, 'I'm so sorry.'

'You've done nothing wrong,' said Liz, trying not to think of the envelope in her handbag.

'That's just it,' said Sam. '*I have.*'

Driving back to Borrowby, Pat reflected on their coffee session in the garden centre. She hadn't meant to get so tetchy, but Liz had been so instantly dismissive of what she'd seen, Sam and the letter and the envelope . . . Not that she thought he *was* the anonymous letter writer, but then it had to be *someone* . . . And someone they knew . . . And maybe . . . maybe Kayleigh *did* have an idea who it was.

She sighed. She had been thinking she might tell her friends about the whole retirement business. Or maybe even that other thing. But that hadn't happened, and moreover she wouldn't think of it today, not when the weather was so much brighter after so many dismal days. Plus, she needed to make something for Sam. There was a rather good Angela Hartnett aubergine recipe she wanted to try. (They were vegetarian, weren't they?) The thought of cooking brought a further sigh as she wondered what sort of state the kitchen would be in; she'd left both Rod and Andrew eating breakfast so at the very least there would be that to clear away.

There was neither van nor car in the yard. Come to think of it, hadn't Andrew and Rod been saying something about fencing posts at breakfast? With a moment of release, she realized she had the place to herself. Getting out of the car, she let the glorious thought wash over her. She could maybe catch up with the *Real Housewives of Land O Lakes*, before starting on the aubergines. And perhaps a cheeky hazelnut latte and maybe even a garden centre Hambleton slice. If the kitchen wasn't in too much of a mess, she thought opening the door, bracing herself for what she might find.

The room was tidy.

Not only tidy but also clean. She only realized how much she'd been bracing herself as she felt the tension release in a slipping, warm rush. The table was clear, the sides wiped and the dishwasher humming. And coming from the utility room was the sound of the washing machine on its final cycle. Going through, she peered at the spinning blur of clothes, obviously more than just Andrew's pants. At that second the machine sighed and stopped, and Pat became aware of a faint but familiar sound, a thumping, muffled and regular noise coming from upstairs. She took the stairs two at a time, thoughts of lattes, housewives and pants banished.

Sitting at his desk, as though he'd never been away, was Liam, before a screen showing some mountain vista. Surveying all from the bed with a look of sleepy proprietorship was Larson.

'Hello, Parentage,' said Liam.

'If you were going to send a poison pen letter, why would you do it?' asked Pat, as she cooked brunch or lunch or whatever category Liam's favourite eggy bread fell into.

Liam didn't even stop to think. 'I'd write to Thelma Cooper and say I know all, repent of your sordid ways.'

'I'm not going to ask if you're going to be stupid.'

She flipped the brown and gold slices onto a plate and set them in front of him, watched intently by Larson.

'This is the St Barnabus anonymous letter writer?' Liam laced the eggy bread liberally with tomato ketchup.

'You may make mock, but a lot of people are getting very upset.' Pat spoke severely. 'One person – well, he nearly topped himself.' *If he wasn't actually the writer,* she added silently.

'Well, to answer your question,' said Liam, 'I wouldn't. Send a poison pen letter. Why bother?'

'To upset someone.'

'I mean why bother in this day and age? If you want to upset someone you can always troll them.'

Pat, who only had a vague idea of what trolling was from her trashy magazines, nodded vaguely.

'Why fanny around writing letters,' he said, 'when with a few clicks and taps you can tell the whole world someone's a total knob brain.'

He was right of course. She well remembered his own bruising encounter with Facebook. But the fact was someone *was* doing it. These letters were a *fact*.

'Anyway.' He pushed his plate aside and flipped open his crimson laptop. 'I've been having a look at Stevie Wonder as your mate Victoria calls him.'

She looked at him blankly.

'Steve Hewson. The Great St Barnabus boiler scandal.'

On the screen was a picture of the man she recognized from her encounter at Baldersby; the mere sight of him, beer in his hand and arm round an improbably sculpted and made-up woman, was enough to give her an unsettling flush of anger and fear.

Round his neck he wore that thick gold chain and Pat could smell that aggressive aftershave. She read the title banner: *You can take the lad out of Castleford . . .*

'What is this?' she said.

'His blog,' said Liam. 'A veritable cornucopia of joy and delight . . . hang on . . .' He scrolled down the screen before reading in a thick Yorkshire accent: 'If foreigners are happy to come to our country and use our NHS, shouldn't WE be free to set whatever wages we want to give them for the work THEY want to do?' He shook his head. 'The man's slightly to the right of Genghis Khan. A reet dodgy eejit as Bern says.'

'I couldn't find anything much about him online,' said Pat.

'And I couldn't cook Nigella's ragout,' said Liam. 'Each to their own. Now, Mother, did you know our Stevie Wonder here actually works for the people who own this wondrous biomass boiler?'

'No, he doesn't,' said Pat. 'No, I know this. Steve Hewson works for Joe Public, or rather he *is* Joe Public, who are a maintenance company. Grandass Finance are a company based in Solihull—'

'Supposedly based in Solihull,' said Liam. 'For Solihull read Eastern Europe.'

'It's them who own the boiler and employ Steve's company Joe Public, to do the maintenance on the boiler,' Pat finished.

'No,' corrected Liam. 'Steve works for Joe Public, or owns it or what have you. But he *also* works directly for Grandass Finance. He's on their payroll. And this Grandass Finance own a whole slew of biomass boilers across the north of England.'

'You see that's what I don't get,' said Pat. 'Why would a finance company own a biomass boiler?'

'Mother,' said Liam indulgently, 'has anyone properly explained RHI payments to you?'

'Our Andrew did. It's money you get from the government for having a biomass boiler.'

Liam nodded. 'An incentive to use green energy. A sound enough idea. And to be fair there's some good outfits going – this one firm near Belfast are doing all sorts of charity stuff.'

'But?'

'But like many things it's open to exploitation,' he said, echoing his brother. 'There's a loophole. The more heat you burn, the more money the people who actually own the boiler get in RHI payments. This is of course on top of the money paid to them by the school.'

Pat frowned. 'So – the more the boiler gets used . . . ?'

'The more Grandass Finance gets. Party time in Solihull. It's been a massive problem in Northern Ireland – you had all these farmers heating these vast empty sheds and making millions.'

'So, Steve Hewson . . .'

'Is going to be on some tidy whack from Grandass Finance.'

Pat frowned and poured herself a cup of coffee. 'Which would explain why the boiler keeps coming on all hours of the day and night,' she said.

Liam finished the last forkful of breakfast. 'You think Matt Barley's been turning it off and on? Maybe taking some sort of backhander from Steve?'

Pat shook her head. 'He says he's been forbidden to touch it. He keeps getting into trouble for turning it *down* . . .'

'So you think Stevie Wonder keeps sneaking into school for a quick burst of green heat?'

Pat frowned. It was hard to see how he could be. But then the boiler was coming on at all hours . . . *Was* Matt involved somehow?

Liam got up and began clearing the plates and cups to put in the newly emptied dishwasher.

'It is so good to see you,' she said.

'I'm going to go and do some work,' he said. Larson stirred himself and disappeared upstairs where Pat knew she'd find him ensconced on Liam's windowsill.

'One more thing,' she said. 'Who's Bern?'

'Behave, Mother.'

'I was just asking.'

'Okay,' said Liam. 'You've rumbled me. He's my lover. I'm giving up uni and the wedding's next month; ask Dad to book the Borrowby Arms, an ice sculpture and a string quartet.'

'Oh, ha ha.'

'I just couldn't see . . . any other way.' Sam paused and for a moment they were both back there on that rainy allotment.

'Sam, you don't have to say anything,' said Liz, trying hard to get an image of a courtroom from her head. (So how much did you actually *know*, Mrs Newsome?)

If Sam confessed to being the letter writer, what on earth was she going to do?

'It's the end of year,' said Sam miserably.

Whatever Liz expected Sam to say, it wasn't that.

'You mean the Year Six ones?' she said.

He nodded. 'The writing levels.'

A glimmer of light, just a glimmer, began to form. A flash of memory; Kayleigh Brittain standing with pride in front of the parents: *We are a Beacon School for writing!*

'You mean the very good results everyone's been going on about?'

'But they're not!' His voice came out as a sort of husky wail. 'I said they were – but they're not!'

'You mean the children *didn't* reach expected levels in writing?'

'No, they did – it's just the ones we said were *exceeding* the expected levels. They're *not*. Well, some of them are – but not the numbers we said.'

Gasp by gasp the story came out – how Jared Keen had been pushing this new method of teaching writing, this new marking technique. How he said the results had the potential of being very good – amazing even. And then Kayleigh Brittain had got hold of this – and all of a sudden there was this expectation of these brilliant results, results that exceeded expected levels.

'I tried telling Mrs Brittain,' said Sam. 'But she got really funny with me . . . started talking about errors of professional judgement – how serious that would be – so in the end I just shut up and went along with it.' He closed his eyes at the memory. 'And now this year, we're meant to be this Beacon School. The one showing everyone else how it's done, with these amazing results. But with this class, there's no way they're going to even get close to the sort of levels everyone's expecting . . . even if I *did* . . .' He paused, dropped his eyes. 'Even if I did do like I did last year. I've been trying hard – extra sessions, new marking techniques – but it's just not happening.' His voice had risen, his hands were nervously bunching the duvet. Any moment now Liz felt sure he'd start biting his nails.

'I've let everyone down,' he said. 'And last night . . . it just got to me.' His voice fell to a dull, flat monotone. 'I couldn't see . . . any other way.'

Suddenly Liz understood what the contents of the letter were.

'Sam,' she said. Her voice was calm, but firm, the voice that had, in the past, solved disputes, explained column addition and provided reassurance that the Great Fire of London could not in fact happen in Thirsk. 'Sam, we are going to sort this all out.'

He looked at her, the tears again brimming.

'But first,' she said, 'you have to sleep.'

He nodded and obediently lay back.

Liz straightened the duvet again and sat back down. Her lips were compressed and in her eyes was an angry glint, such as might have been present in the eyes of a certain warrior queen as she stepped into her bladed chariot.

*

For the third time Thelma tried Kayleigh's number. For the third time she was invited to leave her name, time of call and a brief message, and promised she'd be got right back to. Thelma shook her head and went back to chopping carrots and leeks for the vegetable hot pot she was making for Sam (she was sure he was vegetarian – so many people were these days). Something that would be easy to warm up. She sighed again. Why was Kayleigh not returning her calls? Of course, she could be over in Thirsk even as she chopped, seeing Sam, making arrangements for his cover. But somehow, she didn't think so.

The front door opened. 'Vicar in the building,' called Teddy. He sounded tired.

'Kitchen,' she said, putting on the kettle.

'Good I think,' he said, sitting down without taking his coat off. 'In answer to any questions about how the meeting went.'

She put the vegetable knife down and sat across the table from him.

'A lot of people had a lot of things to say. Which is natural. An online petition has gained nearly 10,000 signatures in a day. The latest according to Maureen is that the Archbishop of Durham may well be prevailed upon to sign it.'

'That's very encouraging surely.'

He nodded. 'I sometimes wonder if the town knew we were here.'

'Now you have your answer.'

'And you? How's that young lad?'

'Sam? He's at home. As is Matt Barley.'

'I kept thinking about them today. On and off. Here we are at college, somewhat set apart from the real world – and yet over in Thirsk very real evil and heartbreak is going on.' He looked seriously at her. 'And are you all right?'

I'm worried about you because I know there's something you're not telling me.

But all she said was she was that she was fine.

When he'd gone upstairs to change, Thelma went back to chopping vegetables, but she'd barely started when her mobile phone went.

'Thelma.' Kayleigh sounded upset, panicky. 'Thelma, you rang. I don't need to ask why.'

'Sam Bowker.'

'Thelma, it's so awful. Have you seen him; do you know how he is?'

'I haven't – but Liz Newsome has. She and her husband were the ones who found him.'

'Found him! *My God.*' There was something like a panicky sob that made the voice wobble into a cough.

'Kayleigh.' Thelma's tone was calm and firm. 'Kayleigh, he's going to be all right.'

'When I spoke to her, his wife said he'd taken some pills.'

'Not many.'

'But he obviously meant to . . . to harm himself.'

'But when it came down to it – he didn't.'

'No.' The voice seemed a little calmer. 'Did he say – has he said – *why* he did it?'

'Not to me,' said Thelma, unaware of Liz's conversation with Sam.

'It's not because of the letter he got?'

'He hasn't said so,' said Thelma.

'It's *got* to be. Why else? I mean *Sam* – he's got so much to live for. That baby . . .' Again, the voice broke into a sob.

'We'll have to make sure he gets the support he needs,' said Thelma. 'And of course, Matt's going to need our support too.'

'Yes.' The voice sounded distracted, almost disinterested – as if

Matt Barley was less relevant in terms of disasters. 'Thelma, who's doing this? Who's sending these letters?'

'I don't know,' said Thelma. She paused a second and then with a prayer for courage asked what had been on her mind. 'Do you?'

Another pause, then . . .

'No, of course not!' The answer seemed both quick and genuine. Too quick? *Too* genuine? *Was* Kayleigh covering for someone? The woman's plaintive tone broke into her thoughts. 'Thelma, I'm frightened. I'm *scared*. I thought I could look after myself. But now . . . I'm not so sure.' There was no trace of the anger of their last conversation . . . just panic . . . fear . . . a frightened child.

After she'd gone, Thelma continued peeling and chopping, onions, parsnips and swede. And in her mind was an image of a red cardboard folder in the middle drawer of Kayleigh Brittain's desk.

She needed to see those letters.

CHAPTER TWENTY-NINE

Baking and perfume are strategically used, and there is a millennial moment outside the head teacher's office.

To the children of St Barnabus's Lodestone Academy, largely unaware of recent events, it was just another Wednesday. In Acorn Base, Sophie Briggs-Buchanan's mother had brought in baby Ena and the class clustered round as she had been changed and let forth an arc of golden wee that narrowly missed Jason Carstairs. In the Nursery playground, the children, togged up against the chilly morning, were energetically hunting objects beginning with 'e', whilst in Elm and Oak classes the very first sketchy start to the Nativity play was being made (after all it's only nine weeks away!)

The various vans parked by the boiler house, the people with their hard hats and clipboards and instruments, plus the festoons of yellow tape barring entry, caused some interest – but otherwise letters, marriage break-ups, near-poisoning, contemplated suicide – all these had as little impact as the storm clouds massing away over the distant Pennines. Only in Rowan and Willow class, where supply teachers struggled half-heartedly with Pineapple Maths were there any doubts and worries about their missing teachers (Mackaly Thorpe reckoned both Mr Berryman *and* Mr Bowker

287

were in prison). But even this was overshadowed by the promise of a forthcoming sex education talk (willies, the lot).

Life, thought Liz, hearing Rowan Class readers for Mr Shah, went on – and nowhere more cheerfully or ruthlessly than in a primary school.

She looked round the otherwise empty school library and checked her watch.

Seven minutes.

Had she time to hear another reader?

In the school office, Pat shifted from foot to foot as the printer hummed into life. Even though she could see the car park on the CCTV, she was nonetheless terrified that Kayleigh Brittain, or Nicole Kirk, or indeed anyone and everyone from a late arrival to the Busy Books man, would come upon her. She wasn't at all sure about this scheme of Thelma's and, watching sheets of paper starting to churn relentlessly from the machine, was wishing she'd insisted on sticking to Linda's original, simple plan.

'Knock knock knockity knock.' As if prompted by Pat's thought, Linda herself appeared in the office just as the printer spat out the last sheet. Pat hastily scooped the pages up and transferred them to her handbag whilst Linda looked exaggeratedly in the other direction. 'I-hope-you-did-not-mind-me-leaving-you-alone-in-the-office-whilst-I-paid-a-quick-trip-to-the-you-know-where,' she chanted in deliberate tones. Pat smiled and surreptitiously checked her watch.

Five minutes.

'So, how's your Matt doing?' she said.

'Fine.' Linda smiled, though she looked pale, haunted even, as she closed down various incriminating windows on her PC. 'Not that I'm telling Rule Britannia that. Let her sweat. Thanks again for the cake.' She gave a fond glance at a Quality Street tin, in which sat an autumn fruit madeira.

At that moment the front door peeped, and on cue Thelma walked in.

Four minutes.

Linda slid the reception hatch open. 'Quite the reunion!' she said. 'Pat's here for her eggs and Liz's hearing readers.'

'How's Matt doing?' Thelma set a Tupperware container on the counter. 'Just some cheese scones,' she said. Linda's eyes brimmed, not for the first time that day. 'People are so blumin' lovely,' she said. 'Thank you. Liz's brought flapjacks, Pat's brought a cake.' She lifted the lid and her eyes sparkled at the golden scones. Pat wondered how many of the various offerings would make it back intact to the farm.

'I called in to see Kayleigh,' said Thelma. 'But I've suddenly had a nasty feeling she said something to me about going to a meeting?'

'She's not back in until tomorrow,' said Linda. 'I can give her a message?'

'Senior moment!' Thelma smiled and tapped a hand to her forehead.

Pat checked her watch again.

Less than a minute.

At that moment the phone started ringing.

'I wonder . . .' said Thelma quickly, as Linda went to answer it. 'Before I go, could I possibly use the facilities? Being a lady of a certain age!'

Linda laughed cheerfully. 'Happens to us all,' she said, buzzing Thelma through, and picking up the phone.

Time.

Nothing happened.

Pat checked her watch. Yes, it was definitely the agreed time. What was Liz playing at?

★

In the library Liz had dismissed her latest reader and strategically moved a library stool into place. She was just steeling herself to do what she'd been mentally rehearsing since 3.30 am. that morning when the library door opened and Jan marched in.

'Okay,' she said in an unsteady voice. 'You and me, we need to talk.'

Liz felt her heart and resolve sinking down to the carpet tiles somewhere. 'Actually,' she began, 'I'm just in the middle of hearing readers for Mr Shah.' But it was as if she hadn't spoken.

Jan turned a library chair the wrong way round and sat astraddle, regarding Liz.

'I'm worried about you,' she said. Her eyes were wide, and Liz could sense tears were not so far away.

'Can we talk later?' she said. 'I have to finish these last few readers.' But even before she'd finished saying the words, Jan was shaking her head, smiling.

'Come on, lady,' she said. 'This is me you're talking to. You've not been in touch; you haven't answered texts.' Liz tried again to speak but Jan carried on. 'This whole business with these stupid silly letters – you can't let it get to you. And we certainly can't let it come between us.'

'Jan,' she said firmly, with a trace of crispness, 'I'm fine, really I am. And I really do need to finish hearing these readers.'

Jan nodded her head, ducked it down. It stayed down.

'Jan?' Silence. 'Jan?'

'I know.' Jan's voice was muffled.

'You know what?'

A single hot tear splashed onto the blue plastic back of the chair. 'I know you're fine. You always are. It's me who's the mess.'

Liz sighed. Part of her heart ached with sympathy; a larger part of her mind was thinking: *You don't half choose your moments.*

She regarded her friend.

A pale, still face puffy from medication. The hot, stuffy ward, the smell of disinfectant. Rubbing the cold hands to try and get some feeling back into the lifeless face.

And now she took her hands again, just as she had in the Friarage secure unit all those years ago.

'You've done so well,' said Liz gently. 'I do admire the way again and again you bring yourself back from those dark places.'

'Those letters,' said Jan.

Liz felt herself tensing up. 'What about them?'

'What if they're aimed at *me*?'

'You?' Jan nodded; another tear fell. 'Jan lovey, a lot of people have had them. How can they possibly be aimed at you?'

'The things they say . . . calling people out – saying they're lazy . . . fat – what if people think it's *me* writing them?'

YOU FAT BITCH.

Of course!

The relief was a warm rushing, pushing aside all those worries about delayed plans.

'Jan, my love.' Liz's voice was strong and calm. 'These letters are aimed at a lot of people. And no one who knows you could possibly think you were the one sending them.' She smiled at her, sure beyond doubt that whoever was doing this was not her maddening, impossible friend.

Finally, Jan looked up to face her. 'I don't say enough,' she said, congested, without a trace of her usual confidence. 'I do appreciate your support.'

'Hey,' said Liz in what she hoped were cheerful but cajoling tones. 'Hey, lady, it's mutual.'

Liz's grip and voice seemed to give Jan strength. She drew a long, shuddering breath and nodded.

'Right,' she said unsteadily. 'Right, this is what's going to happen, no arguments. Next Wednesday night you're going to come round to mine. Halloumi stir-fry, bottle of something fair trade and maybe even that Polish film you've been nattering at me to see.'

Despite never having heard of any Polish film, let alone voiced any desire to see one, Liz nodded. 'Thank you,' she said. 'That'd be lovely.'

'Right.' Jan sprung up with a wobbly, recovering energy. 'I better get into the hall and see what sort of lulu Becky's making of the Nativity play, bless her.'

At the door she paused and looked back. 'I'm glad we're good,' she said.

And in spite of the prospect of a halloumi stir-fry, so was Liz. But what about the plan? Was it too late?

Back at the office Pat had talked about surfboards, the Algarve, fatless fruit cake and the prospect of a Spice Girls reunion tour – anything and everything she could think of to distract Linda from realizing just how long Thelma had been in the You Know Where. What was Liz playing at? Time was ticking and playtime getting ever closer.

In desperation she was just about to propose cutting into the autumn fruit madeira when the strident, insistent beep of the fire alarm drowned out whatever excuse she might have made.

The wailing cut like a knife across the activities of the school. Pencils, crayons, books, Lego bricks were dropped, sentences left half read, pictures part coloured, and in the hall the newly cast shepherds hovered uneasily on stage, unsure of whether to still drop to their knees in terror or not.

A pause.

Then doors opened and children and teachers began spilling out of classrooms as all the electronically locked doors, disabled

292

by the fire alarm, bounced open in the sudden wave of activity. Out in the playground, ragged lines began to form; in the absence of both Mrs Brittain and Mr Berryman there was a certain void of authority, one which Jan Starke was only too happy to fill.

'Line up, guys! Teachers, you need to count numbers!' Even from the library Liz could hear her cheerful, strident voice and despite everything smiled to herself. Quickly she pushed the library stool back into its place and stuffed her aerosol perfume back into her handbag. Not a moment too soon; the library door burst open and there stood Becky.

'Fire alarm, Mrs Newsome,' she said. 'You need to evacuate. There's no one in here with you is there?'

As the alarm wailed on, out in the playground staff began looking uncertainly at each other. *Was* it a drill? With Mrs Brittain, not to mention Mr Berryman, Mr Bowker and Mr Barley away? Could it be for real? Uneasy glances were cast towards the boiler house from where puzzled workmen were emerging. Maybe it was in some way something to do with the boiler?

Thelma emerged cautiously from the staff toilets. If all had gone to plan, Pat should have taken Linda outside, saying she'd seen Thelma in the playground.

Liz was waiting for her. 'I'm sorry,' she hissed but Thelma waved her silent with a hand.

'Stay outside and keep watch.'

Thelma reckoned she had about two clear minutes and although she knew for a fact Kayleigh Brittain wasn't in school, her heart was nonetheless thudding as she pushed open her office door, the lock disabled by the wailing alarm – almost as if she expected the principal to be sitting behind her desk. But the grey room with its big desk was empty, curiously lifeless. She moved purposefully to the desk drawers, taking care to keep herself out of sight of the window. Sending up a quick prayer of repentance for the deception, she tried the top drawer where she had seen Kayleigh Brittain put the red folder.

It was locked.

Of course it was. It made total sense – why hadn't she thought of that? Kayleigh Brittain wasn't going to absent herself, leaving vulnerable material in an accessible place. She scanned the room with some wild idea of picking the lock somehow, but even as she looked, she dismissed the thought as ridiculous. Maybe there was a key somewhere? Hardly likely to be lying about, but even so, she tried the second drawer without much hope. There was nothing there other than a few items of stationery, Post-it Notes, highlighter pens. She put her hand to the back. There was always the vague possibility a key might be secreted there but the only thing her fingers touched was something hard and flat and square that she couldn't place. Drawing it out she saw it was just a coaster. Disappointed, she was about to put it back when something about the design stopped her. There was something familiar about the vibrant colours, the oranges and purples – what was it? She turned it over, on the back was a gold sticker: Lew Carne Gallery, St Just, Cornwall. But no key.

For completion's sake she opened the third drawer, a deeper one full of files.

And on top of them: a red cardboard wallet.

Bingo.

Offering a quick prayer of thanks, she took it out and swiftly set to work.

Hovering out in the corridor keeping watch, Liz felt like life had become one big, panicky heartbeat thudding and crashing in her ears.

'I saw some children inside and thought I better check; I saw some children and thought I better check . . .' she muttered, head turning each way. But for all her scanning she didn't see Becky until the noise of the door from the hall made her turn. On seeing Liz, she stopped dead, her face one big frowning question. Liz opened her mouth to gabble out her pre-prepared line, but before she could speak, the door to Kayleigh's office opened and Thelma emerged.

One of Thelma's favourite quotes was: *With the Lord a day is as a thousand years.* Now, with the three of them contemplating each other – Becky staring at Thelma framed in the head teacher's office doorway as the fire alarm wailed and wailed – the moment certainly had a rather millennial feel to it.

CHAPTER THIRTY

Stylistic differences in expressions of spite and malice are studied.

'She just walked away?' Pat frowned in disbelief. She had to raise her voice slightly over the knitting group at a nearby table; this morning there seemed to be less knitting and more raucous laughter. It was the following morning and they'd gathered in the garden centre for what she termed a 'caffeine debrief'.

Liz nodded. 'I said my bit about thinking I'd seen someone — and Becky just nodded, turned and went outside. We followed her, and that's where we saw you.'

'And she *definitely* saw you coming out of Ms Bling's office?'

Thelma nodded. 'I was literally in the doorway.'

Pat took a bite of her Topcliffe meringue. 'So, she believed you then,' she said. Thelma and Liz looked at each other — they both instinctively thought there was more to it than that. There had been *something* about Becky's face, about the calm, deliberate way she'd simply turned away from them and walked outside.

'D'you think she'll say anything to anyone?' asked Pat.

'No,' said Liz firmly. 'No, I don't.' Thelma nodded in agreement, though she had her fingers firmly crossed.

'Well, there you go,' said Pat through a mouthful of sugary

crumbs. 'We did it, ladies!' She raised her coffee cup in a sort of toast. 'No thanks to Jan Starke!'

They looked at each other. A lot felt unresolved about Becky's action, or lack of it, but nevertheless there was a general sense of a tricky task more or less successfully achieved.

'It's not often I say this,' said Thelma, 'but thank you Amos Lawler.'

They all smiled at the memory of that fraught residential to Robin Hood's Bay, and the 3 a.m. fire alarm courtesy of Amos Lawler and his spraying of Lynx body spray against the smoke sensors.

'Of course,' said Pat. 'Someone could always guess. That library must fair reek of Anais Anais thanks to you, Liz Newsome.'

'I opened the window.' Liz wasn't quite yet ready to joke about what she'd done.

'It was necessary,' said Thelma firmly. 'We have to see those letters, so we had to get into Kayleigh's office, so we had to disable the electric locks.'

'It was Sam I was thinking of,' said Liz. Thelma nodded and by unspoken agreement Pat produced her bag and the first set of documents they'd acquired; the thought of Sam and his distress over the writing levels was enough to end any levity and spur them to start work.

'Now I'm afraid these are going to seem a bit dull,' said Pat apologetically, spreading out the accounts she'd printed. 'After all that effort, I can't really see anything untoward about them. Just a load of people being paid money, food suppliers, stationery, that sort of thing. I mean our Liam said he'd have a look at them, but all these payments are just what you'd expect in a primary school.'

'There's a lot to this Pineapple Inc,' said Thelma, frowning at the list. She remembered a time when pineapples were something one put in a trifle.

'That's this new maths scheme they're piloting,' said Pat. 'I think Chris Cannes' partner is the mastermind behind it.' She found herself wondering how the trip to Belfast had gone but forced her attention back on the list. 'Dance-tastic Academy? What's that?'

'That was the Year Six harvest dance,' remembered Liz. 'I think the lass also runs classes in school.'

'Like I say, it all seems to be above board,' said Pat. 'Nothing like the Kayleigh Bling Seychelles Holiday Fund. Just shedloads going out on the boiler, which if it isn't ethical isn't actually illegal. Though it looks like Steve Hewson is turning the thing on to make more money for the people who own it.'

'How?' said Liz. 'Is he sneaking in and out of school?'

'He doesn't have to go anywhere near the school,' said Pat with the slightly smug air of someone making a significant announcement. 'What he's doing is using—'

'A hive system,' interrupted Thelma without thinking. 'Of course, how clever.' She caught sight of the expression on Pat's face and was suddenly aware once again she'd upstaged one of her friends. 'I mean, that's what he might be doing,' she amended hastily.

'A hive?' said Liz.

'You might as well say, seeing as you know all about it,' said Pat sulkily.

'No, I don't,' said Thelma. 'They just happened to be talking about it at church. Please, go on.'

'It's like Thelma says,' said Pat, still miffed. 'It's a way you can control things like heating via Wi-Fi or whatever. That way he can turn the boiler off and on without even stepping foot in the place.'

Liz sat back and sipped her coffee. 'I can't see how any of this ties up with poison pen letters.'

Thelma shook her head to herself and pushed the accounts away.

'Can you see anything?' Pat was still put out at having her thunder stolen.

Thelma shook her head. 'Like you say,' she said, 'just a list of people paid, which a primary school normally would pay.'

'Anyway,' Liz said firmly. 'The important thing is these letters. It's those we need to look at, after all the trouble we took to get them.'

By unspoken agreement Pat scooped up the accounts and with one eye on the other customers, Thelma discreetly spread the photos she'd taken of the letters out across the table. The hateful words leered up at them in a spiteful chorus. Seeing them suddenly laid out side by side like that gave each of them something of an uneasy jolt.

'There were fourteen letters in the file,' said Thelma. 'Not counting the one sent to Natalie Berryman. And of course, we know there's more than that – ones that weren't handed in to Kayleigh for whatever reason.'

In silence they scanned the documents.

. . . I HOPE YOU REALISE JUST HOW
MANY PEOPLE HATE YOU . . .
. . . YOU FAT BITCH . . .
. . . YOU REALIZE EVERYONE
KNOWS WHAT YOU'RE DOING?
. . . MAKE ME WANT TO VOMIT . . .

The taunting nastiness was a jarring contrast to the Thursday morning atmosphere of the café, the toasties and scones, the swapping of news and gossip, the brightly coloured balls of wool and their emerging jumpers and scarves.

'To think,' said Liz, 'someone actually took time and effort to sit down and write all this filth. It makes me sick to the stomach.'

'I dunno,' said Pat. 'Seeing it all laid out . . . it all feels a bit . . . *petty* somehow.'

'At least,' said Liz firmly, 'I know for a fact it isn't Jan sending the letters.' She looked at her friends as if daring them to challenge her.

'But,' said Pat, bracing herself, 'do we maybe think Sam sent these letters?'

'No, we do not!' said Liz firmly. There was a steely glint in her eye. 'I think it's much more likely he got a letter himself – and thought someone knew what he'd done with the writing results. The poor lad tried to top himself remember.'

'He didn't take that many tablets,' reminded Pat. 'I know this sounds awful, but it could all have been a – well, a distraction. And remember – I did see him with a letter.'

'I know what was in that letter you saw him with,' said Liz abruptly. The other two looked at her. 'He gave it me to destroy. It was—' she dropped her voice '—a note explaining why he'd done what he did.'

'And you looked at it?' asked Pat.

'Absolutely not!' Liz sounded scandalized. Pat and Thelma exchanged discreet glances, each knowing they'd have done differently. 'Anyway,' said Liz challengingly. 'What about Claire Donnelly? Could she not have sent the letters?'

Pat shrugged and looked at Thelma. 'What do you think?' she asked.

'I think,' said Thelma, 'Liz's absolutely right. Claire *did* send that letter to Natalie Berryman.'

Liz didn't actually say the words 'I told you so'; her expression did all the talking necessary. She felt herself relax slightly. If Claire was the letter writer the whole thing became a bit less sinister – sad and squalid yes – but no longer this sense of lurking evil.

'Okay,' said Pat, 'so she sent the others as a sort of camouflage?'

'No,' said Thelma, shaking her head. 'No, I think she sent the letter to Natalie. *I think someone else sent all of the other ones.*'

There was a pause and the other two looked at her; despite the warmth of the café, Liz felt a slight shiver. Sinister was suddenly back in full force. 'Why d'you say that?' she asked.

In answer Thelma brought up the fateful letter on her phone:

SORRY BUT YOU NEED TO. YOU DESEVE
THE TRUTH. A WELL-WISHER.

'The key point,' said Thelma, 'is the differences between that letter and all the rest of them. As Liz said, it was posted – the only one that was. *But it's also signed.*'

'Hardly,' said Pat. 'A well-wisher.'

'*None of the others had any such signature.* And the apology. If you look at it, it's quite different stylistically from these other letters.' She gestured at the papers in front of them. 'No, I think it's as you said. With all the anonymous letters, the poor girl saw a chance to bring an end to Ian and Nicole's carryings on and took it. Never suspecting how it would all blow up in her face.'

Liz sighed, remembering the sobbing figure in the staffroom. 'Silly, silly girl,' she said. 'Typical of her to apologize.'

'She can't even spell "deserve",' said Pat.

Thelma frowned – the words rang some sort of chord in her mind, something she'd noticed but without noticing; but before she could allow whatever it was to take form in her thoughts, Liz spoke. 'You know, it's a bit odd,' she said thoughtfully.

'What is?' said Pat.

'It just strikes me. Looking at them – it's like you say, Pat, they just seem a bit *petty* – like they miss a trick.'

'What do you mean "miss a trick"?' Thelma looked at her.

'This one.' Liz pushed over a letter.

WANT TO LOSE WEIGHT? TRY EATING A BIT LESS, YOU FAT BITCH! NO ONE RESPECTS A WEAK-WILLED FATTY! (Reading it, Pat paused mid bite with her Topcliffe meringue.)

'This is obviously the one that was sent to Tiff, that large lass I told you about. But it doesn't say what we thought it might.'

'What did you think it might say?'

'Margo says she has trouble with her husband – she reckons that's behind all her dieting.'

'I know I'm being very thick here,' said Pat. 'But so what?'

'*So, you'd imagine the letter would make some mention of that.* And here – this one sent to Becky Clegg – it makes no mention of her relationship break-up.'

Frowning, Pat reached out for another letter.

EVERYONE'S SICK OF YOUR SKIVING! YOU DON'T THINK ANYONE BELIEVES YOUR LIES FOR ONE SECOND? DO US ALL A FAVOUR, AND EITHER DO THE JOB PROPERLY OR PISS OFF.

'This must be the one sent to Pesto,' she said slowly. 'Linda was telling me he skives off from time to time because he needs to do stuff for his girlfriend who has a temper on her and smacks him about. But again – you'd think the letter would mention it.'

Thelma was staring. *That was it.* She looked again.

'How strange,' she said. 'These are almost *lazy.*'

'Lazy?' said Pat. 'What on earth do you mean by that?'

'I mean,' said Thelma, 'although they say nasty things, *they could be a whole lot nastier.* I'm wondering now if the one we think Sam got even mentioned the SATs.'

'Does it matter?' asked Pat.

'I don't know,' said Thelma slowly. 'It feels like it should, but I'm just not sure why.'

When Pat got back to Borrowby Liam was hanging out pants (Andrew's), jeans and shirts in the bright, gusty afternoon.

'Don't worry,' he said. 'I'm not going to outstay my welcome. Just been doing a bit of sorting.' She picked up the laundry basket and as they walked to the house, he flung a careless arm round her shoulders.

He'd also tidied the kitchen and cleaned the bathroom. Just the thought that someone else had thought of these things and done them made her realize how difficult it had been since Andrew had ambled back home. Still, she was not going to think about that, nor was she going to think about boilers, carbon monoxide, nasty letters or any lurking, unaddressed darkness. She was going to listen to Jules Bellerby, have a cheeky glass of Merlot and make Angela Hartnett cod with peppers. She was slicing peppers when Liam walked into the kitchen, laptop under his arm.

'I've been having a look at those accounts,' he said.

She looked at him blankly, mind on white wine vinegar.

'The ones you got off Linda. The Great St Barnabus expenses scandal!'

He spread the printouts on the kitchen table, pushing aside the arranged ingredients. The thought vaguely crossed Pat's mind that if Andrew had done such a thing she would have been screaming with inner irritation.

'These companies Kayleigh Bling is using and using.'

She continued chopping. 'They didn't look anything special to me,' she said. 'All things a school needs.'

'You need to look at bit more closely, Mother,' he said patiently.

'What about them? Don't say they're all owned by Steve Hewson?'

'Not exactly. But if you *look* at them, dig a bit . . . Dance-tastic Academy. Run by one Rozalyn Wall. Who according to her Facebook is Kayleigh Bling's bestie. And the decorators they use are in fact Ms Bling's brother-in-law. Plus, We-Shine Windows – that's Rozalyn Wall's partner, the excitingly tattooed Wayne.'

'I see.'

'And of course, in the mix there's Stevie Wonder, Mr Hot Tub himself – and raking it in from his little boiler operation, plus all his various works in school. We're talking thousands here, Mother.'

'So, you mean . . .'

'I mean one way and another, Kayleigh Bling and cronies are doing pretty well out of Lodestone Academy Trust.'

CHAPTER THIRTY-ONE

On a stormy night a landscape is defaced, and a frightened lady gives in.

That night found Thelma again sitting in her favourite chair by the fire, once more listening to the wind outside grumbling up into what the *Look North* weatherman promised were going to be an interesting few days. 'Time to be battening down the hatches, folks,' he'd said cheerfully, pointing at the alarming-looking arrows sweeping in from the Atlantic. 'Storm Fitzpatrick is on its way!'

Earlier on in the programme there had been a segment from Ripon College, where that bonny dark-haired presenter had expertly taken apart the flustered arguments from a Baht'at representative, whilst Josie Gribben and her friends (obviously having the time of their lives) yelled vociferously in the background. A crucial meeting was to be held that Friday and the confident word from Brummie Maureen was that closure plans were to be put on hold. Now Teddy was at an emergency faculty meeting, which was overrunning into the evening; he'd just texted saying not to wait on supper.

Outside the wind was making those unsettling sea-like noises. Looking over at the curtains she could see them billowing out slightly at each gust. From the safety of behind the sofa, Snaffles surveyed the phenomenon with great suspicion.

Thelma sighed and turned her thoughts to that other preoccupation of hers, the anonymous letters. After all their trouble to get a sight of them, she felt very little further forward. *Lazy*. That word came back to her again and again. Why were they so . . . *petty*? But then maybe that was the nature of poison pen letters – spiteful insinuation bothered more about hurting than getting to the real painful complications of people's lives?

Who had sent them? Jan Starke? Or Sam? Or Becky? And *why* had Becky simply walked away instead of challenging her and Liz?

The trill of her phone grabbed her attention. KAYLEIGH B said the call ID. Thelma's first thoughts were panicky ones; what if Becky *had* indeed told Kayleigh what she'd seen? Or Kayleigh had found out about her visit to see her husband?

'Thelma.' The voice was loud, almost breathless, thankfully with no trace of confrontation. 'Sorry to bother you.'

'It's no bother,' said Thelma. 'Is everything all right?'

'Not really. Where are you?'

'I'm at home,' said Thelma as another gust of wind puffed out the curtains.

'I'm so sorry to ask, but is there any chance whatsoever you could come over?'

'To your home?' An alarming vision of the track to Badger's Fold sprung into her mind.

'I'm in school. I've been working late and . . . *I think there's someone in the building.*'

As Thelma drove past the Victoria tower clock on the edge of Ripon, it said five to seven – which in reality meant it was ten past the hour. It was some nineteen minutes later that the twin headlights of the mussel-blue Corsair cut great sweeping arcs across the empty car park at St Barnabus's. Empty apart from the caramel-coloured sports car. As Thelma got out, she could see a solitary figure framed in the doorway.

'Thelma.' Kayleigh clutched at her arm – a dishevelled, nervous figure despite the designer jacket. 'Thank goodness. I thought you'd never get here. Thank you for coming.' She almost tugged her into the school, looking round fearfully. The door almost slammed itself shut, the wind gusting and bucketing against the glass of the reception.

'Have you called the police?'

'That's just it, I can't be sure, so I don't like to. Matt's still off sick of course, I can't reach Terry Meadows. I didn't know what to do.'

'Maybe it's people working on the boiler?'

'They all went at five.'

Thelma realized they were talking in whispers and decided that there was no good reason for this. 'Tell me exactly what happened,' she said in a normal voice.

'I was working late,' said Kayleigh, drawing in great breaths. 'What with being out yesterday and today, there's all sorts cropped up – so I thought I'd clear my desk. Anyway, I was sitting in my office working and, in the corridor, *I heard a cough*. Muffled – like someone was trying to be quiet.' She dropped her voice again and Thelma felt something like a shiver. 'So, I called out "Hello" – I thought it must be someone else staying late. I went to the door . . . but I couldn't hear anything. And I was just thinking it must have been the wind or something when I noticed *the door through to the main corridor was open* . . . And I distinctly remember it was *shut* before. I don't mind telling you, I came over all teazy. I shouted out again but there was no reply, and that's when I called you.' She looked fearfully beyond the lobby into the darkened school. 'I don't know if whoever it is, is still there.'

307

'It's not likely they'd hang around when they saw another car pull up,' said Thelma. 'Not if they were up to no good.' She realized there was more than a little wishful thinking behind her words.

'They must have gone.' Kayleigh appeared to come to some sort of resolution. 'Thelma, I wonder – I really ought to go and check the premises. Would you come with me?'

'Of course,' said Thelma, feeling she hadn't a lot of choice, and also wondering what challenge, if any, two middle-aged ladies could present to any intruder present. She followed Kayleigh into the corridor and as they rounded the corner into the main school, Kayleigh suddenly gripped her convulsively in a way that nearly caused Thelma to have an unfortunate accident.

'There,' she said in a low voice. '*There*. Oh My God.'

Down the corridor, in the black, black depths of the silent school, was a distant glimmer of light.

'Right,' said Thelma. 'We go back to your office, we lock the door, and we ring 999.' But even as she spoke the words, she realized Kayleigh was already moving towards the distant light and she felt once again she had little choice but to follow.

As they cautiously progressed, Thelma reflected on the unsettling nature of a school after dark, the sinister shapes of coat pegs and bookcases where normally there was light, bustle and noise. And even Kayleigh snapping on the electric lights with thunderous clicks, producing dull buzzes as white brightness snapped shapes into being, only served to emphasize how very dark was the night and the unlit areas of the building.

Part way down the corridor they both froze.

'What's that?' hissed Kayleigh.

'It sounds like a door banging.' Again, Thelma realized she was whispering. A gust of cold air and a further bang made them shrink together.

'Come on,' whispered Kayleigh. 'The light's coming from Sam's classroom.'

Approaching the darkened room, the source became all too obvious. A lit torch lay on the carpet, casting an eerie upward glow.

'Left over from a science lesson maybe?' said Thelma, aware of a shake in her voice.

'Maybe,' said Kayleigh but at that moment the door banged again, loud, immediate. They both shrieked and clutched one another. The fire door wasn't fastened. It banged in a sudden gust, which rattled pictures on walls; on the floor scattered papers swirled and turned.

'The cleaners always make sure the fire doors are secured,' said Kayleigh, a tremor in her voice.

Thelma moved to the door, took a quick, timid look outside and firmly closed it.

'Of course,' said Kayleigh and she sounded like she was trying to convince herself. 'Of course with Matt not being here it's always possible there was a mistake.'

'And the torch?'

'Left over from science like you said.'

Thelma took another look round. Apart from things disturbed by the wind, everything seemed in order. *Let's go back,* she was about to say but had no more than opened her mouth when there was another shriek from Kayleigh (and again another near accident on Thelma's part).

'Ohh,' said Kayleigh. '*Ohhh!*'

'What?' said Thelma.

'Didn't you hear it? The front door – I'm sure that was the front door beeping.'

But when they returned to the lobby, all seemed as they'd left it.

'All the same,' said Thelma, 'we need to call 999. Just to be on the safe side.'

'We'll do it in my office,' said Kayleigh. They walked back round the corner to her office door, and Kayleigh waved her fob.

'Funny,' said Kayleigh. 'It normally beeps.' She put out a hand and the door swung open easily.

Too easily.

For the third time that night Kayleigh screamed. For the third time Thelma's body threatened disaster. With a feeling of cold dread, Thelma looked over the other woman's shoulder.

The room had been trashed.

The normally immaculate room had been thoroughly, comprehensively done over, a vase smashed, desk upended, Mukor Bridge ripped, and zig-zagged across with red spray paint. The desk drawers were all ripped out, the contents scattered everywhere, files spread like wounded birds, highlighters spilling like plastic treasure, paper clips sparkling silver. The picture wasn't the only use of spray paint. Across the wall was one violent, horrifying scrawl: *BITCH*.

'Don't touch anything,' said Thelma. 'In fact come away.'

Obediently Kayleigh retreated to the lobby. Thelma lingered a minute longer . . . Was something missing? What? Her mind was registering something not there that should be – but surely everything was such a mess. Then she realized, in the middle drawer, amongst the tumbled stationery, there was no coaster. She instantly dismissed the thought as irrelevant; it must be hidden under the mess somewhere.

While they were waiting to speak to the police, Thelma sat next to Kayleigh, who slumped listlessly on one of the royal seats in the lobby.

'So that noise we heard when we were in Sam's room . . . it must have been whoever it was coming in . . .' Kayleigh sounded totally drained.

'Or going out,' said Thelma. 'They probably waited till we went

310

down to the classroom and seized the opportunity. They may even have been hidden in your office whilst we were speaking.' She wished the thought had stayed unvoiced as Kayleigh emitted a whimpering moan. 'It's all right,' said Thelma.

'What I can't get my head round,' said Kayleigh, 'is what would have happened if I hadn't called you. If I'd stayed here on my own.'

The very same thought had occurred to Thelma. 'Probably nothing,' she said in what she hoped was a comforting voice. But still she couldn't help remembering that last letter Kayleigh had received:

THIS IS YOUR FIRST AND LAST WARNING.

Kayleigh sighed, a deep, weary sigh. Thelma turned to her.

'I want to ask you something,' she said. 'Something I should have asked you some time ago.'

Kayleigh looked at her, the beginnings of a curious frown on her face. 'Go on,' she said.

'The night of the summer fayre. When you received that first letter.'

Kayleigh sighed. 'That night seems so long ago. What about it?'

'Later on, when the raffle was drawn . . . I happened to notice you looked suddenly shocked.'

Kayleigh's face flashed blank for a moment, then the frown returned. 'Shocked?' she said. 'I don't think so . . .' She looked at Thelma. 'I mean I'd received that awful letter saying how I'd upset everyone. Naturally I was very on edge.'

Thelma frowned, but before she could pursue the thought Kayleigh spoke again.

'It had been a long day. I remember thinking I'd had enough.'

'I just wondered if you saw someone? Someone who might be

threatening you – but perhaps you didn't want to say? Maybe to protect them?'

'No,' said Kayleigh definitely. 'I don't remember *anything* like that. Don't you think if I had *any* idea, I'd say something? After all that's happened?' Her voice trembled; was she about to cry? But her voice when it came was calm – flat but calm.

'I can't do this anymore,' she said. 'I thought I could, but I can't.' She turned to look at Thelma. 'Someone's out to get me,' she said. 'I thought I could just ignore it, but I can't take it anymore.' She sighed. 'They've won,' she said. 'Whoever is doing all this has *won*.'

CHAPTER THIRTY-TWO

Thelma asks for help and has her thoughts provoked by horror in the charity shop.

'I can't work out what it is that's happening,' said Thelma aloud in the empty student chapel. 'People are hurt and frightened and I don't know why, and I don't know what to do.'

Outside in the corridor, footsteps sounded and Thelma braced herself, an image of Brummie Maureen or even Josie Gribben coming into her mind, but the footsteps passed and faded into the distance. After all the recent excitement the college was quiet, even subdued, everyone saving their energies for the big meeting scheduled for the following day.

Thelma breathed, and looked round the shabby room, trying to still her restless mind. Since her last visit someone had dumped three cardboard boxes on the chairs opposite. They seemed to be full of files and papers. There was a label written in black marker: *I know about this.* Thelma wondered whether the words were acknowledgement, defence, or maybe even a warning. On a more cheerful note, the faded orange chrysanthemums had gone, and had been replaced by some sombre purple ones.

She tried again to get some semblance of order into her weary thoughts. After an exhausting night explaining things to the police and to Teddy, a very broken sleep, plus an intense phone call first thing from Pat about the school accounts, she increasingly had the need for somewhere to peacefully *think*. Because of the weather it would need to be indoors. Friday morning was messy church at St Catherine's, the cathedral usually had visitors – and then suddenly this place had come to mind.

She felt flooded by events. Flooded, battered, trampled – like the country was preparing to be in the wake of this approaching Storm Fitzpatrick.

'I don't know what to do,' she said again. 'Give me guidance.'

She found herself looking at the chrysanthemums. So purple in the watery sun. Even with everything that had been happening, someone had taken the trouble to replace them, to take out and bin the old ones, refill the vase and put these flowers in.

She took another calming breath and turned her mind back to the matter in hand.

Instead of scrabbling for answers, maybe she should explore the question a bit more.

Unbidden that song came into her mind: *Who where what why; don't forget when . . .*

That was the problem . . . the *what* . . . Or rather the *whats* . . . The many whats.

They lay side by side, full of stuff, much like the boxes in front of her.

Becky's unreadable look. Claire's tears. Nicole and Ian. Linda and Matt. Jan Starke. Sam. *All with their own agendas.*

The break-in, Kayleigh's defeated voice – *I can't go on.*

Then there was what Pat had said about the accounts – not dishonest as such; schools needed painters and window cleaners and dance instructors. But to employ so many friends and family (and, possibly, lovers)? To use one of Liz's favourite sayings, it didn't sit right.

314

But then maybe that was the way of the world nowadays? Maybe it was she, Thelma, who was out of step, reactionary? Maybe there was nothing wrong in making sure things worked financially for all concerned? She thought of the institution she was now sitting in – the jumble of card indexes, the ancient PCs, the splintery wooden desks. It felt to her that currently the college was the financial equivalent of a badly, but lovingly, run church fete.

Maybe it was as Teddy said – maybe this whole place was out of its time?

Like the letters. Not fitting in this modern world of social media . . . and yet with the power to inflict dreadful damage – even to potentially kill . . . And there had been something *else* about them, something she'd subconsciously seen but hadn't fully noticed. She shook her head in frustration.

'What shall I do?' For the third time she said the words out loud, but a third time there was no response in the peaceful room stacked with boxes.

She sighed, picked up her bag – and as she did so her phone buzzed. Half excited, half with dread she snatched it up, scenarios about Sam, about Kayleigh, about Matt tumbling luridly through her mind.

But it was Verna.

FULL OF COLD NE CHANCE U
CUD COVER SHIFT TA

And that irritating crying-with-laughter emoticon she used on such occasions.

Verna may not have been physically there at the hospice charity shop that morning, but her presence was certainly felt. Once again she'd been doing one of her infamous window displays. This one

315

consisted of a great deal of orange fabric draped around the space, liberally scattered with fallen leaves whilst a notice informed the people of Ripon it was the 'season of mists and mere fruitfulness'.

'I'm not sure that quotation's quite right,' said Polly.

Thelma said nothing but regarded the display. Artfully arranged on the clothes and leaves, and round a pumpkin and rake, were a collection of autumn-related objects: mittens, scarves, hats and recipe books (though Thelma couldn't say she particularly associated tapas with the autumn).

'It looks a bit lopsided,' she observed, seeing how the objects were all clustered to the right-hand side, leaving the left almost bare.

'It's meant to be like that,' said Polly. 'I know about that. There's that leaky window frame on the left. Remember those ruined handbags? Until it's fixed, we're trying to leave that side clear.'

'I see,' said Thelma.

'By arranging it like that, it's meant to draw the eye away from the leak; that's what Verna said.'

Across the market place a sudden gust blew a wheelie bin on its side and there was a flurry of activity as people ran to retrieve it.

'They reckon it's going to be bad,' said Polly, peering out at the confusion. 'This Storm Fitzpatrick. I'll make a start on those two bin bags of clothes, if you want to do that bag for life?' She nodded her head at a bag for life with a big rainbow on the side. Thelma nodded vaguely. She was sure Polly had just said something significant, but she wasn't sure what it was. She shook her head. It was so full of *stuff*, she felt a powerful need to somehow take it all out, bit by bit, one by one, arrange the buzzing thoughts like the objects in the window display.

Suddenly she properly noticed the bag. The garish rainbow on the side, maybe half full. It struck her as familiar, but she couldn't quite place it. She checked inside; two new reams of copying paper and a few packets of crayons. Then all at once an image came to her: the hallway of the bungalow by the railway tracks.

'Did you see who brought this in?' she said to Polly. Polly rolled her eyes. 'Some strange lady,' she said. 'Rather wild eyes – a load of pinky-purple hair. I did think she might be a bit tipsy . . .'

Bunty Carter? It sounded like her. But what was she doing bringing stuff into a charity shop in Ripon, when she lived near Thirsk and was staying in Tadcaster?

'Have you taken anything out of there?'

Polly shook her head. 'She was only in a few minutes before you got here.'

Thelma pictured the hallway of Bunty's bungalow, seen through the window that day. 'Was there a second bag with it?' Again, Polly shook her head. 'Just that,' she said.

Thelma took out the paper and the crayons and looked at them sombrely.

The trilling of her phone broke rudely into her grim thoughts.

'It's me again,' said Pat. 'News, hot off the press. I've just heard something from Linda.'

'What?' asked Thelma.

'Kayleigh Bling is leaving St Barney's! After last night, she's decided enough is enough . . . She's not coming back.'

Thelma put her phone back in her bag, staring unseeingly at the packs of crayons in front of her. In her mind, a weary, broken voice – *I can't take it anymore* . . .

'Hi, hi!' The cheery greeting combined with the shop bell made her look up. 'Fancy seeing you here!'

For the second time that morning it took Thelma's mind a few seconds to place something – in this case not a bag but a tubby figure in the purple polo shirt. Church? Certainly not Knit'n'Natter. College? It was the pile of unsorted paperbacks in front of her that made the face click into memory. Of course! St Barnabus's

317

summer fayre. Izzy Trewin? And then she had been at the harvest festival, complaining about being unable to see Kayleigh Brittain.

'I didn't know you worked here,' said Izzy, arch and accusing as though really Thelma *should* have told her.

'I usually work Thursday afternoons and Tuesdays.'

'Ah! Thursday is my "me" day!' A cheerful peal of laughter.

'You work in Ripon,' said Thelma politely, wishing she'd shut up and let her continue pursuing her tangled thoughts.

'I do!' She thrust one of her ample bosoms forward and Thelma saw the logo of the new mobile shop that had opened in the arcade where the barbers used to be. 'Customer service operative!' She managed to make the role sound significant and weighty, whilst also implying the Mobile One Stop was lucky to have her services, though Thelma knew for a fact turnover at the shop was rapid and indeed Contralto Kate, whose nephew also worked there, said you were 'tret worse than a skivvy'.

'I said Izzy Trewin, get yourself back out there and into the world of work – because that world won't come to you, much as you might want it to!' She began looking through the rails, rattling the coat hangers in a practised way. 'Anyway!' She took a rather ghastly blue and pink top and held it up against her. 'What do you think about all the goings-on at St Barnabus's? Talk about the old scandalarbra!'

For a fleeting moment Thelma thought she must have somehow heard about Kayleigh's sudden departure. But then so much had happened at the school during the past week it was much more likely to be something else. Izzy now had hold of a dark crimson creation with a large rosette-type arrangement at the cleavage, which she held wistfully up to the light. 'Still,' she said cheerfully. 'It makes the world go round, so they say. Good luck to them!'

Thelma smiled politely; obviously the particular scandalarbra she was referring to was Ian and Nicole's flight to Acomb.

'I know people have been down on them – I know she could be a Miss Snooty Knickers – but at the end of the day people are people and they have this awkward little habit of falling in love with each other! Especially when they're nose to nose, so to speak.' Izzy smiled, slightly wistfully. 'I remember this school I was working in – a secondary school. There was a similar thing going on, only this was a teacher and a student – talk about kerfuffle!'

A piercing scream interrupted the flow and Polly emerged from the back room at a rate of knots. 'An enormous beetle!' she said breathlessly. 'It just crawled out of the clothes! Oh, it was horrible!'

'It's all right,' said Thelma. 'I'll deal with it.'

'I don't blame you one bit,' said Izzy cheerfully. 'Any sort of creepy-crawly and I go fair teazy. You should see me when there's a spider!'

Izzy Trewin walked out of the shop, ducking her head against the wind, a carrier bag containing the blue and pink top held against her. As she started off down the street, Thelma caught up with her. 'Don't tell me my card wasn't authorized!'

'It's nothing like that.' Thelma spoke loudly against the wind. 'That word you used just now. Teasing?' Izzy frowned, so Thelma repeated the word.

Her then her face cleared. '*Teazy*,' she semi-shouted.

'That's it. Could you tell me what it means?'

'It means you've just seen a blumin' great creepy-crawly!' Izzy laughed loud at her own joke. 'No, it's what they say where Oi came from, my 'andsome.' She affected a thick accent that wouldn't have been out of place in *Poldark*.

Thelma thought back to that warm night so long ago. 'Cornwall?'

Izzy Trewin nodded. 'It means you've had a fright.'

★

319

In the back room of the charity shop she knelt in front of the two upended bags, but despite the blue rubber gloves, she was making no effort to sort the pile of musty clothes. As before, her head was full – but now amongst all those 'whats,' a pattern was emerging, a shape . . . The summer fayre . . . Vague but nasty letters . . . A coaster . . .

Phrases ran through her mind . . . *it draws the eye away . . . talk about kerfuffle!*

That day in the garden centre—

Old Starke-Staring sent them to herself . . . And what else was it that Pat had said? *She can't even spell . . .*

Spelling . . .

She frowned and took out her phone . . . looked through the images of the letters. Finding the two she wanted, she nodded – just as she thought . . . Which meant . . .

A stricken, shocked look . . .

The wind gusted at the skylight . . . *the sound of distant seas.*

The sea.

It didn't take her too long. She was barely online for ten minutes when she found what she was looking for. But she needed to be *sure* . . . and as far as she could work out – there was only one way to do that.

CHAPTER THIRTY-THREE

In a seaside village, shells are collected, pictures viewed and a tale of illicit passion remembered.

'*Cornwall?*' said Teddy. 'Why Cornwall?' He frowned at her in bewilderment. His eyes had gone very blue and focused, the way they did when faced by life's curve balls.

Succinctly, Thelma explained.

'But surely – a phone call would do?'

'I need to do this face to face.'

'But *Cornwall*.' Teddy seemed to be having difficulty in moving beyond this fact. 'What if you're wrong?'

'That's why I have to go there and speak to the person face to face,' she said.

'I see.' He frowned again. 'Do you really need to go tomorrow? It's the big meeting at college, I *have* to be there. If you can wait a day or even two – we can go down together.'

'I'm afraid time is of the essence,' she said. 'Kayleigh will have already left the school by next week.'

'You know there's going to be a storm?' He was staring at her; it was as if it was the first time he was properly seeing her in days. '*Cornwall?*'

★

'It's a long old drive,' said Pat down the phone.

'Seven hours twelve minutes according to Google Maps,' said Thelma.

'There's going to be a storm apparently.'

'Due to die out during the course of the day,' said Thelma.

'And you have to see this person whoever they are, face to face?'

'I do.'

'And what if you're wrong?'

'Then it'll have been a long drive for nothing.'

'You know there's a storm coming?' Liz had distinct overtures of doom in her voice.

'It has been mentioned,' said Thelma. Her decision to tell her friends what she was doing had been one she'd given some thought. Hearing Liz, she wondered if she'd done the right thing.

'No arguments, I'm going with you,' said Pat.

'There is absolutely no need.' This was the last thing Thelma had wanted.

'There's every need.'

'I can only see this person on my own.'

'You won't be seeing anyone if you wrap your car round a tree in Devon.'

'I explained to Pat, I need to see this person on my own,' said Thelma. She had the feeling that events were somewhat running away from her.

'It's the journey I'm bothered about,' said Liz. 'You driving down all that way on your own. There's going to be a storm, you know. Derek's app's giving out double windsocks.'

Thelma envisaged seven hours twelve minutes of Liz worrying about Storm Fitzpatrick.

'It's very sweet of you,' she said. 'There's absolutely no need.'

'*Cornwall?*' From the way Rod spoke, he made it sound at the very least like a war zone of some description. 'Why on earth do you want to go to Cornwall?'

'I don't,' said Pat. 'It's Thelma. She has to see someone, and I can't let her drive down there on her own.'

From their places at the kitchen table Rod, Liam and Andrew looked at her.

'What about Teddy? Can't he go with her?'

'No. He's got this crisis meeting at the college, to do with the closure. So, I said I'd go.'

'You can't.' There was a note of what sounded like panic in Rod's voice.

'It's the other end of the country, Mother,' said Liam. He also sounded worried.

'I know,' said Pat. 'Seven hours twelve minutes. We'll go in the Yeti, we'll be fine.'

'You know there's going to be a storm,' said Rod. 'A bloody big one.'

'I'll be careful.'

'You can't go.' He spoke finally and definitely. 'It's crazy.'

This was the last thing Pat had expected. For the past few months Rod had seemed largely oblivious to her comings and goings. Helplessly she looked at Liam, her usual ally at times like this. But he was looking unsure, bright-eyed, almost panicky, reminding Pat of those times when he used to sleepwalk as a teenager.

'Dad's right,' he said, 'This storm's going to be massive.'

'It's not a bad route though.' Andrew spoke quietly. Pat realized for a moment she'd forgotten he was there. 'A1M, M1, M42, M5, A30.' There was confidence and strength in the way he reeled off the list. 'Motorway and dual carriageway nearly all the way. There may be a few hold-ups, but otherwise you should be okay.'

'There's a sod-off big storm. Gale-force winds. Trees blowing everywhere.' There was an edge in Rod's voice that sounded as if tears weren't so far away. He suddenly looked older. And tired. Pat suddenly remembered it was three months to the day since that last lot of chemo had finished.

'Dad.' Andrew's voice was calm and firm. 'She'll be fine. She's a good driver, Thelma's sensible enough. If it gets really bad, they'll just have to pull in.' He looked calmly at his father and brother. 'And she obviously needs to go.'

'That's done,' said Derek. 'Three people, one night, NightPrem Inn, St Austell. It's in your name and it's given us 85 NightPrem points.' Out of the three husbands he'd been the one – after an initial three-minute wobble – to take the news in his stride.

'Thanks.' From behind where he was sat at the computer, Liz hugged him and planted a kiss on his greying hair. He said nothing but clutched her hands tight.

'And this is all to do with what happened to Sam Bowker?' he said, not for the first time.

'It is.'

'But you don't know what exactly?'

She rested her chin on the top of his head. 'This,' she said, 'is one of those times when you don't know why I'm doing what I'm doing.'

'Promise me you'll take care,' he said, not letting go of her hands.

'Of course,' said Liz. 'I always do.'

'There's a Harvest Pantry attached to the hotel, so you won't have to worry about food.'

'I wouldn't go unless it was really necessary,' said Liz.

'I know,' he said.

In the event it took eight hours nineteen minutes, not seven hours twelve minutes, to drive from Thirsk to St Just; that was with two comfort stops and a protracted crawl through Sheffield where a high-sided vehicle had shed its load. As they passed Birmingham, Andrew rang to tell them of an accident on the M5, successfully navigating them cross-country to avoid the seven-mile tailbacks; as they neared Bristol, Derek phoned to say that the worst of Storm Fitzpatrick had passed.

Like many storms, it had not been quite as apocalyptic as the media predicted but it had been bad, no two ways about it. The wind had, as predicted, raged, shaking the Yeti and obscuring the window with pelting, driving rain that the wipers could barely keep up with. Pat had remained largely cheerful throughout, alternately berating other drivers and singing along to Radio 2; Liz had sat tensely on the back seat clutching her seat belt as if it was a flotation device. And though there was a point near Droitwich where Thelma felt she simply could not stand one more gasp of horror from Liz, or expletive from Pat, she was in the main very glad of her friends' company.

Teddy called no less than eight times, the final time to tell Thelma the college had been reprieved for the time being.

As Derek had said, the worst of Storm Fitzpatrick had largely been over by late morning, though there were disturbing signs of its passage throughout the journey: fallen trees, lopsided signs and even a jack-knifed lorry on Bodmin Moor.

It was coming on for 3 p.m. and a late sun was wearily struggling up through torn and blotchy clouds when the Yeti broached the brow of a hill to reveal the village of St Just spread out below, a jumble of roofs and grey walls, a church tower and beyond, a gunmetal-grey sea.

'Remember,' said Thelma, 'I need to go in alone.'

'I want to go to the beach,' said Liz.

'I hope you've packed your bikini,' said Pat as a belated squall of rain feebly squirted against the Yeti.

Pat dropped Thelma in the village square, which was more of a village triangle, and a lopsided one at that.

'About four,' said Thelma.

'Keep your phone on,' said Liz, peering suspiciously out into the square.

Thelma said nothing but made a mental note to turn it off. The very last thing she wanted was a text from Verna or even – heaven forbid – a call from Kayleigh Brittain during what promised to be a delicate conversation.

The beach turned out not to be a beach so much as a stony slope next to a headland, about a mile beyond the town. From the National Trust car park Pat could hear the waves and smell the seaweed. 'A bit stony for sunbathing,' she said, raising her voice above the wind. Liz, however, donned her fleece and purposefully headed off down the car park carrying two bags for life. Pat didn't follow her. After the long drive she didn't really feel like slipping over a load of wet rocks. Neither did she want to wait in the car park; the lady manning the National Trust stall kept smiling at her and Pat had a nasty feeling given half a chance she'd try and get her to join.

'I'll come back for you after four,' she called down to Liz.

Having parked up in the village she got out of the car, keen to walk off the stiffness of the four-hundred-mile drive. St Just didn't seem to be your archetypal Cornish village, she noted – certainly nothing like Newquay or one of those glossy surfing places you saw on the travel programmes. The shops were practical, workaday – post office, Co-op, baker's, charity shops (four of these). None of those bleached-wood fish restaurants. Nor did there seem to be any of those glass-balconied second homes that caused so much controversy. Indeed, walking round the terraces, seeing the back yards, the Velux windows, the lights coming on in kitchens and living rooms, it wasn't that different from some of the more workaday villages round Bradford.

Down the road leading to the sea was a café-cum-bookshop, The Cookbook. The lit windows looked welcoming in the gathering gloom, and as a sudden squall was blowing up, Pat went in. It was as you'd expect – a couple of low-ceilinged, cosily lit rooms lined with bookshelves, and paintings for sale. A radio was playing – 'Golden Brown' by the Stranglers – and in the kitchen area a woman was washing up, humming along. She looked up when Pat came in, made to turn the radio off.

'Leave it on,' said Pat.

'I've had it on all day,' said the woman. 'I was glad of it earlier. The wind! We're not doing hot food, I'm afraid, the supplies didn't get through, but I can do tea or coffee, and there's some cakes we've got available.'

Pat smiled. 'Thanks,' she said.

As she waited, she browsed through the books and looked at the pictures. The atmosphere was one of peace and tranquillity, added to by the faint strains of music emanating from the kitchen. Some of the pictures looked like the sea, others did not but were probably meant to be the sea. One picture in particular caught her eye because it showed neither the sea nor indeed anything noticeably Cornwall. It was stark, simple, showed the inside of a shed, looking in through the door. Broom propped in a corner, flowerpots on the side, pair of gloves, tea chest, sack of potatoes. Jumbled but at the same time ordered and there was a quality to it that made Pat seem to smell the soil and dust; feel the warm afternoon air.

Another song came on, another one Pat recognized. 'Life in a Northern Town' by Dream Academy. Approaching with Pat's tea (and saffron bun), the woman started singing along.

327

'Makes me think of where I used to live,' she said and as she spoke Pat detected a familiar spike in the accent.

'You're not from round here,' she said.

'Halifax,' said the woman putting the cup and plate on the table.

'A long way from home,' said Pat. The coffee was rich and brown, the bun as good as anything you would get at the garden centre.

The woman smiled. 'This is home,' she said.

It turned out the woman had worked in the planning department of Bradford Council, for years. Spreadsheets, team meetings and data analysis – that had been her life pretty much. 'Every day,' she said, 'I'd stand at that photocopier and say, "Soon be Friday." Years and years.'

'What happened?' said Pat.

'Nothing startling,' said the woman. 'Just one day someone said to me, "You always say that," and I realized, yes, I did always say that. Years and years I spent wishing it was Friday. So – I relocated.' She smiled. 'In films it always happens in five minutes. A few shots of packing up and going. Best part of two years it took me. But I did it.'

'And you manage?' asked Pat. She tried not to put too much emphasis on the word 'manage'.

'Bit of work here, some shifts at the Co-op, some work in the galleries. Bugger all money,' said the woman. 'But I wake up, and I think – ahhh! Tuesday!'

The Lew Carne Gallery was a rather ramshackle building down a back lane that looked as if it had been some sort of workshop at some time, with big windows and a glass skylight. Although the metal frames were somewhat rusty, and the views were of house backs and wheelie bins, you could tell in daytime the room would be light and bright.

The man who had opened the door must have been in his early thirties – reddened outdoor skin, thick curly hair (somewhat paint-spattered) and the bluest of blue eyes, which steadily appraised Thelma as she gingerly sat down on a stool (also paint-spattered; Thelma wondered if it would be rude to cover it with her hanky). She looked around the space. It smelt intoxicatingly of acrylic paint. The spatters of colour and stacked canvases were exciting rather than messy.

'Thelma,' he said. 'Tea or coffee?'

Thelma opted for coffee, not because she particularly wanted one but having a drink tied her to staying a certain amount of time, always useful if things got tricky. Her eyes ranged round the various canvases stacked round the workspace; even if she had not done her homework, she would have had no difficulty in identifying them as works done by the artist responsible for the vibrant seascape that had once hung in Kayleigh Brittain's office. Lew Carne.

Lew Carne returned with the tea and handed Thelma a rather stained Pendeen Mining Museum mug and regarded her steadily with those blue eyes.

'So, Thelma from Thirsk,' he said.

'Thank you for seeing me,' said Thelma. 'I wouldn't have asked to see you if it hadn't been very important to a lot of people. Without going into detail there's been a lot of hurt and upset, and there's a danger of a great injustice being done.'

'Sounds interesting.' His face was giving nothing away.

She fumbled in her handbag and took out her phone and showed him one of the pictures of Kayleigh Brittain, tanned and smiling in Dubai.

Lew Carne looked at the picture for a long moment, face still expressionless.

'Karen McAllister,' he said eventually.

One of the benefits of being a lady of a certain age is that as

329

a rule people generally don't suspect you of having a hidden agenda or ulterior motive beyond the immediately obvious. At no point did Lew Carne seriously consider Thelma of being anything other than what she said she was – a lady from Thirsk out to right a wrong.

Nevertheless, he said, 'All this is strictly off the record, right? I mean I don't want it ending up on social media or nothing like that.'

Thelma nodded gravely. 'You have my word,' she said.

'Anyway, you'll have read it all in the press reports, I reckon.'

Thelma nodded again, thinking of the various press printouts with their lurid headlines discreetly tucked away in her bag. *Teacher's Romps of Shame with Pupil* was one of the more colourful.

'People round here had a field day, you can imagine,' said Lew Carne, sipping his tea. 'And I can't say's I blame them. If it happened to a kid of mine, I'd be effing livid.'

'But she wasn't found guilty?' said Thelma. She remembered the picture of the hunched figure, face obscured, coming out of Truro Magistrate's Court.

'No, I reckoned I owed her that,' said Lew Carne. Suddenly, unexpectedly, his face broke into a brilliant grin. 'Truth was, Thelma – it was bloody brilliant. At first.' He looked out of the window, seeing not the wheelie bins but seventeen years in the past, the smile fading only slightly. Looking at him Thelma had no problem believing the truth in the *Southwestern Herald* headline: *Besotted Teacher*.

He walked across the room to a cupboard, its top a jungle of paintbrushes and palette knives. 'She said she loved me,' he said. 'I suppose everyone says that at some point, but when she said it, I believed her. Trouble was by that time I didn't love her back.' He took out a folder of pictures and walked back across the room.

'I have to make you understand what it was like at school back then. Maybe now as well. You go to school, and you expect teachers to have all the answers. Answers you don't even have the questions to. And round here – well, you realize not only do most teachers not have a clue, most of the answers they did have for us involved either going on benefits or working in some hotel.'

He spread out the pictures from the folder – charcoal, and ink sketches, vivid but slightly naïve: strange figures in armour, viscous tears on stark faces, a hand grasping barbed wire.

'I'd always done pictures,' he said. 'She saw something in them.'

'Was she your art teacher?'

He barked with laughter. 'No way,' he said. 'Our art teacher was someone who used to paint pictures of the Mount and spend the whole lesson bitching about galleries who weren't interested. No, Karen, she was R.E. Citizenship.' He smiled, put the pictures back. 'She was this buttoned-up thing,' he said. 'Strait-laced. We used to rip the piss out of her something rotten. Little shits we were. One day a few of us stuck some condoms in her handbag. We was always doing stuff like that. I went back into class for something I'd left, and she was sat at her desk crying. That was the start of it.'

Again, that look roved into the past. After appearing to consider, he pulled out another picture. This showed a woman with elven ears, sat in a thorny bower, like something from a fairy tale. The woman was naked, and to Thelma's startled eye seemed to have very large nipples. Even with the short hair and thorns (and nipples), she could clearly recognize the figure of Kayleigh Brittain. Karen McAllister.

'I know now what happened was wrong. But when you're seventeen you don't think like that.' His reminiscent smile faded. 'When it came out, I got all the sympathy. Counselling in Penzance once a week, free taxi. Karen was pilloried. Good job they'd got rid of stocks. It was just as social media was getting going, so it could have been worse.' He looked at Thelma. 'Is that what you wanted to know?'

She nodded. 'You've been very helpful,' she said.

'And is Karen okay now?' he said. 'She won't be called McAllister, I guess.'

Thelma didn't say that she wasn't even called Karen but nodded. 'She's very successful.'

He smiled. 'I'm glad. This bother you mentioned – is she involved?'

'I can tell you if you want,' said Thelma.

He looked a long moment at the folder in his hand. 'No,' he said eventually. 'No.'

At the door he said, 'If you see her,' and stopped.

Thelma paused. 'Yes?' she said.

'Tell her . . .' That sudden grin, lighting up the whole room. 'Tell her I'm living exactly the life I want to live.'

Pat was waiting for her in the village square (triangle). Under her arm was a wrapped parcel. 'Did you find out what you wanted to?' she asked.

'I did.' Thelma looked solemn and Pat knew better than to ask questions there and then.

'We better go to the beach and track down Pamela Anderson,' she said.

'Isn't that her now?' said Thelma and indeed there was Liz hefting the two bags, crossing the road with a bright smile.

'What on earth have you got there?' asked Pat.

'Stones. And shells. A bit of seaweed.'

'What on earth for?' asked Thelma.

'Just a little idea I've had.' She smiled.

'You've never walked all the way from Cape Cornwall lugging those?' said Pat.

'A very nice gentleman from the golf course saw me struggling and gave me a lift,' said Liz with dignity.

'Liz Newsome, you dark horse,' said Pat and they retraced their way back to the car park.

CHAPTER THIRTY-FOUR

Professional ethics and their consequences are debated, and in the Gloucester Services (Northbound) a tale is told and a personal fear is shared.

Because Derek was a NightPrem Plus customer, they were given a free drink with their Harvest Pantry meal. Pat had her customary large red, Thelma felt she'd earned a spritzer, but Liz (who always had trouble sleeping in a strange bed) merely opted for a lime and soda. On the flat-screen dominating one corner of the bar-cum-restaurant were graphic images of the devastation wrought by Storm Fitzpatrick, but it wasn't this that the ladies' attention was focused on.

'So back in the day Kayleigh Bling had an affair with one of her students?' said Pat.

'She was Karen McAllister back then,' said Thelma.

'So, she was what?' Pat did a rapid calculation. 'Early twenties?'

'Just twenty-one,' said Thelma. 'It must have been her first teaching job.'

'And how old was the student?' said Liz, tight-lipped.

'Seventeen.'

Liz's mouth tightened still further, and she took a grim sip of her drink.

'Well, I know it's wrong,' said Pat philosophically. 'But these things happen.' The wine was good, much better than the large photo of red grapes and a dewy glass had led her to expect.

Liz said nothing. 'And don't look at me like that, Liz Newsome. Four years. We all know plenty of couples with a four-year age gap.'

'She was his teacher,' said Liz spikily. 'She had a duty of care.'

Through the cheerful first blurrings of the wine, Pat felt Thelma's foot discreetly kick her ankle. 'I'm not saying it's *right*,' she said.

'How would you feel if it was one of your lads?' said Liz hotly.

Another gentle nudge from Thelma reminded Pat of that fraught time Liz's son had himself been mixed up with an older woman. 'So, did Kayleigh Bling end up in prison then?' she asked by way of changing the subject.

'No,' said Thelma. 'It went to court, but there wasn't enough evidence. I gather the lad himself kept quiet. But there was certainly enough to get her banned from teaching.'

'So how come she's in a school now?' said Liz. Again, her tone was indignant, and Pat found herself wishing her friend had also opted for wine.

'She went to Dubai, somehow getting herself employed in an English school there. She must have dodged round the vetting system somehow. And around then she married Mike Brittain, which would have helped. So, by the time she returned to this country ten years later the transformation was complete: Karen McAllister had become Kayleigh Brittain, whose first teaching job had been in Dubai. The Cornwall job had, to all intents and purposes, never happened.'

'But it had,' muttered Liz mutinously.

'As Kayleigh Brittain she got work here, only in primary schools rather than secondary,' said Thelma. 'She was one of those people who find themselves better suited to management rather than the classroom.'

335

Here there was a slight but significant pause as they all exchanged glances; during their time in teaching, they'd all encountered plenty of people like that.

'At some point the Brittains relocated to Yorkshire – and she became a head teacher for Heaton Royd Trust.'

'Where she had a fling with Stevie Wonder,' speculated Pat.

'When Heaton Royd folded, it was taken over by Lodestone.'

'And she ended up at St Barnabus's,' supplied Liz. The lines around her mouth had not become any looser.

'Feathering her nest every Jimmy-Choo step of the way,' said Pat. She rather thought she might have another red.

'What she's been doing at St Barnabus's isn't technically *wrong*,' said Thelma.

Liz nearly spat her lime and soda clean across the table. 'Picking on Jan? Forcing poor Sam to inflate the results?'

'She means with the accounts,' said Pat.

'But that wasn't right either,' said Liz quickly. 'All that work for friends and family . . .'

'Lovers,' said Pat.

'That's a fact of the academy system. What isn't *ethically* right isn't necessarily legally wrong,' said Thelma. 'But whatever the rights and wrongs of it all, Kayleigh Brittain has been in a very lucrative position.'

'Stevie Wonder and the biomass boiler,' said Pat. 'That'll have paid for a few hot tubs.'

'It was all very nice,' said Thelma. 'And the misdemeanour with Lew Carne was all safely buried in the past. Or so she thought.' She took a sip of spritzer and on the flat-screen in the background a dinghy navigated its way down a row of flooded cottages.

'Then one day, completely out of the blue, at the school summer fayre, who should she see but a woman she'd once worked with at the very school where everything had happened all those years ago. She recognized her instantly – Izzy Trewin's a very memorable lady, the sort who doesn't change much over the years.'

'No wonder she looked shocked,' said Pat.

'But why didn't Izzy recognize her?' asked Liz. 'She was stood up on stage for all the world to see, going on about how wonderful the school was.'

'It had been many years, remember,' said Thelma. 'She'd had a makeover, plus a complete change of name. With Izzy it was probably a case of that feeling you get when you see someone, and they seem familiar, but you can't quite place them. But Kayleigh couldn't take any risks. Izzy's certainly not the sort of person to keep her thoughts to herself and Kayleigh was under absolutely no illusions. If Chris Canne had got any hint of what had happened in her past, he'd have dismissed her on the spot. Her whole nice life would have come crashing down round her ears. No wonder she looked so shocked that night at the summer fayre.'

'But what I don't get,' said Liz, 'is where the nasty letters come in.'

'Hang on!' Pat's cry made more than one person look round. 'Wait a minute . . . Suppose someone *else* got wind of what happened . . . and started sending letters to Ms Bling, trying to force her out!'

'We've only madame's word as to what the letters sent to her said,' said Liz eagerly. 'They could easily have mentioned what happened, and Kayleigh destroyed them.'

'And the other letters were a sort of smokescreen,' said Pat. 'And really someone was blackmailing Kayleigh Bling . . . Maybe even getting money from her?'

'No,' said Thelma. 'That's not what happened at all.'

The journey back up north was different again. The weather was much stiller, quieter, as if it had exhausted itself from the exertions of the previous day, and where there were signs of the storm – twisted trees, fields covered in great silvered slabs of water – these were peaceful, still, detached from the chaos they had been born from. In the Yeti they were even able to have the window open from time to time – a growing necessity because of the smells emanating from Liz's bags-for-life in the boot.

On the way up the M5 they stopped off at the Gloucester Services (Northbound) and all three were very taken by the farm-shop style, the turf-covered structure reminiscent of something from the Teletubbies, instead of the usual drab collection of burger bars, coffee stands and amusement arcades. Thelma bought a Gloucester pie for Teddy, and Liz indulged in a Smokey-Joe Scotch egg for Derek and a jar of something called mustard fruit chutney for Jan. Pat stocked up with a whole collection of chutneys and relishes. 'Now it doesn't matter if Rod does decide to cook,' she said. 'I'm all set.' She arranged the jars with satisfaction on the table where they were sitting. Beetroot and horseradish preserve, onion marmalade, cheeky chilli relish.

Liz looked at her friend. 'You've been seeming a bit brighter,' she said. 'More cheerful.'

'I wasn't aware I wasn't being cheerful,' said Pat, immediately guarded. She looked out of the window at the mini hill and reedy pond, which in some way formed part of the Services' eco-footprint. Suddenly the sky was a bright, bright blue, for the first time in what seemed like ages.

'You weren't exactly moping,' said Thelma and her words hung in the air.

Pat picked up the jar Liz had bought. 'Anyway, what's mustard fruit chutney when it's at home?' she asked.

'It's just the sort of thing Jan likes,' said Liz. She sighed slightly. 'For halloumi night next week.'

Thelma and Pat both smiled. 'I know she's your friend,' said

Pat. 'But for the life of me, Liz Newsome, I cannot see why you put up with her.'

Liz smiled. 'Someone has to.' She paused. 'I really did think it might be her, you know. Sending the letters.'

'Why so sure?' said Pat. 'I mean, even I'd struggle to see that.' Liz paused a moment, looked at Thelma before deciding to speak. 'Come on,' said Pat. 'No more secrets.'

'You know she was in the Friarage Secure Unit that time?'

Pat nodded. 'It was a while back wasn't it?'

'You were on maternity leave with your Liam. It was after her marriage broke down – when Dave was seeing that woman, the one from the Vauxhall garage. Jan rather went off the rails. She tipped paint stripper over Dave's car, even set fire to this woman's shed. Destroyed all her garden furniture.' She sighed, remembering sad times from long ago . . . the pain and the hand-holding and more pain.

'In the end they had to get a restraining order on her. If she hadn't had her breakdown that would have been it for her teaching.'

'I never knew that,' said Pat.

'Liz was a very loyal and discreet friend,' said Thelma. 'Hardly anyone did.'

Liz flushed slightly at the warmth in her friend's voice.

'But I knew – *Jan had that side to her nature* . . . so when people she had issues with started getting these letters – well, I wondered.'

'So would anyone,' said Pat.

'May I ask a question?' said Thelma. 'What made you so suddenly sure it *wasn't* her?'

'When she spoke to me in the library,' said Liz. 'And I remembered what Becky had said was in one of the letters.'

'What did it say?' asked Thelma.

'They said someone was a fat bee eye tee see aitch . . .' again Liz flushed slightly. 'And I knew – *whatever* Jan may or may not do – she'd *never ever* body-shame anyone.'

Thelma smiled at her. 'No,' she said. 'You're quite right.'

'Okay.' Pat spoke suddenly, abruptly, with the air of someone making a confession. 'I'm sorry I avoided you both, back at the end of summer.'

There was a slight surprised pause. 'You've nothing to be sorry for,' said Liz, but Pat was shaking her head.

'You were both so brilliant and lovely all that time Rod was ill and having his treatment. But when there's something – *someone* – on your mind, you keep it to yourself, and suddenly it's this massive *thing* . . .' She spoke fast, arranging and rearranging the jars of chutney and relish. 'But . . .' She stopped and looked at her friends. 'That doesn't help, not really. Like you say – secrets . . . they're *toxic*.' Her friends looked at her. They said nothing, there was nothing much to be said – besides Pat was speaking again. 'It's Rod,' she said. 'Rod and the cancer.'

Again, friends were silent.

'I know it was all sorted and I know it's fine.' Pat stared fixedly at the jar of mustard fruit chutney. 'But at some point, *it could come back*. Or I could get it. Or I could get *something*.' She looked at her friends. 'At some point one of us is going to get *something*. And it's all just made me realize . . . I'm nearly sixty . . . and I've more time behind than I have in front.' She looked at the neat line of jars in front of her. 'And that's what I've not been able to get my head round. Time is short.'

There was an understanding pause.

'Finite is perhaps a better word,' suggested Thelma.

'You could both have years,' said Liz. '*Years*.'

'I just wanted everything to go back to how it *was* . . . Him out at work and me pottering around. I never used to have thoughts like this then.'

And still her friends said nothing; because after all, when it came down to it, there was nothing to say. The thoughts Pat was having were thoughts both of them had had from time to time; they both knew such thoughts were an inevitable part of growing older, and to some extent they were inevitable. And being friends as they were, it wasn't about dismissing or belittling or even trying to resolve those thoughts, but about sitting alongside, and putting them into realistic everyday context with chat about families and gardening, shared memories – and of course the intriguing behaviour of those around them.

And now sitting there in Gloucester Services (Northbound), Pat realized something of that, and she also realized both Thelma and Liz knew and would sit alongside her for as long and as often as was necessary.

The journey back took seven hours fifty-two minutes (two comfort stops plus an emergency stop to jettison some of Liz's seaweed that had definitely outstayed its welcome). It was gone seven when Pat walked into her kitchen, busting for a wee. There was, she noticed, no sign of supper being prepared. 'I'm back,' she carolled, heading for the cloakroom.

Rod appeared as she emerged waving her hands dry. He said nothing but put his arms tightly round her and nestled his head into her shoulder.

'What's happened to the hand towel?' she said.

'Our Andrew spilt something I think,' he said. 'Good trip?'

'Yes,' she said, wondering where and when to start. Maybe after supper. 'Our Liam got off back to Durham all right?' She felt the chin nod.

'I missed you,' he said in a small voice.

'Here.' She broke free and handed him the wrapped package she'd brought from St Just. He unwrapped it and looked at the picture of the shed.

'Okay,' he said noncommittally.

341

'Happy retirement,' said Pat.

His arms were round her again when Andrew walked in.

'Oh God,' he said.

'Now,' said Pat. 'If you are going to stay, we are going to have to come to some arrangement about your pants.'

CHAPTER THIRTY-FIVE

*Ambitious people in corporate spaces are
confronted with various truths.*

The headquarters of Lodestone Academy had a decidedly weekend
feel about them that Saturday; no cheery receptionist, no besuited
people going about their business, the mezzanine floor dim and
silent. Chris Canne himself let them in, casually dressed in jeans
and sweatshirt (designer, noted Pat) and guided her and Thelma
through the darkened spaces to the oatmeal office. The photos of
the church renovation were no longer there, Pat saw.

Both she and Thelma refused a coffee; it did not feel like a
coffee sort of occasion. Chris himself took nervous swigs from a
steel flask of water.

'So,' he said with nervous cheer. 'So, I got your email.'

'It's very good of you to see us at such short notice,' said Thelma.

'I'm always ready to listen when people have worries,' he said.
'Any time of the day or night.'

'You got the documents I sent?' said Pat.

'Yes, yes I did, thank you.' He smiled at them, trying to appear
confident, but nevertheless took a quick nervous glug from the
water. 'And believe you me I've been through them with the
proverbial fine-tooth comb! Some serious burning of the midnight

oil I can tell you!' He smiled. 'And I want to put your minds to rest, ladies. Unless I'm missing something, there is nothing here that sets off any sort of alarm bells.'

Neither Pat nor Thelma spoke.

'Okay, on the face of it I can see how this might look a tadette dodgy. Giving out work to associates . . .'

'And possibly lovers,' said Pat.

Chris ignored this. 'But you need to look at it another way. You run a business, like a school, and you're going to want to source the very best resources for that business, often in a bit of a hurry. And at the most competitive price. It's like I said to you before.' He nodded at Pat. 'If you know someone, it cuts corners. Okay, it might not be the fairest thing in the world – but it makes sense.' He smiled, held up both hands expansively.

'What about the boiler?' asked Pat. 'Steve Hewson and the RHI payments?'

The smile slipped slightly. 'We're looking into that too. However, Steve tells me he's no longer on the payroll of the people who own the boiler – it was just a short-term thing. Apparently, he left them some time ago, they just forgot to take his name off the website.' Chris obviously realized how flimsy this sounded, because he leant forward, hands interlaced, face earnest. 'Can I just tell you,' he said, 'obviously I don't know the guy very well.' Here Pat thought of the missing photographs from the corridor. 'But I can tell you he's straight down the line. What you see is what you get with Steve.'

Pat thought of Matt in the hospital bed, Thelma thought of the nervous workers wolfing down their remaindered sandwiches. Again, neither spoke.

Chris regarded them; fingers still interlaced.

'I need to tell you both something in the strictest confidence – which isn't relevant to this in any way, but I'm telling you anyway. Kayleigh Brittain's going to be moving on from St Barnabus's. Poor love, she's been to hell and back, and feels like she's had enough.'

'We heard she was leaving,' said Pat.

'She's not resigning!' Chris gave a nervous bark of laughter. 'We certainly don't want to lose her! But as she in particular seems to have been targeted by this lunatic, whoever they are, we're going to move her to Trust HQ. She wants to move, and, in all honesty, I can't blame her. Down the line, there's a school we're taking on over in Bolton. I think they could really flourish with her skill set.' Another glug from the flask. 'Is it the moral thing to do – cave in to this joker? Maybe not. But in terms of Kayleigh's mental health, it's a no-brainer. And maybe when she goes all this crap will stop.'

'That,' said Thelma, 'is why it was so important we saw you today.'

'All that about the accounts was just background,' said Pat.

After they'd finished talking, Chris's head seemed to be shining more than ever. He attempted to take another swig from the flask, but it was empty.

'That's a very serious allegation you're making,' he said. 'I mean – really serious.'

'I'm fully aware of that,' said Thelma.

'Have you any proof?'

'About the background – yes,' said Thelma. 'But the rest of it – nothing that would stand up in a court of law.'

'But you can see how it all ties up,' said Pat.

'But without proof . . .' He seemed to seize on that fact, frowning in distress. 'I mean it's really serious.'

'I know,' said Thelma.

'What do you expect me to do about it?' There was an almost pleading tone in his voice.

'That's up to you,' said Thelma. 'I wanted to present you with the facts.'

'The alleged facts.'

'Some alleged, some proven,' said Pat.

'What you do now is entirely up to you and the board of Lodestone Trust,' said Thelma.

Chris saw them out of the darkened building; Pat, having witnessed all the water glugging, took the opportunity to nip off for a security wee.

Waiting in the reception area with Chris, Thelma – like Pat before her – found herself wondering exactly what bit of the old church this was.

'This sort of thing,' Chris blurted out suddenly, 'I mean this *alleged* sort of thing – it's exactly what I *don't* want happening here.'

'I don't doubt that,' said Thelma. 'From what I've seen of Lodestone, and yourself – there are very sound principles in place.'

He seized on the words. 'Exactly,' he said. 'That's exactly it. I mean when I worked for the old education authority . . . the *inefficiency* . . . the things not addressed, the things let slip . . .'

Thelma nodded with her own memories of the old LEA – badly run meetings, calls not returned, poorly planned projects. The waits of months, even years, for children to be referred. She thought of the old TFD teachers' centre at Boroughbridge with its tatty carpets and great slabs of pasta bake. She looked round at the room they were in, its pristine carpets, expensive furniture, those studio portraits of children working.

'The problem is,' she said, 'when money becomes one of the guiding principles behind something, there's great potential for corruption.'

Chris opened his mouth to argue, to blurt out, to justify – but

346

something about Thelma's steady gaze woke something of the old Chris, the Chris who used to joke with Victoria, buy his own glue sticks, take the kids walking in the Dales. More thoughts came into his head – the Rolex and the personalized number plates (CCAN 1), that week in New York that was supposedly about education contacts but was in fact everything about sipping cocktails in Times Square with Tony, drunk on Long Island Iced Tea and possibilities.

He opened his mouth again to speak, but Thelma and Pat had gone.

The next morning, a chilly, grey Sunday, the sleek black car with its personalized number plates nosed its way into the car park at St Barnabus's Lodestone Academy and stopped round to the side, out of view of both the road and the CCTV. Kayleigh Brittain got out and scanned round the car park, almost as if she didn't want to be seen. Instead of her customary designer suit she was wearing jeans, sweater and boots (Armani jeans, cashmere sweater and Prada boots). Following her was Steve Hewson, carrying a couple of cardboard cartons.

As they entered the building, Kayleigh moved to deactivate the alarm – but it wasn't set.

'Someone's been careless,' said Steve.

'I'll fire up the computer,' said Kayleigh. 'And clear my office. I don't want to be any longer than I need to.'

'While you're doing that, I'll have a quick whizz through the accounts,' he said. 'Tidy up any loose ends.'

She clicked on the computer (impatiently ripping numerous Post-it Notes from the monitor) and then headed to her office, followed by Steve carrying the cartons.

Opening the door, she was startled beyond words to see Thelma sat in the chair in front of the desk. It was Steve who spoke.

'What the fuck are you doing here?' He turned to Kayleigh. 'This is the woman I told you about, the one who was nosying round your place the other day.'

'Steve.' There was a crisp note of authority in Kayleigh's voice, and he subsided – like a trained pit bull, Thelma thought.

'Terry Meadows let me in.' Thelma spoke directly to Kayleigh, not even looking at Steve. 'I must apologize for just turning up like this, but I needed a word with you.' She stood up and put down the Sunday *Yorkshire Post*, which she had been reading cover to cover in the two hours she'd been waiting here. The room had been semi-restored following its trashing. The furniture was back in place, but the carpet tiles had been taken up, revealing scuffed Victorian floorboards. Stark blocks of thick white undercoat covered the red spray paint.

'She's got nothing to say to you,' said Steve, a nasty tone in his voice.

'Steve,' said Kayleigh. 'Go and wait next door.'

Steve didn't look at all keen to go but there was something in Kayleigh's tone that made him turn. 'I'm just in there if you need me,' he said with a threatening look at Thelma.

After he'd gone, Kayleigh smiled coldly at Thelma. 'I gather you've already met Steve,' she said.

'I have,' said Thelma.

'Though why you felt the need to go and talk with my husband behind my back I'm not exactly sure.'

Thelma said nothing. 'I take it you don't mind if I sit down?' Kayleigh's question was expertly pitched, semi-humorous in a way that served to put ironic quotation marks around the whole encounter. Once behind her desk she surveyed Thelma for a moment 'This is all very mysterious. To what do I owe the honour?' As Thelma opened her mouth to speak, she spoke over her. 'Actually, I think I can answer that question. Some of it anyway.' She paused, gathering her thoughts. 'I had a phone call from Chris Canne late last night. A rather painful phone call for a Saturday evening, quite put me off my glass of wine!' Again, that humorous inflection in the voice. 'He mentioned a couple of things – one being about wanting to see the school accounts. Do you know why that might be?'

Again, she paused and looked at Thelma. Again, Thelma said nothing.

'I take it from your silence you probably do. I'm guessing your friend made another illegal attempt to access school systems.' She regarded Thelma gravely, and then her face broke into a grin. 'But hey! All your friend needed to do was ask, I've absolutely nothing to hide. Thelma! Anything you wanted to know, I'd have been more than happy to talk to you about!' Her voice was still reasonable, though now slightly pained, a lesser person than Thelma could even have been wrong-footed.

'You say he mentioned a couple of things,' said Thelma.

'Ah!' There was a triumphant but weary note in Kayleigh's voice. 'Now we're getting to it. Muck-raking.' She shook her head. 'I take it that's what this is all about.'

'That rather depends,' said Thelma. 'To what exactly you're referring.'

Kayleigh's smile vanished. 'Things in the past. Things that I was cleared of in a court of law. Muck raked up for no good reason.' There was a cold look now in the grey eyes. 'Things that are dead and gone and forgotten.'

'Not by the teaching council, I imagine,' said Thelma.

Kayleigh shook her head sorrowfully. 'You know, Thelma, I thought you and I were friends,' she said.

Thelma ignored this. In her experience comments of this nature were very little to do with friendship and everything to do with manipulation.

'I did speak to Chris Canne,' she said after a moment. 'And I did tell him about Lew Carne. And before I did, I spoke to Lew Carne himself, to check the facts.'

This took Kayleigh by surprise. Her face froze. Her voice when she spoke was slightly hoarse with shock.

'Can I ask just what business of yours that is?' Thelma said nothing, but then Kayleigh gave her little chance. 'I was found not guilty by a court of law. I did nothing wrong. And I shall tell Chris Canne that when I see him on Monday morning with, I might add, legal representation.' She looked at Thelma. 'No, I *will* say this, I wasn't going to because I have a high regard for you . . . But you nosy your way in here, nebbing into things that don't concern you . . . Is it that you can't accept you don't work here anymore? It's sad; it's more than sad, it's pathetic.' She stood up shaking her head. 'I think we're done here. Please leave.'

'Before you call in Mr Hewson,' said Thelma, 'two things.' Her voice was quiet and grave, and Kayleigh found herself sitting back down. 'One, I came here, into school, because you asked me to be a governor. And two: I'm here now not because of Lew Carne, *but because of what you did prevent that knowledge from getting out.*'

Kayleigh regarded her for a moment. 'Go on,' she said wearily, her voice heavy with the implication that whatever was said it wouldn't be worth listening to.

'Since the start of term, a number of anonymous letters have been received by people working in this school.'

'Since the summer fayre,' cut in Kayleigh harshly. 'Three were meant for me remember – even if I didn't get all of them.'

'These letters caused a good deal of upset,' said Thelma. 'Sam Bowker even considered taking his own life.'

'Do you think I don't know that?' There was a real note of incredulous anguish in her voice. 'Thelma, I was devastated when I heard that!'

'I truly think you were,' said Thelma.

'Then just what is it you're saying?'

'I'm saying you sent those letters.'

There was a pause. Kayleigh's face went blank in a way that brought to Thelma's mind that night at the summer fayre all that time ago.

Then: 'That is the most ridiculous thing I have ever heard in my life. You think *I* sent that letter to Sam?'

'The letter to Sam, the letter to Jan, to Becky – and all the other people apart from Natalie Berryman – that one was sent by Claire Donnelly, as you guessed.'

'That first letter – the one to me – was hidden in the raffle prizes. Linda Barley will tell you I'd been nowhere near them.' Her voice was indignant.

Thelma calmly met her gaze. 'I believe that first letter *was* sent by Donna Chivers – or someone from the PTA,' she said. 'And it was that letter which gave you the whole idea. I also think—' her voiced rose slightly as Kayleigh opened her mouth '—you keyed your own car and trashed your own office.'

Kayleigh let her breath out in an incredulous sort of gasp. 'Thelma,' she said. 'I'm being serious, and I'm saying this as your friend. You need to be very, very careful about what you're saying. There is such a thing as a law of libel.'

'I realize that.' Thelma was beginning to feel a bit sorry for the woman. She hovered uneasily, clumsily, obviously wanting to end the conversation yet knowing she couldn't until she heard everything Thelma had to say. She reminded Thelma of many a naughty child in the class who had been caught out doing wrong.

'That night when someone was in school.' Kayleigh almost snatched at the words. 'You were with me when someone trashed my office.'

'There was no one in school,' said Thelma patiently. 'You just pretended there was – like at the governor's meeting, when you pretended to see someone looking in. You trashed your own office before I got here. I remember when I arrived, you stopped me from coming in here by heading off into the school.'

Kayleigh took a deep breath, as if making a laudable effort to stay patient.

'You've no proof for any of this,' she said evenly.

'Nothing that would stand up in court,' agreed Thelma and the woman imperceptibly relaxed. 'But I know.'

'How?'

'Something you yourself said about Sam Bowker. You mentioned the letter he got – *but Sam never admitted getting an anonymous letter*, not even to his wife. The only other person who knew would be the person who sent it.'

'I've never heard anything so ridiculous in all my life,' scoffed Kayleigh. 'Key my own car? Trash my own office? Why on earth would I do such lunatic things?' She tried to laugh incredulously but couldn't quite pull it off.

'So that you could quickly leave St Barnabus's and move to another highly paid position within the trust *without any knowledge of the past coming out*. You recognized Izzy Trewin from your previous school and realized it was only a matter of time before she realized who you were and told everyone about what happened with Lew Carne.' There was a simple certainty and some sadness in her voice.

Kayleigh took another deep breath. Her arms were folded tightly round herself as if she was afraid something would explode out of her.

'You cannot prove any of this,' she said, her words deliberate, low, almost fevered. 'You cannot prove any of this because it is absolutely untrue and if I hear that a word of this ridiculous story has been repeated, I will have no hesitation in contacting my solicitor.'

Thelma stood up.

'I've said what I came to say,' she said. 'I'll let you get on with your packing.' She stood up and opened the door.

'You've got no proof.' It was a question, slightly desperate in tone. It sounded like the question of a spoilt child caught doing wrong.

Steve was standing outside in the corridor, obviously waiting for her to emerge.

'So, what's all this about then?' he said aggressively.

'I've said everything I came here to say,' said Thelma, but he stepped into her path.

'I've asked you a question,' he said quietly.

'Just leave it, Steve.' Kayleigh sounded weary and petulant, but Steve didn't move. He glared at Thelma, reminding her more than ever of a pit bull terrier. She felt her fingers straying to the rape alarm.

'I'm so sorry, have you been waiting for me?' Liz's voice had a bracing yet chilly energy to it. 'Why is it staplers always jam right in the middle of your using them?'

She was looking at Thelma. 'I'm done now. I managed to give Sam's classroom a quick going over, tidied a couple of displays. I'm ready if you are.' She ushered Thelma firmly past Steve Hewson, who automatically took a bemused step back. Thelma said nothing but walked past him down the corridor, feeling his angry stare on the back of her neck as she continued to finger the rape alarm. She thought about the call she'd put through to the anti-trafficking department of North Yorkshire Police; it was by no means certain they would act but they had certainly sounded interested.

At the front door Kayleigh caught up with them.

'Just a minute,' she said, her voice harsh. Liz turned and took a step towards her.

The expression on her face stopped Kayleigh Brittain dead in her tracks.

'You,' said Liz quietly. 'You just make sure you stay all the way away from Sam Bowker.'

Kayleigh took a hasty step back. She tried to stare Liz out with a cold glare, but her face let her down, puckering slightly, tears starting in her eyes.

'Thelma,' she said somewhat shakily, 'you say you saw Lew Carne?'

'I did.'

'And he's – all right?'

Thelma nodded. 'He said to say that he's living exactly the life he wanted to live.'

CHAPTER THIRTY-SIX

Six friends share explanations over supper in Valentino's and under a starry sky there is a heartfelt revelation.

'So, what first gave you the idea it was old Kayleigh Bling who was sending out all the letters then?' Rod took a sip of his lager, facing Thelma with a frowning concentration normally only reserved for *Ice Road Truckers*.

It was a quiet night in Valentino's, as it generally was on a Tuesday in October. The three couples were sat in a table tucked round to the side, by the stairs and the ice cream counter: Teddy next to Liz, Rod across from Thelma and Derek by Pat. Drinks had been brought, orders taken; now it was time for questions to be answered.

'On one level it always made the most sense,' said Thelma. 'The letters turned up everywhere, all round school. And the only person who could be seen literally anywhere without arousing any comment was the head teacher of that school.'

Teddy shook his head. 'In the night he is like a thief,' he said taking a swig of beer.

Thelma shot her husband a swift, concerned look.

'I just don't see why people didn't kick up more of a fuss,' said Rod. 'Tell the police.'

'You'd have to meet Kayleigh Brittain to fully understand,' said Thelma.

'She had everyone in that school just where she wanted them,' said Pat, taking an appreciative sip of her wine.

'She's one of those people who could be nice as pie one minute, then cut you dead the next,' said Liz. 'They were all a bit scared of her. Even Matt Barley.'

'And I rather think she selected her victims carefully,' said Thelma. 'Choosing people she knew she could manipulate.'

'She'd leave them a letter and then pull out all the stops being nice and supportive – knowing full well they'd be very unlikely to want anyone to know about it.' Pat gestured flamboyantly with her wine glass, her floaty sleeve threatening to trail in Derek's Mango H2O. Derek flushed a mottled pink, as he generally did in Pat's company.

'Like the way she manipulated me,' said Liz. 'Inviting me in after it all came out about Ian and Nicole.'

'So, you'd not suspect that it was her?' Derek frowned.

'No,' said Liz. '*So I'd suspect it was Claire Donnelly*. She must have guessed what Claire had done and decided to use the poor lass as a scapegoat. She deliberately sent me down to the staffroom knowing full well I'd see her crying in there – and then she practically put the idea in my head that Claire had been the one sending the letters. I can't believe I was so gullible!'

'No more than me, remember,' said Thelma. 'She asked me to be a governor because she needed a confidant. Someone she could tell all about the letters – so that when the time came to tell the trust what had been going on, she had a ready-made impartial witness.'

'She picked the wrong one there,' said Rod.

'No, not at all,' said Thelma. 'For a long time, I was thinking exactly what she wanted me to think – that there was a twisted letter writer out there, with an especial grudge against Kayleigh Brittain.'

'When all along it was Kayleigh Bling herself,' said Pat, taking another mighty sip of wine.

'So that Bunty Carter you were all fussing over – actually, she had nothing to worry about?' said Derek. There was a pause and the three friends looked at each other.

'I wouldn't say she had *nothing* to worry about,' said Pat cryptically. 'Whatever it said in the letter sent to her made her think she'd been rumbled. It was very much in her interests for everyone to be thinking there was a maniac at large to distract attention away from what she'd been up to.'

'Which was?' asked Teddy.

'Stealing school stock and selling it on eBay,' said Thelma.

'Under the name Big Mama.' Pat gave the title a rather salacious emphasis that made Derek remember those basques and blush yet again.

'There were these huge bags of stuff in her hallway,' said Liz. 'She'd obviously been helping herself for ages.'

'When she got her letter, she panicked, and threw a sickie,' said Pat.

'Eventually she disposed of all the stuff she'd taken round different charity shops.' Thelma shook her head sadly, thinking again how very ordinary evil could be, and how the saddest of lives with the toughest of circumstances can turn to dark paths, albeit very mundane ones.

'Okay,' said Rod a trifle impatiently, 'Okay, I get all that. But what made you see it *wasn't* some twisted nutter sending these letters?'

'To start with,' said Thelma, 'there's the whole notion of poison pen letters.'

'Nasty and horrid,' said Liz. 'But a bit old hat.'

'It's like our Liam says,' said Pat, 'why bother with them when you've got social media?' She drained her glass and Derek unobtrusively topped her up.

'And then there were the actual letters themselves,' said Thelma. 'When we finally saw them, they felt rather half-hearted.'

All three men frowned at this.

'You see, *that's* the bit I don't get,' said Derek. His wife, who'd explained this point at least three times, sighed to herself.

'From what you said they were pretty vitriolic.' Teddy drained his beer. 'With their mouths the godless destroy their neighbours. And with their laptops too.' Discreetly Thelma moved his glass out of reach.

'Vitriolic yes – but not as vitriolic as they could have been,' said Pat.

'She knew *something* about the people she was writing to, but not too much.' Thelma's voice was clear and slow – what Pat called her 'tens and units' voice. 'For example, she knew Margo was stealing coffee – but nothing about her dire financial situation. So, the impression we all got reading them was that they were written by someone who didn't know the staff that well. And as Kayleigh herself said to me, she makes it a point not to get close to the people she works with.'

'But didn't one say something about someone carrying on with someone?' asked Derek.

'In all of this,' said Pat tapping his arm lightly, 'you have to forget all about the letter sent to Natalie Berryman. That was sent by Claire Donnelly and had nothing to do with what was happening, it just muddied the waters a bit.' Derek said nothing but looked in fascination at the bright nails (Jamaica me Happy!) lightly scratching his arm.

'Claire got the idea of sending a letter from the ones already being sent – in the same way Kayleigh did from the letter she got.'

'Hang on.' Derek was looking totally lost. 'How many letter writers were there?'

'Three.' Liz spoke to her husband with her 'keep up at the back' voice. 'Whoever sent the first one, Claire Donnelly and of course Kayleigh Brittain.'

Derek shook his head with a look of perplexed bewilderment.

'It was when I guessed that the first one had *also* been sent by someone else that I began to see things a bit more clearly,' said Thelma.

'And how did you guess that?'

'Spelling. Or the spelling of a certain word.' Thelma brought up her phone, and flashed up the photo she'd taken of two sentences side by side.

*I HOPE YOU REALISE JUST HOW
MANY PEOPLE HATE YOU.*

*YOU REALIZE EVERYONE KNOWS
WHAT YOU'RE DOING?*

'Look at the spelling of "realize". People generally don't tend to spell the same word differently. So that indicated the first letter was written by a different person from the others. I then started looking at the whole thing a bit differently. Not what was happening – *but what was happening as a result of what was happening.*'

'Which was?' said Rod.

There was a dramatic pause; the three men stared at her, fixated.

'The net result of these letters being sent,' said Thelma, 'was *Kayleigh Brittain was going to leave St Barnabus's with salary and reputation intact* – and indeed a good bit of sympathy from the board at Lodestone.'

At that moment the first courses arrived and there was a brief hiatus whilst the confusion with Teddy's deep-fried mozzarella and Pat's whitebait was resolved.

'And she wanted to move from the school because of this scandal in her past?' said Teddy.

'Lurve,' said Pat in a way that almost caused Derek to choke on his minestrone soup.

'Right,' said Rod, diving into his garlic mushrooms. 'Right, so Kayleigh Bling had an affair with someone way back down the line – yeah?'

'A pupil she was teaching,' said Liz grimly.

'And she was afraid it would all come out?'

'It all goes back to the night of the summer fayre,' said Thelma. 'Back in July. I saw Kayleigh suddenly looking very . . .' She searched for the word.

'Surprised,' supplied Liz.

'Discombobulated,' suggested Teddy, slightly too loudly.

'Shocked,' said Thelma decisively. 'Shocked to the core. She'd suddenly a seen a woman from Cornwall where she'd started out as a teacher.'

'A woman who knew her and about her fling,' said Pat.

'A woman she knew had the power to ruin her reputation.' Thelma discreetly moved her husband's bottle out of his reach. 'She considered leaving – her husband told me she met with her financial adviser – but she had too much to lose.'

'Plus, all the nice little earners for friends and families,' said Liz grimly. 'Like with that Steve Hewson.'

'Then she must have thought of the anonymous letter sent to her at the fayre. All the shock and upset it caused – and it made her think . . . really it must have seemed like some sort of sign.'

'The love of money is the root of all evil,' intoned Teddy, pushing aside his mozzarella largely untouched. Thelma nudged a glass with water over to him.

'So how on earth,' said Rod, oblivious to the general activity, 'did you realize Kayleigh Bling had come from Cornwall in the first place?'

'One word,' said Thelma. 'One little word. Teazy.'

'It's Cornish,' said Liz.

'It's Cornish for discombobulated,' said Pat with a laugh.

'I heard both Izzy and Kayleigh use the same word – quite unconsciously. Izzy told me it was Cornish, and I realized that at some point Kayleigh Brittain must have spent some time there. I immediately thought of the seascape Kayleigh had moved from her office after recognizing Izzy Trewin, and then of course there was that coaster I found in her desk.'

'Lew Carne Galleries, St Just, *Cornwall*,' said Liz.

'And when Izzy mentioned a scandal in a school she'd worked in when she lived there, it didn't take a lot of digging to find the case of Lewis Carne and his teacher. But the teacher had a different name, so the only way I could be sure was to go and confront him with a picture of Kayleigh. There weren't any in school – she'd been very careful like that – but of course there were plenty of her in her house.'

'Yes, but,' said Derek frowning, 'all this with the letters . . . Couldn't she have just asked for a transfer?'

'Or got another job?' said Teddy.

'These things take time,' said Pat. 'And every day she was at St Barnabus's was a day she risked running into Izzy Hoojamaflip.'

'She didn't dare be anywhere she might meet her,' said Thelma.

'Parents were already commenting they hadn't seen her that term,' said Liz. 'She didn't even dare have her photo taken for the lobby noticeboard.'

'Of course,' said Thelma, 'to an extent she was a victim of her own success. St Barnabus's was this Beacon School.'

'She'd made a humongous song and dance about how wonderful

she was and how she was improving the place,' said Pat. 'Why on earth would she suddenly want to leave?'

'Sending letters would give her the perfect excuse,' said Liz. 'Dreadful woman.'

'Evil flourishes as the green bay tree,' said Teddy. Thelma signalled to the waiter for another jug of water.

'Okay.' Derek was still frowning. 'But then why send the letters to everyone? Why not send them just to herself? She could still make out someone was out to get her.'

'Because if it was just herself,' said Pat, 'there'd be pressure from people to call the police. But with other people involved – so many of them didn't want a fuss.'

'Or be like Sam, and not even admit to having had one,' said Liz.

'It was really a very clever scheme,' said Thelma.

'Wickedness often is,' pronounced Teddy. 'Clever and successful – and needs facing head on.' His wife poured him another glass of water.

'So,' said Rod, leaning back. 'She's got away with it all scot-free, has old Kayleigh Bling.'

'Oh no,' said Thelma.

'I wouldn't have thought you could prove any of this,' said Derek.

'She's going to be sat in that hot tub of hers laughing her head off,' said Rod, shaking his head.

'She's lost her job don't forget,' said Pat.

'She'll blag her way into another,' said Rod. 'People like that always do. Ess aitch eye tee floats and all that.'

'It's true she won't be brought to book for what she did,' agreed Thelma.

'All the pain and suffering and upset she caused.' Liz shook her head.

'But what you have to remember,' said Thelma, 'is that we *know* what she did – and so does Chris Canne in spite of all his protestations. *And she knows we know.*'

'Do you honestly think that'll bother her?' asked Teddy sadly.

'I think,' said Thelma choosing her words carefully, 'there's a woman called Karen McAllister, who fifteen years ago fell in love, deeply and passionately in love, with a young artist called Lewis Carne . . . and *that* woman, who no matter how much money, how much power and status she has achieved, has never got over that love – *that* woman will know that there's people out there who know exactly what she did to try and maintain her lucrative lifestyle.'

Her face was sombre; her voice intoning judgement was low. Those listening to her found themselves remembering their own loves, their own dreams and the good and bad they had done in their such short lives.

'She knows,' said Thelma. 'In our eyes she'll forever be the woman who sent poison pen letters.'

'They who have turned to crooked roads, no one who walks along them will know peace,' said Teddy.

'Hear, hear,' said Derek.

Rod tapped his spoon against his plate of tiramisu. 'Things is, folks,' he said, 'at the end of the day, it's not about what other people get up to, it's what you yourself do – how you spend the time you have. I know that better than most.' In the dim light he looked almost younger – certainly healthier than they'd seen him in a while. They all remembered the times when he'd looked so weighed down by the illness and its treatment – but tonight there was something hopeful and optimistic about him.

'So,' he said. 'Let's just be glad we're all here tonight. Together. Cheers, everyone.'

'Cheers,' they all said.

★

Thelma had known there was something on her husband's mind; she'd known it all evening. Walking down Blossomgate, she looked up at the clear October sky and said a quick prayer; for what, she wasn't exactly sure.

'A good night,' she said as they turned up Trinity Hill. 'Being with the others, seeing Rod looking so well,' she added hastily in case Teddy thought 'good' referred in any way to the story they'd shared.

Her husband nodded, or rather thirty-two years of marriage told Thelma that he did.

'It's a beautiful night,' she said again, looking at the bejewelled sky.

Again, he nodded, and this time he took her hand.

By now they were passing the college, set back behind and beyond privet and lawns, lights a reassuring twinkle in the dark. Teddy stopped, looking at the buildings.

'Tonight,' he said, 'when I heard the full story . . . what you and your friends were involved in . . . it crystallized something I'd been feeling for some time.' He paused and sat down on the bench overlooking the grounds. Thelma sighed; she guessed this had been coming. Steeling herself she sat beside him, the bench was every bit as cold and damp as she'd anticipated.

'All these years,' he said, 'all this time – I've been working at the Vicar Factory.'

'You've done good work,' said Thelma quietly.

'I know,' he said simply. 'I know it's been good work. And I know there's still good work to be done.'

'But?'

'When it looked like the college was closing . . . my first sensation was . . .' He paused, staring at the lit building, and Thelma knew better than to speak. Somewhere away in the distance a fox barked. 'A sense of *anticipation*,' he said. 'If the job had gone – the prospect was an exciting one.'

'I see,' said Thelma. She thought of the folder on the coffee table. Maybe he had been going through it after all. 'You mean to retire?'

'No.' The negative had firm conviction. 'No, I'm not ready to retire. Not yet.'

'You mean?'

'I mean,' he said. 'I want to find another job.'

EPILOGUE

Ho ho ho! Staff Xmas night out BACK ON! Running buffet plus Abba-tastic! Sandal Farm, Friday December 10th.
£15 deposit to Margo ASAP!

November

The stormy weather of the past weeks had largely subsided into something more settled, but even so the wind was stirring the lime trees outside St Barnabus's in a way that made Chris Canne cast anxious glances in the direction of his new Chevrolet Corvette. It was barely three weeks old and fear for the paintwork often outweighed the pleasure of acquisition. He forced himself to focus back on Becky Clegg's words as they walked down the corridor together.

'The autumn data is looking very promising,' she was saying briskly. 'Miss Ahmed is proving a really strong staff member – the kids all love her – and she gets on great with all the staff.' She paused reflectively. 'A much-needed breath of fresh air,' she said.

'Good,' said Chris eagerly. 'That's good. And . . .' He caught himself slightly. 'And how are the staff?'

Becky didn't answer him immediately. From within the hall they were passing could be heard the sound of an enthusiastic female voice. 'Christmas bells go ding ding *DING*!' There was a cheery but distinctly hysterical edge to the words.

'Nativity practice,' she explained. 'Jan Starke does throw herself heart and soul into these things. And to answer your question about the staff – healing. Having the pressure taken off us – the Beacon Schools and all that – was very helpful. Thank you.'

Chris nodded, regarding the composed figure next to him, her mane of red hair caught back in a sober French plait. She was, he thought, proving a more than adequate acting head teacher. Already that morning she'd fielded questions about Foundation baseline assessments with a calm, knowledgeable confidence he'd found impressive.

They resumed their way down the corridor to Willow Class and when they were approaching the door, he spoke again.

'And Mr Bowker? How's he doing?'

'He seems fine,' said Becky. 'As I said, he insisted on coming back to work, said he'd much rather be in school – which I can understand.' Chris didn't miss the faint flicker of darkness that crossed her face. 'But of course, I am keeping an eye on him. As are others.' She suddenly smiled, a tired but hopeful smile. 'Really, the way everyone has come together these past few weeks has been so lovely.'

She paused, her hand on the door handle of Willow Class. 'And Mrs Brittain?' she said carefully.

Chris replied equally carefully. 'Mrs Brittain no longer works for Lodestone Academy Trust,' he said. There was a pause; Chris felt something more was expected from him. 'There was absolutely no proof of anything,' he said, rather desperately. 'Without proof my hands were tied.' He looked at Becky, who nodded. 'Staff don't know everything that went on, do they?' he asked. There was a definite note of unease in his tone, as if he was seeking reassurance.

She shook her head. 'No,' she said. 'That is to say, there is talk.' She smiled faintly 'Which is inevitable in a school – but no, no one knows everything apart from myself.' She looked at him steadily. 'I do think it's better that way.'

Chris nodded, relieved, and followed her into the classroom.

Thinking about it later, the best way to describe the atmosphere in Willow Class was as if some sort of spell had been cast. The lights were off; the low November sun slanted into the room, giving it an ethereal, almost enchanted feel. The noise of the sea could be heard gently in the background, obviously playing on the sound system, but so powerful was the atmosphere in the room, it felt almost as if the sound were emanating from the light and peace. And was it his imagination, or was that a faint ozone-salty smell in the air? He had a sudden, poignant flashback to childhood summers on the beach at Aberaeron.

The children were writing. In front of every child was a pebble or a seashell, some were being clutched by children as they wrote, hands and heads and backs arched intently over the task in hand. Some faint grains of sand from Cape Cornwall beach trickled across the writing books and tables.

Sam Bowker was moving quietly but purposefully round the room. 'Tell me,' he said, his voice low and compelling. 'Your image . . . What is it your stone or shell can do? This is the stone that – *what*? What is it?'

Sat to one side of the room was a greying woman working quietly with a group of three. She'd written various words on a whiteboard and was gently encouraging the children sitting with her.

'That's it, Jacey,' she was saying. 'See if you can finish the whole sentence on your own.'

Chris lowered his voice. 'This is marvellous,' he said enthusiastically. 'Of course, I know the teaching of writing is Sam's strength. I presume he's using Jared's marking scheme?'

Becky looked apologetic. 'No,' she said. 'No, I don't believe he is.'

Chris looked at one of the boys. He could see he was utterly immersed in the world he was bringing to life through his words.

This is the stone, he had written in uncertain handwriting, *that tumbled from the crown of the Mermaid King; the king of dreams and wishes.* The stone in question was clutched tightly in his left hand, his white knuckles contrasting with the sandy black pebble.

'Oh well,' he said. 'As long as he's getting the results.' The woman working with the group looked up at Chris, who felt some further comment was needed from him.

'And of course, it's all about making that sustained year-on-year progress, isn't it?'

'No,' said Liz. 'No, it really isn't.'

AUTHOR'S NOTE

In writing about an actual area, it's important to point out what's real and what is fiction. There *was* a school in Baldersby St James, which has sadly had to close due to falling numbers. However, this closure was unavoidable and the very highly regarded Trust that ran the school is in no way, shape or form anything like the Lodestone Trust.

ACKNOWLEDGEMENTS

To me, a writing career feels akin to walking on a floor made of smoke: I'm never entirely sure from one moment to the next whether my foot is going to go through. Every word of support and encouragement has made that floor of smoke that bit stronger for me, and I'd like to thank everyone who has emailed or messaged or spoken to me at events – anyone who has in some way communicated their appreciation of book one, which has in turn given me confidence when writing this second outing for Pat, Thelma and Liz.

I'd like to give a special shout-out to this brilliant new (to me) world which I've tumbled into – that of independent bookshops. Part library, part community hub – much-needed places of cheer and hope in so many communities. Their encouragement and support, their open-hearted welcome, has also gone such a long way towards strengthening that floor of smoke. Thanks in particular to the St Ives bookshop, the Stripey Badger in Grassington, Truman Books in Farsley, Darling Reads in Horbury, the White Rose bookshop in Thirsk and of course my original number one supporter, the Little Ripon Bookshop. You're all doing a terrific and much-needed job, you're all well worth a visit.

During the writing process I'm become very aware (and appreciative) of all the 'team' behind me. Thanks again (and again!) to all the people at Avon, not least to my brilliant editor Cara, who has that rare quality of being able to develop and sharpen a manuscript whilst consistently communicating her enthusiasm and passion for the work. Also, a big thank you to Charlotte for her work on the audio book and to Becci, who expertly steered a nervous first-time author through the labyrinth that is promotion and publicity. Thanks as well to Maddie and Ella, who worked on the marketing and of course to Caroline, who has done such an amazing job designing the cover.

Massive thanks as always to my wonderful agent Stan, whose insight and guidance has provided many a signpost at just the right moment.

I also want to give mention and thanks to Julie Hesmondhalgh for her inspirational talent; the enthusiasm and warmth she brought to the audio-reading of book one gave the story a whole new dimension – one which has been so valuable to access whilst writing novel number two.

Thanks as well to the brilliant Gary Brown of the BBC, the person who first opened my eyes to the dramatic possibilities of academisation; his ongoing advice and critiquing has given me so much confidence as a writer as I tread that smoky floor.

Much-needed focus and perspective on the whole subject of the academisation of schools was provided by Pat Thomson; I found her excellent book *Whistle Blowers* invaluable as a resource. Thanks also to Isobel Ashmead and Pippa Davies for their many many conversations on the subject.

Once again, a big shout-out to my team of early readers – to the Grammar Police! Thank you to Maureen from church and to Peter Dodd. Thank you to my solid gold friend and writing buddy Catherine Johnson for her endless support and encouragement, both now and over the years, and not forgetting the evergreen Audrey Coldron, patiently reading through yet another of my stories.

And of course, my English teacher Sandra Appleton. Like all good teachers, she's had a profound effect on my life and I can't say how brilliant it has been to have her 'marking' my work, just as she did in the 1970s.

This brings me onto the subject of education, where it's been my privilege to spend much of the past forty-odd years. Throughout the vagaries and uncertainties of writing, it's been of inestimable benefit to have that solid ground of primary schools underlying that floor of smoke. I'd like to salute the teams of woman whose work and lives I've shared, who've encouraged, admonished, laughed (many times!) and sewn up holes in my clothing as required. There's too many to name, but you know who you are; as I'm writing this, I've a big smile on my face remembering the staffrooms of Peel Common, of Oakworth, of Sanders, Ryecroft and of course fantastic Foxhill up on the tops where I've been privileged enough to spend the past 25 years.

Finally, I'd like to thank my friends and family for their help, support, encouragement and empowering belief in me both as a writer and a person, especially on those days when my own belief was somewhat flickery. Thanks to Louise Fletcher for all the creative fuel in my tank, to my cousin Ruth and to my lovely Aunties, Mary, Catherine and Lee.

Thanks also to Caitlin and Andy, Conor, Niall and Jess, Sally, Maisie and Elyse, to Babs, Tracey and the rest of my brilliant family.

And finally to Judith, my number one cheerleader, and of course to Simon, my support and gardening guru. The floor is never stronger than when you're around.

**Introducing the three unlikeliest sleuths
you'll ever meet . . .**

Every Thursday, three retired school teachers have their 'coffee o'clock' sessions at the Thirsk Garden Centre café.

But one fateful week, as they are catching up with a slice of cake, they bump into their ex-colleague, Topsy.

By the next Thursday, Topsy's dead.

The last thing Liz, Thelma and Pat imagined was that they would become involved in a murder.

But they know there's more to Topsy's death than meets the eye — and it's down to them to prove it . . .

**Don't miss J.M. Hall's debut cosy
mystery — available now!**